THE VOICE LIKE WATER

Alora's Tear, Volume III

NATHAN BARHAM

BARHAM INK
MOSCOW IDAHO USA

Table of Contents

For Mom, who taught me that women are stronger.

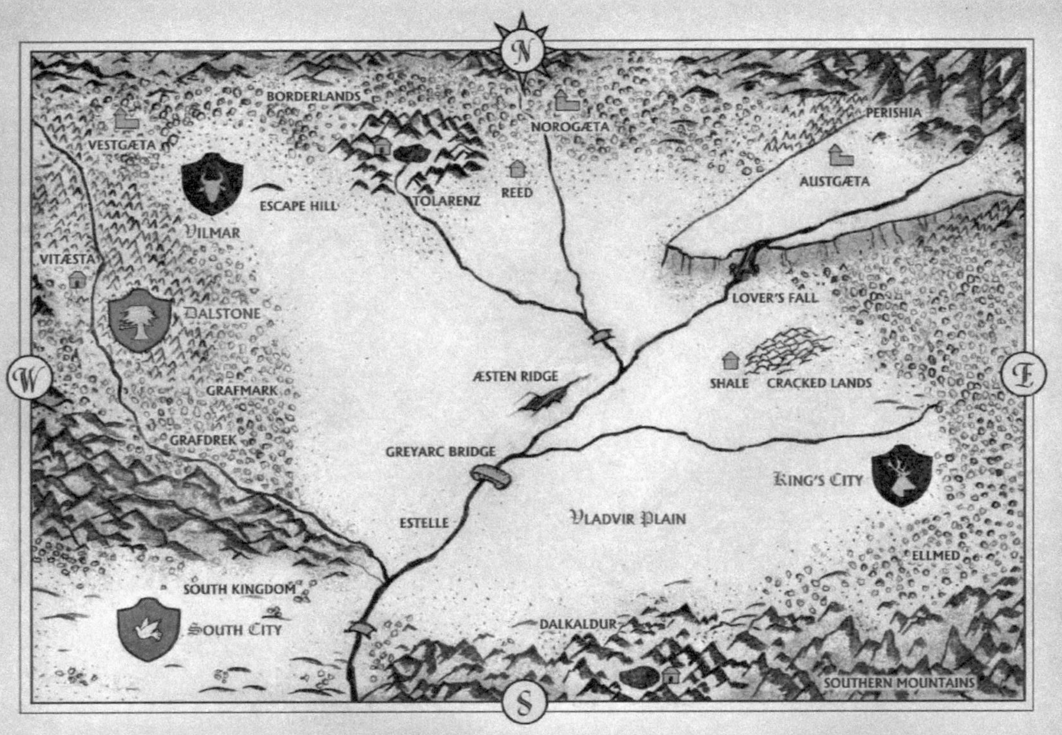

N
W
S
E
BORDERLANDS
VESTGÆTA
NOROGÆTA
PERISHIA
ESCAPE HILL
TOLARENZ
REED
AUSTGÆTA
DILMAR
VITÆSTA
LOVER'S FALL
DALSTONE
ÆSTEN RIDGE
SHALE   CRACKED LANDS
GRAFMARK
GREYARC BRIDGE
KING'S CITY
GRAFDREK
ESTELLE
VLADVIR PLAIN
ELLMED
SOUTH KINGDOM
SOUTH CITY
DALKALDUR
SOUTHERN MOUNTAINS

THE VOICE LIKE WATER

CHAPTER ONE

Grafdrek

Three days had passed since they set out from Dalstone. The slow, churning current at first lulled, then grated, and finally bubbled entirely out of conscious thought. In the afternoon, ripples shimmered in the sunlight, reflecting the heat onto the boat's passengers. In a matter of hours, they each had sunburns as severe as any acquired through fieldwork or soldiering. Keeping covered as best they could, only a few areas—foreheads, noses, necks—were affected by the deepest burns. By the time the boat emerged from the protection of the trees, those foreheads, noses, and necks had all peeled, leaving them tender and pink.

On the first day out from Dalstone, the river ran quickly. Askon learned only a few hours after leaving John at the dock that the river's name mirrored that of the surrounding forest; Grafdrek—originally Grafdrekka—meant "the drink of the dead." To Askon, the name hardly seemed fitting as the lively stream chuckled along, sending them onward to the South Kingdom. At the first afternoon's rate, they would have been within Apopsé's domain in no more than a day and a half. Not all of the Grafdrek would be so easily ridden.

They woke on the second morning to sluggish slack-water thick with green tendrils of algae and slime. Thousands of frogs and millions of insects filled the air with their chatter. A lazy sun lingered behind the surrounding mountains while the boat slowed to a crawl. Its oars were replaced by long poles which Edward and Thomas used to drive the vessel through the currentless mire.

As he awaited his turn at the poles, Askon observed movement on the western bank. At first he had been wary, making quickly for one of the bows they had taken with them from Dalstone. But, after a moment's consideration, he saw the brightly colored feathers. All along the shore, Brâghda's fighters had followed them; for what purpose, Askon was unsure. Thomas concluded that the Norill had come as a precaution, though Edward maintained it was to watch the half-elf—whom they so revered—leave the forest. Personally, Askon preferred the former explanation and welcomed the chance to escape the strange elf-worship practiced in Grafmark's heart.

The next two days had proceeded in similar fashion, though sometime in the middle of the second, the Grafmark Norill had gone. The first night was simple. They exchanged watches, drawing straws to see who would sit up first. Elise had drawn the shortest, but unsurprisingly, Thomas had volunteered to watch in her place as well as his own. She acknowledged his chivalry and planted herself at the prow of the boat upon the setting of the sun. She refused to move until Thomas fell asleep.

After that, they could no longer rest properly on the boat. They all found it uncomfortable, but it was the work during the day which made it impossible to stay aboard. For hours they would push the poles through the slime and sludge, traversing hundreds of yards before the stream finally came free of the weedy shallows and ran more briskly. Then, sometimes after only a few minutes, the boat would slow and the slog would begin again. Doing so for only one day brought them all near to exhaustion. They tied the boat to the shore at the edge of one slow section and cast themselves heavily onto the beach. There, under long fingers of cypress, they fell into deep sleep. None could stay awake to sit watch.

When morning came, they awoke bug-eaten and tired. Onto the boat they climbed again to suffer another day filled with the swift stream, slow stream, push poles, rest a while monotony. Now—on the afternoon of the fourth day—Askon lay with his arms dangling limply into the clucking water. The burn in his muscles, which he had begun to feel even before they set out from Dalstone, thumped along numbly.

He drifted in and out of sleep while Edward manned the rudder. The last slack-water stretch had nearly broken them, taking most of the morning and early afternoon to traverse. But it was not the distance that brought the difficulty; it was the depth. In the last hour, the river had become so wide and so shallow that they were forced to maneuver the boat in a serpentine pattern, the hull all the while scraping against the bottom of the stream-bed. At the back of the boat, Elise lay wrapped in Thomas's arms, both their mouths hanging open in the freedom from self-consciousness felt only by the very weary or the very old. Once again, Askon closed his eyes, shutting out the blinding reflection of sun on water.

"Askon."

"Yes, Líana?"

"When are you going to get married?"

"Probably not for a long time. Not many girls want their husband off fighting wars most of the year. They want someone who can tend the fields or make things to provide for the family."

"Well, then if you had to get married today, who would it be?"

"I don't know."

"Yes you do! Would it be Læna? Or maybe Irina?"

"They're both nice girls. Yes, I suppose either would be fine."

"That's not very romantic."

"No, I guess not."

"Oh, come on! There has to be someone. Right?"

"I'll know her when I see her."

"Really. That's a little better. How will you know?"

"I'll just know. And she'll know when she sees me. That's how it works in all the stories, isn't it? I'll see her, and right then I'll be ready to stop soldiering, build a house, and fill it with children."

"See? I knew you could do it."

"Oh, it's alright for me to end up tending a farm but not for you to end up tending a house?"

"It was your answer. If I'm a soldier, I can just marry a soldier, and then there will be no reason for either of us to stop."

"Right. Go to sleep."

Askon opened his eyes, and the blinding sun had gone. It westered somewhere behind the steep slopes that fell, almost barren, down to the water's edge. They had passed beyond the borders of Grafmark. In the glow to the east, the Vladvir plain stretched out for miles, broad and flat, until it vanished in the horizon's haze. Somewhere over those distant miles, the Estelle pounded its way south, where the Grafdrek would eventually join with it. Beyond that was Codard's city. Even now it was likely the king had gathered his forces—and those of his Norill allies—readying for battle with Lord Apopsé. The far greater threat, Lord Iramov, likely rallied his forces somewhere west of the Estelle.

The best news was that the water had deepened. Here, the current was slower than it had been when they left Dalstone, but it was steady, and the water seemed free of the muck which had held them back for the last several days. Seated beside him, Edward knocked softly on the board where Askon's head lay.

"Askon. Are you awake?"

"I am."

"Shh. Thomas and Elise are still asleep. I don't think they'll be waking up any time soon. Would you mind steering for a bit while I get some rest?"

"Of course."

They traded places: Edward asleep near the front of the boat, Askon at the rudder scanning the steep mountainsides to the west and the flat plains to the east. Before long, Askon began to wonder how they would locate Morrowmen once they arrived in the South

Kingdom. Morrowmen had seemed confident that they would indeed find him, but in the back of his mind, Askon could not help thinking they would encounter problems at the gates. After all, they had met difficulties at Austgæta, King's City, and Dalstone. Even in Thomas's own village they had been forced to sneak inside.

Askon's half-elf eyes and ears and angular features had caused trouble for him since the day he was born. And though he had devised a good many strategies to cope with being recognized as such, he sometimes wished he had only the human bloodline in his veins. He shook off the feeling and instead tried to devise a way they could enter the city without his race being noted.

In the west, the golden sun dimmed to silver then to gray. Stars blinked into the night sky, and from around the straggling trees at the edge of Grafmark, a lurid, bulbous moon glowed, casting a sheen over the plains grasses. Askon pulled hard on the rudder. The boat swung lazily around, drifting on the steady current of the southern Grafdrek. As the nose poked the shore, grass and bulrushes hissed in protest. Gently, Askon guided the vessel to the bank, stepped out, and secured it—sleeping passengers and all.

When he awoke the next morning, the others were gathered around a small cooking fire. He rose from where he had clumsily tossed the bedroll in the dark and made his way toward them. A yawn pried his mouth open and mashed his eyes shut. Reaching out with both arms as if to embrace all three of them, he stretched wide. Instantly, he retracted his limbs, curling them to his chest like a dead spider.

The soreness had not yet left them, though he felt more awake and alive than he had in many days.

"That swamp must have really taken it out of you yesterday," said Edward cheerfully. Thomas, seated on the stump of an overturned tree, scooted closer to Elise, making room for Askon, who sat heavily, shaking the stump and jostling them.

"It did," said Askon. "And unlike our friends here, I didn't get the chance to sleep it off on the way to camp."

Smiling, Thomas tended the small cooking fire. Edward sat opposite them, across the ring. On a flat rock, a pair of filleted fish sizzled. Thomas poked at the pieces, flopping them over carefully.

"It's a good thing we did sleep, sir. Otherwise there'd be no fish for your breakfast," Thomas said.

"And no one to have kept the first watch," added Elise.

"Hm," Askon grunted. "If John were here, I'm sure he'd have a few words for my being the last awake."

"He probably would," said Edward.

For the next few minutes they did nothing more than gaze intently into the flames, listening to the hiss and pop of fish against hot stone. When Thomas flipped the meat again, one side thoroughly browned but not black, he quickly sliced the two fillets in half and placed them on another stone away from the heat. A few moments later, they ate greedily. Another ten minutes and the pieces of fish, along with some nuts and other provisions were gone. Thomas overturned the stones while Elise filled the waterskins. Edward and Askon carried the full bottles into the boat, discussing what their next move would be.

"As far as I know," Edward said, "the worst part of the Grafdrek is behind us now. It never picks up again, like when we left Dalstone, but it stays wide and smooth until it meets the Estelle."

Askon slid the bags farther to one side of the boat, making room for the waterskins. "Then we have a choice to make. We could stay on the water, which could be dangerous considering how fast the Estelle runs, or we could take the main road and follow it until we reach the South Kingdom."

"Either way we'll enter the kingdom quite a number of miles before we reach the city," said Edward. "On the river we'll have to go west across country, while on the road we'd just follow it right to the gates." Edward handed another bottle to Askon, who stuffed it under the plank where he was seated.

"We know that Iramov and Codard have men—and Norill—patrolling the northern parts of Vladvir," Askon said without looking up. "How far south they've come is another question. If I'm right in my reckoning, we should be a little more than a day's hard ride south of the Greyarc. So another small force, similar in size to the one John's bowmen defeated on the bridge, could easily have made its way this far by now."

Edward looked from his friend to the bank some yards away. Thomas knelt at the edge of the river, helping Elise with the last of the waterskins. She gazed up as though it was the first time she had laid eyes on him; a broad smile bloomed in the frame of her black hair.

"I think it best we stay out of sight for as long as possible. Who knows? We could be carrying precious cargo," Edward said with a small smile.

Askon laughed. "There hasn't been time."

"Oh, there's always time," said Edward.

"John would've said that better, I think."

"Most certainly," Edward agreed. He put on his best imitation of John's gruff delivery. "Ain't a day in a man's life where he can't make time for the like o' that! I'll tell ya, a day's worth o' fightin' can't hold a candle to a day's worth o' feastin', and *that* can't hold a candle to a day's worth o'—"

"So when are we off?" Elise interrupted, stepping onto the boat. The men looked uncomfortably from one to the other; Thomas stepped in behind her.

"Oh we'll be makin'—I mean—prepar*ing* to leave any minute now, my lady," stammered Edward.

Elise seated herself at the boat's prow, as did Thomas. Askon grinned, holding back laughter. Had the fragment's power taken him at that moment, on her face he might have read, "I know exactly what you two were talking about." Color filled Askon's cheeks, and he looked away, but Elise's eyes were clever and cold. She reached across the boat, wrapping Thomas's hand in her own.

CHAPTER TWO

The River or the Road

Edward's memory served them well enough. The slowest going along the Grafdrek was just out from their camp. For a short while, they even had to use the poles again. But soon they came through to the other side of the shallows and drifted for the rest of the day on the river's lazy current.

Marten, who had stayed clear of the boat in general, flew ever further from them now. With the plains sprawling out to the north and east, the hunting was too good and the space too open for him to remain nearby. A flicker of falcon-shaped shadow signaled his brief moments of return, and then he was gone again. His distant flights troubled Askon not at all; a boat like this was no place for a bird like Marten.

By late afternoon, they approached the confluence where the Grafdrek merged with the Estelle. Edward, taking his third turn at the rudder, guided them to the southwest bank and secured the boat. The steep mountainsides that only a few miles upstream had dived straight into the churning water, had begun to pull away from the shore. Here, the slopes gave way to long rustling grasses and rolling hills like those of the plains following the Estelle down from the north. With its rippling stalks and soft earth, this side of the river now looked much more like Vladvir than Grafmark. For that, Askon was glad.

"We should get out and stretch, maybe even walk a little," Edward said. "But before we do, I think it's important that we make a decision."

Elise frowned. "You're wondering whether we should go on foot from here or try to navigate the Estelle." It was that calculating voice, the one that veiled a quick temper and ruthless wit.

"We both are," Askon said, stepping out of the boat. "I feel responsible for the two of you, now that you've decided to come with us." And he did. Ever since they had left the castle, in the mad dash to escape the twisting halls behind the throne room, Askon had felt responsible for Thomas. Now he felt the same for Elise, no matter how independent she might appear.

"Here is what I propose," he continued. "We take Edward's walk, but go our separate ways. Take some time to think. I'm sure you two," he indicated Thomas and Elise, "will go together. But Edward and I will take our own counsel. We meet back here in one hour. Then we decide: the river or the road."

Thomas and Elise wandered away, hand in hand, toward Grafmark. Some several hundred yards in that direction, Askon had seen a cluster of drooping willows, out of place on the edge of the straggling cypress forest that followed the Grafdrek. He knew the cool shady canopy would be their destination.

Edward had gone directly south where only gentle hills and long grasses lay. It would be enough for Edward. Askon assumed his friend already knew which position he would argue. The walk would be more for the couple's benefit than his own. Askon turned to watch Edward go. The prince stood with his head hanging back loosely, face to the sky, deep breaths slowly lifting his shoulders and chest. His cloak flapped around him in the breeze, the bright blue stag against black amidst fields of pale gold.

Askon's path led him along the water's edge. His boots pressed into the saturated earth, leaving deep footprints trailing along behind him. Not far from here, he assumed, must be a crossing of some kind. The Greyarc was a wonder, certainly, and useful to almost all of Vladvir's people, but Askon now stood many miles from the clever stonework where he had come face to face with Christopher. Surely a bridge of some kind had been built nearer to Apopsé's city. If Askon was right, it would be close to the confluence.

Then there was the matter of Christopher himself—and Patrick and Victor. Askon cast his mind back to the night of the battle. There had been thunder and lightning. He had come out of the Norill ranks at the edge of the forest, Grafmark no less; that alone made him doubt what he had seen. Those staring, blank, emotionless faces. Men who should have been dead. Even as the sun bathed him in warm light, Askon shivered. How were they alive? Was that even the right word? And where had they gone? After seeing them in the trees and falling so deeply under the power of the fragment—that sluggish feeling where the rest of the world moved with such terrible quickness—he had not been able to spot them again. If nothing else, Askon had to tell the others. He resolved to do so as soon as they had made their decision about how to enter the South Kingdom.

Last and most pressing was the river. The combined waters from the Grafdrek and Estelle would be dangerous from here on: first because the farther south they traveled, the less they knew the terrain and nature of the land; second because Askon's limited knowledge about the lower Estelle told him of great falls, sharp rapids, and impassable sections that stretched on for miles. On the other hand, that same, mercilessly swift current would also be the fastest way to arrive within the borders of the South Kingdom.

Or they could take the road. Going would be easy and direct. He had never been this far south, as most of his military service had been at the northern border fort, Vestgæta. He plucked a flat stone from the grass and turned it over in his hand. Tiny mineral flecks glinted all across the smooth rock. Tossing it lightly up and catching it, then repeating the process a few more times, Askon's mind wandered.

Ever since they had entered Grafmark, he had felt disoriented. He remembered further back to the king's reaction concerning Tolarenz, so cold and almost flippant. Codard was a man Askon had served with honor, risking his own life many times for the king's causes and purposes. And John. John who had fought by his side for years—longer even than Edward, though not by much. John who had taken command of Askon's company in the face of almost certain defeat, who had stood by while the king threatened to execute Askon for desertion, but who in the end had saved them from Christopher's men on the Greyarc.

So much had happened, and Askon saw no end to the confusion, no end to the battles, no end to the mystery surrounding the Tear. Here they were, a young man only recently old enough to join Codard's army, a girl of similar years who would follow him anywhere, a prince now openly fighting against his father's forces, and Askon, one of the last remaining half-elves and one of only two survivors from the tragedy at Tolarenz. None of them knew the road nor what defenses had been built around Apopsé's kingdom. Even Edward, who had the most extensive education in such matters, knew precious little about the kingdom to the south.

Askon caught the stone, stared closely again at the speckled surface, and listened to the sounds of the gurgling Grafdrek. He tossed the stone again and it rose slowly up, a foot or so above his open palm. Then it stopped. The river was silent. The grass by the waterside leaned with the gentle pressure of the wind, but the air did not shift. Rustling, buzzing, trickling, all ceased. And there was the stone, frozen in midair—like the arrow had been.

That was enough. Without examining the fragment beneath his shirt, he knew the pulse of light within it had stopped. So too had the world around him. As clearly as if a teacher had spent weeks instructing him on the nature of the world and its workings, Askon saw the subtle signs of the seasons. Leaves of grass were paler, the water level of the Grafdrek had once been higher. The sun's path moved lower across the sky, and in the distance where only Askon's eyes could see clearly, new snow had fallen on the remotest moun-taintops. Summer's last gasp would soon pass away into autumn. Codard and Iramov would have to move their armies and strike before the first snows came.

Askon reached up and plucked the stone out of the air, where it hovered—utterly still. He cocked back his arm and fired the spin-ning rock into the Grafdrek. It met the surface at an angle, a spray of tiny droplets bursting outward. And for a split second it stopped there, halfway below the surface but not breaking it. The water, flexed and dented like a battle-tested armor plate, conformed to the shape of the rock while the droplets hung in the air all around. It remained there, frozen, stream and stone and grass and sky. Askon turned away, marching back toward the boat, his hour expended. Behind him, the stone skipped five times across the water and plunked into the stream. The wind blew, and the grasses hissed rest-lessly.

Askon returned first. Against the shore, the boat bobbed and clunked. They hadn't traveled far, but one of the waterskins needed filling. He pulled the slack leather-wrapped bag from beneath the gunwale and carried it to a small, clear stream which trickled into the steady waters of the river. When the skin was full, he capped it and slung the carrying strap over his shoulder. He turned back to-ward the boat and saw Edward, with his long strides, on the crest of a rise to the south. There was no sign of Thomas or Elise.

Edward took his time in crossing the remaining distance to the meeting place. As he drew near, Askon held out a loaf of stale bread and gestured for the prince to sit. Along the edge of the stream, chunks of driftwood had collected in piles. One sun-bleached log sat alone, left behind when the water level had been much higher. Edward lowered himself onto the log next to Askon and took the bread.

"I figured we might as well eat it now," said Askon. "It won't keep much longer, especially if we continue down the river."

Edward chewed and swallowed the tough mouthful with an effort. "What makes you think we're taking the river?"

"When I was down there," Askon pointed southeast toward the confluence, "the fragment's power came over me again. I'm certain we should follow the water."

"So the fragment gives you advice now?" Edward asked.

Askon shook his head. "No. But it does help me see things more clearly sometimes, like in Codard's throne room and with Mark and Eldred." He plucked the bread from Edward's hand and tore it in half before giving it back. "Down by the water, I saw how close the end of the summer is. Time is running out for Apopsé. Iramov and your father will make their move soon. We should get to the South Kingdom as quickly as we can, and that means the river."

Tossing his half of the loaf into the air, much as Askon had done with the stone, Edward waited a few moments. Just as Askon was about to press the prince for his thoughts, Edward caught and held the bread in his hand. He turned to Askon. "I disagree."

A moment of silence passed. Askon waited to hear if there was more to his friend's response, and Edward waited to be sure Askon's temper wouldn't flare.

"We know next to nothing about the nature of the river once the Grafdrek and the Estelle join together," Edward said slowly. "Yet all four of us have significant training in woodcraft and experience going unseen on foot, with possibly the exception of Elise. But her time with the Grafmark Norill, her time spent hiding from her own people, counts as much as Thomas's short career in my father's army. We'll be safer on the road."

Despite Edward's efforts, Askon felt the anger kindle inside him. It was not the same fury that surfaced when he thought of Iramov or the powdered circles in Tolarenz, but he was convinced the fragment had helped him see the clearer path. "We'll be slower," he snapped, a little louder than he had intended. "Apopsé will need all the time we can give him to prepare, and you'd spend that time plodding along the road. There are probably patrols between here and Apopsé's city. How long will it take if we have to stay off the path all the way to the gates? Days? A week? More?" He pitched the remaining hunk of bread over the grass in a wide arc. It fell out of sight amongst the stalks.

The prince remained calm. "That may be true, but between the four of us we have almost no experience on the water. These last few days have exhausted everyone. By all accounts, the lower Estelle is far more dangerous to navigate than the Grafdrek. What if the boat breaks up or capsizes and we drown? Then who will come to help Apopsé? And what about Elise? I was joking earlier, and I don't know any more than you do, but what if we are responsible for more than just four? We should take the road. It's safer."

Askon stood, now even more annoyed. "What good will it do if we show up too late for our news to matter? The South Kingdom will look like Austgæta or worse, like Tolarenz." Saying the name out loud cost him more than he expected. His voice cracked. "I will not be too late again," he said with an effort at finality.

Edward took a deep breath and looked up at his friend. "I'm sorry about what happened, Askon, but at the very least we need to wait and see what Thomas and Elise decide. Perhaps a vote will be more fair."

"There are four of us," Askon said shakily. "That's an even number."

Edward smiled. "Something tells me Thomas and Elise will vote as one."

Then, as if some outside force had come along to tap the two men on the shoulder, to lightly remind them of the surrounding world, both Askon and Edward forgot their argument.

It had been much longer than an hour since the party had decided to separate.

"Where are they?" Edward asked.

CHAPTER THREE
A Calculated Decision

Both men rose from their driftwood seat. The log rocked unsteadily, scattering hundreds of tiny bugs into the shadows between its rotting surface and the soft earth below, but Askon and Edward did not notice. Each had drawn his sword, Edward's in the right hand, Askon's in the left. Together they jogged west along the stream. As they moved, one or the other would stop to point out signs left behind by Thomas and Elise: footprints, broken stems, crushed leaves. The couple had not been careful.

Soon the signs led them to the willow grove. Askon had guessed already that they would have come here. What he hadn't considered was how vulnerable his friends would be. Thomas, though brave and sometimes surprisingly intelligent, had too little experience in combat to fight a group of any size by himself. When traveling together, Askon forgot how intimidating a party of armed men wearing military emblems could be. A young man and woman traveling alone would be a much more tempting target for highwaymen or other opportunistic criminals.

Askon and Edward approached the willow trees with caution. They slowed, stepping so quietly neither could hear the other over the river. The willows waved slightly, dangling tendrils of powdery blue leaves that rubbed noisily against one another. Askon quietly pulled back the curtain of foliage. They looked inside.

Thomas lay sprawled on his back in the shadows. He did not move. One of the blankets from his bedroll lay askew over his lower body. Above it his chest was bare and his eyes closed. Elise, also bare to the waist where the blanket covered her, lay face down against Thomas's shoulder.

Realizing their mistake, Askon and Edward stepped back. But in their haste, both made more noise than they intended. When they looked up again, Elise was awake.

She sat bolt upright and wary, her black hair tousled and uneven. Making no effort to cover herself in any way, she looked around, her dark eyes landing on the parting in the leaves where Askon and Edward stood. Recognizing them, she still made no modest gesture; she merely glared, her eyebrows rising in an arch that said: "Why are you still looking at me?"

Askon and Edward, both red in the face, quickly averted their eyes as Thomas began to stir. With their backs to the willow grove, they heard Elise's voice, not the whisper, but the keen-edged command she had used with the guard back in Dalstone.

"We didn't think you'd sneak up on us like thieves in the dark," she snapped. "And I thought the two of you had more decency than to stand there gawking. Wasn't it clear enough to you?"

Thomas mumbled something incoherent; then they heard him sit up quickly.

"You were supposed to be deciding where we would go next!" Askon barked back. "How were we supposed to know?"

Edward placed a hand on Askon's chest. Askon glared, but said no more. Instead, Edward continued in his place. "We apologize for intruding Elise, but we worried you might have been harmed or taken. It has been much more than the hour we agreed upon."

The response came not from Elise, but from Thomas. "I—I, we—we're sorry, your highness, and Askon, sir. I must have fallen asleep. We can—I can, just give us a moment."

"There's no need for 'your highness,' Thomas," Edward said laughing. He and Askon kept their backs to the willow grove. "Why don't you take a few minutes to put yourselves together, and we'll continue with our meeting as planned." He pulled roughly on Askon's cloak. "Let's go."

Askon and Edward sat side by side on the driftwood log near the boat when Thomas and Elise emerged near the little stream that met the river. Decidedly more composed than when Askon had seen them last, the two walked hand in hand. Elise's black hair still looked slightly disheveled, and in places Thomas's clothes were crooked or hastily fastened. Both walked lightly, Elise standing tall, her hair flying loosely, and her face distant. Thomas came along more sheepishly, his head down, swaying from left to right. Every few steps he glanced up from beneath his brows. But he smiled all the while.

They took their time, Elise directing their pace. At intervals she would stop, release his hand and gesture widely at nothing in particular. Though Askon could see their mouths moving, the wind carried their voices and the words of their conversation away. Whatever was said, it was clear they did not yet agree on the direction the party should take.

By the time they reached the meeting place—twice the allotted hour after they had stepped out of the boat and onto the shore—Askon was altogether annoyed and showed no interest in hiding it. Even Edward, though still calm and quiet, seemed impatient. Thomas sat in the grass across from his friends. Elise lowered herself slowly and sat cross-legged, her hands folded in her lap. Fragment or no fragment, Askon could see it plainly. She had won the argument. But for which side?

"Well, let's get on with it," Askon said, shifting uncomfortably on the old log. "Before we go on, we have to decide. Do we take the road or the river? Edward and I have already discussed our choices. We disagree." He rubbed his forehead with his shirtsleeve. In the time between leaving the boat and gathering everyone together again, it had grown hot.

"I think we should stay in the boat, use the river's swift current to our advantage," he said confidently. "Safety left us weeks ago. It left me months ago. Nowhere is truly safe anymore, especially not for me. So the simple answer, that the road would be safer, makes no difference. All paths are dangerous now. If we get to Lord Apopsé and Morrowmen more quickly, they might have a chance of defeating Iramov and Codard. Under no circumstance should

Iramov be allowed to acquire any more fragments. The damage he's done with the Death fragment is more than enough." Though he didn't realize it, Askon was staring northward, barely acknowledging his audience. He was thinking of Tolarenz.

"Not just the Death fragment," Edward added. Pulling Askon back into the group and out of his dark thoughts. "Remember too that if we are right, Iramov needed my father's help to be in so many places so quickly; he needed the Space fragment as well. Even so, I say the road is the better choice, but not for its relative safety as Askon implies. It's true the road may be safer than the river, but it is our combined skill sets that worry me most if we take to the water."

Thomas nodded, looking pointedly at Elise. She ignored him. Askon's eyes had drifted northward again; he'd heard all of this before.

"None of us have experience navigating a boat other than what we've done these past few days," Edward continued. "But all of us—all of us—have experience staying hidden in the woods. Getting to the South Kingdom quickly is important, but getting there alive is more so."

"It's about probability," Thomas added, as though he might not have another chance to speak. "Is it better to get there, or to *possibly* get there faster? The likelihood of us reaching Lord Apopsé's city is much higher by taking the road."

"Unless they're waiting for us." The words were like a steel trap snapping shut around Thomas's mouth. Even Askon turned to face the group, jarred from his reverie. "It's simple," said the cold, calculating voice. "If Iramov knows we're headed south, and I think he does know, then with these fragments he would easily be able to intercept us." The wind had whipped several dark curls over Elise's face. She pulled them back, revealing her eyes, almost black against her pale skin. "Edward is right. The road would be safer if not for this, but our enemies will not expect us to take the water, may not even know it is an option. Askon is right but for the wrong reasons. It is not speed that makes the river our best choice. It is surprise."

A moment passed. Askon folded his arms across his chest, unable to enjoy her support, annoyed further that Elise had agreed with him while still making his decision look poorly considered. Edward, opaque as ever, hardly moved. He sat thoughtfully, saying nothing.

"Thomas agrees with me," Elise said finally. "We vote as one."

Now Edward came to life; his hearty laughter whooped into the riverside breeze. It continued into wheezes and finally silent twitches. He wiped a tear from his eye and looked to Askon. "Didn't I say they would vote together?"

Askon, his pride still injured at having been out-strategized by Elise, did not find the situation as funny as Edward. Yet he begrudged the prince a forced smile.

"That settles it then," he said rising from his seat. "We follow the Grafdrek to the Estelle and on into the South Kingdom."

CHAPTER FOUR

Riding the Rapids

Edward's continued fit of laughter reminded Askon of John. Many times, John would find a situation to be so funny that even hours later, Askon would catch him chuckling to himself. Edward might laugh now, but something told Askon that his friend still had misgivings.

As they floated the Grafdrek's final miles, Askon thought again of its name: the drink of the dead, thought of its origins, how it poured out of the forest by the same name. It was in that moment he remembered the vacant, expressionless faces in the trees surrounding Dalstone. He remembered the three who should have been dead.

His voice was unsteady over the distant rush of the Estelle. "There's something more," he said. "Something I haven't told you all." He laughed, a short dry burst of air. "It makes Elise even more right about why the river is the right way for us."

"So tell us," said Edward shortly.

Askon hesitated. The Tear and its fragments were capable of many things, but what he was about to say went beyond healing wounds, transporting people from place to place, even killing without blood or pain. All of these were extraordinary. But bringing someone back from the dead? Only in old stories or fairytales had he heard of such a thing. Then again, the Tear itself came from one of those stories. He closed his eyes.

"Never mind," he said. "It can wait until we meet with Morrowmen."

Edward looked doubtful. "Then why bring it up now?"

"Just tell us," said Elise. It was more command than request, and it was the reason why Askon couldn't tell them. He didn't trust her. She knew so much about the Tear, and what did he know of her? Little more than a girl, Elise had been taken from her people and had chosen to remain with the Norill. Then with almost no time together, she and Thomas had fallen in love. It all seemed so unlikely, now more than ever. And her voice. Sometimes she spoke only the softest words, alluring, enchanting almost. Other times, she sounded every bit a hardened commander of men, like the General when Askon had met him in his hidden chambers beneath Austgæta.

He shrugged it off. "It can wait. Morrowmen will be able to put us at ease. If I tell you now, it will simply give us cause for worry. I'm sorry I said anything." He turned to face the confluence of the rivers. If anyone could read Elise's true loyalty, it would be Morrowmen. "The current is picking up. We should stay focused. Everyone grab a pole or an oar." They did, and the rush of the colliding rivers grew louder.

The change happened more quickly than Askon expected. One minute they floated serenely over the wide, flat surface of the Grafdrek's slow-moving waters; the next, sprays of foam shot high over sharp-pointed boulders. Under the stress the boat creaked and scraped as it ricocheted through the rapids.

Then the river relented, smoothing but not slowing its course. On the shore, trees and shrubs, animals, even a fisherman's tent whisked by. Askon smiled to himself. The feeling was akin to the power of the Time fragment: moving along faster than they ought, traveling through a world that seemed to stand still. He reached down and twisted the end of his cloak. Dripping from the spray, it looked more black than green. Water drained in a stream, then dribbled from the cloth.

"I think it would be wise for us to stow the cloaks," said Edward. The Estelle's first set of rapids had soaked him as well. "In fact, after that, I think we should bundle all our gear. Tie it tight, so that if we go over, it will stay in the boat and not around our necks."

It was a good idea. While they awaited the next round of whitewater, they collected the most valuable items and wrapped them in their cloaks. Elise, who wore no cloak, used a blanket instead. Around the bundles they twisted twine, knotted in Norill fashion with Elise's help.

Without his cloak and leather armor, Askon felt awkward and exposed. Edward and Thomas appeared as though they felt similarly. Askon tried not to look at Elise. The first rapids had drenched them all, and her dress, though not revealing when dry, now left little to the imagination. After his mistake in the willow grove, his awareness of her had been heightened, but he won the battle to avert his eyes.

Edward and Thomas had tied their swords to the bundles. Askon could not bring himself to part with his own weapons. On his belt, the long, curved hunting knife still hung securely in its sheath, and his sword remained on the opposite side. If he drowned, then so be it. They had not been lost to the fire in Tolarenz, nor would they be lost to the waters of the Estelle, unless Askon himself were to be lost with them. He tightened the belt, and the eerily silent current became a rumble and rush as they approached the next series of rapids.

This time, they were ready. Poles and oars came out like spears from a shield-wall in the battles of old. And like the men who stood behind those walls, the four grinned at each other, eager for the coming onslaught. They anticipated each stone, each slope of sliding water, each jarring shift as the prow dove down and popped up. At one point, Askon called across the boat to Edward, but the noise of the river was too great. This battle, they would fight without ears and without voices. When the work was done, the enemy lay defeated behind them, its cries receding quickly into the distance. Once again, the calm stillness of the resting river took over. Drenched from head to foot, their hair clinging to their faces and trickling beads of water into the boat, they laughed together and cheered their victory.

Edward shook his head, scattering a shower of droplets into the air, and Askon remembered Roland, the Tolarenz smith, whose dogs would often emerge from the lake in similar fashion. Grinning, Edward rocked the boat left and right in his exhilaration. "I do stand corrected," he said loudly. "Perhaps I should have chosen the river if only because it's much more fun than the road. Riding at full gallop is fast. But this, this is far faster, and the water keeps you cool all the while."

"I could almost enjoy it if I could forget that we're all likely to die at any moment!" said Thomas, not nearly as pleased with the ride. He looked worriedly at Elise. But to Askon, it seemed Thomas did so without cause. She smiled, exhilarated with the speed and the danger, strikingly beautiful. Askon caught himself staring and turned away again.

"I guess it's good that you're enjoying yourself, Edward," he said. "The river goes on and so do the rapids. You'll be of a different opinion, I think, by the end of the day."

And the rapids did go on. There was another, smaller series of rocks, much less dangerous than before, but still enjoyable—even to Thomas. On the other side, Askon's prediction came true. Arcing over the lower Estelle was a tall, sturdy wooden bridge. The materials made it strong; large trees that looked to have been taken from the depths of Grafmark made up the bulk of the construction, and Askon wondered how the builders had moved the immense pieces of wood so far. Instead of projecting directly from the bank of the river, the approaches to the bridge started a hundred yards or more from the edge. A latticework of beams lined either side, curving like a rainbow over the water. Six of the giant trees stood on end beneath, though it seemed that even if the water washed them away, the complex structure of crossbeams could keep the bridge aloft.

When they passed under, it was nearly nightfall. If Apopsé, Iramov, or Codard had men on guard, Askon guessed they wouldn't notice the shadow of the little boat passing by below. Whether there were actually any guards, Askon never knew, but they floated between the great tree pillars and downstream nearly a mile before they heard the familiar roar of whitewater. Thomas, whose turn it was at the rudder, directed them to shore.

Their camp was small and kept near the water with no fire to warm their food, and little said between the travelers. Thomas and Elise wandered off down the river, hand in hand as always. Thomas had promised to return before the night's watches began; he had drawn the first. As the two figures vanished amongst the riverside trees, Askon turned to Edward.

"I don't trust her," Askon began. "There's something about her that doesn't seem right. It all happened so quickly."

"Sometimes it does," said Edward. "I bet if you asked John, he'd say that's the best way for it to happen. Of course, he'd probably think it ought to end quickly as well."

They laughed, but Askon's doubts remained.

"What about the two sides of her? One minute she's sweet, quiet, meek almost. The next she's firing off orders like an instructor at a training ground." He shook his head. "Even her voice changes."

"You act like you've never met a woman before."

"Now you really sound like John," Askon replied. "I thought a prince would see more nuance."

Edward chuckled. "To be fair, you could say the same about men. Take yourself for instance. Have you heard how different you sound when someone's pushed you over the edge?" He waited a moment. "Of course you haven't because you're you."

"I suppose you're right," Askon said. "But I'm also not quietly whispering half the time either."

"No, you're not." Edward looked up at the sky. "So what was it you had to say?"

Askon tilted his head. "What do you mean?"

"Just before we reached the Estelle today, you mentioned there was something you hadn't told us. It seemed important. Now I know why you wouldn't say it; you didn't want Elise to hear."

Edward waited, shifting to lean on one elbow, still looking at the sky. "Out with it."

For a moment, Askon considered keeping the secret to himself. What could the knowledge do to help them? Nothing. All it could do was bring about fear and panic. How would they fight an army that could just rise from the dead when the battle was over?

Then another thought occurred to him. He remembered Caled's face as the rain began to pour in Tolarenz. It was an intentional sacrifice—this much, Morrowmen had told him. There were so many questions Caled could have answered, but now he was gone. What if the same thing happened to Askon? What would happen to his information if he died? The answer was simple. In the words of his father, the best answers always were. The information must be shared. Edward, as strong a candidate as anyone, should know.

And so he explained the faces he had seen in the forest, the faces of the dead. He told his friend about their blank, expressionless stares, how they seemed fearless, unaffected by the threat of swords or arrows or battle itself. Reluctantly, he even told Edward about the wild shifts in the fragment's power, how one minute he'd been fast enough to cut down dozens of Norill before they even knew he was there, and the next minute so slow he barely noticed the entire force marching past his hiding place. He went on to tell of the battle's end, of the arrow and saving Brâghda's life.

"But I never saw the dead faces again," Askon finished quietly. For a moment, Edward said nothing. Then he sat up.

"You said there were three?"

"Yes."

"That bit seems to me like relatively good news."

"Why?"

"If Iramov could raise an army of the dead, bringing back all our fallen enemies and friends, wouldn't he have done so by now? Think of all the forces he has defeated already."

Askon stared out across the river where the moon's pale reflection rippled and wavered over the surface. "But what if he's just hiding them?"

"Then why not send more to Dalstone? If he could raise them all, he'd have hundreds, Askon. There must be some kind of limit to what he can do. Otherwise, we'd be dead by now and fighting in his army."

In that moment, as Askon gazed out upon the lower Estelle, a dreadful thought crept into his mind. What if Christopher, Patrick, and Victor were just a handful of a much larger group? What if somewhere, Roland the smith worked Iramov's forge; Halan trained airborne spies; Askon's father drew designs to engineer Iramov's victory? Askon breathed deeply. What if somewhere, Caled—Knight of Vladvir—sharpened his sword for battle?

"No!" Askon roared, and the echo pinged off the opposing shore, wailing into the distance.

"Shh!" Edward's finger was pressed against his lips. "What are you doing?" he whispered. "There could be guards near enough to hear you." He looked warily from left to right, then back over his shoulder toward the bridge.

"I'm sorry," Askon said, embarrassed at his outburst. "It's just—when I thought about my father or Caled or any of the others from Tolarenz fighting for Iramov, I—"

"You have no way of knowing," Edward said. "And going by the way you described the three in Dalstone, it's not the people who are brought back, just the bodies."

Though well meant, Edward's consolation helped Askon little. Looking down at the blurred shadows of the tall grass, he sighed.

"We need sleep," he said and Edward nodded.

Thomas came blundering through the brush and trees a few dozen yards away. The young man's gear was again askew, and Elise appeared in roughly the same degree of disarray. She followed a few yards behind, with much less urgency.

When Thomas stumbled into full view, he still had his hands at his belt, tightening it. He looked surprised to find Edward and Askon sitting calmly by the waterside.

"I—uh—I heard a shout. Is everything alright? We—I mean, I thought something might be wrong."

"No, nothing is wrong," said Edward coolly.

"Then what was all that noise about?" Elise demanded, in the cold commander's voice.

Thomas placed a hand on her shoulder.

"It's alright Thomas," Askon offered. "I was just talking with Edward about what happened in Tolarenz. The anger, the grief was too much."

Elise batted Thomas's hand away and marched forward. "You should know better," she scolded. "You might've been heard by the guards back at the bridge. A commander, and elf-kind at that, should keep himself under control."

"That's enough," said Thomas. Askon and Edward looked at one another, eyebrows raised. Neither had heard him speak this way to her before.

"It's one thing to be concerned," Thomas continued, "and another to be disrespectful. I'm sure Commander Askon knew his danger, and if not, already knows his mistake."

Elise said nothing, but her face grew dark. Even in the pale starlight, Askon could see it. Her black eyes seemed somehow blacker, and Askon was glad he had not revealed everything to her. She drew back, clasping Thomas's hand, and cast her gaze to the ground.

"I think it's best we get to sleep now," said Edward. "Thomas, you'll be on the first watch."

Thomas snapped to attention, nodding tersely in the military style. "Yes, sir," he said.

With the stars splayed out overhead, Askon wondered at the bright points of white, curiously visible only when surrounded by endless black.

CHAPTER FIVE

Dark Waters

Thomas was shaking him, stammering something unintelligible. Was it sunrise already? The light in the distance seemed like it might be. Now the shaking was more vigorous. Askon put out a hand to still Thomas's efforts. Edward moved slowly a few feet away. Elise was nowhere in sight.

"What is it, Thomas?"

"Askon!" the young man whispered. "I didn't want to speak."

"Why?"

"Guards, they must've heard you. They've got torches, and they're coming this way."

Askon scrambled to his feet. "We need to go, now." He turned to Edward. The prince was already standing.

"Move, then!" he said.

Hardly more than shadows, they hissed through the grass down to the boat. Askon turned to Thomas.

"Where's Elise?" he said coldly.

Thomas stared back with wide eyes. "She went into the bushes, to—uh, you know." He paused awkwardly. "A few minutes later, I saw the torches and heard voices."

Askon turned to Edward. The two exchanged a knowing glance, but said nothing. Marten dove unexpectedly out of the sky, fluttering inches from their faces. He perched restlessly on the prow of the boat. It was the first time Askon had seen him since a full day earlier. "You're a little late," Edward said to the bird.

Seconds later Elise came crashing through the brush. She looked harried, her eyes wild. "Guards!" she choked, pointing upstream to the torches. Thomas caught her in his arms as she tripped over a loose stone.

"We're all here," Edward said. He waved them on toward the water.

The moon and starlight illuminated the boat's path well enough. Each star had a twin reflected in the river's surface making the banks easy to detect, black masses looming up against the scattered points of light. Askon's eyes adjusted quickly, and though the river's many dangers were visible only as shades of gray, he thought he could see well enough to guide them down the stream.

They had stopped to camp because of the dark, had gone as far as they could before encountering whitewater that none of them, not even Askon, could see. Those rapids rumbled now, drawing closer. Out of nowhere a jagged rock formation appeared, and they collided with the stone. Boards and planking creaked and popped, but the boat held together. With poles and oars at the ready, they straightened the little vessel, bracing for another shock.

All around them, the water swirled and churned, roaring ever louder. Suddenly they found themselves sideways in the stream. The boat slammed against another group of jutting rocks. This time, Askon was sure he heard something snap within the hull, but no water came in from below. With a jolt, they dropped another several feet.

Then the river calmed. On their last fall, the boat had taken on a great deal of water. In a few places along the edge, the boards had been nicked and cracked, but the planks in contact with the water held strong. Using clothes, oars, and hands they bailed the excess water from within.

"Perhaps we should have stayed on the water, even in the dark," said Edward as he scooped from between the seat planks.

"Looks like it," Askon replied. "We barely took a scratch in all of that. I'd say it was the biggest we've ridden yet."

Edward put his hands on the gunwale, breathing heavily. "Maybe you were right about taking the river after all."

But they hadn't been listening. After tumbling off the last swale, the roar of the river should have lessened. It hadn't. As though the words were ripped from his mouth, Edward, now seated at the front of the boat, dropped clean out of Askon's sight. Before he could react, Askon too was falling, head over heels. And then he was in the water.

The splashes as they had floated down the rapids felt cool and refreshing, but now the river was icy cold. Askon surfaced, gasping, and it pulled him under again. In the twisting current, he slammed into a flat rock, jarring his shoulder. At his hip, the sword yanked him from side to side as it clacked against riverbed and stone. It was holding him down. And he was running out of air.

With all the strength he could muster, Askon drove his boots into the nearest foothold. He shot out of the water to chest height and sucked in a ragged breath. Another series of boulders battered him as he went under again. Then the stream smoothed for a moment. He began to swim. He gagged and coughed, struggling against the current and the weight of his gear. But the river wasn't finished. It pulled him down a third time, and he felt his strength fading. He pushed up once more, his legs shuddering with the attempt. Exhausted, he flailed in the water, slowly losing ground and gasping for breath, pulling in mouthfuls of water that burned his throat. He retched and twisted as his muscles cramped tight, and the blurry gray night ebbed toward black. His arms grew heavy, refusing to lift for another stroke. He felt the stones of the river bottom, but his feet slipped stupidly over the slimy film. The roar softened as he went under. All he could do was stretch toward the black sky and shivering stars.

And then there was a hand, firm and strong. It gripped his wrist and pulled. At first it seemed that the help had come too late, that his exhaustion would make him too heavy to rescue, but the hand did not relent. Askon pushed against the current and the sliding rocks with what little strength remained to him. The hand pulled fiercely, and Askon burst through the surface of the river, flopping like a fish onto the bank. He coughed and spluttered, a gush of water pouring from his mouth. Tears burned unbidden in his eyes and he heaved again, this time the water only a trickle. He shuddered, wheezing, and blacked out.

"Askon."

"Yes, Liana?"

"You forgot to say goodbye."

A pounding pulse thumped like war drums from within his chest. His eyes and ears throbbed. He was sitting up, drenched in sweat. Wait. Not sweat. Water. Her voice still echoed in his head. He lifted his hands to his face; they resisted the command. It was cold.

Slowly, thickly, like honey dripping from the comb, his senses returned. The smell of the river and musty dirt and crushed leaves. Shadowy patches of grass. A lurid rippling flicker on the water that looked like laughter. The feel of soft earth beneath him and the weight of sodden clothes. In the distance, a great drone of water falling in gallons by the thousand. He tried to shut it out.

Where was he? Someone had pulled him from the river. Where were they now? And his friends, what had happened to them?

He was on the western bank, though his sense of direction felt scrambled, his head woozy. The moon was slightly to the north, in the same direction as the crashing falls. However far they had gone, he felt they would be safe from the guards who had come from the bridge. Even if he were to scream or shout, even if he had a bugle chorus from the king's court, they would not have heard him over the booming falls.

From where he sat, a trail of muddled footprints led back toward the river. He followed the oblong shapes with his eyes, shaking his head as the world pounded in and out of focus. Some distance away, he saw the packs, two bundles wrapped in cloaks and strung with twine like parcel deliveries. From each, a gleaming sword protruded: one for Thomas, one for Edward. Askon sighed with relief. Willing his legs up to his chest, he stood with an effort. Still dizzy, he took a step toward the packs. His head swam as though his eyes had come unhinged in their sockets, rolling like loose marbles. The sensation sent him reeling, and he slammed into the ground. Blackness took him again.

"Askon."

"Yes, Líana?"

"You should have said goodbye."

"I—I'm—"

"Now, wake up."

This time he heard voices first. Then they were gone. Hours had passed. The moon hung low to the northwest, and though no light grew yet in the east, the horizon would soon be afire with the coming of morning. He felt better, still groggy, still dizzy, but better. It took him only a moment to get to his feet. The packs were still there, but he ignored them now. He needed to find his friends.

With unsure feet, Askon stumbled downstream through tangles of grass and reed. Amid the broken rushes a trampled path led up and down the bank, treading along the river, turning now and then to the water's edge. Whoever had traveled this way had made little effort to conceal their steps. Sets of heavy bootprints stood out clearly in the mud, and in some places wide swaths of grass had been flattened. The trailblazer was looking for something, or someone.

With his senses and his balance returning, Askon moved faster through the waterside foliage. When he found his voice, he let no worries of pursuit stifle him.

"Edward!" he shouted. "Thomas! Elise!"

Nothing.

He followed the path to its next bend, where the searcher's tracks went back to the water again. At the shore, an eddy swirled slowly against the current. The circular formation of rock and mud sloshed gently, only just loud enough to be heard over the distant falls. The water churned, oblivious to Askon's urgency, the need to find his friends.

"Edward!" Askon bellowed, as loud as he could muster. Then more quietly to himself, "Where are you?"

He knew it was pointless, foolish even. If for some reason there happened to be enemy soldiers nearby, he would surely be found if they heard him. But they had been through so much together. Thomas, whom Askon had saved from the darkness beneath the Austgæta caverns. Elise, whom they had taken from a life amongst the Norill. They couldn't just be gone.

Then there was Edward. Askon's friend when he had had none. When even John stood against him—in the king's throne room and all those years ago at Vestgæta—Edward stood by his side. Unshakable Edward. The artful politician, cool, level-headed. Not easily enraged, like Askon; not too quick to act, like Askon; smart enough to choose the road and not the folly of the river. Gone.

Askon stared into the spiraling countercurrent. He inhaled, ready to shout again, but nothing came. It was as though his chest was empty, his energy spent. He flopped down onto his knees, defeated.

At the edge of sight, something came floating down the stream. He had almost missed it. He stepped out into the water, and the object became clearer. It was a boot, black with silver buckles. No, it was a pair of boots and something knotting them together. Askon lifted it from the stream. The whole knot came up at once, trickling water into the eddy where he stood ankle deep. He examined the boot first and slogged back to the bank, his feet plunging deep into the fine silt.

His heart sank. Buckles of this quality were rare indeed, silver, not steel or some base metal. Fine etchings interlaced one another along the outer edges. And they had been well cared for. The boots themselves were of the highest craftsmanship and finest sturdy leather. Even soaking wet, Askon knew to whom they belonged. Next he went to the shapeless mass that bound the boots together. A fine, but travel-worn shirt, probably black, though any cloth would have seemed so in the dark, fresh out of the river. But the worst detail was there on the end of the sleeve. A bright blue stag embroidered in the style only the best seamstresses could produce. It all belonged to Edward.

Behind him, Askon heard the crunch of heavy footfalls and the murmuring of troubled voices. His will and conscious mind wanted only to give up, to let them capture him and do what they would, but instinct won out. He spun into a hollow of branches near the edge of the eddy and popped open the clasp on his sword belt. With fingers poised above the hilt, he waited.

CHAPTER SIX

A Determined Farewell

In the waning moonlight the two figures did little to conceal their movements, though their faces were obscured in the dark. They spoke in hushed tones. Askon's vision was hazy, his mind still fuddled by sleep and his narrow escape from the river. From the covert, Askon sized them up as best he could. On the right walked the taller of the two: broad shouldered, hunched, and uncertain. The other was shorter, obviously the leader, one step ahead all the time. With little hesitation, the two moved forward, retracing the path along the river. When they came to the eddy, they stopped. Kneeling, the leader reached down to inspect the pile of sodden clothes. Askon cursed himself for leaving them behind.

He told himself to remember Morrowmen's words, Caled's manner, and Edward's self-control. Perhaps, if he could remain calm, remain focused, he could fight the two searchers, even as exhausted as he was. With the help of the fragment's power, it might even be easy. He concentrated steadily on the glimmering boot-buckles, and felt the quiet calm begin to settle in. Then it shattered, exploding into a thousand broken pieces, and rage snarled into its place.

The leader had examined the buckle, slipped it off the boot and pocketed it. They were stealing Edward's belongings like filthy grave robbers. With the anger already blurring his vision, Askon watched in disgust and horror as the larger figure reached back and tossed the boots and shirt back into the river where they landed with a dull, dead *splat*.

Askon's fingernails bit into the wrapping of his sword hilt. He ground his teeth and unleashed a scream like a wild thing. The blind fury had control now, and he brought down his sword blade with every ounce of strength that remained to him. The larger figure looked up. It was Thomas.

Askon tried to reverse or deflect the direction of his sword, but it was too late. *"I'm sorry. I'm sorry! Stop it!"* his mind wailed. But he couldn't stop; he could only close his eyes. Without mercy, the sword came down in the dark.

Lightning. It was the only way to describe it. And in later years, that is exactly how Askon would tell the story. In a flash, faster than he had ever seen a person move, Thomas lifted his sword and stopped Askon's steel as though the half-elf had struck a boulder. With that same unnatural speed, Thomas gripped Askon's hand and turned the point of the blade down, speaking calming words all the while. Askon never remembered what was said, but when he finally could understand his friend, Thomas was saying, "It's alright. It's alright. It's me, Thomas. Askon, it's Thomas."

So it was. Next to him, looking perplexed, knelt Elise. She rose, brows furrowed over coal-black eyes, and cautiously handed the silver buckles to Askon. Her hands brushed against his. And to his surprise he found himself holding her right hand in his. Not holding, clutching. She tried to pull away, but he did not release her.

"It was you!" he said, stunned.

Now Thomas looked confused. It was as if Askon had forgotten they had just drawn swords against one another.

"It was you," Askon said again. He stared at the buckles.

Elise ripped her hand free and stepped back, slipping slightly behind Thomas. She looked afraid.

Askon laughed, a wild, half-crazed sound. "I'm such a fool. We never should have come this way. Now he's gone. I didn't trust you. But I should have, and now what will we—"

"Askon!" Thomas almost shouted. "What are you talking about?"

Askon smiled, looking a little less crazy but just as delirious. "Elise pulled me from the river. Without her I'd be dead. As dead as—"

"Don't say it." Thomas stopped him. "We don't know where Edward is."

But Askon was still stuck on Elise. He spilled it all. "I didn't trust you, Elise. That's why I didn't tell you everything before we crossed onto the Estelle. It's true; Morrowmen will know what to say, but I withheld it because I couldn't believe how quickly the two of you fell for one another. I thought it was a trick."

They both looked wounded, Thomas most deeply. Elise's face changed quickly though, almost as fast as Thomas's sword had been. The black eyes seemed to freeze Askon where he stood. "You'll know better next time, won't you elf-kind?"

It was the second time she had used the Norill term for the elves, but Askon knew now that it was only part of her nature. The girl was no more sinister than Thomas himself.

"Or maybe next time there won't be a hand to drag you and your precious weapons from the bottom of the river." She stomped off toward the packs.

Pain still lined Thomas's face. He followed her slowly, looking once back at Askon before turning away.

"I'm sorry," Askon called to his back. Then to the river and the void where Edward should have been, "I'm sorry."

Hours passed. The morning grew old and hot. Their clothes, which had been sopping wet in the chill before sunrise, dried within the first hour and became uncomfortably stiff. There was still no sign of Edward.

For miles they followed the stream, and within each mile there were rapids large enough to severely batter anyone traveling through them, boat or no boat. With each crown of jagged rocks, Askon grew more and more certain that no amount of searching would ever lead them to his friend. He did not know how close they were to Apopsé's city—if they were close at all—but he knew it lay somewhere to the west. By now, Iramov's forces might already be standing at the gates.

Tired and hot, the three sat heavily. The lower Estelle rushed by only a few feet away. Thomas and Elise had said little to Askon since the altercation by the eddy. In the king's army, he had often felt outcast and alone, but the isolation had fueled his desire to achieve, pushed him to take greater risks—like going after an imprisoned prince. Now, after he had grown accustomed to the friendly interactions and shoulders with which to share heavy burdens, he felt almost as singular and powerless as he had in the pouring rain of Tolarenz.

Yet he remembered how it had all begun. The Austgæta assignment was to be his last. Finished with his duties, he would head back and lead his people. Caled meant to turn over his office, and Askon would be the one to take it. It was not a position of immense power—though at the time he did not know the fragment would be handed down as well—but it was a position of great honor. Tolarenz had become nearly autonomous in the years under Caled's care, and that is how it would have remained. Askon was meant to be its new watchman and symbol of protection, young and strong, like the city itself.

But he could not protect the little valley anymore. That opportunity had passed. Before him, the rippling water streamed along. He thought of the Time fragment, green and gleaming beneath his shirt, and he laughed. The gem could speed or slow his perception of time—even stop it—but it could not take him back. He could not save Caled or his parents or his sister, or Edward. It was time to protect those who still lived and to let those who were gone rest.

To himself, Askon said his goodbyes. Again and again he apologized to Edward and thanked him for his help, and still the river rushed on. Then Askon reached into one of the packs—Edward's pack—and removed his armor and cloak. He pulled the gear over his chest and arms, tightening the clasps and buckles, then rose with his back to the river and snapped the cloak out before him. He wrapped it around his neck, the hood spilling limply down. Marten, who had been hopping through the grass nearby, leapt to the shoulder guard. At first, the others didn't even look up. They were lost in thought and grief and the daze of weariness.

"We're done here," he said.

Thomas was the first to raise his eyes. There stood Askon in his flowing cloak, falcon perched upon his shoulder, silhouetted against the sparkling river. He was like one of the Glittering Host, called forth by Caled himself in the years beyond distant memory. And indeed, in that moment, he was. Thomas spoke not a word and rose instantly. Then Elise followed suit. Her black eyes resisted for a moment, but gave way to the command of Askon's voice and the pull of Thomas's hand.

"Edward is lost," Askon said. "I would like nothing more than to find him and give him the memorial he deserves. But it is better to honor what he would have wanted, and he would have wanted us to reach the South Kingdom before Lord Iramov and before Codard. We have to go."

With another glance at the stream, Thomas turned west and led Elise back toward the road. He turned once more to look upon Askon in all his gleaming, sparkling glory, but the spell was broken.

Marten had flown, the river had fallen below the bank behind them, the sun beat down, and Askon had lifted the hood to cover his downturned face. All Thomas saw now was a tired, weatherbeaten man. But even in the hooded shadow, the eyes—one green and one blue—burned with unfailing determination.

When the angry afternoon heat finally exhausted itself, the travelers were grateful. At one point, still early in the day, Thomas had suggested they find shade and rest until the sun faded, but Askon had disagreed, still absorbed in his newly focused effort to reach Apopsé. He saw far at night, much farther than his companions if the light was right, yet in the daytime he saw even farther. And so they stayed the course. If they happened upon the city, Askon would see it sooner, much sooner than if they traveled at night.

But the sun proved to be even more fixed and determined than Askon. On the horizon's edge in the west, craggy peaks rose up, siblings of the range that flanked Grafmark. At times, when atop one of the rises that bulged here and there from the plain, he could see all the way to the foothills. Though neither Elise nor Thomas knew it yet, in those hills, a forest began again. Under the trees, long shadows cooled the ground beneath. The going there would have been much more pleasant. Askon said nothing, and instead directed their course to the nearest clump of dry twisted trees, stragglers of various breeds collected around a spring.

They cast themselves onto the ground in the meager shade. Thomas and Elise did not wander away together this time. There was nowhere for them to go and the day's march combined with the previous night's trial and tragedy left them without the will or the energy to go on. Askon rolled over onto an elbow to face the others.

"We rest. No watch. It's a risk, but sleep will do us all good," he said. "I can see the road now at times. By tomorrow it will be close enough for us to follow whether we choose to walk it openly or travel alongside." He turned away from them and closed his eyes.

In the night, Askon dreamed. They were on the river again, caught in the rapids with no means of escape. Poles snapped and oars broke as he pushed hard against the rocks. John was there and helped for a while, but then he fell out of the boat, his hand waving goodbye into the distance. Marten held a tiny oar in his talons, swooping and diving between the rocks, but he dropped the oar and flew away. Thomas and Elise sat together, holding hands and staring into each other's eyes while Askon frantically tried to steer their course. Then they were gone.

He was standing between the towering oaks of the town hall garden in Tolarenz. It was raining hard. Before him, spread out like an enormous tablecloth lay the powdered circle where he had perceived the fates of his family members and the people of his city. It began to dissolve before his eyes, and he reached down quickly to touch the circle again, hoping it would show him the faces of those he loved once more. But the air resisted.

Pushing hard against the force, he screamed, a primal, animal sound like he had made when coming out of the bushes by the riverside. The force gave way, and his palm made contact with the fading circle. Nothing happened. He looked up and saw a blond ponytail bounce lightly above the maze of hedges. He heard a child's laughter.

The rain came down harder than ever, and a flood rose to cover his hand, then his wrist, his elbow. He stood, lifting his hand to his face; it was covered in blood. He glanced back at the rising water and it too was blood, warm and red. With a start, he jumped back. The rising tide and its horrible red surface became utterly still, flat as a windowpane.

Caled stood there, feet firmly planted on the motionless red sea that surrounded him. The rain had stopped and all was totally silent. Caled reached out and handed him a bright green gem that dangled from a silver chain. Then he began to sink. Desperately, Askon reached out from the boat to pull Caled back, but he had already gone under. Askon hesitated, then plunged his hand into the blood-sea, grasping for Caled's outstretched arm. He felt something and pulled hard. When it came up, he saw the faces of Patrick and Christopher and Victor, three faces and yet one face.

He released them, his hands and arms drenched in blood, his fingers slick with it. At his neck the gem pulsed, then flickered, then glowed bright, the green sickly against the endless expanse of red. Then Edward stood upon the surface, as had Caled, arm outstretched. But from behind Askon, a warm musical voice spoke slowly.

"The cur of Tolarenz is dead. His whelp will be next. Then all of the filth will be washed away from Vladvir."

Askon spun in the boat, and there—a wicked sneer slashing across his face—stood Iramov, bald head gleaming, crimson bull emblem ruddy against his black leathers. Askon found that he had already drawn his sword. He brought the blade down hard and fast. Iramov vanished in a flash of smoke and cackling laughter. The green light of the fragment went out.

When Askon turned back to the red sea, Edward had already been swallowed up. Only his fingers protruded from the surface. Askon lunged for him, crying out, and his blood-filmed hands clasped his friend's. He pulled. But the blood was too slick, and his hands came free. Suddenly the stillness broke and the flat sea became a roiling current. Edward's hand rushed away, beyond Askon's reach. And then he awoke.

CHAPTER SEVEN

A Welcome Diversion

It was early morning, and not yet light. Askon sat up, his head reeling from the dream and his body recovering from the river's beating. He reached for his waterskin and took a long drink, gulping as the cool liquid trickled down his face. Glancing around, he found that he was alone. For a moment, panic began to rise within him. Then he heard them, speaking softly to one another, some yards away, behind a clump of gnarled brush and short, hardy trees.

"I don't think I'll come over there this time," Askon said loudly. "See that you are ready to leave soon. We eat while we walk. I think you've had enough time to—" he paused, "rest." He thought of John. John would have had something better, something wittier. It would have lifted Askon's spirits. He thought of Edward. Edward would have laughed.

By noon they could all see the road clearly. It lay like a flat leather strip ready to be cut into bootlaces. People traveled the road, but only in small groups, none large enough to be a patrol or military force from either side.

But that was only on the road. An hour after setting out, a larger group—Askon thought he counted ten—had appeared southwest of their position. They wore black or some other dark color. One member of the party was decidedly smaller than the others, a head shorter in most cases, and the four largest figures carried something. Whatever it was stretched several feet in length. They went carefully with their cargo, but not slowly, and they moved south.

Over the last few hours, all three travelers had become obsessed with the group. At one point while the morning was still young, they had even turned directly south in order to keep the others in view. Elise and Thomas saw them as a black dot at vision's edge. Askon could discern individuals, sometimes better than others. But try as they might, they seemed never to gain or lose ground.

"Do you see anything new?" Thomas asked for what must have been the hundredth time.

Askon sighed. "Nothing."

"Perhaps they've seen us following them," Elise suggested. She had again taken on the affected whisper, the one that reminded Askon of an owl's wings in the night. He ignored it, but responded in kind.

"That would be very unlikely. The two of you can see them, so they might be able to see us, but the sun is at our backs. It would be in their faces if they looked this way."

"Then why aren't we closing in on them?" asked Thomas.

Askon laughed. "Because we aren't moving very fast." He stretched with a groan, twisting at the waist. "We're tired and, to be honest, slow. It's not surprising we can't catch them. If we want to investigate, our best bet is to wait until they stop to rest and continue toward them."

So they did. Just after noontime, the dark group stopped, most likely to eat, Askon judged. The three travelers continued even as the heat grew, not so hot as the day before, but still uncomfortable. They narrowed the space between the two groups significantly, though the others were still a dark mass to Elise and Thomas. Askon, however, could see them more clearly now, when they weren't behind the slope of a hill or patch of trees, both of which had become more common as they moved south. The details he had seen earlier were confirmed, and their clothing, uniforms he now saw, were definitely not black. At the remaining distance, the color still eluded him, but it was for certain the same across the entire group.

By morning the gap had narrowed a great deal. All day the travelers had continued their pursuit, maintaining their distance. At sunset the others made camp. Askon and his friends pressed onward, lessening the gap until evening turned to night. With his clear vision, Askon led them forward confidently yet carefully, knowing his followers would have to rely on his directions and the pale moonlight. When they could go no farther, they decided on a two-shift watch. Thomas volunteered to take the first.

Askon slept peacefully, no dreams of blood or lost faces disturbed him. He awoke to a bleary-eyed Thomas, signaling his turn to sit up. When Askon felt fully alert, he gestured toward Elise, who lay sleeping nearby. Askon and Thomas said nothing to one another, and the younger man stumbled over to her and fell promptly to sleep.

In the distance, where the darkly dressed group had set up their camp, a small fire burned. Above it a trickle of smoke meandered lazily into the star-peppered sky. Askon was sure they would set a watch of their own, as many as three watchmen per shift. With this in mind, Askon and his friends had refrained from building a fire themselves. Close enough that such a fire would now give away their position to the others, Askon wondered if they had been spotted anyway.

A few hours later, Askon woke Thomas and Elise. Before stopping to rest, they had agreed to a short night. Only the faintest stirrings of light stretched along the eastern horizon, but for Askon it was enough to see quite far. In fact, he had seen much already.

"They check the cargo from time to time with great care," he said as they gathered up the packs. "Whatever it is, it seems to be important."

"How long should we follow them?" Elise asked.

Askon thought for a moment. "I've wondered the same. I think we follow them long enough to determine if they are hostile, or we follow until they stop heading southwest, toward Apopsé's city. From what I know, it isn't far. We might be able to see it by the end of the day."

On they went. For the first few hours, they gained on the group ahead of them. It had taken longer for the others to pick up camp than Askon had expected, giving him and his friends time to close in. Then, at approximately the same time as on the previous day, they stopped to eat. With the others seated around a large lonely oak, Askon stopped his own party.

"That's close enough," he said, holding out a hand.

They too halted under the shade of a single tree, this one a sycamore. Askon was reminded of the gardens back in Tolarenz. Thomas leaned against the tree's thick trunk, and Elise already rested between two large exposed roots. Marten perched in the branches, picking at the remains of a snake.

"Askon," Thomas began tentatively. "I've seen you with Marten before. Sometimes he seems to communicate with you somehow, like back when you had to leave our mission to Norogæta so you could get to Tolarenz."

Askon frowned. Too many times he had been forced to address this topic. It was a sore one, one that often led to suggestions about the nature of the elves. "What of it?" he said.

"Well, if he can tell you things, why can't we just send him on ahead to scout this group?"

"For one, he doesn't *tell* me things," Askon replied, still terse. "He shows me there is something that needs attention. I have to discover and interpret what that is, but it's usually danger of some kind."

Elise shifted against the tree, trying to get comfortable. "So he wouldn't be able to help us understand if these people are friends?"

"No." Askon lay down in the grass beneath the shady tree. He put his hands behind his head. "He would let me know if they meant to attack us, but other than that, he'll be of little help."

No more than a quarter of an hour later, they were on the trail again. Walking carefully, and staying behind cover when possible, Askon and his friends kept pace with the others for the rest of the day. In some ways, being close gave them an advantage. All three could now see if any of the others stayed behind or looked suspicious. However, in many cases, they wished they had remained at a greater distance. Every pause the others made became a recognition, every glance back, a confirmation, but the dark group continued on their way whether they had seen the three travelers or not.

Immediately after setting out from the shade of the sycamore, Askon recognized the uniforms. In make and design they were akin to those worn by the Darts of Grafmark. Even Thomas noted this detail, as he now wore the armor himself. It was lighter even than the leather worn by the king's scouts, yet strategically fortified for dueling or archery, as the Darts fought little in large-scale battles.

The color too became clearer as they drew closer, but it was not that of the South Kingdom or Lord Apopsé, whose symbol was a white dove on a sky blue field. Askon had always thought a hawk would have been a better emblem, and John had often mocked the choice, but these soldiers wore no doves. They wore purple. If it could even be called that. In the open sunlight, Askon and Elise had agreed upon the matter. Thomas insisted it was simply a trick of the distance, that the uniforms were clearly black. And almost all the time, Askon felt the same. But against the deep green and gold of the plains grass, especially on the short cloaks and leggings, the color, like the faded skin of a ripe plum, became faintly purple.

For the third time since they had left the river, since they had left Edward, the sun sank below the western mountains. They crested another of the increasingly frequent hills, its mottled ridge sprinkled with purple and white hyacinth, and saw the jewel of the South Kingdom spread out before them: Apopsé's city. Towering pillars and domed rooftops rose above a massive wall that stretched expansively and gleamed white as ivory even in the receding sunset. Elise gasped and Thomas gazed in wonder. Even Askon slowed his pace in order to look upon it. Left unchecked for years, Apopsé had been busy indeed. Behind the wall thousands of lights burned amongst the city's buildings, an orange mirror-image of the coming stars.

Deep within, past the countless rows of market stalls, homes, forges, taverns, and every other type of edifice Askon could imagine, another wall separated the palace from the city proper. It too had been built with the same marvelous white stone, and were such a thing possible, Askon thought that the Tolarenz town hall could be placed upon wheels and rolled through at least three of the arches. One of these was so large that he guessed the same could be said even for the Dalstone meeting hall.

Beyond the second wall stood the palace itself, with wide domed rooftops similar to those along the battlements of the outer wall. In some ways the palace was larger than Codard's castle, though not as tall. King's City had several towers that stood nearly twice the height of Apopsé's highest domes, but the city of the South Kingdom spread over nearly twice the area. Askon thought to himself that perhaps the designers here were wiser, in that more of the space in Apopsé's palace would be usable to its inhabitants, while Codard's towers, though impressive, were less functional for daily life.

"How far do you think it is?" Thomas wondered aloud.

The thought had already occurred to Askon. "A day and a half," he said. In truth, he was sure they would take at least one full day to reach the outer wall, but that time could be lengthened depending on the dark group ahead of them. At most, they were two days from their destination. Somewhere in that pearly white city, Morrowmen waited, hopefully with answers, hopefully with a plan.

The others again built a small camp for the night. Against a pink sunset, Askon watched the smallest member of the dark group pace across the camp to the long white object they had carried ever since Askon first noticed them. They were close enough now that he could make out faces, even in the fading light. This one had sharp features that cast long shadows over his face and nose, making it difficult to see his eyes. Like the others, he wore the modified Darts of Grafmark armor, but as did only two of the dark party, this one wore a hood.

The small soldier moved deftly, and knelt by the long white object. Reaching down with gloved hands, he pulled back the covering, something Askon had seen various members of the party do whenever they halted for food or rest. Until now though, he had been unable to see what they were looking at under the wrapping. Lifting the cover, which Askon recognized as nothing more than a thick white sheet, the soldier revealed what it was they had been lugging across the miles of grass and scrub brush into the hills of the South Kingdom.

It was a person. A body. The soldier leaned down and pressed his hand against the forehead, then ran it gently alongside the face. With the other, he dipped a white cloth into a small bucket nearby, and with the utmost care, squeezed drops of water into the partially opened mouth. Then he dabbed the cloth at the cheeks and temples. After looking on for a moment, he rose slowly and lifted the sheet, the white cloth billowing out with the cool breeze. In the split second when the soldier's shadow moved away from the body, the remaining light of sunset glowed on the face below. Askon stared in disbelief, joy, suspicion, anger. The cargo that the dark company had carried all this way was Edward.

CHAPTER EIGHT
The Dark Party

Askon wondered if Thomas and Elise had even seen him go. For a few minutes, they had all stared out at the city, mesmerized by its beauty. Then, Thomas and Elise had wandered away to a place more private. Askon did not know where they went, did not want to. They would only have slowed him down, maybe even tried to stop him. Now, he decided, was not the time for discussion or debate. Edward lay in the hands of armed men. It would not take long for them to realize that at the very least, they held captive a person of nobility.

Amid the spare trees and shifting grass, Askon knew he would be virtually invisible to the others. Whatever their intent, they would not see him coming or hear his footsteps. Around the first hill, far enough away from Edward's captors that he would not be detected, he practically sprinted, his clear sight availing his purpose in the dark. Around the second hill, he slowed his feet and his breathing for the approach toward their camp.

Then he could see them and hear their chatter. A few were already asleep, their bodies curled atop bedrolls or under blankets.

Others though, remained awake, eating, drinking, laughing. At three points around the makeshift encampment, sentries manned their posts, staring out into the rustling hills, waiting for a sign of movement. Askon would give them none.

Crouching low in the grass, he found a larger party than he had reckoned. Either by a trick of the light and distance or by some strategy practiced amongst the group, they had managed to conceal their numbers, bringing Askon's count to twelve. This detail left three on guard, three already asleep, and six awake but unaware. Given the right conditions, and help from the Time fragment, it was not more than he could handle. He felt for the gem under his shirt. He pressed it against his chest with the heel of his thumb, rolling it back and forth. As he did so, the voices in the camp became clearer.

"I hear princelings fetch a high price, if you know where to advertise," said a gruff voice.

"Don't go talkin' like that again. We got our payment comin' just as right as right when we get back," said another, this one nasal and sharp.

"If ya ask me," said a third, "he's heavy enough, we should'a just left him in the drink back there. Nothin' anybody can do for him now."

The man with the gruff voice didn't seem convinced. "He's alive ain't he? Probably come around one o' these days. What's the code say about a live prisoner anyway?"

"It says take what ya need and leave 'em for dead," said the third voice through mouthfuls of food.

"Well, the code isn't always the most profitable option, now is it?" the nasal one snapped. "Specific orders supersede the Bandit's Code."

"Don't call it that," said the third voice. "You make it sound less than it is."

"You want to talk about code?" the gruff one said. "Code says our new recruit has to pass the test."

Laughter echoed all around.

"Not for this one. Our wise leader can't bring himself to order it done. I think he's afraid."

"All the more reason to take the test. We can't have recruits out on assignments who haven't proven themselves. It's a danger to the lot of us."

"Well, you know the rule. Recruits fight the first captive."

Askon's breath caught in his throat. Edward was their captive, and even if he woke up, he would be in no position to fight, even against an untested youth. Perhaps especially that sort, as it was clear that these mercenaries were little more than highwaymen. A young recruit in their ranks would be vicious and cruel, with little to lose. He pulled the fragment from within his shirt. In the dark it glowed dim green, shedding only the tiniest light within his half-closed palm. He stared at its facets, followed the links of the silver chain, and watched as the heartbeat rhythm gradually slowed.

"Do they have to kill?"

"Code says they do," the gruff voice laughed.

Askon tried to focus, but the next words—from the grating nasal voice—broke his concentration. "Doesn't say the captive's gotta be able to fight for himself does it?"

"No, it doesn't."

Another round of laughter.

The fragment no longer mattered. Thomas and Elise, back on the hillside, no longer mattered. Even his mission to reach Morrowmen, to stop Iramov, no longer mattered. On the Grafdrek, it had been Askon's decision to stick to the river. It was his fault Edward had fallen into the waters of the lower Estelle. And now, it would be his fault if his friend were killed in some base execution by thieves and robbers.

He rose from the grass, hood shadowing his fierce eyes and face. In the darkness he was a looming shadow, sword in the left hand, knife in the right. He took a step forward and was driven hard into the fragrant grass.

Two sets of hands wrapped tightly around his arms. A third twisted his wrists until his weapons came free. Askon thrashed against them, slamming his head into one of his attackers. He heard his weapons ping against the ground and the third set of hands took the place on his right.

"Let me go," he growled through clenched teeth, still struggling against the hand.

"An' where would that get us?" said the one on his left, foul breath hot and sickly on Askon's ear. "Look what ya did to Thal, down there. A headbutt is no kind of greeting for a guest to make." They dragged him, kicking and struggling, into the firelight.

"Oy!" shouted the one on his right. "We found the third one!"

It was then Askon paid the price for his hasty decision to come down from the hilltop. Out of the shadows, three more men in purple uniforms emerged. Two held Thomas and the third, Elise. His friends looked mostly unharmed, but Thomas struggled with what strength remained to him, his eyes wild and frantic. He did not even seem to notice Askon. Elise stood straight, chin up, stoic against the hands that held her own behind her back.

"Eh?" crooned the nasal voice. "Now this one's a fighter. Have a look. In better shape he is than the gangly one there with the girl." He paced over from the fire pit and looked Askon up and down. With a snap, he yanked the hood from Askon's head. "Oh, and you're an elf," he added with some amusement. "Well, half an elf anyway."

A snarl curled over Askon's face as he lunged at the nasal-voiced man. Stepping back, the man lifted both hands, palms out, smiling.

"Whoa," he said. "This one surely is a fighter indeed. Hey, Mot?" He looked back toward the fire pit. "Remember how we were talkin' about that test we give to the new recruits?"

"Like it was just a minute ago," said Mot, the gruff voice from before.

The two laughed, though no one else did. Askon's mind whirled, contemplating his own escape and the rescue of his friends, but the mercenaries' grips were tight.

"Let's get the recruit then. This'll be more fair, I think. And more fun. Fightin' a half-dead princeling is hardly an entertaining proposition," said the nasal-voiced man.

When the recruit appeared, Askon was not surprised. It was the smaller soldier he had seen tending to Edward. He thought it strange that such a seemingly kind caretaker would have fallen in with thugs like these, but the recruit looked not the least bit timid now in the flickering firelight.

As had been the case for as long as Askon and his friends had followed the dark party, the recruit wore a hood. None of the others present did so. Whoever the second hooded soldier Askon had seen from the hilltop had been, he would not be present for the test.

"Hey Green Hand, be careful with this one. I hear the half-elves like to cheat," a voice called from the ring that had formed around Askon and his opponent.

"Yeah, Tolarenz is gone now, so you might let this one live. He could be the only one left."

"Nobody would notice anyway."

Anger twisted inside Askon. How dare these brutes, these spineless thieves say such things? But he knew he had to control it, to focus.

"Don't think of a salamander."

He glanced around, trying to find something to fix his concentration upon, but the ring of laughing faces made it difficult. Then they threw the sword in front of him. It clattered against the dirt and rocks amongst the grass.

"Don't you have any little forest friends to come help you out?"

"Where's your magic? Show us your magic!"

"Your daddy give you that sword, elf? I hear they can't do anything for themselves. Gotta stay under Mommy and Daddy's wing till they're grown men. Near all of our boys have seen under the skirts of most the half-elf women by the time they even get to leave the nest."

"Bah, just kill him and get it over with. Good riddance to the half-man. Looks like it's only a coward's half."

He tried again to concentrate, but like a dry twig in the summer sun, something inside him snapped. He rushed the skinny recruit, snatched the sword, blade gleaming. He did not notice the flicker of the exposed fragment or the quick movements of the ring as they stepped back from his rage.

With his face contorted in anger, he flew at the recruit. Like a bird, like Marten in fact, the hood perked up and the legs bent into a fighting stance. And then the recruit's blade was out, clutched and angled in the left hand. Just before Askon collided with him, he breathed, leaning back, then lunged.

At least Askon thought the recruit would lunge. Instead, Askon hit the dirt. His sword remained in his grasp, but his arms and legs sprawled awkwardly about him. Somewhere in the distance the ring of onlookers cackled with laughter. He whirled up from his fallen position, blade level with his eyes, ready to deflect any attack. None came.

The recruit stood with head cocked slightly, weight on one hip. He looked around. In the roar of laughter from the surrounding ring and the haze of the fragment's world-quickening effect, Askon thought he saw the recruit join the laughter, the purple hood bobbing up and down. Anger welled inside him, clawing and scratching like the terrible beast it was, and everything became blurrier, faster, harder to track.

Without warning, the recruit shot across the ring, and sword clashed against sword. Askon shuddered at the impact, but it was not the strength of the attack that worried him most, it was the speed. In a blast of slashes, the recruit's sword flicked before Askon's eyes. Instinctively, Askon defended himself. Not a single stroke made contact. But before he could counter, the recruit shoved him away.

They stood five feet from each other. Around the ring, the laughter faded. Again the recruit stood up and looked around, then with a wave of a thin hand, signaled Askon to attack. The insult cut to the bone, and the laughter swelled again, louder than ever. With only a sliver of control, and with a great deal more fury, Askon went on the offensive.

An overhead cut with all the force he could muster. Blocked and shrugged off. He staggered. An upswing to the right hip. The recruit's sword was there almost before Askon made the decision to strike. It was as though his mind were an open book. A stab, parried. Back-cut, evaded. Lunge, too far. A rain of wild blows: blocked, dodged, ducked, blocked, parried.

Slash. It came off the parry so quickly Askon had not even seen it. The recruit's sword bit deep into Askon's right leg, just below the hip. He screamed in pain, dropping to one knee, and his opponent jumped back, pulling the sword free. The recruit lifted a hand to his face.

As he did so, the purple hood fell away. There, in the dancing shadows of the fire, two horrified eyes stared back, one green and one blue. The features were angular, and the ears sat high on the jawline. Their points stuck up sharply like knives against the shimmering blond hair which had been pulled back into a tight braid. The recruit was no man at all, but a half-elven woman.

Askon was stunned, and the world whirled around him as the fragment flickered faster and faster. "How could you?" He heard himself shouting. "How can you let them say those things when you are one of us!"

The woman said nothing. She just stood there, with her hand held to her half-open mouth and a tortured look twisted across her face.

"We should fight *them*," he roared. "They hate us! They will always hate us!" He stood, clutching the deep cut in his leg. "I'll kill them all before they hurt Edward, before they hurt my friends. Especially a traitor like you." And he spat into the dust and grass.

He charged her, and she deftly spun away. Their swords clashed, and he heard her try to say something, but he would be the fool no more. With blinding quickness she blocked and parried, ducked and evaded. It was like he fought his own shadow, only much faster, a shadow that could predict his every move.

Then, pain in her eyes, Askon watched helplessly as she whisked the flat of her blade down, pressing it hard against the cut she had made previously. Askon doubled over in pain, and fell again to his knees.

"Finish it then!" he screamed, his voice ragged, breaths coming in gasps.

"I—"

And then came a strange sound. Behind him? He did not know. It was distinct, and the laughter was gone. All there was in the fire-lit circle was the half-elf woman, mouth agape, and the rustling grass. Around them, the other men stood silent. The strange sound rose up above the wind in the long stalks and over Askon's rasping breath. A whistling.

Crack!

Sharp rocks dug into his back, and the mounds of grass pushed and prodded his beaten body. He stared blearily up into a sea of stars and wondered if these brigands, with their traitorous half-elven re-cruit, would be the ones to end his life. If they did, would he pass into those stars that now, so high and distant, looked coldly upon him? It was said that Alora herself had been lifted up by the gods to become the Breaker of Hearts. Her constellation shone out through the wisps of cloud above, her fingers in light contact with her lover, Heraphus the Mender. Unable to stand, Askon stared into the sky, waiting for death.

A hooded figure loomed into view. It was the same hood the elf woman had worn. He grimaced. "Do it, then," he snarled, his head reeling.

"And what would that be?" said a new voice. He had not heard it in the fireside conversation or leading up to the duel. "Kill you?" It was not a woman's voice. "That might put *me* out of my misery, if I was rid of your blundering idiocy. But I'm not sure it would do you much good at all." The figure reached down and held the fragment between two fingers, its chain halting the gem a few inches above Askon's chest.

"Have you forgotten what this is?" said the figure. "I mean, logic says even a dimwit would recognize that you carry one of the five fragments. Apparently, however, logic is forsaken in that thick military skull of yours. Perhaps I have forgotten, and actually instructed you to run about with it swirling in the breeze shouting, 'My name is Askon, village idiot of Tolarenz! Come have a look at the miraculous fool who carries a piece of Alora's Tear!' At least then you might've done the opposite."

In a flash, the figure yanked back his hood, exposing his face to the dim light. It was hideous, like a skull, all sunken eyes and gaunt cheeks. Over the bald head, a few thin strands of pure-white hair twined crazily like drunken spiderwebs. Curling lips flecked with white bits of loose skin rose above a horrid mouth and the grotesque smile continued to the raised eyebrows that said, "*Are you so stupid as to still not know who I am?*" The gruesome face stared for a second, then with a look of disgust, turned away.

"Morrowmen?"

He phrased it as a question, but already knew it was true. Surely, a reprimand of some kind would come, but Askon could think of nothing else to say. In the shadows Morrowmen cast his arms out wide, flipping his hands at the wrist. And just like that, the ring of mercenaries dispersed. Morrowmen stood with his back to Askon in the same long robes he had worn in the Tolarenz town hall. He was still shaking his head.

"We're doomed," said the old man. "Iramov is on his way with a Norill army, Codard—the spineless jellyfish—is helping him, and you're running around as tightly wound as a schoolboy with too many rules to break. Have you learned absolutely nothing at all? If I didn't think it would become infected and cripple you for life, I'd leave that wound open for the rest of the journey, just so you could remember your own stupidity." He snorted and his shoulders twitched. "At least you made it here alive. Wonder of wonders."

Slowly the world came to rest before Askon's eyes. He frowned and took a step toward Morrowmen. Hearing the footsteps, the old man cocked an ear and pivoted on his walking stick. "Something to say?" he asked. "Can it speak?"

Askon tried to ignore him. "Why do all this, Morrowmen? Why kidnap my friends, fall in with these common bandits who clearly do not support the cause of Tolarenz and its people? Why make this woman fight me when you knew I wouldn't be able to control myself. You played me like a hand of cards. Why?"

Morrowmen sighed, looked at his walking stick, thought better of it, and rolled his eyes. "Think about what you say, Askon. Just this once—at least to start with."

"I don't know." And the whistling.

Crack!

"'I don't know' isn't an answer. It takes no thought whatsoever. Try again," Morrowmen commanded.

Askon fell to his knees. A long, unintelligible *hrmph* escaped his shuddering mouth. Tears trickled down his face.

"I have tried," he snapped, his voice cracking. "I don't know!"

Again, the whistling.

But this time, the stick never reached him. Instead of the now all-too-familiar *crack* as the gnarled wood connected with Askon's bruised skull, all he heard was a dull *clunk*.

"That's enough, Morrowmen. Leave him alone," said a voice, familiar yet somehow alien. In the lingering haze of the fragment, which still refused to fully release Askon, the sound was like cool water in a sweltering desert. And like water, it slipped through the fingers. A delicate hand lay on his left shoulder and a sword shone out, half buried in the wooden staff.

"What do you know? I'll leave him alone when I'm ready." Against the refreshing sound of the half-elf woman's voice, Morrowmen's croaked like a toad or a crow. He wrenched the walking stick free.

"No," she said, stepping in front of Askon. "I've seen enough of pain, enough of suffering. I won't watch you torture him anymore."

"Or else what?" cawed the crow.

She turned the sword so that the moon's reflection slid down the length of the blade. The water became ice. "Or I'll cut that jewel from your wrinkled fingers and heal him myself. Now do it, so he can think clearly, before I decide to take the whole hand."

Morrowmen's shriveled face contorted into the same sickening smile Askon had looked upon as he lay on his back. With a flourish of his robe, Morrowmen presented the Life fragment. "Now that's logic," he said with a dry laugh.

"You should do this, dear." He handed her the purple case. "It's good practice, and it does take so much out of me anymore. We'd be days getting back to Apopsé." He twitched again at the shoulders and neck. "You're a little violent and a little angry, but logic is logic, nonetheless." He smiled again and Askon felt nauseous. "Now if we could just get your brother to show some—even a little—we'd all be much better off for it."

Askon gaped. Speechless.

"Oh yes," said Morrowmen as if it were a trivial detail in a larger, more pressing argument." Askon, say hello to your sister Líana. Didn't I say that you wouldn't recognize her?"

CHAPTER NINE

The Other Survivor

When the Time fragment worked in Askon's favor, he gained clarity of perspective and the ability to leave the slowing world behind. He reached conclusions before others did, and destinations as well. Upon reaching Morrowmen's encampment, two days out from Apopsé's city, this ability came and went, and though he tried to master it, Askon found little success. If he let his emotions win out, the fragment worked against him, punishing him.

In their duel Líana bested him easily, a situation humiliating enough without the knowledge that his opponent was actually his ten-year-old sister—who now looked the part of a twenty-five-year-old woman. More so than it ever had, save perhaps when he had seen the vacant faces of Victor, Patrick, and Christopher in the trees surrounding Dalstone, the fragment refused to allow him the chance to concentrate, moved everything around him faster than he could comprehend. Now he saw the details.

Her skin was lighter than his, more like their mother than their father, but not so light and pale as Elise. A long blond braid arched above her head slightly and fell down her back almost to waist length. When last he saw her, he had been able to reach down and ruffle the blond curls that fell all around her head. Now she stood only a few inches shorter than he did, and the braid was pulled tight. She was still thin, but as before, neither weak nor frail. He smiled, remembering their mother. She was always trying to get Líana to eat, "thicken her up a bit" as she would say.

The sword she carried at her right hip and held in her left hand, as Askon did, was very different from his own. Askon's blade, several inches longer and half again as wide, was completely straight from hilt to tip and had a strong wrought-iron cross-guard to protect his hand and wrist in battle. Líana's more closely resembled the traditional elf-blades that Codard's army frowned upon. The edge had only one side, the steel curving back ever so slightly starting several inches above the guard, which encircled the base of the blade rather than extending outward. The grip was shorter and meant for one-handed use, a fine weapon, one of which their father would have been very proud and their mother appalled if she had seen it in her daughter's hand.

For quite some time he said nothing, only stared, trying to take in what she had become, while discovering all the reminders of what she had been. He stopped at the eyes, one green and one blue, like his though opposite: blue on the left and green on the right. Suddenly he felt overwhelmingly comforted; with her presence, he ceased to be alone. On multiple occasions since the tragedy at Tolarenz, he had heard people say there were other half-elves still alive in Vladvir. Some were in King's City, some out on their own in the wilds, some maybe even lived in the South Kingdom. He knew not whether his people would be accepted by Apopsé's, nor whether any lived in the sprawling city that glittered in the distance.

But here was someone who understood—and family no less. He wrapped her in an enormous hug, half-tackling her, lifting her off the ground. Pain lanced through his wounded leg, and he toppled into the grass.

"So much for thinking before acting, eh Askon?" Morrowmen said with all the same exasperated annoyance as ever.

"I'm glad to finally see you, too." And there was that voice again, like cool water. He knew now why it refreshed him, made him feel stronger. "But, that cut needs tending." She shot out an open-palmed hand in Morrowmen's direction.

From his place on the ground, Askon watched as Morrowmen reluctantly produced the fragment case. It fell into Líana's hand with a soft sound. The old man seemed to shrink and shiver as the fragment left his possession, but he remained upright, looking older than ever.

Líana closed her eyes, her fingers curling around the deep purple case that held the Life fragment. She waved it over his injured leg, her breathing slow. Starting at one side and moving to the other like a bell swinging in the high towers of King's City, she followed the full path of the cut. With a release of breath, she opened her eyes.

Nothing happened. The wound, still open and black with drying blood, lay unchanged. She stared at it, the same fierce light in her eyes that had burned within Askon's as he and his friends walked away from the lower Estelle. Frowning, she shook her head and tried again. This time, she reversed the pattern and held her breath as she waved the stone back and forth. When she opened her eyes again and the ragged bloody flesh looked the same as it ever had, she balled her fists and threw them violently to her sides, clenching the stone in her left hand. Water welled in her eyes, and for the first time since Askon saw her for who she really was, she looked more a frightened child than a warrior woman.

"Don't think of a salamander," Askon said quietly.

"What?" She looked confused. "What are you talking about?"

Askon smiled. "I said, don't think of a salamander."

Líana looked back blankly, frustrated.

"Remember that game Father would play? He said it would help us concentrate. It's hard to stay focused, but it's even harder to try *not* to focus on something that is bothering you."

Recognition dawned on her face. She brushed at her eyes with the back of her hand. "You always won that game."

"I'm much older than you. You were at a disadvantage."

She smiled and closed her eyes. Two slow breaths brought her shoulders up and down, up and down. Her eyes popped back open. Her woman's face looked again like a little girl. "Do you think it will work if I actually think of a salamander?"

Askon laughed. "Maybe."

With the smile still on her face, she passed the stone again carefully over Askon's leg. This time, around the seam where the two clamshell pieces of the case came together, Askon saw a faint purple glow. She made another pass for good measure, then opened her eyes. The smile faded and her shoulders dropped heavily. The cut was still there.

"I guess it didn't work," she said sadly. "I really thought it would."

Askon reached up and put a hand on her shoulder. "It will. I think maybe you just need practice with it. Obviously I still need it with my fragment, and I've carried it every minute since…"

"Since what happened back home," she finished.

"Yes."

Morrowmen shuffled closer. He looked unbalanced, weak. "Oh that's right!" he said, with some vigor returning. "While all this is quite touching, I think you've missed a very important detail. You see this?" He slipped the point of his walking stick into the silver chain at Askon's neck, lifting the fragment into the air a few inches.

"Sometimes," he continued, "these blasted things interfere with one another. Caled and I found this out the hard way. Though, as far as I know, we're the only ones who ever did."

Askon sat up carefully to avoid aggravating his injury. "What do you mean by interfere?"

Morrowmen's head rolled wildly, and he fell to one side. He caught himself with the cane, but it wobbled precariously under his hand. Líana gave back the Life fragment, and he steadied in an instant. "These two fragments are bound together in some way. I've never let anyone else use it besides her." He indicated Líana. "Never had a reason to. But Caled and I were always close, always working together, even when we disagreed fundamentally with one another. Once, it went a little too far. I was young, no more than fifty, just a boy practically. What can I say? I got angry. He was always so infuriatingly calm!"

Askon pointed at the old man's chest. "Isn't that what you're always trying to get me to be?"

"You? Calm? Don't be ridiculous, Askon. The day you're half as calm as Caled, I'll be a six-year-old girl frolicking through a field of flowers."

Líana giggled.

"I'm just trying to get you to think. For. One. Second. That's all I ask." He paused, reconsidering. "That, and also don't sit there pondering like a drooling ignoramus."

Askon raised an eyebrow. "So think more, but not too much?"

Morrowmen refused to dignify him with an answer. Instead, he continued his story. "Caled was hurt. I let my emotions get the better of me, and then he was lying on the floor. There may or may not have been a lot of blood."

"Gods! You attacked the Knight of Vladvir?" Askon looked up to find Thomas standing not three feet away with Elise on his arm.

Morrowmen shot him a glare. "And who are you? No. Never mind. I'll deal with you later." He turned back to Askon. "I may or may not have let him sit there for a while, just to learn his lesson. Like I said, the foolishness of youth was upon me. When I felt he understood my side of the argument, I tried to heal him with the fragment."

"And nothing happened," said Thomas. Askon smirked, then winced as his leg spasmed, the muscles clenching.

Morrowmen let out an elongated sigh. He looked at Thomas, then back to Askon. "And. Nothing. Happened," he grumbled irritably. "I started to panic, not meaning to kill my friend. By this time I was quite adept in using the fragment, but I didn't know what to do. Of course Caled, the tranquil bastard, wasn't even upset by any of it, which only made it more difficult to concentrate."

"Sound familiar?" It was Thomas again. This time, Elise slapped him lightly on the stomach. Askon's smirk became a grin. Whether it had been directed at himself or Morrowmen, Thomas was absolutely right.

"Anyway," Morrowmen continued, now through gritted teeth, "Caled grabbed the Time fragment from where it hung around his neck, broke the chain, and threw it across the room."

Their eyes went wide.

"I had the same reaction," said Morrowmen. "But, as happened more often than I would've liked, he was right. He told me to try it again, and sure enough, it worked as well as it ever had."

Askon already had the chain off his neck. He offered it to Morrowmen, who shook his head. "I don't like that thing," he said warily. "You keep it away from me."

Puzzled, Askon stared back at him. "We need to try. I can't just go on with this gash in my leg. Besides, you had the fragment in Tolarenz, before you gave it to me."

"Most traumatic day I can recall," Morrowmen said. "And that's a lot of days to compare against. Give it to Mr. Bright Ideas over there. He looks trustworthy enough."

Thomas looked left, then right, then pointed at himself. "Me?"

"Yes, you," Morrowmen croaked. "Just take it so we can get on with this."

Slowly, and with more reservation than he expected, Askon handed the dangling green gem over to Thomas. When it came into contact with the young man's skin, he flinched. A look of sour disgust washed over his face. Askon felt annoyed and somehow compelled to take it back. Such a reaction was disrespectful, offensive in some way.

For the second time, Morrowmen released his own fragment into Líana's care. His face showed similar anxiety to that which Askon himself was feeling, but Líana took the purple stone without even the slightest negative response, in fact, Askon thought she somehow looked brighter, more vibrant when she held it. She looked at Askon's wound, then back to Morrowmen.

"Why can't you just do it?" she asked. Askon could hear the worry in her voice, the fear that she might get it wrong.

Morrowmen shook his head. "I told you. It takes too much out of me. And besides, our prince over there will need my skill if he's going to survive. I don't want to waste all my energy on your incompetent brother."

She frowned, glaring back at him. "Maybe I could just heal them both," she said under her breath.

Morrowmen smiled, and Askon looked away. It was so horrible, all transparent skin and decaying teeth. "Pretty confident for someone who was afraid to try only a moment ago. Let's see how you do with this one first."

"Don't think of a salamander," Askon added quickly as she closed her eyes.

"Foolishness," said Morrowmen, swaying on his cane.

Líana smiled, her eyes still closed, and began moving the stone back and forth across the gash in Askon's leg. As it had before, the clamshell seam glowed faintly purple. Deep in the tissue and bone, Askon felt a tickle, then an almost uncontrollable urge to bolt. He looked away from his sister and instead stared at the Time fragment, now in Thomas's hand. The young man held it aloft, looking at the facets and the mesmerizing pulse of its light. Askon did the same, but behind the image of the fragment, he saw Thomas's face, the sour expression never leaving it, even as he studied the gem.

"Done," said Líana proudly. And it was done. The leg, which only moments before had been bloody and would soon have become infected, looked as though it had never taken a scratch. Askon knew that in healing the cut and damaged bone beneath, he had given up some amount of time from his life. He laughed to himself. But what would it matter if the Time fragment would keep him alive as long as it had Caled? He turned back to Líana.

"Thank you," he said warmly. "Did you think of a salamander?"

"No."

"Then what?"

"I tried to imagine Morrowmen's face and count the wrinkles."

Askon chuckled. "And?"

"Too many."

CHAPTER TEN

Answers

Some time later, they gathered around the fire-pit with the men Morrowmen called his "agents." Askon had been introduced to Mot, the gruff-voiced man, and Thal the unfortunate receiver of Askon's headbutt. Rickard, the man with the nasal voice had come last to introduce himself. The remainder had either gone back to sleep or to collect the three travelers' things from the hill.

Thomas's complexion had improved, now that he had relinquished the Time fragment, and Morrowmen had a bit more spring in his step. Líana hadn't said much, aside from during the quick introduction Askon gave to Thomas and Elise. He did his best to explain what had happened to his sister: the attack on Tolarenz, the enormous bonfire of their possessions, her journey into the flames. The last, Líana herself told haltingly. Not even Askon had known what she endured. Venturing too near the fire in an attempt to rescue her own belongings and finding the blaze too hot, her possessions too far to reach, Iramov's men had appeared. It was here that Líana could no longer continue. Askon finished the tale with his sister's rescue and recovery under Morrowmen's care and the Life fragment's power. They accepted the story, though Elise now watched Thomas closely, with narrowed eyes.

They were situated around the fire: three of Morrowmen's agents, Askon and Líana, Thomas and Elise, and Morrowmen himself. Thomas looked troubled.

"I mean no offense," he began, then faced Morrowmen, "but if Askon's sister aged fifteen years or so in body—" Elise cocked her head toward him, one eyebrow raised archly. "Physically—I mean, generally. Would she still be, still have—uh—the mind of a ten-year-old?"

Morrowmen said nothing.

"My friend and rescuer," Líana said, nodding in the old man's direction, "thinks my wounds were deeper than just the damage to the flesh."

Elise shifted uncomfortably. Thomas laced an arm around her shoulders.

Líana continued, completely unaware. "He says my mind was damaged as well. So, when the fragment healed me—"

"Your mind matured along with the rest of you!" Thomas interrupted, finishing her sentence.

Askon laughed. Elise glared into the crackling flames of the fire. Morrowmen was still as stone, but for his unsettling smile.

"I mean—um," Thomas stammered.

Líana looked past them into the starlit sky. "It's alright," she said. "The whole ordeal has been very—" She paused. "Strange. Sometimes I feel like my mind aged even more than the rest of me did. Other times, I feel like the same girl who sneaked through gardens and pulled the tails of stray cats just to prove I could do it."

Askon grinned. "It was good practice."

"Hmm."

Turning to the three agents who huddled together, Askon changed the subject. "Rickard is it?" he asked.

"Yeah."

"I still don't understand. Why did you say all of those things about the elves if you're working for Morrowmen?"

Morrowmen perked up. "Should I get the walking stick, Askon? If you're going to be asking questions, we might need it." Líana elbowed the old man hard in the ribs. "Alright. It was only a suggestion."

"You already gave the easiest answer. We work for Morrowmen," said Mot.

Rickard seemed unhappy with the explanation. "What Mot means is that we were acting on orders. The plan was to grab all three of ya and bring ya back here. Morrowmen thought we'd have a little fun with the whole sister-who's-fifteen-years-older-than-when-you-last-saw-her bit. The old man said we're supposed to give ya a hard time once the duel started. Ya know, try to mess with your head and everythin'. It was him who came up with callin' it a test."

Askon rocked back on his haunches, the fire warm and smoky in his face. "So the test was actually for me," he said flatly.

"It was," Morrowmen cawed. "And you failed as miserably as I could have imagined!" Líana gave him another elbow, and the old man scooted away from her with a huff.

"And the Bandit Code?" Askon asked.

Eager to be heard again, Mot spoke first. He leaned forward. "Oh, that's real as real Mr. Half-elf. Bandit Code's as good as any."

Rickard shook his head and thumped the larger man on the back. "What Mot means to say," he began, as he had before, "is that Morrowmen decided his people, *agents* as he calls them, would follow a modified version of the Bandit Code. We do have our recruits fight our captives, usually enemies, but we don't kill them. We've got the Life fragment anyway, don't we? Enemies are usually more valuable alive than dead, as long as ya can keep 'em in check."

Askon poked the fire with a stick. Sparks rose into the air above them. "I think I know what you mean. Morrowmen isn't much of a believer in kings and armies, so he wouldn't structure his men that way. Real bandits do a terrible job of following the code, but that doesn't mean the rules themselves are the problem."

Without warning, Morrowmen reeled on the large piece of wood he shared with Líana, then fell with a *thud* into the grass. He lay on the ground, motionless.

"Morrowmen?" said Askon, concern lacing his voice. "Morrow-men!"

The old man popped up with a gasp, his chest heaving. The hideous smile spread across his ancient face, and he stared into Askon's eyes as though he had just seen a ghost.

"I think I may have just had an episode," he croaked, panting. "It seemed like you constructed an entire series of ideas that made sense. And then I blacked out."

Askon's face went flat. The skin-wrapped skull grinned back, and the others began to laugh.

"Fine," said Askon. "At least I know now why they said those things. For a moment I thought you might be working with such hateful men intentionally."

"There's the intellect I've come to expect," said Morrowmen dryly.

After nearly an hour, Morrowmen called an end to the campfire. His agents vanished quickly, hoping to avoid their watches. Thomas seemed tired. Since posing his questions to Líana, he hadn't spoken again. Elise looked happier and had even offered a few questions of her own. Askon decided to let them rest, volunteering to take the first watch. Líana jumped up from the fallen log to join him. Askon's heart warmed at the familiar presence. Another agent covered the east side of the camp, while they went to the west. In the darkness, a crooked mass of shadowy, purple robes shuffled along unnoticed behind them.

"Askon."

He hesitated. Hearing the actual voice, even if it was slightly changed, older, more mature, was like living the dreams that had haunted him since he first left Tolarenz. For a moment, he simply wanted to let the words fill the air around him.

"Yes, Líana?"

"Are you worried about Edward?"

"Wait. I need to tell you something, now."

"Alright."

"I'm sorry."

"For what?"

"When I left home, they came to get me in the night. You were still asleep, and I didn't say goodbye."

"I was very upset at you the next morning."

"I'm so sorry."

"Askon, don't cry. That was so long ago."

"Two months. Three at most."

"Not for me."

"I wish I could take it back. Do it over again."

"You can't, but I forgive you."

The words washed over him. He let them soak into every inch of his body and mind. She forgave him. And in those words he knew what she meant. She forgave him not just for goodbye, but for leaving at all, for not being there to help her when Iramov and his men came, for not being able to save their mother and father. He smiled and closed his eyes. She was looking at him.

"Now tell me about Edward. Are you worried?" she asked again.

"I'm worried about a lot of things: Iramov, for one; the king and his foolish alliance; Edward too, but not for his health. With the Life fragment here, and Morrowmen to wield it, I'm sure he will be fine. For Edward, I worry most about what he will choose to do after we've spoken to Lord Apopsé."

"You think he won't follow us?"

"He'll want to, but he is in a unique position. If he betrays his father, the king might say anything at all about him. Even if we can fight them and win, Edward's reputation will be so poisoned by Co-dard's lies that he could never take back the kingdom."

"That didn't answer my question."

"It didn't?"

"No, it didn't. I asked if you think he'll follow us."

"Honestly, I don't know. Edward is a man of honor. But there are two things to honor here. One is his kingdom. It's his responsibility, when his father is gone, to care for his people. The other is us, his friends, and choosing what is right, even if it means difficulty for the same people he is supposed to protect."

"Do you think if I heal him, he will be more likely to side with us?"

"You mean instead of Morrowmen? I suppose. He knows us, has met you. And no one would argue that your face would be a much more pleasant one to wake up to than Morrowmen's."

"Now that's just rude." The crow-call shattered Askon's waking dream like a stone through an aging windowpane. The old man hobbled over on his cane. "Is that a blush on your cheek Líana?" he croaked.

Askon looked at her. The old man was right. "Wait," Askon stammered. He recalled earlier in the night, two hilltops away, when he had watched the small soldier tending to the man under the sheet. Then it dawned on him.

"No." A word like a hammer stroke.

"Ha!" Morrowmen crowed. "Her talk jarred loose the coagulation in that thick skull of yours, did it? Thinking about why she's so worried over our comatose prince?"

Líana looked away abashedly.

"Líana, he's fifteen years older than you. He's my age—"

Morrowmen slapped him on the back. "Oh it's just a little crush. And anyway, you're going to have to get used to this. She turned out to be quite pretty, didn't she?"

"I'm standing right here," Líana protested.

Askon scowled.

"What? I think their children would be adorable."

Before the final word escaped the ancient mouth, Askon's hands clutched the old man's throat. "Take it back," he growled through clenched teeth. Under his shirt, the fragment began its work, but he did not let go.

Morrowmen choked and coughed, but he seemed unruffled; he was laughing. Askon's fingers tightened, then relaxed just enough to let him speak. "What are you going to do?" Morrowmen gurgled. "Kill me? I'd like to see you attempt that." The old man cast his arms out to his sides. "Go on. See what happens. I'm sure Apopsé will let you in without me."

Then Líana's hand was around Askon's wrist. She twisted it hard. The fragment flickered. Suddenly his arm was behind his back and he again looked up from the ground at the thousands of twinkling stars. Líana drove her knee into his chest, and the air rushed out of his lungs. She leaned down.

"What's gotten into you? Morrowmen is right. You need to think before you act."

The words stung, mostly because she was right, but also because he had truly made himself the fool this time. In that moment, with

Morrowmen still spluttering next to him and his newly rediscovered sister pinning him to the ground, Askon decided no matter what it took, he would find a way to control the Time fragment, to limit its power over him, so that he could use it against Iramov.

"You see?" said Morrowmen, regaining his composure. "I tried to tell you. But, as expected, you don't listen. Now your sister has beaten you twice. Let him up Líana, I'm alright."

"But he was choking you. What if you had—" She stopped.

"Died?" Morrowmen laughed. "My dear, it would take a lot more than his angry little fingers to kill me. As long as I carry the fragment, I'll be just fine. Now if you see him snatch that away from me in one of his little rage-fits, then you should worry."

"I'm sorry," said Askon slowly. He couldn't bring himself to look at Líana.

"Oh, shut up," Morrowmen barked. "It's clear to me now you're going to need some kind of training in order to manage this…problem." He readjusted his robes. "Give me some time tomorrow, and I'll decide what needs to be done about it."

Morrowmen turned and looked at Líana. She stood there, shorter than both men, but powerful and wary. In the act of throwing Askon to the ground, the tail of her braid had fallen in front of her, snaking down over the shoulder and across her chest. She glared at them.

"I'm not going to apologize," she said, crossing her arms and pinning the braid against her body. "It's—"

"My fault," Askon interrupted. "I have to learn that you aren't my ten-year-old sister anymore."

"No," said Morrowmen. "You have to learn that she both is and is not your ten-year-old sister. In some ways, she may have a wisdom you do not possess, an advantage, if you will. In others, she will be the same."

Líana remained, arms crossed, jaw set.

"Like right now?" Askon offered.

Morrowmen nodded. "I followed you two over here for a different reason, but solving these two problems: that of Líana's age, and that of your self-control, will be enough for now, I think." The ancient eyes flicked back to Edward's covered form several yards away. Askon noticed Líana's eyes were already there. Morrowmen gazed for a thoughtful moment, then turned back to the distant lights of Apopsé's city.

"Tomorrow we set out to see the Lord of the South Kingdom," he said. "There is much for you to learn between here and there, and much to learn after. I hope Iramov does not cut our time any shorter in his haste."

Askon was still looking at the sheet under which Edward lay.

"Líana," Morrowmen commanded. "Your watch is over. I want you rested for tomorrow if you are going to try to heal our prince."

She nodded and followed him back toward the center of the camp, leaving Askon behind, alone, staring into the wind.

CHAPTER ELEVEN

Water in the Desert

Night's cloak encircled the camp when Thomas came to relieve Askon of his watch. Over the last few hours, the lights in Apopsé's city had winked out one-by-one until only a few watchfires remained. Askon found the process soothing, peaceful, but his mind had been anything but. Within him, he knew, he held more than just simple anger; his drive to defeat Iramov came from more than just a desire for revenge. It was wrong that the people of Tolarenz had died, and it was somehow even worse that no one had come to their aid. Who could have? It had all happened so fast.

He wondered if Caled could have saved them. The Time fragment's powers were great. For Askon it had virtually stopped time, allowing him to pluck the lone arrow out of the air before it struck Brâghda. Caled had carried the fragment for much longer than Askon; surely he could have commanded the same power. Líana and Morrowmen seemed to have similar degrees of control over the Life fragment. So why would he and Caled be any different? Even Codard might have saved Tolarenz, either by spiriting Iramov away or by bringing forces of his own to defend the village. But Codard was weak, already turned to Iramov's side. And what good would an army have done? What good had it done at the Norill colony near Austgæta?

Askon stared into the dwindling lights of the city. The night had grown cold not long after Morrowmen had sent Líana to bed. Askon laughed to himself. For his little sister—the one he had left in Tolarenz without saying goodbye—such a command would not have been out of the ordinary, but for the fierce warrior with the long braid, it seemed quite ridiculous. As Thomas approached, Askon pictured Morrowmen giving the same command to John. In his mind, John moped away like a sullen child. Askon chuckled again to himself.

"Sir?" Thomas asked tentatively. He circled around and sat in the grass.

Askon leaned back to get a better look at the young man. "You know, I think the time for 'Sir' is over. I am no commander in Codard's army any more than you are a footman. That world is far behind us now."

Thomas straightened. "You're right, Askon," he said awkwardly. "We have left that life behind, but as has ever been the case, I follow you. So title or no, you are my commander, Sir."

"If you say so," Askon said. "But I'd like to add this. If you ever feel that my actions go against the greater good, that I've somehow lost my honor or perspective, I—as your commander—order you to help me correct my mistakes."

Thomas thought for a moment, arms wrapped about his knees. "What if it means, physical intervention?"

"Then I will need your help more than ever. Tell Edward. He will understand."

"And if I can't change your mind?"

Askon turned back to the city's lonely watchfires. "Then you should leave."

"Where would I—where would *we* go?"

Placing a hand on Thomas's shoulder, Askon rose from his place in the grass. He looked down upon his young friend, and his eyes were heavy from lack of sleep. "You go wherever it is that I ought to be going."

Thomas wrapped his cloak tightly about his shoulders and turned to face the city. Askon walked back toward the center of the camp. With practiced hands, he unwrapped the bundle, laid out the bedroll, and was asleep almost as soon as his head came to rest.

He dreamed again. The rushing river, broken oars. John was no help, he just waved goodbye. Tolarenz. Líana's laughter. A rising tide of red water that was blood. Caled appeared, sank, slipped away.

Here the dream changed. He still stood strangely suspended on the surface of the blood. Edward would be next, waiting to follow Caled into the depths. But before he came into view, Askon felt something. Another body, another person, standing back-to-back with him. He turned, hoping to see who was there. Yet, no matter how hard he tried, how quickly he turned, he could not see. And then Iramov was there, bald and imperious, the dim glow of the Death fragment blending with the troubled surface of the blood sea.

Remembering his mistake, Askon twisted around, leaping to retrieve Edward, to save him from sinking. He clasped his friend's hand and wrenched him up. Edward, his face twisted with fear, pointed with outstretched hand at Askon's chest. There, in the green glow of the Time fragment, Askon saw the end of a long, golden braid.

Darkness descended, heavy and cold. The braid pulled up and slipped off his shoulder. Behind him, the presence, the weight of the other person vanished. Iramov cackled wildly. The blood sea turned black. Edward turned black. Askon was thrust to his knees, and the world turned black. Then there was a blinding flash of purest white. An explosion more terrible than the crushing darkness. Beneath it he was revealed, scared and alone.

His hands were covered in white powder.

Askon awoke with his fingers scrabbling in the dust. Brilliant light seared his eyes, forcing him to lift his hands to his face. He squinted, blinked, then sat up. All around him Morrowmen's agents dismantled the camp. He heard them more than saw them in the bright light and unexpected heat. How late had he slept? Tents came down, their poles and tarps clacking and flopping dully. Voices babbled and laughed at one another as the work continued. Somewhere to his right, Rickard was regaling Mot on the finer points of tent care and storage. Elsewhere in the quickly vanishing campsite, Elise—in her keening commander's voice—lectured Thomas. It ended with "Keep your eyes to yourself!" Even without seeing them, Askon knew she didn't mean Thomas should keep his eyes off her.

Morrowmen's cane came down with a *thump* in the grass, mere inches from Askon's face. It swished a little in the spindly stalks. "Left to my own devices, I would have had you awake and training your mind at sunrise." His voice was like an eyeful of sand, its grit aching to be rubbed away. But like the sand, addressing it only made the discomfort worse.

"I've had a long couple of days," Askon said dumbly.

"Ha!" Morrowmen laughed, and the sand scraped again. "Don't tell me about long counts of days."

Askon decided to hold his tongue. Usually with Morrowmen, it was better not to speak at all than to say something the old man would find irritating or unintelligent.

"Nothing else to say?" Morrowmen asked.

Askon rose and scanned the camp's perimeter. His eyes came to rest upon Edward. The sheet was so similar to the one Morrowmen had used on Líana back in Tolarenz. Askon wondered what would become of his friend. Would he age as much as Líana had? And how would it affect his mind?

Then there was the other detail. Kneeling beside the sheet, as he assumed had been the case since she awoke, was Líana herself. She stroked Edward's forehead with the back of her hand, dabbed it with a cloth, repeated the process. Had the camp been quieter, Morrowmen's agents less eager to move on with their journey, Askon would have heard her singing.

He turned to Morrowmen. "Will Edward age like my sister?"

The old man shuffled ahead a step or two. "I think not," he said. But something in his voice sounded unsure, less confident and forceful than usual. "You see, I'm well versed in the effect the Life fragment has when under my control. With her, things are…less predictable."

"What do you mean?"

"She's new to it, and as I told you back in Tolarenz, the fragments work differently depending upon who wields them. Our young Iramov is as good an example for that as any. His father could not do the things he has been able to. Your sister has a knack for getting to the fragment's power, but how it will manifest, that is another question. Only time and experience will clarify for us."

Askon considered leaving it at that, but his entire journey up to this point had been directed toward finding Morrowmen and reaching the South Kingdom. He took a deep breath.

"What about me?"

Morrowmen's eyes narrowed. "What about what?"

"Did the Time fragment affect Caled the same as me?"

"Of course not. The fragments affect no one the same as anyone else. It's like asking if he rode a horse the same, or parried a sword stroke the same, or wrote his name the same. Your bodies, minds, skills, experiences, they were all different. So too with the fragment."

Askon sighed.

"Why? What have you been able to do?"

Askon thought for a moment. "Well, there's the problem we talked about last night. When I get angry or act too quickly, the world seems to speed up all around—"

"Oh gods!" Morrowmen choked. "I thought you just became a fool out of control. This is worse than I imagined. If the fragment is tied to your blundering stupidity…" He threw his hands in the air, the walking stick waving through the air.

"Caled never—"

"I told you. Caled was so calm that he sent me into a rage more times than I can count!" The old man was clearly flustered now, out of sorts. "We need to get Edward on his feet and you to work on your exercises."

"Don't you want to know the other effects?"

Morrowmen drove the point of his cane into the dirt. "Will any of these other effects cause us to be endangered or killed because you can't keep your temper in check?"

"No."

"Then I have more important things to worry about, don't I?" He stormed off in Líana's direction. Around him the purple robes fluttered and flapped as he limped along, the wind twirling his wispy white hair. Askon looked on helplessly. Líana once again had her hand on Edward's forehead. She raised her eyes as Morrowmen stomped through the grass.

"Why won't you just let me heal him!" Askon heard her say angrily when the old man approached. Morrowmen mumbled something, but it was covered by the noise of the wind and the voices of his men. Askon started toward Edward.

"I'd like to observe, if that's alright." It was Thomas. He looked a bit sleepy, but the time he had spent resting before he took the final watch had clearly done him some good. He stood a bit taller, seemed slightly less travel-worn.

"And where he goes, I go," said Elise. Thomas put a comforting arm around her.

"I don't see why not," said Askon, and they crossed the remaining distance together.

When they approached, the sheet had been pulled completely back. Edward was stripped to the waist, his feet bare. Askon kicked himself for having left his friend's clothes back at the river. It all seemed so far away now. In Askon's mind, Edward had been given over to the water. But somehow Morrowmen and his agents—Líana included—had found the prince and brought him here, not two days hard marching from Apopsé's city.

Had Morrowmen and Líana not shown every indication to the contrary, Askon would have thought Edward dead. Would he have been convinced enough to bury him? Askon wondered how many soldiers they had buried who might have been alive, as Edward was now. All color had gone from his face, and the skin looked like stone or the surface of a cold gruel. His dark hair had been parted and straightened about his face, most likely by Líana, but it hung lank and disheveled on the stiff boards they used to transport him. About his ribs and lower abdomen, several deep bruises discolored the skin, as purple as Morrowmen's robes. Just below the knee, the dark cloth of Edward's trousers had been shredded. Strands of thread and torn fabric hung loosely away from a series of deep cuts, each of them as severe as the one Líana had healed for Askon. She knelt there, waiting to begin. Morrowmen's shadow, long and cold, towered over her.

"What if it doesn't work properly? What if I make it worse?" Líana murmured, not looking up to address the old man.

He produced the stone case. In the morning sun, Askon saw thin dark veins spreading like fingers through the deep purple. When he had seen the case in Tolarenz, it had been indoors, and the night before it had been dark. The smooth violet surface that Askon had perceived before became mottled and uneven in the daylight. It looked much more like Morrowmen.

The case dropped into Líana's quivering hand. Again it fell with that soft sound Askon had heard the previous night. Morrowmen's shadow shrank and wavered. "In all my years, I've seen one thing when it comes to this fragment," he said. "It does good or it does nothing. So what's the harm?"

Askon shot him a confused glare. "Morrowmen I tol—"

Crack!

"She needs to concentrate. Self-control lesson one: shut up." He pushed Askon away with the tip of the walking stick.

With the stone case in hand, Líana closed her eyes. The sun shone off the loops of her braid, which had again fallen over her shoulder, its tip hovering above Edward's chest. Slowly, her hand passed over his body, and despite the brightness of morning, Askon could see the line of purple light glowing through the seam.

As though they had never been there at all, the bruises vanished. The cuts puckered, knitting themselves back together. The process was bizarre, similar to how Askon felt when the world around him moved too fast or too slow. It was as though Líana, with the fragment's help, pulled Edward forward in his life to a day when the wounds would be gone. Color bloomed first at the chest and then across the body. Cheeks and forehead grew rosy with life. And last, the breaths became full and regular. The stone stopped.

Líana toppled backward into the grass, the end of her braid curling limply on the ground. The Life fragment's case clattered noisily against the gravel and dust.

"Líana!" Askon raced to her side, scooping her up as though she were still the small child he had left sleeping in their parents' home. She didn't move.

Morrowmen stooped, still shaking, and grabbed the Life fragment. He steadied himself, then sauntered over to Edward. "He looks better," the old man said.

"What are you doing?" Askon shouted. "Help her!"

A long, deep breath filled Morrowmen's frame. "Rule. Number. One!" he said without turning from Edward. He waited a moment. When Askon said nothing, he began again. "Good. Your sister appears to be in danger, and yet you managed to restrain yourself from choking anyone. I suppose that's a start."

"But she's not waking up," said Thomas worriedly. Elise clamped down on his wrist.

"Did anyone ask for your input?" snarled Morrowmen. "No. They didn't. But since I'm feeling generous today, I'll offer this. Líana will be fine. She healed quite a bit of damage, and as I said, it takes a lot out of a person to do so." He paced back to Askon, indicating he should release her. "She'll sleep for a bit and be good as new when she wakes up. Well, at least that's how it always seemed to happen for me when I overdid it."

Askon lay Líana back into the grass, placed a hand on one knee, and stood with an effort. "You told me the fragments affect us all differently. What if you're wrong?"

"I'm never wrong."

He turned away again, back toward Edward. The prince still lay on the boards. He looked healthy, and all the wounds were sealed, but there was no sign he would awaken. Morrowmen fished into his robes, searched a moment, and produced a pipe. With a flash of his horrid smile, he chomped down on the stem. Then as though he were a sack of vegetables Morrowmen wanted to shift aside, the old man kicked Edward in the stomach. Air rushed out of the prince's mouth, and his breathing shuddered as it returned to normal.

"Hmm," Morrowmen grunted through the pipe. Askon was speechless. In two long strides he had ahold of the old man's robes, pulling him forcefully away from Edward.

"I knew it," the ancient face said, pipe wobbling. "Too good to be true."

"Maybe if you leave him to rest, he'll wake up, like you said Líana would." Thomas seemed hesitant, but sure in his reckoning. Elise scowled as she had since Líana's fall into the grass.

"Not him," Morrowmen said. "The fool who is—once again—trying to strangle me."

Askon released him.

"Self-control rule the second: stop and think."

Thomas smiled. "Isn't that two rules?"

Morrowmen grunted and glared back at Askon. "Your friend has some sense," he said. "Too bad none of it has worn off on you. Leave these two for awhile. We'll come back in an hour to see if they wake up. If not, I'll finish the healing process myself. How does that sound, Askon?"

Askon said nothing.

"Ha!" Morrowmen cackled. "He learns!"

An hour later, when the camp was nothing more than a memory and a few smashed clumps of grass, they returned to Edward and Líana. Askon had been unable to ignore them, even as Morrowmen drilled him in his newly conceived rules of self-control. He watched as Edward breathed rhythmically, showing no signs of movement other than the rise and fall of his chest. Líana had lain perfectly still for a quarter of an hour, Askon's worry increasing with every minute. Finally, just as he was about to berate Morrowmen for his apathy toward her, she too began to breathe, slowly at first, then faster and fuller until she and Edward moved perfectly in time with one another. All the while, Morrowmen poked and prodded, physically and mentally, at every soft spot he could find in Askon.

It was infuriating, and only further exaggerated his failure. Morrowmen could arouse Askon's anger and rage at will. It seemed he hardly had to try. An anti-elf comment here, an off-color crack about his sister there, a string of seemingly thoughtless remarks concerning his leadership abilities and choices in their journey. It felt as though it would never end. He did not do well.

With the hour spent, the entire party collected around Edward and Líana. Askon bent down, gingerly trying to awaken his sister. When she gasped, her eyes snapping open, he jumped back. She looked around wildly at the gathered faces. Suddenly she looked very young and very afraid.

"It's alright. You lost consciousness after trying to heal Edward," Askon said quietly.

But she pushed him aside, stood, and strode across the ring of onlookers to where Edward lay. Her eyes narrowed, and she pulled at her braid absently, looping it around one finger, then slipping it through each of the rest on her right hand. Back and forth it traveled. It was as though she had forgotten any of them were even there.

"It's not his body," she said to no one.

Askon stepped forward. "Líana. Why don't you—"

With one hand, Morrowmen raised the walking stick. With the other he held up a single finger. Rule number one: quiet. Askon stopped. Then the old man added a second finger to his count. Rule number two: stop and think. So he did.

With a bounce of her heels like a tavern boxer, she lifted one arm over her head and hooked the hand with the opposite fingers. She stretched this way, then the other, bounced again, and this time the braid followed suit. Her left hand shot out to her side, the palm open in command, not invitation. Morrowmen winked as Askon frowned in silence. The old man tossed the stone in her direction, but it went wide by several inches. Without turning to look, Líana's hand twisted like a striking snake, and Askon heard for the third time that same, soft sound. Whether she had found the fragment or it had found her, Askon did not know.

Morrowmen wobbled on his cane, and after a breath, took a few steps toward Líana. His back straightened and he stood more still than before. Líana, unaware of the crowd, leaned over Edward. She was right. His body looked as though it hadn't seen a day's combat in his life. But still he did not awaken. She settled near his shoulders and leaned in close. Her hips rested in the grass, her legs half-bent along his side. She rested her weight on her left hand, and the braid fell to length just above the ground. She moved closer, placing the stone case on Edward's forehead. Then in a graceful, floating series of movements, she tensed, lifted both hands to the case, and flicked it open. She tossed the empty purple clamshell aside and pinched the bare gem between the thumb and forefinger of her right hand.

Morrowmen cocked his head to one side, intrigued. He looked back at Askon approvingly. He hadn't moved, or said a word. The crowd was eerily silent. Even Elise looked on with wonder.

Líana let her weight rest again, holding the fragment in her fist which hovered just above Edward's eyes. None of the onlookers saw her close her own, but when they retold the story around the campfire in later days, they all remembered the glow.

What had been only a faint, purple-pink line in the case became a beacon in Líana's hand. The light shone through the skin and flesh and bone until it illuminated the whole area to arm's length around her. It was a light unlike any Askon had ever seen. Not even the Time fragment at its most powerful, brilliant green in the frozen moment before the walls of Dalstone, glowed so brightly. Then suddenly, like a man who miscounts his steps on a stairway in the dark, the light fell away.

Líana shivered, but her eyes remained fixed on Edward's face. All around, the world grew still. Askon pulled the Time fragment from inside his shirt, but it pulsed its heartbeat rhythm steadily. Then the quiet peace was broken. Líana placed a hand on each side of Edward's face. Beneath one delicate palm, the Life fragment pressed gently into the stubble and skin of his cheek.

"Wake up," said the voice of cool water, the voice of cold mountain streams, the voice that gave life when a man was dying of thirst.

And Edward awoke.

CHAPTER TWELVE
Distractions

When Edward's eyes opened, only Askon and Morrowmen still looked on. Every other face in the party, from Thomas and Elise to each of Morrowmen's agents, had turned away. Such a moment was not meant to be seen by outsiders, but Askon saw it.

Edward blinked, awestruck wonder washing over him. He said nothing. With a gaze that ignored the outside world, he studied Líana's face. Then carefully, as though she might shatter at his touch, he placed his hand on her cheek in a mirror image of her hand on his. And for a fleeting, liquid moment their faces, their lips, their eyes moved toward one another. Askon watched, an intruder, frantic to stop them but powerless to speak.

Líana drew away quickly and rose to her feet. She looked around and stepped awkwardly behind Morrowmen, she seemed to shrink as she cast her eyes to the ground and color rose red in her cheeks. Without looking up, she handed the bare fragment back to him. He peered into its dim purple light thoughtfully.

The members of the crowd began to turn back, curious to see what had happened. One by one they discovered Edward was alive and awake. A cheer rose among them. All at once Askon discovered how many there actually were. He had found on his own that they used some sort of skill to conceal themselves, appearing to be a group of no more than a dozen. Now they numbered nearly twenty-five, and all of them cheered the newly revived prince of Vladvir.

"Water," Edward said and they fell silent.

Morrowmen turned abruptly. "Go on, now," he croaked. "Start walking. We'll follow you." The agents dispersed, grabbing packs and supplies, starting their march toward Apopsé's city. Askon and his friends remained, Líana still cowering sheepishly next to Morrowmen.

"The water," Edward said again. "It dragged me, beat me. I felt myself breathe it in. Everything was dark, or light, or both somehow. Then came that voice. Gods! Such a beautiful sound. It pulled me away. I had to follow." He paused, shaking his head. "Who are you?"

Askon crossed in front of Morrowmen and Líana. He helped Edward to his feet, handing him a shirt from the bundle Thomas and Elise had retrieved from the river. "This is Morrowmen," Askon said, indicating the old man. Then he bent down, picked up the Life fragment's case and tossed it in Morrowmen's direction. The old man snapped it up, dropped the fragment inside, and hid the case in the folds of his robes.

"Not him," Edward said, entranced. "You described Morrowmen to me before, his identity is obvious enough." He took a step forward. "I mean her."

Líana peeked from behind Morrowmen's shoulder, revealing first her green eye then the blue. She drew back again as Edward's eyes grew wide.

"It can't be," he said.

Askon put a hand on his shoulder, firmly. "I'm afraid it is."

"Yes yes, it's Líana, Askon's little sister," Morrowmen said hurriedly. "Big surprise, alright, everyone's surprised. But 'Look at her,' you say; 'She's so attractive now.' She's a woman; he's a man; she saved his life, and on and on. You'll have to get over it, Edward. We simply don't have time." He looked around the group as though that would be enough, as though he had communicated all that was necessary to understand the situation.

"How did you find me?" Edward asked, still slow, sleepy.

"An excellent query," Morrowmen answered brightly, but the question had not been directed at him. Edward leaned to one side, trying to get a better look at the girl who stood behind the man in the purple robes. Morrowmen continued, unaffected.

"We found you because we've been watching your progress this whole time," he said.

"Who was watching us?" asked Thomas.

"And when," Askon added skeptically.

Edward leaned farther. "You were watching over me." It wasn't a question. He pulled the shirt over his head, eyes still fixed on Líana, and slid his arms through the dark sleeves.

"Well not the whole time," Morrowmen admitted. "On and off since I arrived here, I've been keeping track of Askon's movements. I told him to come to the South Kingdom but didn't trust he could follow instructions. Indeed it has taken him long enough."

"But how did that lead you to Edward?" Elise asked. It was the first time Askon had heard her speak all morning.

"Simple," said Morrowmen. "He was with you, and then your idiot leader decided to float the rapids in the middle of the night. When he went into the water, my men were already patrolling the river, waiting for Askon to show up. We had similar groups placed on the road. They saw the prince, picked him up, and by then Líana and I were already on our way out of the city."

Askon was unconvinced. "Why didn't we see you?"

"Um—"

"No, Thomas," Morrowmen snapped. "It's too late now." He smiled. "Your watchman here should have seen us, probably did, in fact. He just didn't say anything."

Thomas and Elise both looked away. When they looked back, Askon was waiting. "So?" he said.

"Thomas and I were otherwise occupied," Elise said, not in the least bit embarrassed. "If you must know, we—"

"Saw them arrive," Thomas interrupted awkwardly. "But I wasn't sure, so we tried to count the next day. I couldn't be certain that there were more of them." He bowed his head. "I'm sorry."

"Don't be," Morrowmen said before Askon had a chance to chastise the young man. "We all have our…distractions. The real problem is that once again, your leader has asked the wrong question."

Askon shrugged. "What?" he asked. "What is the right question, then?"

Morrowmen shook his head. He held up two fingers.

"Technically, it's three," said Thomas. "Shut up, stop, and think."

Morrowmen ignored him.

So Askon thought. And the question at which he arrived, when it finally occurred to him, seemed obvious, painfully so. "How were you watching us?"

With a start and a little snort, the old man lifted his head. "I'm sorry. What was that? I may have fallen asleep. Old age, you know."

Líana giggled. She peeked around again at Edward who swayed slightly to the music of her voice.

Askon sighed, Morrowmen was actually going to make him ask a second time. "I said, how were you watching us?"

Morrowmen nodded. "Yes, that's the right question. And the answer should be quite simple for anyone whose mind isn't made of soup."

"It's the fifth fragment." The response did not come from Askon, rather from Thomas. He said the words as if they were incontrovertible. As though he had seen it himself.

"So it is, young Thomas," Morrowmen replied. "How do you know?"

Thomas hesitated, looking to Askon for help or advice. Askon nodded.

"We know there are five fragments," Thomas began. "Codard has one: Space, we think, because it seems to be moving people around. Iramov has another: Death. Askon has Time and you," he pointed to both Morrowmen and Líana, "have the Life fragment, as we all just witnessed." He grinned. "That leaves only one: Sight."

Morrowmen slapped his ancient hands together slowly, applauding Thomas's deduction. "Again Askon, take notes on this fellow. He seems to be the only intelligent member of your group. Well, he and his lady also, I'm sure."

Above them, the sun had climbed well toward noon. By Askon's calculations, they were nearly two days from the city. If they didn't set out soon, the total would come to three. Certain that Morrowmen already knew this, he held his tongue. And instead of asking whether or not they should be going, he simply started off in the direction of the larger party, who now had drawn away several hilltops' distance across the plain.

"Yes," Morrowmen said as Askon started toward the city. "I can explain Apopsé's fragment as we walk. And more besides. There is much that you five should know before we arrive, but time is also short. The South Kingdom will need our help whether by sword or mind or politics. It will need the help of the Time fragment and I fear more immediately, the Life fragment. Let us discuss on our way."

A few yards ahead, Askon stood alone. Marten had landed on his shoulder. Behind him came Thomas and Elise. Morrowmen shuffled along on his own as Líana drifted back to Edward. Askon heard their voices, soft and shy, but could not discern the words. Soon Edward was speaking louder and Líana was laughing.

CHAPTER THIRTEEN

The Hateful Thing

In spite of his promise to talk as they made their way over the rolling hills, Morrowmen said little. He grumbled about the heat and picked at Askon, trying to trigger an emotional response. Once, he had expressed his lack of total disgust in Askon's ability to control himself, but the old man always found a way to get to him in the end.

Thomas suggested that it was only Askon's first day practicing these exercises, thus proving his progress significant; however, Morrowmen knew better. He had seen in the Sight fragment Askon's earlier attempts to control his emotions and so control the Time fragment. Thomas's suggestions were wasted on a man deaf to excuses. There had been plenty of time already for practice.

Much to Askon's growing irritation, Líana and Edward remained at the rear of the group. Long after Morrowmen, Thomas, and even Elise had fallen into step with him, Askon's sister and Vladvir's prince stayed behind. At times he had looked over his shoulder to find Líana dancing about, chattering like a schoolgirl as Edward smiled at her story. Once, he saw her shuffling along in an eerily accurate impersonation of Morrowmen. Askon could not help but laugh at this; Edward laughed, too.

They crested another rise and found Morrowmen's agents waiting on the next hilltop. There, a clump of dense trees had grown like a silvery green wall. Askon heard light footfalls approaching. Líana crashed into him from behind, almost sending him face first down the slope.

"Piggy-back for old time's sake?" she laughed. Askon shrugged her off and regained his footing.

"No," he said, though a smile already brightened his face.

Her face darkened, eyebrows knitting together. "Oh," she said softly. Then Askon heard another set of footsteps.

"Come on, Askon," Edward's voice boomed. "I thought it would be funny."

"She's not a child anymore."

Líana laughed tentatively. "That was the point. That's what makes it funny, right?"

Edward nodded in agreement, but Askon saw only the approaching line of trees, not so thick as the edge of Grafmark nor as wild as Ellmed but an obstacle nonetheless. In its lengthening shadow, Rickard and the rest were gathered. Some sat or crouched around their packs, playing at cards or dice. Others napped in the shade or nibbled at bits of food. One or two sharpened their swords, the smooth scraping sounds dry and raspy in the quiet of the trees. Rickard came forward, into the sun.

"Did our half-elf learn something on the way?" he said, addressing Morrowmen only.

"There are two of them now, one of which—I'm quite certain—is incapable of actual human thought. The other is Líana," Morrowmen replied.

But Askon wouldn't bite. He knew the old man's tricks now, if only somewhat. Instead of acknowledging the slight, he addressed Rickard directly. "You are familiar with the South Kingdom and our relative danger. Should we take a route through the trees or travel northwest along the edge until we meet the road?"

Rickard looked to Morrowmen who shrugged, his pipe leaning upward as he pursed his lips. The agent considered the choice for a moment, then turned back to the trees. "Hey Mot!" he shouted.

"Eh?"

"Which way's the fastest back to the city, you think?"

"South road's closer than the north," Mot called from behind a hand of cards. "Forest ain't bad though. It's cooler in there."

Rubbing the bridge of his nose, Rickard thought for a moment. "It's up to you, Askon, unless Morrowmen is leading us. Like the big man says, south road's faster, but the forest is cooler."

"What do the rest of the men want to do?" Askon said.

Morrowmen limped between them. "There you have it," he said to Rickard. "His intellect only gets him so far. And not very far at that. Any fool knows a leader shouldn't poll the group. That's why they have a leader." The old man grinned his skin-over-skull grin. "But Askon knows better than that. He's had command of his own men for quite some time now in Codard's army. If I had to guess, I'd say it's our two lovebirds who are the problem. He's been distracted by them all morning."

"Who?" asked Rickard. "He's been traveling with them for weeks. Ought to be used to it by now, I say."

"Not them," Morrowmen said, indicating Thomas and Elise. "Our handsome prince has been smitten by his rescuer, whether she be Askon's little sister or no."

It was another trap. However tangled his feelings might be, Askon was not stupid—no matter how often Morrowmen suggested it. He said nothing. There would come a time that he could speak with Edward privately. Then he would explain his point of view and make the appropriate threats. He would follow rule number two: stop and think. At the very least he could stop, for now.

"Well, if you woke up to a girl like that, you'd be followin' her like a drooling puppy too. Am I right, Morrowmen? I mean, seriously, the eyes, that face, and not to mention the—"

Whatever Rickard thought needed mentioning stuck in his throat like swollen bread. His face turned red, then redder, then purple as Askon drove the flat of his hunting knife into the man's neck. Morrowmen kicked Askon in the ribs, pushing him off Rickard. The skinny man rolled in the grass, gasping and clutching at his throat.

With lightning quickness Morrowmen snatched the Time fragment from its place inside Askon's shirt. He held it up before Askon's eyes. The old face twisted, not in the ugly smile, but an even more terrifying look of anger.

"Look," he commanded, and Askon did so. For a few seconds the fragment flickered from light to dark in rapid succession. "That is the signal which should tell you that, yet again, you are a miserable failure." He threw the gem down. It struck Askon's shirt soundlessly. "You think I haven't coached all of my men in how to train you? Caled felt you were worthy of the Time fragment. Does *this* look like someone who is ready to lead a city? An army? A people?"

Askon glared up at him sullenly. "No," he said. The others looked on as he and Morrowmen argued. "Maybe Caled chose wrong!" Askon shouted. "Maybe you're right, and I'm too rash or hasty or stupid to do what you want!"

Now even more than before, Askon came under the fragment's effect. Like a snake coiled to strike, Morrowmen snapped up the hunting knife.

Searing pain shot through Askon like fire as the old man drove the point of the blade into the soft tissue of Askon's shoulder. Paralyzed by the fragment, he could do little more than watch while Morrowmen bared his teeth and yanked hard on the hilt, slicing through muscle and sinew just beneath the joint in his armor. The knife turned back, tearing deeper into the flesh. Askon screamed in pain and tried to kick the vile assemblage of skin and skull and purple robes off him. But the fragment made him so slow, and he was so angry. His vision throbbed and the pain mounted, burying him in agony. When the world began to fade, the old man was beating the hilt of the knife with his fist as a hammer strikes a nail. Each blow drove it deeper into the bone.

Then the weight was gone, the horrible face somewhere far enough away to stop hurting him. Askon smelled blood. He felt his clothes grow damp with it. And then he heard the voice like water.

In only a few moments, he was healed. But the time felt like hours as anger, fear, and doubt churned and sloshed within him like a raging sea, a sea of blood. He was angry still at Rickard's remarks, angry at Morrowmen for attacking him, for berating him again and again, for nearly cutting off his arm. He found his anger directed too at Edward, who only reacted as anyone might have done. And he found it directed unexpectedly at Líana, for having grown so beautiful so quickly without him there to guide her, to protect her. And then he understood. The anger grew greater, more forceful.

Swooning from the pain and the blur of the fragment, he saw the beast that clawed and scratched within him, traced its grotesque shape with his eyes, heard its voice, smelled its stench. He hated it. More so than he had hated Mark and his whining voice, more than he hated Codard for betraying his people and his son, more than he hated Iramov, he hated the thing inside himself that hulked and screamed in fury. Peering closer, drawing nearer, aiming to kill it while he could still hold it in his mind, he saw. The thing's face was his own. And for that he hated it all the more.

"Askon." It was Líana. "Wake up. You're alright. He won't hurt you anymore." Her jaw was set, and tears tracked crooked paths over her cheeks. "I won't let him."

Opening his eyes, Askon found himself lying in the shadow of the trees, the rolling hills of the South Kingdom spreading out to the east. His shoulder felt unharmed, though his shirt still smelled of blood, its cloth still shredded. Morrowmen sprawled in the grass some fifteen feet away. The purple robes did not move.

"He'll be fine," said Líana. "Though I'm not sure why we should care."

In a semi-circle around him were Thomas, Edward, Elise, and of course, Líana. They now stood with swords drawn, Elise holding Askon's knife, awaiting a response from Morrowmen's agents. Askon assumed that however the old man had come to be unconscious on the grass, it had not been peaceful. Rickard approached them warily.

He lowered his sword. "If you ask me, he had it comin' to him by now. Never knows when he's taken it too far." Across the larger group, the men in dark uniforms nodded, voiced their assent. A few even shouted approval at Líana, who had apparently been the one to remove Morrowmen from his perch atop Askon.

"You can put the weapons down," Rickard said.

Askon expected them to look to Edward for direction, but they deferred instead to the woman with the golden braid. She gave a terse nod and sheathed her sword. With the weapon still loose in the scabbard, she approached Morrowmen.

"I didn't want to do that," she began. Askon rubbed at his terrorized shoulder while he watched. No pain lingered there.

Morrowmen lay still, his breathing slow. Líana handed over the Life fragment and looked down upon him. "You'll feel better holding that, I think."

And so it seemed he did. The pile of purple robes collected itself, and the old man sat up weakly. He surveyed the stern face above him, then turned his gaze to Askon and his friends. "Your brother doesn't understand yet," Askon heard him say.

Líana was quick to respond. "If that is how you intend to teach him— through torture—you'll have me to answer to. And them." She waved a hand at the others. "Even your own men agreed you had gone too far. I have lost too many of those I cared about. You will not torment the one who survived."

"Is this true, Rickard?" Morrowmen asked. The thin man kept his nasally voice quiet this time. He nodded and looked around for support.

"Yeah, that's what we said," hollered Mot from somewhere within the group. "Mr. Half-elf isn't figuring things out too quick, but stabbin' him ain't gonna get us nowhere."

"Fine," Morrowmen croaked. He stood shakily and locked eyes with Líana. "I won't *stab* him anymore." Tremulous hands smoothed the folds of his robe, and he turned away.

"No," Líana commanded. "You won't hurt him anymore."

"Alright. Have it your way."

A momentary silence took hold as everyone waited to see what would happen next. In that moment, Askon made a difficult decision. He remembered the beast, the thing he had seen and felt when the anger came to call. He remembered its face, his own face, ugly and twisted, but more than that, thoughtless and stupid. Above all else, controlling himself would be key to their victory. An army was useless against the Death fragment; they had seen that already, and what Codard could do with his own fragment, they could only guess. Morrowmen and Líana could both wield the Life fragment, and Apopsé obviously had power over Sight. The only remaining piece was Askon. He and the green jewel hanging at his chest would be the deciding factor. Even if he could control the Time fragment, Iramov's power seemed almost too much to imagine.

"Wait," he said. "Morrowmen is right."

Líana was horrified. Her eyes widened and her mouth dropped open with a soft click. "You can't be serious." Nearer the trees, and with his back to them, Morrowmen smiled.

"Líana," Askon began again, "thank you for helping me. You were right to do so. And Morrowmen was wrong to attack me." He stepped forward. "If we are to defeat Iramov and Codard, we will need all the resources we can muster. The Time fragment is one of those resources. I think, when we get to Apopsé's city, I should spend some time with Morrowmen alone. Maybe in the days or weeks we have left before the enemy comes, he can teach me to manage myself and the fragment's power."

He turned to Edward and Thomas. "Think what might have happened if I hadn't stopped the arrow in Dalstone. Luck won us that battle. By chance I had the fragment on my side. Without it, Brâghda would be dead and Dalstone still at war. Codard and Iramov's forces might even have returned to destroy both factions."

His friends nodded their agreement and Morrowmen's smile widened. He still said nothing, but Askon knew that inside the old man danced a victory celebration.

"Is this really what you want?" Líana asked. Pain etched her features, pain Askon would need to endure if he meant to help at all in the coming battle. A long silence lay awkwardly amongst them. For nearly a full minute, no one spoke.

"Of course it's not what he wants." It was Morrowmen. He seemed to have recovered from whatever injury Líana had given him. "But he understands now, perhaps, it's not just about what he wants. He needs someone to train him. He needs to be able to use the fragment. And he needs me to do it. Does that sound about right, Askon?"

It did. They crossed into the small forest, eager to avoid the heat and to stay out of sight. Morrowmen and his agents felt they would be safe this far south, and with the morning's events—and the energy the Life fragment required to do its work—they decided the shelter of the trees would be best.

As the last of them entered the cluster of thin trunks, Morrowmen whispered to Askon. "I think for now, we take a break. Until we've spoken to Apopsé, you will suffer no training. But after that, you should hope you truly mean what you say."

"I do," Askon replied.

When night fell, hours later, they stood on the opposite edge of the small forested area. Less than a day's travel remained between them and the city. Its outer wall rose high above the harvested trees and stubble of grass. Askon's reckoning had been close, but the passage through the little forest was easier and faster than he had expected. It was decided that none who had used the Life fragment that day, and none who had been healed by its power, would sit a watch. So Edward, Morrowmen, Líana, and Askon all slept a heavy, dreamless sleep.

CHAPTER FOURTEEN

Sticks and Stones and Broken Bones

In the morning Askon and Edward hunkered over a weatherworn blanket and an equally weatherworn breakfast. Much had been lost to the river, but a square of hard cheese which had survived the trip made the main course, followed by several hunks of stale bread. A few nuts and berries, found the day before in the trees, rounded out the meal. Morrowmen, after rummaging through one of his agent's packs, produced a handful of hardy fruit. According to the old man, such fruit were of plentiful supply in the south.

Through a screen of trees, the final leg of their journey lay before them, gold and green under the morning sun. At one time, the little forest had stretched all the way to the city's outer wall, but now it had been pushed back as the wall and everything within it grew higher, wider, and stronger.

Behind them Líana sat next to an uncomfortable-looking Elise. Seated side by side, there could scarcely have been two more opposite women: Elise pale as powder, with brooding, dark features, raven hair, and peasant's clothing scavenged or sewn in the Norill settlement of Vitæsta; and Líana, golden haired and bright of face, in a combat uniform, sword laid out to one side. Líana was saying something to Elise and glancing briefly in Edward's direction. It seemed the blue and green eyes settled on the prince more and more, and in turn the black eyes glowered less.

Thomas had been selected for the middle watch and so was still sleeping as the others ate or prepared for their departure. He lay only a few feet from the two women while Marten flitted from tree to tree, eager to resume their travel over the windblown plain.

With no introduction, fanfare, or even a polite request, Morrowmen flopped down beside Edward. Askon looked across the blanket at him. He shifted his robes, held up another handful of the small fruit, placed them in a neat line next to the nuts and berries, and looked up into the trees. His spiderweb hair floated inertly above his splotched scalp.

"Loyal bird," he said pensively. "Common with the elf training. Caled kept birds for a long time. He got tired of them dying. Decided it was better to not get attached."

Askon and Edward eyed one another, unsure whether to speak or be silent. Morrowmen provided their answer.

"With me it was the dogs," he went on, "almost like people, if you find the right one, and I found a great many. Oh sure, I could keep them alive a good deal longer than an ordinary dog, but it's hard to keep one around who more or less looks like this." He pinched the loose skin at his neck, jiggling it like an obscene convulsing rooster.

Askon winced and set down the piece of bread he had been gnawing at. Edward did the same.

"I suppose they felt that way as well. Too bad really, so I stopped keeping them. Aside from Caled, I stopped caring about most anyone. I cared for the kingdom and its people of course, though I sometimes wonder why. But individuals? It was too hard to lose them over and over." He shook his head. "Obviously Caled felt differently, building Tolarenz, supporting all those half-elves—even a few true elves—during the Scouring. He was better than me in a lot of ways."

He stopped. Askon wanted to reply, to say something that would comfort the old man, though he had rarely done the same for Askon. But he knew that anything he might say would ring hollow because it was true, Caled would have been a better teacher, a better trainer, a better leader.

"I'm sure you know what they say in the kitchens and the laundries of the castle," said Edward. Askon smiled. Edward always knew what to say and how to say it.

"I probably do," Morrowmen grumbled. "But I'd like to know anyway."

Edward crunched a round nut no bigger than the end of Askon's little finger. They were green, and fell in profusion throughout the surrounding grove. The night before, the watchmen had roasted hundreds of them over the fires. He flicked a spent shell into the grass.

"'Playing at cards is an exercise in life,' I once heard a baker say. 'And playing at life is an exercise in cards.' I took that to mean that our hands are dealt at the game's beginning and that to some degree our victories and our defeats are dealt then as well. Some hands keep a poor player in the game longer than he should be, while some cast out the game's most experienced in the first few rounds. But we see those who play the poor hands well as the heroes, and those who play the great hands poorly for what they are, the fools."

"Hmm," Morrowmen mumbled through a bit of fruit. "A wise pastry chef," he smacked. "Perhaps there is hope for our friend Askon after all."

Behind them a series of loud *clacks* rang out through the trees. Askon turned to see Líana and Elise standing face to face. The latter arched her back, raising her weapon, and launched a flurry of savage blows. Her black hair had been tied tight behind her head, but a few strands dangled loosely in her face. *Clack, clack, clack!*

Now came Líana's turn. From Askon's vantage, he could have sworn her green eye shone brighter than the blue. With surprising force, and unsurprising speed and grace, she battered her opponent. A downward stroke, blocked. *Clack.* A back-cut, anticipated. *Clack.* Pirouette. *Smack!*

The stick which Líana had been using as a makeshift sword struck Elise across the face, and she fell to one knee. Thomas sat up, wild fear in his eyes. But this was not the quiet whispering girl they had met in the cluster of Norill hovels. No, this was the cold commander who ordered the guards at the gate, the one who lay just beneath the surface behind the black eyes. With a bit more hair loose from its tie, she stood, a long red streak rising against her pale skin.

Líana's mouth moved, but they could not hear what she said. Elise spun an awkward imitation of her opponent's previous strike, and brought her stick down on Líana. With focused precision, Líana met Elise's stroke and effortlessly twisted the mock blade from her pale hands. It thumped into the grass. Fluidly, as though gravity were only a suggestion, Líana's toe slipped under the stick and kicked it lightly into the air. Elise caught it with a pleased, giddy smile. Her eyebrows bounced, and a small laugh escaped her lips.

Líana repeated the lesson, this time as the aggressor and much more slowly. Elise met the stroke and turned it aside, though Líana's stick stayed in her hand. Thomas looked on with wide eyes as they continued. Askon wondered what the young man would do if Elise ever became a proficient swordsman. *Swordswoman?* Askon mulled the word and smiled. Whatever Thomas did, he would certainly be even less argumentative with her than before.

"While we are all mesmerized by ladies with swords," Morrowmen said, like a schoolteacher in a room full of distracted pupils, "you can stare on your own time." Askon and Edward turned to face him, playing their parts as scolded children.

"I didn't come over here to talk about my dogs or baker's wisdom. And I certainly didn't come over here to watch girls play with sticks," he said.

"One of those girls had you sprawling in the dirt yesterday," Edward said.

"So she did," the old man grunted. "Still, we have more important things to worry about before we're on our way."

Askon cracked open another of the green nuts. "For instance?"

"If you'll give me a chance to speak without your incessant interruptions!"

Askon wagged a finger. "I thought you said we were taking a break from training until we reach the city?"

Morrowmen smoldered for a moment, then started again with a huff. "The Life fragment. I needed to see you two up close, but now I'm sure of it. Líana uses it differently than I do."

"What do you mean?" Edward asked.

The old man reached over and grabbed Edward's shirt, lifting it up to expose the ribs. Reflexively Edward pulled away, aiming a skeptical look at Morrowmen who went on as if he hadn't noticed Edward's reaction. "Look here, both of you," Morrowmen said.

They did.

"Yesterday bruises covered this whole side of your ribcage Edward," Morrowmen went on. "Since you were unconscious, you wouldn't know that. The Life fragment healed them."

Askon pried apart the shell of another nut. Whatever Morrowmen was getting at, he was beginning with the blatantly obvious. "We all saw that yesterday. Líana healed him."

"I remember that," Edward said wistfully.

Morrowmen nodded. "I know," he said. "But we needed to begin with a point of fact." He lowered the shirt and turned to Askon. "How long do you think it would have taken our prince here to recover from those wounds on his own?"

"A few months if there were broken bones, weeks or days if it was just bruising," Askon said tossing an empty shell aside. "Why?"

Morrowmen pointed to Edward's leg. "Now, what if I told you that the bones of his knee had been utterly destroyed in addition to the lacerations you saw?"

Askon's eyes widened; Morrowmen had his attention. "At least a year. Probably never. I've seen soldiers take pikes to the knee; most never return to battle. Some can't even work the fields or forges when they go home."

Thwack!

"Ow!" hollered Edward. "Why would you do that?"

Morrowmen smiled. "It's good as new now, isn't it?"

"Yes," said Edward, rubbing his knee. "But I'd be happier if you didn't hit me anymore."

"I won't," said Morrowmen, and no one believed him.

Shaking his head, Askon stared out toward the city wall, its ivory surface like a bone laid bare in the sun. "So Líana healed him more than we thought. Like I said, if it was possible to return from such an injury it would take a year or so."

Morrowmen's eyes lit up and the skin-over-skull smile stretched tight. "And what if I said his back was broken in four places, one of which—just above the hips—had severed the tissue inside the backbones. How long would that take?"

"People don't recover from such injuries naturally, Morrowmen," said Askon frowning. He remembered a boy back in Tolarenz. The boy, no older than Líana had been when he set out for Austgæta, had been climbing the cliffs north of the town hall. Children, especially boys in the gray areas between childhood and their coming of age could often be found there, testing their strength, exercising their bravado.

The news had come swiftly and cruelly. He had fallen, breaking his back. The women and physicians thought he might have lived, had his fall been on grass instead of stones. Askon remembered them saying that the cord of life had been cut.

Morrowmen's head bobbed up and down. "Well," he said, "that's mostly true. There have been isolated cases where men have gone on to live after such an injury, but they never again walk upon their legs, and certainly not with four fractures in addition to the tissue damage."

Edward looked ill. He flipped the blanket up over the food and looked away. "So you brought me back from the dead?"

"Gods no!" Askon had never seen Morrowmen look so aghast. The effect on his ghoulish face verged on frightening. "Necromancy is a myth perpetuated by fools, like those who say Askon's people can call down rainstorms or hold pure fire in their hands. It's nonsense. The dead stay dead, my prince. You just weren't quite dead yet."

Instantly Askon's mind cast him back to the woods outside of Dalstone. In the pouring rain, three faces disproved Morrowmen's assertions. Patrick, Christopher, and Victor had all—as far as he knew—been dead. But then again, he would have said the same had he found Edward as he had been under Morrowmen's white sheet. Askon raised a hand to interrupt, desperate to see if Morrowmen would have any answers for him. "I—"

"Askon," Morrowmen said sternly. "Your training is on hiatus, but would it kill you to try not to break my concentration? This is important. Besides, you're next."

"What?" Askon was confused, still thinking of vacant staring faces.

Morrowmen rose and hobbled over to him. "Alright," he said, and flicked the walking stick into Askon's healed shoulder. "Point number two. I did enough damage to this shoulder for you to never recover from it. Between driving the metal into your bones and severing all of the major tendons, I think I did a respectable job."

Frowning, Askon wondered what Morrowmen would find disrespectful.

"Anyway," the old man continued. "It was enough to prove my point. You should both be older. Especially you," he indicated Edward. "With those injuries, you should look like your new friend Eldred back in that festering hole of a town in Grafmark. But you don't." He rounded on Askon. "And you. You should at least have a gray streak or even a strand in that mop on your head, but there's nothing."

"Could be a family trait," Askon offered.

"A family of simpletons!" Morrowmen snapped. "Excuse me," he corrected. "Old habits. Have you ever heard of a family trait in which the members recovered from quadruple spinal fractures?"

Askon hadn't.

Staring into the dirt he had exposed by folding the blanket, Edward reached behind him, running the back of his hand up and down his spine. He started to say something, but the words never came. Morrowmen, triumphant now, paced through the scattered brush.

"You see," he said. "It's different. She's doing it differently. I don't know how, but she seems to be using the Life fragment without the negative side effects, and it heals almost instantly. I've healed many people with that blasted rock and not one of them has come through the process nearly as quickly and utterly unchanged as the two of you. And since our test subjects couldn't be more different, aside from the fact that you are both male, the only possible conclusion is that the difference rests not in the recipients but in the wielder of the fragment."

Thomas had made his way over to them from the impromptu sparring ground. Glancing over his shoulder one last time, he approached Askon. Another series of *crack, crack, crack,* punctuated by a *smack!* and a high-pitched yelp, echoed through the trees. Thomas sat down.

"I thought I'd feel better if I came over here," he said. "Líana told me not to worry, that she would heal Elise before we started for town, but it's still hard for me to watch."

"Interesting," said Morrowmen, drawing out the word so the others would take notice. "Thomas," he said, after gaining their full attention, "did Líana say anything about how the fragment would affect Elise?"

"No."

Morrowmen tossed the young man one of the fruit from the blanket. Thomas caught it and bit into the skin, grateful for something new to eat in the face of their waterlogged supplies. "I was just telling your friends that I think Líana can use the Life fragment to heal without the adverse aging effect that has plagued me for so long."

Thomas nodded. "I wondered the same thing. Neither Askon nor Edward looks any older, and those were some very severe wounds. Edward's were much worse, of course. I kept thinking he would wake up looking like the man from my village, Havard, the one we call the Grandfather."

"Ha!" Morrowmen squawked. "That's right. He should have, but he doesn't. I don't know how to describe it. Exercising the Life fragment's power with no apparent ill effects? Who knows what that might mean?!"

While Morrowmen stood wonderstruck at his discovery, Thomas snapped up another of the small tender fruit. He chewed thoughtfully for a moment, then swallowed, his eyes wandering here and there. He scratched at the emerging stubble of beard on his chin and picked up another fruit. Opening his mouth, he lifted it, then stopped, agape.

"Morrowmen?" he asked, his eyes still moving about like drag-onflies over stagnant water. "What if she isn't healing them without ill-effect?"

"What else could she be doing?" Morrowmen barked. "You've seen these two. If anything, they're younger than they were yester-day, certainly in better shape."

It was true. Even though Askon didn't feel any younger than he had the day before, his shoulder had never felt better. Years of swordplay, battles, and injuries had taken their toll on his body.

Nagging pains pestered him from time to time, but not in that shoulder, not now. The healing was complete, not only knitting up the damage done by Morrowmen's vicious attack, but restoring the joint entirely, like his arms had felt when he was a boy helping to build gardens in Tolarenz.

"That's not what I mean," said Thomas, popping the fruit into his mouth. He continued through his chewing; the lump pushed his cheek into a round bulb. "When *you* use the fragment, it takes time from a person's life, right?"

Morrowmen looked dubious. It was the same tactic he had used to begin his discussion with Askon and Edward. "Yes."

"So they get older right before our eyes. But, taking time from someone's life might instead be deferred. Say, instead of looking five years older, you just die five years sooner." Thomas reached for another of the fruit.

"Where did you find this boy?" Morrowmen said to Askon. "He's brilliant! Such an idea hadn't even occurred to me."

Thomas smiled timidly, but Askon did not look pleased in the least. "So I just die early? That's it?"

Edward's face grew worried. "What does that mean for me?"

Morrowmen stopped his pacing. "We don't know for sure if our young Thomas is correct. If he is, Askon has nothing to worry about. But for Edward, time may be very important indeed."

Time. There was that word again. It reminded Askon of the gem dangling against his chest and of the arrow in the fields near Dalstone. He remembered Thomas being fast enough to bat his hand away, and Morrowmen so quick he could steal Askon's knife right from his hand. Morrowmen had promised to help him once they reached the city, and he had promised to allow that help. They just needed time.

CHAPTER FIFTEEN

The Secret of the Dead

Askon rose from his seat. Whether he and Edward would have shorter lives than without the Life fragment, he did not know. What he did know was that without it, he would have been irreparably maimed while Edward would have been dead. And that reminded him again.

"We need Líana and Elise," he said.

Thomas jumped up, without so much as a second breath, and jogged over to the sparring women. He waited for them to pause. Líana now had a welt or two of her own where Elise had made contact. Later Askon found that this was merely positive reinforcement by an excellent teacher. In single combat, only an expert swordsman could ever hit Líana. When they had finished, he spoke first to Elise, pointing to the blanket around which Askon, Edward, and Morrowmen sat. She nodded, pulling her hair loose so that it fell all around her face. Líana nodded too, tossed the sticks aside, and followed them.

The women unbalanced the discussion. When they sat down opposite Edward and Thomas, sweat still beaded on their skin and dampened their hair. They sat with their upper-bodies rising and falling, rising and falling, their breathing still accelerated from exertion. Meanwhile, both Thomas and Edward were transfixed by the opposing pair, watching as they traded drinks from a waterskin before sampling from the quickly dwindling breakfast that lay before them.

Beyond their immediate distraction, Thomas and Edward both seemed concerned. Líana, dressed in uniform, seemed mostly unaffected by the sparring match. She had taken a few hits, but only one mark stood out on her cheek. And though Edward asked Líana if she was alright, a note of protective care in his voice, Askon smiled proudly, nodding his approval. Such a blow was not easy to take, even from a beginning student. His sister, he decided, would be just fine.

Thomas had more cause for worry. Líana was already a promising teacher and surprisingly expert with a sword, and she had not been gentle with her student. Elise's face, striped with red against the pale white skin, already showed the signs of bruising. As they had walked toward Askon and the others, she limped, favoring one leg. But behind the dark locks of hair, she smiled contentedly.

"She's beaten Elise silly," Thomas was saying. "I don't know if this is the best idea. Elise, do you really need to learn how to fight with a blade?"

The smile flattened and her dark eyes snapped across the blanket. "Why not?" she asked, and a threat bubbled beneath the surface. "Do you fear what I might be capable of, given the chance?"

"No," said Thomas quickly. "I—I just—it's," he sighed. "Well, the wounds on your face."

"Can you not love me if my face isn't an unmarked beauty mask?" Her words were laced with venom and warning.

"I—she—"

"What about *her*?"

"She's hurting you!" Thomas blurted. The others drew back.

Líana placed a hand on Elise's knee. "Thomas. I can heal her. There will be no sign we ever even crossed swords, or sticks."

"Yes," Elise rumbled, then drew back into her musical whisper. "You'll have your pretty face to look upon once again. Will that make you feel better?"

Thomas trembled at her words. "It's not about the marks or the scars. It's not about how you look." He turned to Líana. "Can you take back the suffering from when you strike her?" he said, his voice cracking. "I heard her cry out in pain. Does the Life fragment erase that?"

Líana looked away sheepishly, saying nothing.

Elise broke the silence. "Before you came along," she said with the strange lack of care or self-consciousness that she so often showed, "my life was painful in many ways. None too terrible, of course, but starting anew in a city full of creatures so different from you can be—" She paused. "Difficult. All of those small hurts and slights strengthened me, taught me, so that I could help when

Brâghda brought in new men and women from Dalstone. These," she pointed to the welts, "will help me to learn. Their little bits of pain will quicken my eye and strengthen my hand so that one day, I might protect myself as Líana can. And that will be very valuable indeed."

It was a speech Askon had given many times to recruits as he battered them with a blunted sword. Over and over again, they would make the same mistakes. A missed block here. A flinch and closing of the eyes there. The wounds were more brutal, but the philosophy was the same. Each stroke the student did not turn would be a reminder to do so the next time. And not coincidentally, Askon thought, he had given a similar speech to a much younger Líana in the fields near their home.

"While this is all very inspirational," said Morrowmen, "it's time we were on our way to the city. Apopsé is waiting for us, perhaps watching for us. Askon called you ladies over here. Did you have something to say to them that I need to hear, or can I go and deal with more important matters?"

Important matters. Askon almost laughed at the thought. What could be more important than the faces he had seen outside of Dalstone? But he didn't laugh. He pressed the pads of his fingers together and tapped the forefingers against his mouth.

"This is very important, I think," he said.

Thomas scooted around so he could better see Askon. A beam of light had sneaked through the branches overhead and now fell upon Thomas's face. He squinted, then moved again. Líana, who already sat next to Askon, looked up. Her eyes had remained downcast after Thomas pointed out the pain she had caused Elise. Edward glanced at Líana briefly as she lifted her eyes. Then he looked back to Askon.

"Out with it already," said Morrowmen.

Askon grinned. "Now who's the impatient one?"

Morrowmen was not impressed.

"Outside of Dalstone—Líana, do you know what happened there?"

"Of course she does," Morrowmen interrupted. "She watched in Apopsé's fragment just as I did."

"Alright," Askon continued. "After I attacked the enemy near the trees, I found myself on the opposite side of their ranks."

"For once you had the fragment working in your favor," said Morrowmen.

It was true. The fragment's power had allowed him to cut down a large number of the enemy without them even knowing it. He hoped Morrowmen could teach him how to better control that power. "For once, I did," Askon said. "But not for long. It started to rain, and I looked farther into the forest. Lightning flashed. It was only for a fleeting second, but I saw them."

Líana reached out and touched his shoulder. "I remember. You looked so afraid. I didn't understand what was so terrible about the reinforcements."

"The reinforcements weren't terrible, just men, though I was surprised to see Codard's stag alongside Iramov's bull."

"Then what was it?" asked Thomas.

"Those who should have been dead," Askon replied. "In the ranks of reinforcements, I saw three faces I never thought to see again in this life: Victor, who led us from Tolarenz to Austgæta and who led me many times before; Patrick, who Thomas and I said goodbye to on the slopes between Austgæta and Norogæta; and Christopher, who I watched Edward kill with my own eyes. John's men were to bury him near the Greyarc bridge. I think they did not."

Morrowmen stood abruptly, his purple robes flowing around him.

"Nonsense!" he said with a grunt. "No more than a few minutes ago we discussed this. Necromancy does not exist. And even if it were true—which it is not—what would we do about it?"

"I think it is important that all of you know what I saw," said Askon.

"What you thought you saw," Morrowmen corrected. "It could have easily been a side effect of the Time fragment working against you. I saw the gem flickering in the image Apopsé showed us just as plain as if it had been in front of my very eyes."

A shadow crept over Askon's face, but he said nothing.

"Enough of this," said Morrowmen. "Thomas, Elise, go gather your things. The day is wearing away already. Líana, tell Rickard to marshal the others. They'll be bored by now, I'm sure. Edward, I'll not give orders to the prince of Vladvir, at least not right now. So you do what you want."

Edward gave a quick nod and followed Líana, catching up and falling into stride beside her. Askon and Morrowmen stood together under the leaves.

"You can't just ignore this because you don't believe in it," Askon said forcefully. "I don't know what those blank, empty faces are capable of, but I doubt they are harmless."

"Shut up!" snapped Morrowmen. "Some things are meant only for us to know," he continued in a whisper. "Caled and I kept many secrets over the years. Some of those became rumor, some common knowledge. But some will never be known."

Askon looked out on the vanished camp. His eyes followed Líana, and as such, Edward. He tried to ignore it, but he still felt uncomfortable about the way his friend and sister acted toward one another.

"Are you saying you knew about this power?" he asked.

Morrowmen, also watching Edward and Líana, adjusted his robe. "Absolutely not. But while we are unsure about it, the others are best left with the minimum of information. Walk with me today. We will discuss exactly what you saw, and if we are lucky, we will have a ready explanation when we arrive at Apopsé's city. As the Sight fragment's guardian, he should know as well."

With the sun still hiding behind the thin trees, they set out. Morrowmen's agents took the lead, with Rickard at their head. Thomas and Elise found friendly conversation amongst them, and for most of the day's early hours traveled within the group of shadowy purple uniforms. Líana, who knew Morrowmen's soldiers well already, flitted from one to the next for most of the morning. She laughed with Rickard and Mot, shared burdens with some of the others, and spent significant time talking seriously with Elise. Askon noticed that during this particular conversation, Elise waved Thomas away.

Edward, personable and unrestrained, weaved a path through the purple uniforms, getting to know each of them. Askon's training told him that by the end of the day, Edward would be able to recall all of their names and most of their backgrounds, including which villages or cities they came from and if they had families to return to. Askon had tried to do the same with his own men in Codard's army, as was suggested of all leaders. Edward, however, had always been much better at remembering, even after months or years.

More troubling to Askon was the amount of time his friend and his sister spent together. They both filtered through the larger group, but they seemed to accidentally cross paths again and again. At first they both acted surprised, as if they had happened upon one another in the crowds of some large city. But as the sun climbed to noon, it became a game. She would smile, he tip an imaginary hat. Askon tried to think of a time he had seen Edward wearing a hat and could not recall ever having witnessed such a thing. A helmet in battle, certainly, though often the prince—and Askon as well— had eschewed helmets in favor of wider range of vision. Many times they were sent as reconnaissance or to set an ambush and as such needed as much acuity of sight and hearing as possible.

Hat or no hat, the game went on. Soon, Edward was taking her hand by the fingers, placing a gentle kiss in the flat space above the knuckles. She would smile, nod, and give a polite wave before heading off in another direction. More than once, they fell in together, laughing and talking. When Líana would bounce or even skip away, Edward watched her go and on more than one occasion glanced back at Askon before continuing on his way through the group.

Whatever his feelings toward them, Askon was certain he had the poorer company. For hours he trudged along with Morrowmen, recounting the events near Dalstone over and over. Each time, Morrowmen demanded more details, and Askon did his best. But by the time their shadows shrank into the tufts of grass, the story of the dead faces had changed very little.

"There are no other details," Askon said, exasperated. He tried to remember how many times they had been over the story, but could not.

"How did they fight?" Morrowmen asked—for at least the third time.

"I've told you, I didn't see them fight. They stood amongst the ranks in the trees, their faces emotionless, blank, unfeeling. I ducked behind the tree, and they charged with the rest of the reinforcements. They must have fought, but when I made my way back to the battle, I was never able to find them again."

Morrowmen pinched the bridge of his nose, breathing noisily. "What are we going to tell Apopsé, then?" Askon had heard this question already as well.

"Morrowmen," he began. "There is only one thing to tell."

"And that is?"

"We tell him what I saw. Maybe he has seen more in the Sight fragment." But Askon had said this before, too; he knew where it led. "I know, as surely as a man can know, that Patrick and Christopher were dead. As for Victor, I only had the information second hand, from John. But if you had seen their faces, the way they stared. Whatever animated Patrick and Christopher, so did it animate Victor."

Morrowmen stopped. He put his boot on one of the many stumps that littered the area, remnants of the little forest that had once reached all the way to the city walls. "It's not much to tell," he said.

Askon kept walking, his words fading away with every step. "There are dead soldiers fighting in Iramov's army. It may be a short sentence, but the information is important. We have to let Apopsé know, if only to see what he can find out by using his piece of the Tear. If you think I don't have enough detail, you can say so, as I'm sure you will, but I won't keep this to myself." He left Morrowmen brooding over the stump.

CHAPTER SIXTEEN

Advice

As they drew nearer to the city gates, the outer wall loomed up, brilliant white in the hot sun. The sea of stumps and grass gave way to fields, some bare, some growing grains or other crops. They also began to see people on the road. Such contact became unavoidable the closer they came to the wall. Upon striking the road, they passed through a collection of travelers headed north. Led by a small, mean-looking man who claimed to be a merchant, the travelers said little of where they might be going. Edward warned them to keep an eye out for trouble, though he too withheld specifics. The mean man pointed sharply at two large brutes at the back of his company. Askon wondered what quality of protection two such guards would give if the travelers were attacked. He said nothing, keeping his head down and his hood up.

The South Kingdom, Morrowmen had explained, had yet to coalesce around a single attitude toward Askon's people. For some, the old prejudices were alive and well, while others, mainly concerned with their own livelihoods, paid little attention to such matters. According to Morrowmen, the city housed a modest number of half-elven families, regardless of what he had told his men to say in order to set Askon's anger alight. No. Askon and his sister were not the last of a people. It was a relief to hear, but Askon wondered if the existence of half-elven families in the South Kingdom made any difference. Iramov would come here to wipe them out, just as he had done in Tolarenz.

"Have you met any of them?" Askon questioned his sister. The wheat and barley had been replaced by stalks of corn on either side of the road. Men worked in places throughout, but with harvest coming soon, most were inside the city preparing tools and organizing workers.

"I've been to their quarter of the city," Líana replied. She sounded sad. "It's not like Tolarenz. And it shouldn't even be called a quarter at all. They live in tiny houses with one or two rooms. For the most part, their entire homes are no bigger than our sitting room. Everything is so close together in the city, and very brown. I know it looks white from out here, but inside, especially where the half-elves live, it's a lot of dirt and dust."

Askon surveyed the white outer wall. She was right. From here, it did look like everything in the city would be made of marble or ivory. But he also remembered how neat and green Codard's inner gardens were, and the tangle of wild brambles that grew between the city proper and his castle gate.

"Do they keep the same customs?" Askon asked.

Líana thought for a moment. "No. I talked to a few of them, and I think they'd like to, but water has to be carried in every day from much farther than in Tolarenz. Morrowmen says the city was built on blasted land where nothing would grow. So the half-elves here keep no gardens."

Askon frowned. The family garden was an enormous part of the culture in Tolarenz. It gave each dwelling a personality which spoke to the individuals living inside. Every year families spent countless hours tending to these living representations of themselves. If a hard year came and more time had to be spent in the fields or tending to floods or dealing with the rare drought, the gardens were smaller, less meticulously managed, but never empty. Something always grew in front of a family's home. He wondered what would become of the gardens now.

Thoughts of vacant homes loomed up like the white wall before him. He saw Iramov's maniacal face, heard his echoing laughter. In order to keep the memories at bay, Askon changed the subject.

"Why are you teaching Elise to fight?" he asked. "I mean, I heard her reason, and it makes enough sense, but there must have been some reason you would offer."

Líana blushed, hiding her face behind her hand.

"I knew it," Askon said smiling. "She wouldn't have come to you first."

"No," Líana said. "She wouldn't. I don't think she likes me very much."

Askon laughed, the kind of deep rolling laughter that only comes after one has been too serious for too long. "Of course not," he said while the laughter rolled on.

"Why?" Líana asked. She looked very confused and a little wounded. "What's so funny?"

Askon regained control of himself and put his arm around her. "Morrowmen is right," he said. "In some ways you're older and wiser than me, and in others, you're still that little girl I left back at home."

"What do you mean?"

Askon gestured out ahead of them. Thomas and Elise walked together while they talked with Rickard. Thomas waved his hands animatedly in some retelling of their adventures.

"You're her competition now," Askon said. "Until you arrived, she was the only woman in Thomas's sight. There was no other."

"I don't think of Thomas that way!" Líana said, a bit too loudly. She raised her hand again to her face.

Askon let his arm slide off her shoulder. "I wasn't under the impression that you did. But he has noticed you. They all have."

"Who?"

"All of these men," Askon said with grin that was half amusement and half a sign of his own struggle to accept the fact. "They all see you for what you are now, a beautiful woman."

Líana blushed again and slapped Askon's shoulder. "But they all know what happened to me. They know how I got this way."

"It doesn't matter," said Askon flatly. "You know, the Grafmark Norill have a saying for it."

"For what?"

Askon's smile widened. "Well, for everything really. But it applies here as well as it does anywhere."

"What do they say?"

"The world is how it is." He repeated Brâghda's words with slow reverence. "The men see you as you are, not as you were, no matter how hard they try." Askon had tried hard enough himself, but even for him it was true. Once in a while Líana said or did something that reminded him of the little girl sneaking through the bushes in front of the town hall, but the rest of the time she was a grown woman, and there was nothing he could do to change it.

He went on. "And Elise sees you as a threat. Who can measure beauty? Only the admirer, it is said. If Elise thinks you more attractive than she is, then to her you must be."

"Oh," said Líana quietly. "I hadn't really thought about all that."

"So, as I was saying, you must have been the one to come to her about the sword training," Askon resumed. "You didn't think I would forget my question did you?"

She had. He could see it on her face. "No. I just—it's just—"

"About Edward?" Askon suggested.

"Yes," Líana mumbled. "I didn't know how to act or what to say, so I went to Elise. There are no other women here. Just talking to you about it now is uncomfortable enough."

The corn stalks vanished, replaced by rows of orchards, each tree carrying dozens of the fruit Morrowmen had provided at breakfast. Askon understood now why he had been so free with them.

"That explains why she would even talk to you, and I suppose her advice would be as good as any. But what advice do you need with men anyway, you're just—"

"A little girl?" said Líana pointedly. She had crossed her arms, and in that moment looked surprisingly like a well-armed, blond version of their mother. He almost expected her to scold him about his manners. But she had caught him. How could he in one breath tell her that "The world is how it is," and in the next pretend she shouldn't be interested in Edward, or any other person she chose, for that matter.

Now it was Askon's turn to feel the color rise in his cheeks. "I'm sorry," he said. "I'll have to let that go, I suppose. It isn't going to be easy, you know."

"I know," Líana said, her arms still folded.

"But you haven't answered my question about the sword-fighting. That hardly counts as womanly advice."

Líana lowered her arms and the vision of their mother faded. "It's a trade. She gives me advice, and I give her advice. She knows about being a woman, and I know about hitting people with sticks." She laughed and Askon joined her.

CHAPTER SEVENTEEN

South City

When they reached the gate, Askon could not help but be impressed. Back in King's City, he had often marveled at the high walls, tall turrets, and strong stonework. But Apopsé's wall was another marvel entirely. Standing nearly a third again as high as the ramparts of Codard's castle, it towered over passersby, and the huge doors of the gate used a complicated mechanism of wheels and gears in order to open and close. When the city was sealed, the metal workings slid out partially to reinforce the hinges. Such a gate seemed nearly impenetrable.

The surface of the wall itself, which had appeared to be pure white at a distance, actually more closely matched the color of canvas. He decided the effort must have been massive to construct such a wall. Across its entire surface, the white layer had been spread like mud, then hardened in the sun. To the touch, the coating was as hard as stone, though Askon could see a few places where it had flaked away, revealing a more traditional stone-and-block construction. Whatever it was made of, the layer served more than just a cosmetic purpose; it created an almost perfectly smooth surface. Scaling the wall during a siege or even in secret would be practically impossible.

On the inside of the western facing main gate, a wide square opened before them. Líana's description of the half-elven quarter could not have been more different from what Askon saw there. Beneath their feet lay a broad, tiled mosaic depicting the white dove on sky blue. Each tile had been carefully enameled and not a single piece showed a crack or chip. Morrowmen later explained that Apopsé had any scratched or shattered pieces replaced frequently to provide the appearance that the tiles never broke. Around the far edge of the mosaic, a series of shops lined the square, all covered in the same white layer as the wall. In one display case, gems and precious stones sparkled on links of chain and rings equally precious. Another had fabulous cloth of brightest color and lightest weight. Pottery of unparalleled quality there was, even tumblers and goblets made of transparent glass. The glorious white row of shops showed no sign of food vendors, fishmongers, or butchers anywhere, just lovely, extravagant objects for customers to purchase.

Before Askon could investigate the wares further, they were approached by guards bearing the white dove. Half capes hung loosely from pins on their shoulders; the fabric shimmered like ripples on a windblown lake. Their armor, a combination of steel plates and tightly linked chain mail had been polished to a mirror finish. The leader, a tall man with a plume of white feathers, fell in next to Rickard—after first talking with Morrowmen. He now led them toward the center of the city.

All along the main street, vendors sold their wares. Just as in the wide square before the gate, all the buildings had been covered in the canvas-colored substance, making everything appear clean and well cared for. Unlike the main street in Codard's city, this one did not run straight. The guard explained that when the city was designed, the builders had decided that a lane from gate to keep made for a poor defensive strategy, even if the gate itself was unlikely ever to be broken. So they snaked their way over nearly a mile's worth of paving stones, turning left then right, sometimes running parallel to their destination, other times approaching it directly. Once or twice, Askon had caught a glimpse of the neighboring streets. There, Líana's description could not have been more accurate. Leaving the splendidly white main path meant a descent into dirty-brown, bare wood, and shacks or sheds.

Though they had seen the palace from a distance, it now lay obscured from view. They could, however, see the second wall, just as white as the first but not as high. Rounding another of the sharp corners, the gate came into view. Black bars, spaced a few inches apart, formed a barrier between the palace grounds and the rest of the city. Following the man in the feathered plume, they approached. Askon recalled their previous luck with gates and laughed to himself. Of course they had walked easily through the impregnable barrier of wood and steel and strange machinery, but now before a row of simple iron bars, they halted, unable to go forward.

It was here that Rickard and Morrowmen's other agents said goodbye. They turned aside and slipped down a side street in pairs or threes. Before Askon had the chance to see where they would go, they disappeared into the alleys and narrow paths of the city.

The feathered guard approached the wall and tapped three times on its smooth white surface. It made no sound, as behind the thin layer it was likely made of solid stone. Askon glanced at Edward, puzzled. Stepping away from the wall, the guard took a few paces to his right, turned and tapped again. He waited. After a moment he repeated the procedure. Askon watched as Morrowmen thumped his cane impatiently against the pavers, and wondered what the old man would say to rules number one and two now. He decided to let it go. They would have plenty of time to practice and argue over Morrowmen's maxims of self-control.

After the third series of knocks, a narrow slit slid open just inches from the guard's closed fist. He said something into the opening, then nodded, plume swaying and fluttering above him. Moments later, a series of clicks issued from the wall around the gate. A whirring sound arose, like a swarm of angry bees, and rather than swinging open on hinges, the gate slid apart, its two halves disappearing inside the wall. Morrowmen let out a disgusted sigh.

"Apopsé and his machines. A simple door would make more sense," he said.

Askon glanced again at Edward who watched the whole process with a measure of interested respect. Across from them, Thomas pressed his face against the gap into which the leftmost half of the gate had vanished.

"That's amazing!" he said, pulling back from the black space. "I wonder if it's a smaller version of the mechanism in the main gate. If so, imagine what you could do, the things you could build."

The others did not share Thomas's interest and instead followed the feathered guard. After they had drawn some distance into the palace grounds, Askon heard the swarm of bees again, only this time farther away. Thomas uttered an exclamation of wonder and amazement as the gate's two sides came to rest against one another.

"Truly extraordinary," he said breathlessly, trotting up behind them. "I wonder if Lord Apopsé will allow me to study some of these machines."

Morrowmen waved his cane through the air, pointing vaguely around the palace grounds. "Once your giddy blubbering about them reaches his ears, we'll most likely never hear the end of the infernal contraptions. I'd rather you kept your questions to yourself for the sake of the kingdom. We might never accomplish anything if the two of you spend morning to night wandering around discussing gear ratios and pulley weights."

Just inside the sliding mechanical gate, a gentle slope rose to a wide plateau. It occurred to Askon that he had seen no green or growing things anywhere along the street or in the square. Apopsé's gardens began and ended on the palace grounds, and they were like nothing Askon had ever seen. Almost nothing grew on the ground. Everything hung from tall stone pillars connected with long thick crossbeams. Many of these were made of cinder-dark wood, though the largest were of stone that matched the pillars. Red and blue petals dangled from hanging pots or troughs built into the sides of the crossbeams. Vines of green with tiny white buds encircled many of the pillars and draped the structure in a living curtain. Throughout, Askon heard the faint trickle of water.

Beneath the hanging gardens lay another wide floor made from the same enameled tiles as the giant mosaic in the square. Nothing grew there, only above it. The effect was intoxicating, the plants towering over them as they walked, the perfume of a thousand flowers drifting down upon them. Askon breathed deep and was nearly swept away by a memory of Tolarenz in full bloom.

He opened his eyes and continued to survey the cleverly designed growing system. The crossbeams, which at first appeared to be perfectly level, actually slanted downward slightly. Some doubled back, angling earthward and away from the entrance. The topmost crossbeams on the lowest tier of the garden were fitted together into four rectangles. On this tier, the beams were made of wood, held in place by metal pins and straps. Though the floor of the garden was mostly flat, it rose ever so gradually to the palace entrance. The rise helped with the second tier's height, but even so, when they passed beneath it, the gardens dangled farther and farther above them. The pattern continued: two rectangles, then one, where Askon had expected the construction to end, but it did not.

The final section of the garden was comprised of three squares. While the other tiers had been set horizontally in comparison to the outer walls and the palace within, the last were vertical, and each rose several feet higher than the one before it. By the end, the garden structure stood twice the height of the sliding gate and nearly level with the colossal outer wall. At the end of the series of squares,

Askon found himself under what had at first appeared to be an enormous tent or awning. It was in fact, an immense bronze dish. How it had been constructed or even could be constructed, he did not know, but there it was, held up by ten pillars of similar make to those in the garden itself.

Up close Askon understood the purpose of the bronze bowl immediately and why he had heard water trickling along the length of the garden. Above him, where the bronze had been carefully molded, two streams of water, as narrow as the opening of his waterskin, poured down onto the first set of stone crossbeams. The top surface of the beams had been notched to accommodate enough water for the plants growing on that tier as well as to send the remainder down to the successive tiers below. Starting at the top, where the plants grew large and lush, the garden thinned until the lowest level where only a small amount of the water reached. Even then there was enough for plants to grow, but what had seemed full and verdant when they had entered on the first level, now looked sparse and pale as they stood beneath the enormous bowl.

Either because he had spent too much time in the palace already or his sense of duty disallowed it, the feathered guard gave the gardens no more than a second glance. He marched Askon and the others up the gentle slope, then to the stairs between the final three overhanging squares, and finally under the bronze watering bowl to a deep, shady archway. Out of the darkness four additional feathered guardsmen appeared. They divided the space between the archway and stood at attention, long shining spears in hand. The guard who had led Askon's party from the city's entrance broke away from Morrowmen and took his place at the center of the others.

"Welcome Edward, prince of Vladvir!" the guard announced, and together, five spear shafts pounded the tiles. "He is accompanied by the Lord Morrowmen and his guests. Please, enter."

With a click of booted heels, the guards pivoted and marched to opposite sides of the arch. The leader stayed in the center, prepared to show the way into the palace. The guards, and their introduction, reminded Askon more than a little of the sliding mechanical gate they had used to enter the grounds.

Thomas gaped in wonder. He walked backward, still staring at the series of tiered gardens. "The minds it must have taken to design this," he said excitedly. "What else might they have built? It would be impossible to know if this would work without testing it." Straggling behind the others, he slipped into the darkness beyond the archway.

Suddenly the shadows gave way to a cool, well-lit space. Almost perfectly circular, the room spanned the width of the Tolarenz town hall and the Dalstone meeting hall combined. By sheer space alone, Askon thought Codard's main hall might be larger, but something about this room's shape made it feel more open. The ceiling rose high above them into a domed roof similar to many of the city's largest buildings. Starting ten feet above their heads, in the walls as well as the roof itself, countless openings of varying sizes had been cut to allow plenty of natural light to enter. Placed at odd angles, none flush or in line with the others, Askon guessed they deflected rainwater while also allowing heat to escape.

"Beautiful isn't it?" The voice came from a man standing at the opposite side of the room. His words echoed in the vastness. "The skylights at the center are glass panes an inch thick, but the others are open-air. They're designed to channel the rainwater out to the bowl and into the garden."

He was a short man and wore a wide brimmed hat, even inside. Beneath it, his face was narrow and brown with a small nose and weak chin. His clothes, made of the same shimmering fabric as the guards' half-length capes, hung loosely like robes but more closely resembled trousers and shirt made for a much larger man. Small delicate feet peeked from below the folds, covered in supple shoes that looked to Askon like the boots sewn for newborns in Tolarenz. Rings covered the man's fingers, and several necklaces overlapped onto his barrel chest, each one of extravagant make and immense value.

"Where are my manners," he said. "I am Lord Apopsé."

Askon guessed that he was no taller than Líana, maybe even an inch or two shorter, and his voice held little power within it. Recalling how Caled would command the attention of the entire town, or the way even the king demanded respect in his aggravated, forceful manner, Askon wondered how such a soft-spoken man could have overseen the wonders that lay strewn from the immense outer gate to this circular sunlit hall.

Apopsé cleared his throat and spread his arms wide. "Welcome to the South Kingdom, Prince Edward of Vladvir and Askon of Tolarenz."

CHAPTER EIGHTEEN

Apopsé

He scuttled across the polished floor as though he could not lift his own feet, knitted boots sliding noiselessly over the stone slabs. In a strange combination of awkwardness and practiced precision, he slipped from one end of the hall to the other and came to an abrupt stop a few feet from Askon. Líana stood beside him, her purple hood buttoned across her shoulders and the long braid tumbling down her back where it curled slightly, just above her belt.

The little man in the slippery shoes bowed low. With a precarious wobble, his wide hat nearly fell from his head. He cleared his throat, a thick, viscous sound that made Askon's face tighten. He smelled strongly of lavender water. "And how could I possibly, forget," he said, his voice like syrup over a griddlecake, "the lovely and talented Líana, of Tolarenz as well." Spreading his hands out wide, he drew his face even nearer to the floor until his too-large shirt-sleeves fell limply onto the stone. Then, with an unexpected quickness, he snapped up Líana's hand and kissed it lightly, his opposite arm hovering outstretched at his side. Two bulbous blue orbs looked up from beneath the hat brim, his thin lips turning up into a smile that was very nearly taller than it was wide. And it was there that Askon first beheld the Sight fragment.

The hat, made of tightly woven straw, covered Apopsé's head and face, until he looked up. Just below the band of his hat, a tight circlet pressed into the brown skin of his forehead. Loops and whorls of silver coursed through the mouse-brown hair where, here and there, Askon saw flecks of gray. Patterns like leaves, similar to those wrought in the Time fragment's setting, littered the circlet's surface. But they concealed greater, more intricate designs: men with bows, galloping horses, and a strange combination of both, the like of which Askon had never seen. Each man and horse-man had loosed an arrow, the needle-thin bits of silver traveling along the circlet to the center of Apopsé's brow where a jewel glowed steadily, blue as the clearest sky over the Vladvir plain. As Morrowmen had once said, it was smaller than a chicken's egg but larger than a robin's. Its strong inner light cast faint hues over the brown forehead and pinched features. Líana blushed and gave a small smile, then turned away. Apopsé rose, slowly tilting his head toward Askon.

"I suppose that's progress," he said, lazily emphasizing the sibilance. "When they set out she didn't smile." And his frog's-eyes clicked wetly.

"Lord Apopsé," a voice called. If the little man's words were raindrops, these were a coastal shore. "I came not to exchange in pleasantries." Edward stepped from the shadows behind Morrowmen. He stood tall and stern before his host. "The tidings of war in the north come to you, and for the part of Vladvir, I bring an offer of friendship."

As the prince spoke, Askon saw Líana, eyes wide, lips slightly parted. She took an unconscious step toward Edward, and in the huge emptiness of the hall, Askon heard her breathing quicken. He also saw Apopsé, who watched Líana from the shadow of his hat brim. The little man puffed up under his loose-fitting clothing and, looking more frog-like than ever, addressed Edward.

"Prince of Vladvir," he began, but the initial sound popped too hard from his mouth, a bit of spittle flying before him. "You think your arrival brings news to the South Kingdom? Let me instead inform your highness." Again he let the sibilance sing long after the word had ended.

Morrowmen looked from Apopsé to Líana where the small man's eyes seemed irresistibly drawn, then to Edward where Líana's eyes seemed irresistibly drawn. He lifted an ancient, bony hand to his forehead, pressed the fingers into his eyes, and sucked in a deep, rattling breath. Seeing it all, Askon understood. This would be a problem.

Like one of the ice-dancers Askon had once seen traveling out of the far north, Apopsé came sliding along. He stopped within arm's length of Edward. More than a foot shorter than the prince, he looked up comically, and his hat flipped off the back of his head. A thin cord caught the hat, and the shining blue light of the fragment was laid bare.

"You see this?" he hissed. "Even if you do, I see more. I see what's inside it. Your little tumble into the water, Askon's spectacular lapses of temper, Codard's slow descent into servitude."

"Watch what you say," Edward paused a beat, his voice the rumble of thunder, "Lord Apopsé."

"Or what?" It was like hearing a cricket chirp before an oncoming storm. Tiny, and utterly pathetic. "South City is the seat of my kingdom!" he squeaked. "I issue the commands here. Kindly show some sensibility."

Bewildered at the chirruping cricket, almost bemused by the response, the gods of thunder rolled back and Edward looked to Morrowmen. The old man did not speak, and Askon, in an attempt to practice patience and control, chose to follow suit.

As he did so, the steady calm of the Time fragment settled upon him. Apopsé was, by all ordinary appearances, totally alone and unguarded in the cavernous room. But with the fragment helping him, Askon saw the unmistakable shimmer of the guardsmen's white half-capes. Spearpoints gleamed in the darkness, quavering only a hairsbreadth, but Askon saw them. He stared at them, counted them: one, two, three, four, and the fifth at the back: the feathered man who had led them into the palace. Apopsé appeared to perceive no threat, but his men shuddered with anticipation. Askon didn't like what he saw.

He considered his options, and the effect grew stronger. It would be simple—at this distance—to grab Apopsé and threaten the guards to stand down, but that would do no good. They needed

Apopsé's goodwill, no matter how insolent he was to Edward. Another possibility would be to grab Edward and get him out of the room, but his full support would also be important if they were to succeed, and he needed to make an alliance with Apopsé in order to play his part.

As Askon began to consider his third option, he saw—very slowly—a spearhead move in Edward's direction. The guard was young, too young to be appointed to a ruler's personal detail. He had little experience wielding a spear, his grip resembling more closely that used with battle-axes or perhaps a mace. A bruiser. His face, visible only through the visor of his plumed helmet, showed Askon everything else he needed to know. This man, young as he was, had won his position by acting on instinct. So far, it had been a boon, but he had now made a grave mistake. Hoping to win glory in defending his insulted lord, he meant to assault the prince of Vladvir.

But Askon saw this man too clearly, had considered how he might react, had even chosen not to speak in his friend's defense. When he made his choice, the green of the Time fragment glowed as strong and steady as the blue on Apopsé's brow. The overaggressive guard found himself suddenly unarmed, as though the spear had simply vanished from his grip. He stumbled forward clumsily, and looked around. His brethren also found themselves instantly weaponless. Each man looked at his empty hands, then to Apopsé. The little man stood gaping at a pile of neatly stacked spears. Between Apopsé and Edward was Askon, his blue and green eyes sharp and dangerous as the gleaming spearpoints at his feet.

"Did you see *that* in your stone?" he asked, pretending to examine a nicked fingernail. "You aren't the only one with a fragment of the Tear." And then the whistling.

Crack!

"While I could absolutely applaud your ability to shut your mouth for two heartbeats, allowing us all a moment's peace from your evergreen stupidity, I have to put a stop to all of this before the three of you bring about all of our deaths in addition to those of any well-meaning citizen in Vladvir or the South Kingdom!" Morrowmen lifted his arms like a huge purple vulture. "Get out," he cawed at the guards, then rounded on Apopsé.

"Without these two men, your pretty white city will be ground to dust beneath Iramov's boot. He cares not about your money or your confounded contraptions. And I'll kindly ask that you scoop your slavering tongue off the floor, as I'm afraid our volatile half-elven friend will place a sword blade between your teeth if you don't peel your eyes away from his sister. That is, if she doesn't place the blade herself. You're a lord, by the gods! I've even heard your people bandying around that idiot title Edward's father uses. So if you'd like to appear as a true ruler should, pull yourself together and honor your guests before we're all run down by the crushing darkness."

The room went silent. Then Askon heard the guards creep quietly away, their armor creaking and rattling as they went. The sounds lingered in the open air. Apopsé straightened his long, loose sleeves, then turned back to Líana.

"I apologize, my lady," he said. "I should know my manners. Please, Edward, Askon, everyone, come with me. This room makes me feel small. I'm afraid my guards have misinterpreted our conversation, and I have embarrassed myself. Thank you, Askon for showing me how a fragment of the Tear ought to be carried. I hope you will have such control when we face Lord Iramov."

Morrowmen, already ruffled by the bickering, peacocking leaders, limped along behind them. "Oh yes, because stacking spears and demanding applause is going to help us," he rasped. "Maybe next time you could even announce what it is that you carry a bit sooner, and louder. Then we wouldn't have that pesky element of surprise getting in the way."

Thomas and Elise followed awkwardly, as though both felt they should not be a part of such events. Apopsé led them across the circular hall to an ornate door. At its center was a blue circle blazoned with the white dove. Below it were depictions of stacked gold coins, jewels, and other valuables. Above it all, snaking vines of green lay sprinkled with flowers of blue and red. The work, as fine as any Askon had seen, was but one such door in Apopsé's palace, all of them with the same themes: greenery above, dove in the center, gold below. Yet each door was in some way different from the others.

This one had a small lever at the center, just below the dove's tail. Apopsé reached out and pulled. The lever receded, and a rhythmic *clunk, clunk, clunk,* beat within. Slowly, in a jerky series of motions, the dove rotated. When it faced the floor, the door opened inward without the help of human hands. Thomas was beside himself.

"How does it work?" he wondered aloud. "The intricacy of the mechanism must be exceedingly elaborate."

Apopsé seemed to gain several inches of height. "Yes, it is. My father designed the door, with the bird and the gold and the green, I mean to say. But," he paused for effect, "I designed the machinery."

With his face lit up like a candelabra, Thomas approached the door's right side, where the rotating blue circle came to rest with its now overturned dove. "That's amazing," he said, running his fingers along the smooth, round surface. "How does it work?"

Apopsé tapped a small brass switch with his knitted boot. It clicked. Then with a slightly different series of *clunk, clunk, clunks,* the door swung back into place. The little man looked up at Thomas who, though not as tall as Edward, still towered over the lord of the South Kingdom.

"I must second-guess your ability to understand such a complex design," he hissed lazily. His hat toppled again from his head.

Thomas frowned, a wounded look rather than an angry one. "Oh," he replied, his hand still sliding up and down the closed door. "I was thinking it might be a succession of offset pulleys with a reconnecting linkage, possibly spring-driven on the return. But it's probably much more complicated than that."

Apopsé's eyes narrowed. "Well, when you say it that way, of course it sounds simple," he huffed. "Machining the gears and wheels is a complex process. Without getting that right, none of it works."

Fascinated, almost as though Apopsé wasn't even there, Thomas said, "Side by side arms would twist the axle twice the amount, applying more rotational distance on the engagement assembly. With that additional torque, the disc would turn more smoothly." He smiled happily. "And no shuddering!"

With a splutter, Apopsé replaced his hat. "Of course, I've thought of that already," he said, straightening his sleeves. "I just haven't had time to implement it yet."

Morrowmen, who hadn't even paused momentarily at the mechanical door, called back to them from the end of the long hallway. "You two can talk about clockwork door hinges later. We have more important things to discuss." He jammed the tip of his cane into a recess at the hallway's end. By the time Thomas and Apopsé had caught up with them, another door swung open. "And Thomas," said Morrowmen. "Stay with Elise, and keep your engineering comments to yourself. I'm afraid the Lord Apopsé cannot resist debating the value and construction of these clatter-boxes of his."

CHAPTER NINETEEN
The Vulture and the Frog

They entered a relatively small room with a large wooden table made to seat twelve. Only the two chairs at the ends had backs at all, and those were short and round. The rest of the seats were more like stools than chairs. Askon stood waiting by the table, allowing Líana to pass, then Edward, followed by Elise and Thomas, and finally Apopsé. Morrowmen, already seated on the opposite side of the table, drummed his crooked gray fingers impatiently.

To Askon's surprise, Apopsé plopped down on the nearest stool, and looking to Líana, drew out his open palm, which he held for a moment above the seat next to his own. He smiled and winked one frog's-eye with a click. Líana looked to Morrowmen. His thin white brows were pinched, his shoulders hunched. Without a word, he jabbed a pointed, bony finger into the seat next to him and farthest from Apopsé. Líana took her place.

Edward, having regained some of his composure and awareness of decorum, eyed the proceedings carefully. He sat across from Apopsé, on the same side of the table as Líana but at the opposite end. He did not look in her direction. Askon filled the space between Edward and Morrowmen while Thomas and Elise took places on Apopsé's side of the table. At the back of the room, another mechanical door clicked, and two servants filed out with drinks and food. Askon wondered when Apopsé had signaled the servers.

"I hope you don't think this unaccommodating," Apopsé said. "We try to eat light in the late afternoon here. It gets very hot sometimes, and too much food can adversely affect one's disposition when combined with the heat."

The servants cleared the room. After everyone had taken a bit of food from the trays, Morrowmen rapped his cane against the side of the table. The old man, it appeared, would be in control of this discussion. He twisted his head to one side, stretching his neck until it cracked softly.

"After our incident in the entry hall, I've decided that three fools with only a thin bit of sense between them are not the best choice to conduct a meeting of the minds such as ours. So, I'll direct our talk from here on, and if any of you feel like volunteering a derisive remark, I'll thank you to keep it to yourself." He rapped the stick again. Edward, still as a lake on a windless day, said nothing. Apopsé sunk lower on his stool, easily the oldest member of their council aside from Morrowmen but by mannerism the youngest and most sullen.

Askon watched them all with interest, and as yet no anger, though he did worry that if Apopsé sunk any lower, his face would be below the table. Out of the corner of his eye, he saw Elise eating daintily, straight-backed and proper, sipping on the goblet the servants had provided. When he saw Líana mimic Elise's posture and poise, he almost laughed aloud. Instead he only smiled, shaking his head; it was like watching a bobcat in a tiara. Though, aside from her uniform, Líana had all the looks of a lady at court: fair skin, well-kept hair and the like. She had ever been at odds with their mother on the manners of polite company. She ate like a soldier on the trail, sat like John at a tavern bar, licked her fingers clean, and sometimes belched audibly at table. Askon had wondered if her transformation had changed any of these traits. Watching her now, he knew it had not, but he found her attempt to appear ladylike highly amusing.

All of Líana's efforts, intended obviously for Edward's attention, went unnoticed. For the first time since he had awoken under the glow of the Life fragment, Edward's focus seemed not at all on Líana. He had taken on the air of royalty, an attitude Askon knew to be a tool rather than a natural state, and all of his will was directed at Apopsé. Edward had either an alliance to establish or an enemy to make.

Morrowmen rapped the stick a third time. "According to our most reliable information, Lord Iramov discovered his ability to use the Death fragment against others more than a year ago. Some of his men began to defect. In the spring, South City saw a handful of high-ranking military types arrive seeking refuge, but the majority of Iramov's men stayed loyal to him. Once we became fully aware of Iramov's abilities, after Caled's sacrifice, we began asking questions. The stories we heard from the defectors were grim. By using the power of his fragment, Iramov is essentially able to convince all but the sternest resistance to join him. Those who won't follow him become—"

"Rings of white powder," Askon interrupted thinking of his dream, the one in which his hands and arms were covered in the substance.

"Well, dead anyway," continued Morrowmen. "He has since been gathering a host of brigands and mercenaries to his cause, thus increasing his military might. As far as we can tell, Codard came into the picture a few months ago, not long before Tolarenz was taken. Using the Sight fragment, we were able to understand his reasons plainly, but I had already guessed at the cause."

"He was afraid," said Edward flatly. "You knew that before seeing it because it is always the case. Afraid of the oncoming winter, afraid of too much rain in the spring, afraid of one year's economic instability or another's plenty, my father is always afraid of something." He turned to face Morrowmen. "Do I have it right?"

"You do," said the old man. "Specifically, he fears two things: one, that Iramov will attempt to take control of his lands—so at least we have that on our side; and two, that Lord Apopsé means to expand the South Kingdom beyond its namesake region and into the Vladvir plain."

Apopsé sat up, the gem in the silver circlet casting shadows of warbling blue. "Which is preposterous," he said, with as much authority as he could muster. "Edward, there is nothing of value in southern Vladvir. It's why the South Kingdom's border has remained the same since it was first established. The forests and mountains of Grafmark might hold some hidden treasure: gems, gold, silver maybe, but it's so difficult to work in those trees, or even to clear them, and so far from South City. There's no reason for us to make such an expansion."

No one contested him, but no less than three of the others knew enough about the lands of Vladvir to see through his words. Askon felt certain that Apopsé had at least explored the idea of expanding to the north. If not, he would have been less specific about the value of the lower plains and Grafmark. Kingdoms, especially one as recently established as Apopsé's, needed land, and aside from the unknown wastes east of Ellmed, Askon knew of none that had yet to be claimed. Of course, much of Vladvir and its surrounding areas were uninhabited wilderness, but every year the settlements grew larger, the fields spread farther, and the wilds receded.

Apopsé may not have been flawlessly truthful in his self-defense, but to Askon, that was not the most interesting revelation thus far. It was something Morrowmen had said. Or rather something he had not said. Askon allowed the conversation to continue, only glancing in Morrowmen's direction. For now, he would practice rules one and two.

"Everyone at this table believes you, Lord Apopsé," Edward was saying. "But that doesn't mean my father does. Who knows what Iramov has told him, what lies or threats he has made. Fear motivates my father more than anything else. It has kept his kingdom safe for many years—reacting to threats based on his worries—and it helped his forebears as well." He addressed Morrowmen next. "What else have you seen?"

Morrowmen rubbed his scalp. The white remainders of his hair fell limply over his splayed fingers. But it was Apopsé who answered. "*We* have seen," and he emphasized the first word heavily, "Codard sending his men after you and Askon. We have seen John and his men saving you on the bridge, the events at young Thomas's village, and the battle for Dalstone. We see Askon quite clearly, and Codard as well, most of the time."

Edward leaned forward. "Why only 'most of the time'?" he asked.

And there it was. Askon had been waiting to hear how either Apopsé or Morrowmen would explain their earlier omissions. Morrowmen had specifically said they had *seen* Codard in the Sight fragment, but only *heard* what Iramov was doing. They had information about Iramov's movements and his army, but had actually watched Askon pluck the arrow from the air in Dalstone. He wondered how fully Morrowmen would clarify.

"It's like the Life and Time fragments, isn't it?" Thomas, who had been quietly listening, now spoke up. He had made a habit of such theories, and was usually right.

Apopsé's eyes darted around the table, as if he were about to be attacked. He hunkered a little, drawing his hands to his chest.

"It's alright Apopsé," said Morrowmen. "Everyone here knows as much about the fragments as the others. There's no need to guard secrets with these five." Askon cocked an eyebrow, remembering Morrowmen's reluctance to share Askon's information about the dead men who fought in Iramov's army. Morrowmen was playing at some game in which none of the others present knew the rules.

How much did Apopsé know about the fragments? Morrowmen had only said that everyone at the table knew at least as much as the South Kingdom's leader, but who knew more and how much? Apopsé was a valuable piece in Morrowmen's game, as were Edward, Líana, and Askon, even Thomas and Elise. But Morrowmen seemed to be the only one playing the game for their side, and Iramov was his opponent.

"We have discovered," Apopsé began haltingly, "that the fragments can interfere with one another in certain cases. We cannot be sure which ones conflict with the others or in what ways, but as Thomas says, the effects of Life seem to be somehow neutralized by Time. What we have come to believe is that in addition to those, Sight may also conflict with Death."

Askon nodded. He had been right, and was now glad he had waited to speak. "So you can't see Iramov."

The bulbous eyes glowered beneath the wide-brimmed hat. "No, I can't." He scooted his stool forward and lifted a hunk of bread, opening his mouth wide, exaggerating his frog-like appearance. Then he stopped. "But," he said, still holding the bread an inch from his lips, "we can loosely guess where he might be. It's a painstaking process. We find someone who we *can* see and follow his movements. When our subject comes too near the Death fragment, we lose track of him. By noting the areas we *cannot* see, we get a rough estimate of the enemy's position."

"There's a map, Askon," said Morrowmen. "Since I spoke with you in Tolarenz, we've been marking locations that go dark, even if it's only for a short while. Apopsé sees the carriers of the other fragments as clearly as if they were sitting here with us now, and average people come through blurry, like colored shadows."

"Iramov, or more accurately the Death fragment, is blackness. For miles around sometimes, everything is black. I see nothing," Apopsé said, continuing what Morrowmen had started. His features sank as though the fault was somehow within himself. Askon thought of the yard in Austgæta, the prisoner there, and the crushing, brutal nothingness that came along with the Death fragment's power. By the emotions on Apopsé's face, Askon guessed that some of that cold, empty darkness came through the Sight fragment whenever the lord of the South Kingdom attempted to track Iramov.

But Apopsé had not finished. "By tracking Iramov's movements, we know only that more and more men are being gathered to his cause. Dalstone still stands, thanks to Brâghda and the Grafmark Norill. The Darts have taken well to their new leader. They now fortify their defenses in preparation for another attack."

The news concerning John came as a great relief to Askon. Now, with Morrowmen and Apopsé in the same room, they were able to answer so many questions he hardly knew where to begin. Just knowing that he had not made a mistake in leaving his friend behind improved his spirits greatly. For a moment, he imagined what the meeting at Apopsé's table would have been like if John had followed them south. He smiled. John would have wanted action. Morrowmen would not have approved.

"Will Iramov and Codard strike Dalstone again?" asked Elise. She still sat upright and poised, and the question came as if it were nothing more than a query about the latest fashions in the market-place.

Apopsé hesitated, straightened his sleeves, and rolled a small piece of fruit between his fingers. Morrowmen seized the opportunity to answer her. "I think not," he said. "Dalstone will be the first, maybe the only, place where Iramov has met an organized resistance. His army, based on what we can gather, is large enough to make an assault on South City directly when combined with Codard's."

"What about the Norill, the ones Brâghda's people call, the Lost?" asked Thomas. "They fought with Codard and Iramov at Dalstone and against the king's forces at Austgæta. Brâghda said they want to reassemble the Tear, that they worship it."

"They do," said Morrowmen. "They will fight alongside Iramov as long as they think he intends to bring together all of the fragments. And that is exactly what he means to do."

Líana, in her best attempt to emulate Elise's courtesy, placed her hands in her lap and looked down her nose toward Morrowmen, who sat hunchbacked beside her. "But why try to reassemble the Tear?"

The old man smiled, as warmly as his skeletal face could smile. "So many reasons," he said shaking his head. He closed his eyes. "Power, for one. Think of what Iramov could do if he controlled all of the fragments. Askon, Apopsé, you, me, we can all do amazing things with the help of just one of the gems. Imagine having all five at one person's command.

"But there's a much more important reason for Iramov to reunite the pieces. This reason drives him more forcefully than power ever could, and it solidifies his bond with the Norill. Codard, I think, has not even realized his ally's true motivation, and that may be to our advantage."

CHAPTER TWENTY

The Great Darkness

Morrowmen drew himself up, gazing at the wall on the opposite side of the room. At first, Askon thought he might be examining something in the stones, but then he understood. Whatever Morrowmen was seeing, it came from long ago, further back than any of their minds could reach, further than their parents' minds would reach had they also been seated at the long table.

"When Caled brought the complete Tear to the old king, in the time of the Great Darkness, he was given a hero's welcome," the old man began in a vague whisper. "We had no way of defeating the creatures of the dark. There were thousands of Norill, but they were the least of our enemies—the cockroaches who would go on to survive the fire. Monsters out of the blackest nightmares had raided the old cities, laying waste, killing without mercy. They didn't even take slaves, as was the fashion of the time. Some of them ate their victims. Others practiced a similar tradition to the Norill you know as the Lost. But instead of wearing the bones of their victims as rudimentary armor, these creatures wore the bloody, rotting hearts of our fallen, whole hands that had died still gripping their swords, even broken faces.

"They burned everything to the ground and killed any who could not flee. Fortress after fortress fell to the creatures of the dark. Our weapons and armor were not as they are now, our defenses less clever, but truly it was the fear the enemy brought with them that defeated us again and again. Each time our terror grew as news arrived alerting us to another defeat." Morrowmen paused, his face deeply lined with age, his eyes watery and clouded.

Askon had heard stories of the Great Darkness many times. All of Vladvir's children had. Always distant, told with a smirk or a wink to remind the listener that none of it was real. The stories of the Great Darkness, the Knight of Vladvir, and the coming of the elves were nothing more than tales sprung from the clever mind of the storyteller. But hearing Morrowmen recount the events was altogether different. He had seen with his own eyes these monsters and remembered them now. He had stood on the earthen walls which protected the collections of hovels they had called cities. Told from Morrowmen's perspective, it all became real, vivid, and unquestionable because he had lived it.

Apopsé chewed noisily on a bread crust at his side of the long table while the others listened in rapt silence. Morrowmen still stared at the wall. He said, "When the last of our outer defenses had been destroyed, those who were able to escape made their way into Vladvir's southern mountains. Many died on the road, run down by Norill or other stronger, faster creatures. Some made it as far as the first snows below the mountain peaks before they succumbed to the cold, all the while feeling the monsters drawing nearer, following them through the dark. For a precious few, the journey found its end in the sloping bowl of Dalkaldur, the cold valley. There, the sun shines brighter than on the crags above, and a small settlement had grown up around the valley's central lake and towering keep.

"The keep's builders, gone long before the valley had been settled, used practices similar to those which went on to build the Greyarc and Codard's castle. Though not as precise or sturdy as the structures that would come after the arrival of the elves, Dalkaldur's keep—though old—was the strongest we had in our time of great need.

"It was in this hidden fastness that the remnants of Vladvir's cities gathered. Together we might have populated Dalstone as it stands today, but we held little hope for victory. The old king, who had no heir or any named successor, sent several of his knights into the depths of enemy territory to seek the source of their power or the reason for their unrelenting attacks. All were killed save one.

"Caled once told me his greatest achievement, even more than the building of Tolarenz, was finding his way back through the snows of the southern mountains to Dalkaldur. You see, when the knights left, our haven remained hidden. The creatures of the dark knew we had fled into the mountains, but they knew not where. By a stroke of luck, the winter was hard and longer than usual, making it even more difficult for the enemy to locate us. And though sometimes bitterly cold, the four seasons still touched the lonely valley.

"Caled and the other knights set out when the snow-covered rim surrounding Dalkaldur had receded as far as we could guess it might. We hoped the creatures would not trace their steps back to us. For a year they searched, listening quietly to the conversations of the Norill and other evils who had taken root in Vladvir. Caled claimed to learn to understand if not to speak the Norill language. They were searching for the Stone of Mountain. An artifact of great power, which you know as Alora's Tear. But our knights found it first.

"The Norill were closing in on the Tear's location. Caled showed me once. It was hidden, guarded by priests a thousand times more fervent in their beliefs than was your friend John's father. Each one of them had tattooed a teardrop somewhere on their person. By the time I saw their temple, the priests were long since dead, but it is still there, if you look closely. Beneath the pool at Lover's Fall, a grotto no wider than this room."

"Lover's Fall?" Thomas interrupted. He slapped his hand against the table's thick boards. "Askon, we camped beneath the falls on the way to Austgæta. To think, we were so close to such an important place, and I didn't even know it! I wonder how many of the men knew—or how many didn't."

Askon smiled and gently tipped his head toward the old man at the head of the table whose already impatient face had shifted from irritation to glowering frustration.

"Indeed," the ancient voice grumbled. Then it pitched high, as if it had made some new and exciting discovery. "The world is simply brimful with endless wonders hidden just beneath our—" and here the feigned, childlike awe ceased, "backwater ignorance, oblivious blundering, and blatant disrespect when our betters attempt to relay important information!"

Thomas stopped, his lips parted as if a question might have been captured between them. Askon gestured with an open hand toward Morrowmen as if to imply his younger companion should have anticipated such a reaction. The soft *pop* of aged knuckles cracking one at a time filtered through the now silent room. Morrowmen steepled his fingers and eyed Thomas who looked from Askon to Elise and back to the head of the table.

"May I continue?" said Morrowmen, still staring.

Thomas seemed to shrink. He took a quick breath as if to answer, thought better of it, and simply nodded.

Morrowmen cleared his throat noisily and began again.

"As I was saying, with the Norill drawing ever closer, Caled and the other knights begged the priests to let them take the stone to Dalkaldur where it might be safe, warned them that the creatures of the dark would stop at nothing once they arrived. But the priests refused. Caled debated with his men late into the night. It did not matter. The creatures arrived with moonrise, killing the other knights and the priests. Caled, who had remained in the grotto, arguing with the leader, took the stone and escaped through a long dark tunnel that opened somewhere in the forest of Ellmed. The last priest closed the way behind him.

"When the snows began to lessen, Caled rode again into the mountains, but he did not know what we knew. Dalkaldur had seen a harsher winter than the Vla'dvir plain, much harsher. The path became unclear, blocked with snow, shrouded in clouds of frost and flying bits of ice. When his horse died of exhaustion, he used its body to keep warm. After his supplies ran out, he collapsed in the snow.

"But something in the gem that he carried would not allow such a thing to pass. Instead, when our patrols found him—less than a mile from the rim of Dalkaldur—he lay in a patch of green grass, ice and snow six feet deep all around him. Tiny white flowers bloomed in the green, but his body was weak, his mind in some distant place, maybe in the place where more of the white flowers bloomed. We carried him back to the keep, and when we looked behind us, the greensward was covered in ice, the flowers buried under six feet of snow.

"He awoke nearly a week later, after much care and worry on my account. The old king felt that Caled's return was an ill omen. He wanted me to bury the knight somewhere beyond the rim and to keep the stone that he carried. Having seen the greensward around Caled with my own eyes, I would not allow any harm to come to him, and eventually he came around.

"He woke hysterically, shouting to me that he had found Alora's Tear and that it would save us from the Darkness. We did not believe him, especially the old king, as few still knew the story of Alora and Heraphus. But the old king sent men out to deliver a message to the refugees and natives of the valley. It commanded anyone with information concerning Alora's Tear to report to the keep, and they did. In droves, we heard stories upon stories, many of them fabricated on the spot. Rewards were requested: food, building materials, weapons, and more. None were given, as none of the information helped us in any way. Whatever power had kept Caled alive now lay dormant.

"Then, when we thought the endless tales would never be exhausted, an old man came before us. His body looked to me as mine does now to all of you, unfathomably ancient, gray, and battered. He smiled and asked a question we had already heard many times, 'Has Alora's Tear come to Dalkaldur?' The old king, tired and frustrated by the useless string of storytellers, berated him, shouted, spat, and denied that the Tear was indeed only a few rooms away. But even in my relative youth, I saw the old man's wisdom. His weathered face smiled; he saw easily through the king's lie.

"The old man turned to go. As he hobbled to the door he said a handful of words that would change Vladvir forever. 'You will find them by the waterside.' In his fury the king had his guards seize the old man, but even under threat of torture the crooked mouth stayed tightly shut. With the king angrier than ever, the old man looked directly at me, ignoring the guards who dragged him to the door. He said, 'Send him to find me, the one who holds the Tear.' And they tossed him into the street. The king, who had stormed off to his rooms, did not hear the old man's final words.

"Caled regained most of his strength, but not quickly enough. The next morning we received news that the enemy had found the pass through the mountains, that their entire army had gathered in the foothills and would soon follow their leaders to Dalkaldur. The king rode to the rim. The day was clear and cold. Miles and miles below, he saw the throngs of creatures, a squirming black mass snaking into the pure white snows. They would be upon us in days.

But in the sweeping winds of the rim, the old king was blown from his horse. He fell, breaking his neck upon the rocks, and there died while the Great Darkness poured into the mountain pass.

"I rode back to the keep and warned Caled, telling him everything: of the countless stories, of the king's death, and finally of the old man. I told him what the man had said, 'You'll find them by the waterside.' And Caled's eyes lit up like fire in the night. I told him the rest, of the old man's cryptic demand to seek him out. As though possessed, Caled combed the settlement. All the while, the creatures of the Great Darkness gathered below the rim, waiting hungrily for the rest of their army. They would destroy us here utterly. None would walk from Dalkaldur alive.

"When the army had nearly reached its full muster, Caled found the old man. Our own army, kingless and in despair, had manned the point of entry along the rim's northern edge."

CHAPTER TWENTY-ONE

By the Waterside

Morrowmen's eyes broke suddenly away from the gray stones of the wall. He looked around as if he found the room unfamiliar or foreign. Glancing at each of their faces he seemed not to recognize them. Líana placed a delicate hand on his forearm, and he came back again to himself, nodding slowly to her. "What comes next are Caled's words as closely as I can recall them. When he found the old man, I rode with a column of ill-equipped peasants and healers in order to tend to the wounded.

"Caled began the story always by saying that the old man found him, not the other way around. In a small house with mud-lined walls and paneled roof, the old man had waited. The army, or what we told ourselves was an army, had already headed out to the rim while the women and children stayed behind. They were few. Caled had exhausted his strength and now worked his way back toward the keep, hoping that after rest and food he would be able to find the old man before the Great Darkness broke our defenses.

"As Caled passed the mud-spattered house, the door creaked open and the old man called to him from within. Caled approached warily, ducking inside the candlelit room. Dalkaldur's cold wind snapped the door shut behind him, and he stepped further inside. There sat the old man, his chair propped against a wall. When Caled told the story, he never failed to note how warm it was inside the little house. Whether it was by clever design or some other power, he never knew.

"He crossed the room to the man in the chair, aware that it could be none other than he whom I had described. 'Come closer,' the old man said and Caled did. 'Do you have Alora's Tear?' the old man asked, and Caled said that he did. With a shudder, the ancient face smiled. Before Iramov came to Tolarenz, Caled told me that my smile had become almost as pleasing as was the old man's smile in Dalkaldur. I didn't take it as a compliment.

"With another tremor, the old man produced a key, not a special key, just an ordinary piece of brass forked to match a lock at the far side of the room. Pointing to the door, the old man directed Caled to open it. Inside, a series of steps led down into the cold bedrock. It had been previously thought that at any depth greater than for growing crops, the earth was too hard to excavate. No houses in Dalkaldur had cellars, except this one.

"Caled climbed down the steps into a narrow hallway. Every few feet, small rooms like expanded closets opened in an alternating pattern, left and then right. Books and papers and scrolls lined each room: large tomes, thin volumes in series, single leafs stacked one atop the other; it was an underground library. But something, maybe even the Tear itself, pulled Caled to the end of the hallway.

"At its point of termination, the hallway opened on a semi-circular space with a single stone plinth at the center. When Caled explained the room, he made sure to emphasize how cold it became. One step he was in the hallway's warmth, similar to that of the house above, and the next he felt as though he stood in the winds of the rim with the defenders of the cold valley.

"On the plinth lay a rolled parchment, exceedingly ancient and obviously treated with the utmost care. It was bound with a lovely chain of thin silver." Morrowmen turned to Askon. "You might recognize it, I think." Askon lifted the Time fragment from beneath his shirt, where it hung from what must have been the very same chain that bound the parchment.

Morrowmen said, "Caled picked up the parchment and uncoiled the silver. The page sprang open like one of Apopsé's doors, but it was only parchment. On it were written words in the common language, the letters reminiscent of the old king's official script, only with longer lines and intricate flourishes. Caled spent many years trying to copy that script. He never was satisfied with the result. In the cold, empty room, he read the parchment aloud:

Wait for them.
The morning light be blinded by.
On mirror lake or crystal stream,
As long as things of green reside,

If you seek them,
They will find you
By the waterside.

"Then Tear and paper began to vibrate together. Caled described it as a hum, deep and cool, like a choir singing in a building far away. The sound alone might have been enough to convince him that our salvation lay within those words and that stone, but time was pressing. He curled the parchment back around itself, preparing to bring it to me, hoping I might be able to understand. He raced through the hall, weary and frustrated, through the warmth, past the doors, up the creaking stairs, and into the house.

"The heat began to stifle, almost as if someone had left a fire burning too brightly in the hearth, but the cinders there were dead as stone. In his chair, the old man sat, gazing distantly at the cellar door. 'Parchment paper!' Caled shouted at him, but he only stared. 'Beasts in the thousands gather at our doorstep and you send me for pressed reeds and faded ink? What is the meaning of this? The king is dead, and so shall we be too. There will be no reward, only darkness.' And still the old man looked on quietly.

"Caled crossed the room with no purpose other than to shake the old man into speech. If they were to die by the will of the Great Darkness, this ancient fraud would answer for himself. With the parchment tucked lightly in a pocket, grasping the old man's collar, Caled shook shirt and cloak and man within. 'What is the meaning of this?' he asked again.

"But the old man did not speak. He only stared. His head fell loosely to one shoulder and the mouth opened to reveal a limp gray tongue. Eerily, the eyes seemed fixed on the cellar door, cloudy orbs focused only on their final task. Caled pulled back from the dead man's face, his frustration greater than his bewilderment until he found that he could not let go. Something powerful and heavy, like an adult's hand guiding a willful child, held Caled in place.

"He felt his head turn sharply, guided by the invisible hand. There on the table next to the dead man's chair were several deep scratches in the soft wooden surface. The words were upside down, but Caled saw also the hand which had made them. On the backside of the palm, between the splotched wrist and the withered knucklebones, an emblem had been tattooed in blue ink: a simple teardrop.

"Without a second glance, Caled snapped the parchment from his pocket, uncoiled the silver chain—your silver chain, Askon— and watched as the parchment unrolled itself again. There, in the lower right corner of the page, the dropsical punctuation after the final word, was the same simple teardrop. Again Caled felt his head pulled toward the scratches on the table. But he was already on his way.

"Rotating the circular piece of furniture with a twist, Caled watched helplessly as the dead man's body slipped from its chair, the hand scuttling along the wooden surface. Murmuring a half-hearted apology, he rolled the table until the words became legible. It said:

Heed the words.
They will save us.

"But Caled, knight of Vladvir, did not know how to heed the words. He turned to the old man's corpse, hoping to find some clue or hint beyond the teardrop marking on the aged hand. But there, beside the table and toppled chair, only a pile of dirty rags lay. The clothes remained, but the body was gone."

A rush of air that might have been a stifled laugh puffed across the table. It came from Elise. A smirk worked its way across her face.

"I wonder if our historian hasn't ventured too far into embellishment," she said dryly.

Morrowmen fidgeted, clearly ruffled but undeterred. He raised a crooked eyebrow. "Perhaps when you've lived through such darkened times, you can structure the recollections as you see fit. I on the other hand, have already done so, and once again, your interruptions fracture the story for those who would see it told in full."

Elise shrugged, her curtain of black hair shadowing her face.

"In the time he had spent inspecting the vanished body and scrawled words," Morrowmen said, returning to the tale, "the room had grown warmer, much warmer. Beads of sweat gathered on Caled's forehead and his clothes felt heavy and damp. He realized how hot it had grown and drew back a step from the table. Turning full circle he saw thin trails of smoke curling sinuously from the mud-lined walls. Then the smoke began to fill the room, choking him. He stumbled a step, then two, and found himself inches from the hearth.

"Suddenly the dry ash leapt into flame, and pulsing heat pressed down on him. Again he faltered, falling to his knees. From the ground he tried to drag himself to the door, inch by painful inch, all the while strangling in the smoke. When he felt he could do no more, he saw the latch, but he began to lose consciousness. The last thing Caled ever remembered of the old man's house was the powerful force of the hand, lifting him up to the door-latch, turning the handle and casting him out into the chill of the empty street."

CHAPTER TWENTY-TWO

The Rising Sun

"Whether by his own strength or the invisible hand—which we later believed to come from the Tear itself—Caled awoke in the blackness of night. His lungs burned, but the air was clear, the night cold. Along the rim, nearly a mile above him, the first attacks had begun. The creatures of the Darkness swarmed over our defenses, but we felled many as they came on undaunted. Yet even had every arrow found a mark, every spear a target, and every rolled boulder killed a hundred, another thousand enemies would have taken the places of the fallen. They saw through the dark, those creatures of night, and they waited until the world was at its darkest to strike, but neither did they fear the light. When morning came, they hoped to feast on their victims under the warmth of the sun. We did little to slow their progress.

"Caled lay heaving and shuddering on the south western side of the bowl. He pieced together his location by the shadow of the ancient stone keep and the order of the stars. In his hand, the Tear glowed with inner light, pure white. Lifting the parchment before his face, he read again the words the old man had commanded him to heed.

Wait for them.
The morning light be blinded by.
On mirror lake or crystal stream,
As long as things of green reside,
If you seek them,
They will find you
By the waterside.

"In the circle of light, he saw that indeed there were things of green all around: mosses, vines, shrubs, and an army of bulrushes like sword-blades at the edge of sight. And he knew he had been led there for a reason, only a few feet from the clear central lake of Dalkaldur. He waited for the hand to guide him, but needed it not.

"In the east, the sky grew gray with the sun's awakening. Caled saw the shattering of our defenses, watched as the creatures of the Great Darkness poured over Dalkaldur's rim, our broken army fleeing in terror before them. Like a flood of oil they descended the slope, spreading slowly, glutinously across the north side of the rim. Some stayed behind to crack the bones of our greatest retainers or to make ghastly trophies of their mangled bodies. Who would see these grisly trophies, we did not know, for all of the defenders would soon cease to be.

"Across the lake, due south, Caled could see the settlement, small and flimsy before the towering keep, our last bastion. The women and older children had gathered there with what weapons they could carry and many torches.

"Down the steep sides of the rim came the enemy, leaping, cackling, frothing at the prospect of the oncoming slaughter. The flood spread, painting the entire north face of the rim in black, even as the sun stirred from its sleep. Our men, tired from the battle, afraid, and unwilling to lose their honor, turned to face the enemy a mere hundred feet from the scattered huts and mud-lined houses of the settlement. From behind, the women and children filled the ranks, side by side with their fathers and husbands and brothers. And then, the sun broke the edge of the rim.

"So bright was the coming of the morning that the defenders looked away, covering their eyes against its piercing light. The enemy seemed to surge with it. Seeing our soldiers gathered with their women and children sent them into a frenzy like nothing I had seen before or have seen since. They slashed at one another with weapons and open claws; from the wounds, thick blood pulsed which they smeared over their bodies or lapped with serpentine tongues. And with each hideous motion, the taste of our fear intoxicated them.

"But to the west, Caled stood shakily by the water's edge. In one hand he held the parchment and its silver chain, in the other, Alora's Tear, still complete and unbroken, a gleaming star fallen from the heavens. He opened his eyes to the rays of the sun, took them in as the starving devour bread and meat. The reflection off the shimmering lake ought to have blinded him for life, I always said, and if not for the Tear, I think it would have. But in that searing light,

Caled said he saw acres of tiny white flowers, speckled like the first flakes of snow on the fading grass, and that the lake too became home to the white petals and twisting green stems.

"Then he felt their presence behind him, heard the clink of armor and the cold scrape of steel. Our weapons were of baser metals and so our armor. Not these. In the field of flowers, an army rose at Caled's back, glimmering as though the metalwork they wore had been wrought from the very rays of the sun. They were swift and light on their feet, fearless in the face of the blood-crazed enemy. Their swords were long and two-handed, with a single razor's edge sloping gracefully from hilt to tip. Some carried bright shields, polished to a mirror finish and smaller one-hand versions of the gleaming blades.

"Farther back, Caled said he heard distant thunder, and then the flood of black erupted into flame from the slope of the rim to the edge of the lake. As the hillside glowed orange and the enemy shrieked in pain and horror, the field of flowers disappeared, revealing again the cold, still surface of the lake. But many of the creatures remained, many more than the defenders of Dalkaldur could possibly defeat, even in disarray.

"Without a rearward glance, Caled marched ahead. Determined to add his own blade to the final conflict. Whatever the old man had done to save them had not been enough. The darkness was too great, the enemy too numerous. He took three steps then collapsed on the grass with tears in his eyes. He could go no farther. Dalkaldur and all the realm of Vladvir now belonged to the darkness, to the evil, twisted creatures of night.

"Daylight ebbed, pulsing before Caled's eyes while he struggled to regain his feet when a powerful hand clasped his collar, lifting him upright again. 'You carry the Tear, knight of Vladvir,' said a voice. 'No harm shall come to you.'

"With that, Caled felt a warmth like nothing he had ever experienced, unlike that of the old man's house, unlike even the embrace of a loved one. The stone shone out white against the brilliant day and he felt stronger, nourished, and healthy once again. He looked up and found himself surrounded by an army clothed in shining gold, the army of the morning. Their eyes were sharp and green, and for those who elected not to wear the gleaming golden helms of their brethren, elongated ears rose prominently to points from stern faces. Gazing about, Caled saw not only the angular features of men, thick-shouldered and powerful, but women warriors as well, their faces seemingly even more stern and distant, their limbs lithe and their blades sharp. In the form of an army we came to call the Glittering Host, the elves had come to Vladvir.

"With speed and precision unrivaled, they raced to the aid of the defenders. Hope kindled within us then, but we did not yet dare to fight. It wasn't until the elves made contact with the enemy that we came full into our courage. Something in their sheer presence made the enemy quail. Some of the creatures shuddered and died before any stroke fell, their mouths foaming white spittle and their yellow eyes bulging in the sockets until they burst like thin-shelled eggs. The others attacked wildly, but their heinous armor protected them little against the weapons of the elves, and countless enemy blades cracked and broke against the glittering mail of our saviors.

"The elves swept across the whole of the rim, and everywhere they went, the strange convulsing, rupturing deaths continued. We followed them, easily killing the weakened creatures that were left behind. The strongest of them twitched and snarled, trying desperately to finish their war, but their blows were meek and without force, like a sleeping man swatting flies while he dreams. Those that still had their eyes stared past us into the sky or the dirt, and some flailed uncontrollably, though many of those had dropped their weapons, their movements no longer their own. But we kept on, methodically killing any that still stood against us. Then the bodies that had fallen dead on the spot began to burst. Something inside had inflated the chests and protruding bellies until, like so many overcooked sausages, they exploded. It was then that our awe of the elves first kindled to fear."

Morrowmen had slowly drawn inward over the course of his story, his features darkling, his voice quiet. He looked up from his lap where his crooked hands turned the Life fragment over and over between the fingers. "And it is that fear, now turned to hatred, that truly motivates Lord Iramov." His shoulders rose and fell in a deep, heavy sigh.

"Iramov wants to kill the half-elves," Thomas said with wonder.

As does the crow at the sound of danger, Morrowmen's head turned with a snap. "Partly right, young Thomas. The half-elves of Vladvir are only the beginning. Iramov aims to reunite Alora's Tear so he may pass into the field of flowers and annihilate the elves not just from Vladvir, but from their original home. And with the power to separate the Tear into fragments, namely to isolate the Death fragment, he just might be able to accomplish his goal. Using our ancient enemies, he could destroy our greatest allies. If he can do that, he will turn against the Norill and Edward's father in an instant, wiping them from the face of Vladvir forever, leaving only his hand-picked survivors to live under his unchallenged rule."

CHAPTER TWENTY-THREE
The Palace

That night, Askon sat with his friends under the trickling greenery in Apopsé's garden. Morrowmen and the lord of the South Kingdom had been closeted for hours after the meeting, discussing the appropriate defenses for South City. During that time, a handful of servants had shown Askon and the others to their rooms, lavish apartments with featherbeds, smooth sheets, and ornate curtains. Thomas and Elise took one room, while Askon, Líana, and Edward each had their own private space. But in the heat of the afternoon and early evening, the apartments were stuffy and uncomfortable, despite their expensive decor. The cool breeze of the garden and the quiet chuckle of water over stone were infinitely more pleasant. With a servant on hand at all times, wine flowed in ample supply, golden and clear like honey and yet fresh and crisp.

Any doubt that Edward would side with Apopsé had vanished at the end of Morrowmen's tale. The damage done at Tolarenz and Dalstone was enough, not to mention Austgæta, Norogæta, and villages like Thomas's everywhere in between. However, the prince had not been persuaded to fight against his father. In nearly the same breath, he had both condemned Iramov and demanded Apopsé provide a messenger to send to Codard directly. As long as the king wasn't side by side with his new ally, the Sight fragment would allow them to piece together his location.

They were not so lucky. Without hesitation, Apopsé had removed his silver crown and peered into the sky-blue stone, searching for the king. A heavy look of despair or fear had fallen over his round face; in the stone he saw only darkness. Wherever Codard was, the Death fragment was nearby. In desperation, Edward had ordered that the messenger be sent anyway, either to King's City or a location between Iramov's last known position and South City. Apopsé had agreed, and Edward had left the long table to instruct the messenger personally. Askon did not hear what Edward said, but Apopsé had also spoken with the soldier. When his questions were finished, he was content that Edward had not attempted to conspire against the South Kingdom. This, in turn, had sent Edward into a rare display of anger. He stormed out of the room after Apopsé.

Askon understood the need to be certain of Edward's allegiance. Even though Askon would entrust his own life to Edward, Apopsé had no reason yet to believe the prince. When Apopsé returned to the table, none of the guests were surprised to find that Edward had been completely truthful. The messenger would go bearing the white flag of peace with a retinue of soldiers in case they met trouble upon the road. When they found the enemy forces, the guards would remain hidden while the messenger went alone to the king.

Assuming Iramov was to be present for the message, which Edward believed he most certainly would be, no tactical information had been included. The words were simple: "If you choose to stand against Lord Iramov, you do not stand alone. The South Kingdom will fight by your side with no intention to expand beyond its current northern border. Edward, prince of Vladvir, son of Codard sends this plea in hopes that his father will change his mind."

They all knew Codard would refuse the message on sight, especially if Iramov heard it as well. The king's fears, and Iramov's volatile temperament would be enough to assure a dismissal. Apopsé's greatest worry was that his messenger would not escape the enemy encampment unharmed. But they had no other way of communicating with Codard, and even the seed of resistance might be enough to sway the cowardly king to their side.

Askon lifted the sparkling wineglass to his lips and sipped on the honey-gold liquid. He stretched out to full length against the carved stone pillar, crossing his ankles, allowing one foot to dangle off the side of the bench. Across from him, Elise sat in similar fashion, though her legs were draped over Thomas's lap. Next to Elise and Thomas, Edward and Líana sat together near the center of their bench. Only a few inches separated them, but their backs were straight, heels and knees together with their goblets cradled in front of them. Askon stifled a chuckle at the sight, not that he had any desire to see his sister sprawling across his friend as Elise did with

Thomas. The contrast between the two pairs, however, was irresistibly humorous.

Apopsé's baths had been kind to them. After being shown their rooms, the servants led all five travelers to the end of a long hall. Set behind another of Apopsé's curious mechanical doors was a room with two partitions. The women went to one side, the men to the other. Steaming tubs filled with hot water waited for them; they undressed and washed away the miles of grime and sweat. Askon refused to remove the fragment and instead wore it around his neck, where it sank an inch or so into the water.

In a bustle, the servants had carried off their traveling clothes and armor. Askon had been hesitant at this, but allowed them to do so after extracting an assurance that the gear would be returned safely to their rooms.

As they relaxed in the tubs, Askon and the other men could hear Elise and Líana talking as they reclined in their own baths. Askon was glad that the partitions separated them, but it felt odd hearing the women speak without seeing their faces. Once or twice the two groups called to one another through the partitions, but more or less, the conversations stayed on one side or the other.

When Askon had scrubbed himself from head to toe, feeling cleaner than he had in months, and the others had done so as well, he placed a hand firmly on each side of the tub. Rising up out of the water to waist height, Time fragment sparkling with clinging droplets, he looked around. Pausing, he looked again, then lowered his body back into the water.

"There are no replacement clothes," he said to Edward.

Edward surveyed the room. He shook his head. "Maybe they forgot?"

Thomas had also been looking for a new set of clothing, leaning this way and that, checking for an obscured shelf or cabinet near the partition. There were none. "Elise!" he called over the divider. "Do you ladies—uh—have any clothes over there?"

Líana answered. "There aren't even any towels to dry off."

On the other side of the room, Askon heard water slosh as the two women stood up, then four wet slaps as their feet touched the floor, followed by water trickling. Then Elise said, "Maybe they mean for us to walk back to our rooms like this. I hear the customs are very different in the south. Perhaps we are supposed to let the water dry in the open air. It is very hot here."

Elise had already shown a lack of modesty concerning her own body when Askon had gone looking for them at the confluence between the Grafdrek and Estelle. Whether it was an innate characteristic or a result of her time spent with the Norill in Vitæsta did not matter to Askon. At the very least, he would feel awkward walking naked back to his room, especially with the others and certainly not with the men and women together.

But Edward and Thomas were already up and out of their tubs. They looked at each other with a shrug, let the water run to the ground for a moment, and started for the door. "Are you just going to sit there, Askon?" Edward asked. He turned and stepped out from behind the partition. Líana giggled, her voice bounding off the walls and stone floor tiles.

"Stop!" Askon commanded and Edward stepped back. "Get back here. We'll wait until we all freeze before you go naked through the halls with my sister."

Behind the other partition, the giggle turned into the wild, combined laughter of both women. One of them clapped twice, loudly, and the servants appeared again. As the women gasped for air between bouts of laughter, Líana called across the divider. "I've lived here for months now Askon," she shouted. "Do you think I'd actually wander around without my clothes? How would the palace even function if that's what all the people did?"

Askon glowered. Thomas and Edward had joined in the laughter, though not quite as raucously as Líana and Elise. The servants held towels for each of them to use in drying off. Then, on Askon's side of the partition, they handed them each a shirt and pair of trousers made from fine white linen. The fabric was cool on the skin, a welcome relief from days spent in sweltering leather and rough, stiff traveling clothes. In the time it took to dry off and clothe himself, Askon felt the fragment of Alora's Tear grow cold on his chest. He lifted the chain from beneath the linen shirt and tried it in front, visible, pulsing green over white. Then he put it back under and felt the chill of gem and chain against his skin. Again he lifted it out, this time allowing it to stay outside the shirt. In bare feet, they headed for the door.

When the men rounded the partition, all three stopped suddenly as Elise and Líana emerged from their side. They wore dresses of purest white but not of linen. The fabric was different, lighter and very thin. Askon worried that the dresses might reveal too much in the sunlight, but his fears were misguided. The feminine forms beneath the garments were too clear for his liking considering who wore them, but the white was as opaque as plate mail. Above all, they were beautiful. Something in removing the dirt and sweat of the road had transformed them. Askon was reminded of just how striking Elise was, and proud at how lovely Líana had become. He smiled, while Edward and Thomas looked on vacantly. Líana raised a closed hand to her mouth and turned away while Elise put on a smirk. She hooked Líana's arm and stepped lightly from the steaming room into the lighted hallway.

The men followed them.

CHAPTER TWENTY-FOUR

A Night Among Friends

After the baths they had returned to their rooms, found them stiflingly hot, and instead gathered outside beneath the leaves and vines of the garden. For some time they had spoken little. The wine had come after the first servant passed by. He asked what they would prefer, and Edward, always willing to accept the manners of the culture to which he was a guest—even if it meant traipsing up and down the hallways naked as the day he was born—asked what the lord of the house found to be his finest drink. When the servant returned, he brought the glittering glasses, each one nearly brimful of the honey-gold wine.

"I still have one question about Morrowmen's story," said Thomas, adjusting Elise's knees so he was more comfortable. "The elves outright destroyed the enemy army at Dalkaldur, but the Darkness had already taken every city and village in Vladvir. How did they reclaim them? And why didn't Morrowmen tell us?"

Edward looked up from his glass. Líana scooted away slightly. "My guess," he said, "is that we already know the truth of that part of the story. Morrowmen would be loath to tell us something we already knew—unless, of course, it helped him prove some argumentative point. So, the end of the Great Darkness must be just as everyone tells it: the elves marched through the cities and villages one by one until all of the creatures were dead. Only a small number of Norill escaped. Their descendants make up the Lost and the Grafmark Norill."

"Right," said Thomas. "But I keep thinking about the way Morrowmen described the deaths in Dalkaldur."

"It sounded like a really awful way to die, even for creatures of evil," Líana said.

"And disgusting," added Elise.

Thomas's face lit up. "That's exactly what I mean. The convulsions, the mindless staggering, the bursting corpses and eyeballs—"

"Thomas, stop it!" Elise said, looking nauseously at her wineglass.

"What I mean is," he began again, "that it sounds familiar. Think, Edward. Do you recognize it?"

Edward's brows knitted together, a deep crease forming at the center of his forehead. He stared into the golden liquid, swirled it a few times and let it come to rest. "It's like a pestilence," he said distantly. Earlier in his life, Edward had made a study of the medical arts, hoping to find a cure for his fatally ill mother. He had found no cure, but in his memory, some of the study remained. "Only much worse than any I've ever heard of."

Thomas pushed Elise's legs gently off his lap. He leaned forward. "That's what I was thinking," he said. "Vladvir has seen several plagues in its history. I'll spare the details, but some of them had similar effects on the victims. Never all at the same time, though."

"Or so violent, if what Morrowmen says is true," Edward added.

Askon arched his back, scratching an itch between his shoulder blades against the stone pillar. He looked up into the curling fronds and colorful petals. Marten was perched there, looking uncomfortable amid the flowers. "We were always taught that it was the superior technology of the elves that won Vladvir back from the darkness, not a disease," Askon said.

"As was I," said Edward.

"And us as well," said Elise, referring to both Dalstone and Vitæsta. Líana went on staring into her wineglass, running her thin finger back and forth around the rim.

"We all were," Thomas said. "That doesn't mean that it was true. Elven technology was certainly superior. They used steel instead of iron or bronze. They used stronger, faster-drying mortar in their stonework. Their forges were hotter, their armor designs better reinforced while also lighter and more comfortable. They used advanced mathematics in their construction that our wisest did not even understand until new generations had been educated in the practice. Almost nothing in the elves' technology was even on par with our own. It was all categorically better."

"You forgot Morrowmen's hillside full of enemies bursting into flame," Edward said.

Thomas smiled, almost as if Edward were falling into some sort of trap. "I did, and many other things besides, like their sword-making practices for instance. Every decent smith in Vladvir now uses some variation on elven sword-craft. As for the fire, I'd say some sort of mechanical device similar to a catapult threw it out across the hillside. How they built something that would burst into flame, remain on fire long enough to incinerate a large number of the enemy forces, and still cover that much area, I can't say. I think they must have kept that particular secret to themselves because we have yet to see its like anywhere in Vladvir."

Líana looked up from her glass, her eyes continuing on into the foliage above. She smiled as Marten hopped from one crossbeam to another and back again. Her long braid hung over her shoulder and down along her side between arm and body. "All you've done is tell us how wonderful elven technology was. It sounds to me like they could have defeated the Darkness with all of those things," she said.

"That's where you're wrong," Thomas responded, a bit too forcefully. The trap he had set for Edward seemed to have caught Líana instead. "Many elves came into Vladvir that day, but all accounts have them as a large army. The creatures of the dark are always described as numbering in the countless thousands. No amount of technology that I can think of could even such odds."

Elise swung her legs up onto the bench again, this time bending them just enough to fit between Thomas and herself so that her toes rested against the outside of his thigh. "Maybe it was magic," she suggested.

"The elves had no magic," Askon said with finality. "They had none then, and we have none now. Statements like that make people believe and say all sorts of things about us." He took a deep breath, thinking of Morrowmen's rules for self-control. "I'd prefer you refrain from adding to the misinformation."

The dark-haired woman of Vitæsta did not like being told what she could and could not say; Askon read as much on her glowering face and in her black eyes. But she did not speak.

Thomas interrupted the staring match. "It wouldn't have to be magic," he said to both of them and the group at large. "If they were able to use a plague as a weapon, they could wipe out a great many more enemies merely by exposing the creatures to the sickness during battle, maybe even without combat."

Edward nodded, his gray eyes clear and thoughtful. "That would also explain why all the creatures were eradicated, including whatever spawn they were able to produce in the time that they occupied our cities."

"The Glittering Host would not have killed women or children, if the creatures of the Great Darkness could even be called that," Askon said, setting down his glass. A moment later, a servant appeared and whisked the sparkling goblet away. He returned promptly with another glass filled with golden wine. Askon continued, "My father was as expert in the old traditions as anyone yet living—aside from Marten's trainer, Halan perhaps. According to their lessons, no elf would risk the damage to his or her honor.

Women might fall in battle if they donned the raiment of war." At this he glanced at Líana, both proud and sick to his stomach at the thought of her joining in combat. "But never in their homes or in front of their children."

With a flick of her fingernail, Elise's glass rang like a bell, pinging over the tiles and up into the leaves. "Wouldn't a disease weapon be just as dishonorable?" she asked in an oddly restrained version of her cold commander's voice. "Killing someone face to face is more honorable than infecting them from a distance. At least with a sword, you look them in the eye."

Askon smiled. It was another of his lessons to Líana. When he had said it to the little blond girl in Tolarenz, he had been comparing swordplay and archery, but the meaning held in this case as well, perhaps more so as bows were a mainstay of warfare in Vladvir while using a sickness intentionally to defeat an enemy was unheard of.

As they talked and sipped from their glasses, darkness crept up as it will in the company of friends, draping its blanket over the world while words and laughter, smiles and shouts go here and there. Askon looked around and saw Elise curled up against Thomas, shaking ever so slightly from time to time. It had grown cold quickly in Apopsé's garden, and they had been so focused on their conversation that none of them had even noticed. But in the shadows cast from the ring of torches lit all around the lavish garden, Askon saw that even Líana showed signs of the chill. She had sidled, bit by bit, closer to Edward. Now their sides pressed ever so slightly against one another. She did not shiver. Neither of them made any detectable movement at all.

But Thomas was not finished. He only paused to think, and to rub Elise's shoulders as she trembled in the swift, oncoming chill of night. "What if it wasn't a weapon?" he asked the group.

No one said anything. They heard only the distant music of croaking frogs, from hiding places unknown, a multitude of voices casting echoes about the garden.

When it appeared he would receive no response, Thomas tried again. "What if the elves didn't know they would make the creatures sick? It has happened here before with simple border conflicts between villages. One militia becomes ill while they travel, some fatally so, but by the time they reach the battle, most of the members are well again. Then the opposing force catches the illness, and even if they win the fight, many die from the combined strain of their injuries and the disease." He rubbed his hands together, blew into them, and placed one on each of Elise's shoulders. "Maybe that's what happened with the elves. Whatever contagion they carried didn't affect humans, but it laid waste to the creatures of the Darkness."

"Except for the Norill," Edward said, careful not to move toward or away from Líana. "They were more like us and so it didn't always kill them as it did the other creatures. Some of them survived and fled."

"It makes sense," said Askon. He looked at his half-emptied glass, lifted a finger, and pinged a nail against the crystal as Elise had done. The sound was different, as hers had been empty, but still pleasing to the ear, like a well-wrought chime.

"And I'll tell you something else," said Thomas excitedly. He dropped his hands from Elise's pale arms, gesturing animatedly with fingers and open palms. "If I'm right," he said, pointing skyward, "I think I know why so few elves remained after only a relatively short number of years."

Líana's brows furrowed and her mouth turned down. "There were many elves in Vladvir before the Scouring. That's why they did it." She had leaned forward, pulling just inches away from Edward. She sat back slowly. When her shoulders fell against the bench again, she leaned against him, this time a little more obviously than before.

"Ah," said Thomas, pressing his palms together, "but those were half-elves, at least for the great majority. The original Glittering Host was long gone by then and their descendants too." He stood up, too excited to stay seated. "I think something in the illness changed, turning it from Norill back to elf. Soon there would be so few original elves left that they would have no choice but to find mates with the humans, especially if having human blood would protect their children from the disease." He placed his hands on his hips, like a hero's statue in a city square.

"I suppose you're very proud of yourself," a voice croaked. Thomas whirled around, surprised at the sound. Between the torchlight and the garden, a robed, purple shadow emerged from the palace. "I hope you're all enjoying Apopsé's wine. We have work to do, and it begins in the morning."

Elise and Askon stood, turning to face Morrowmen. The chance to relax and simply talk without worry had been a blessing, but now they felt a hint of shame at taking the afternoon and evening with such leisure. Edward and Líana stayed seated, maintaining their precarious contact.

"Thomas has it right," the old man declared. "After the battles to take back our cities, the elves decided to return to Dalkaldur, doing most of the work to clear the area of the dead creatures who hadn't been burned to ash. At first all was well. Then the elves began to sicken and die inexplicably. Their healers conferred, and with some sadness at leaving the place where they entered this world, they vacated Dalkaldur forever.

"They were unsure whether the pestilence would spread to the human population. One of their healers once told me they might predict such a transition, but only with instruments of the world from which they came. So, all those living in Dalkaldur—both elf and human—were evacuated. No one has ever since returned there." The ancient face pulled back into its gruesome smile. "Happily though, no new cases of the disease emerged after that day, but as Thomas has so astutely observed, the elves had no choice but to mingle with the humans."

Heads nodded all around the group. Thomas grinned like an idiot.

"The end!" Morrowmen barked and they all jumped, startled. "Now go get some sleep. We will be busy from here on out." With that, he turned on a heel and limped off in the opposite direction of their rooms, his walking stick clicking intermittently against the tiled path.

When Askon looked back, Thomas and Elise had already vanished down the darkened hallway, eager to return to their room. He stood alone under the highest tier of the garden, two steps above where they had been sitting for the majority of the evening. Behind him, he knew Líana and Edward still sat together, each of them afraid to pull away from the other. With a massive effort, he set his jaw and started toward the hallway. "Goodnight," he managed through clenched teeth.

"Goodnight," Líana said quietly.

Step by agonizing step, Askon made his way toward the hallway entrance, the night sky dark and sparkling above, the water trickling over the crossbeams, the frogs a choir of life in the cold darkness. Slowly the archway came into view, and he passed beneath it. Then, without warning, his resolve snapped, and he turned back. Beyond the blaze of torchlight, under the open blooms of Apopsé's garden, Líana lifted her chin and kissed Edward beneath a sky full of stars.

Nearly half an hour later, Askon leaned against the wall across from Edward's door. One at a time, he cracked the knuckles of one hand, then the other. His back lay flat against the cool white wall, and his ankles were crossed in front of him. Shadows danced over his sharp features while the torchlight glinted from the green of his left eye. The white linen hung loosely over his body, and the heartbeat glow of the Time fragment pulsed on his chest, its chain gleaming silver like the overhead stars. Beneath the white, a threat deep as cold night's shadow lurked.

At the end of the hallway, Edward's outline appeared against the darkness of the garden. He stood tall and whistled a tune, as yet oblivious to his peril. Soon he was only a few feet from the door.

"What'cha doin'?" said Askon musically. It was not his custom to speak in such a manner, and in truth he had lifted the words from John, who might have spoken a similar phrase several times a day.

Edward stopped. Feet, hands, body, eyes, breath: all stopped. No words came.

"Gettin' pretty cold out there," Askon went on. "Did'ya go talk to Morrowmen?"

No response. No breath.

Askon's form seemed to grow, like a huge owl or other nighttime predator. Edward did not move. With the hidden threat revealed, Askon's sword-hand fell upon the back of Edward's neck. "I think you know what happens if any harm comes to her," Askon said, and all the music vanished from his voice.

Edward managed a quick nod.

The hand lifted, and the threat dissipated into nothing. Askon was gone.

CHAPTER TWENTY-FIVE

Powerless

It was still dark. The sheer inner curtains fluttered in the open windows of Askon's room. Past the field of tree-stumps, beyond the rolling hills, over the Estelle and the Vladvir plain, a meeting took place. Codard stood shivering next to a dark figure with a crimson bull emblazoned on his tunic. Standing almost a full head higher than the king, it would have been easy to mistake the shorter man for the subordinate.

Iramov's face was wicked and gaunt, a twisted wreck of steely resolve and calculated vengeance. His eyes, steady and black, froze the king in place. Behind the eyes, though, a wild cacophony of wrath, rage, and hatred seethed.

Shining like a ball of glass, his head stood bare against the pink fringe of mountain sunrise. Around his neck and chest, a sash of blood red undulated in the wind, a portent of the slaughter to come. He held no weapon, and neither the long ebony staff nor its glowing red gem were anywhere to be seen. Behind him his army waited, ready to move, to destroy whatever might next stand pitifully against them.

With contorted fury, the face opened at the thin-lipped mouth. A shout should have burst forth, but only flecks of wetness flew from tongue and teeth. They landed on the smaller man who cowered visibly. It seemed the king's army had not yet prepared itself fully for the final battle. Nervously, Codard turned the blue Space fragment over in his hands. It pulsed weakly against the hard blackness and florid pink. He looked uncertain, which might have been the closest he had ever come to defiance in the face of a threat. After another bout of screaming, Iramov stomped down the slope, leaving the shrunken king on the hilltop.

The bald man walked nearly a mile, the pink growing ever more vibrant behind him. Ahead, the forms of an army came into view, black as shadows in the moments preceding morning. Some were Norill shapes, others men, but their number had increased far beyond that of Iramov's original forces. Another hundred yards and rank after rank stretched into the darkened distance. With every step, the darkness grew, in contrast to the coming sun. Then Iramov stooped into the folds of a tent, black with the outline of his crimson bull. Inside lay the staff. For a flickering instant, the Death fragment glowed like a blood-filled chalice of purest glass. Suddenly, silently, all was black.

Codard stood on the hilltop gazing out at the fading pink horizon. The sun would come soon. He smiled, a weak, defeated smile. In the first rays of day, the sparkling Estelle was revealed. Codard's eyes traveled from the far distant mountains surrounding the valley of Tolarenz, all the way to the Greyarc bridge, a child's toy in the plain below, and then finally to the mountains in the south.

With a heartbeat's hesitation, he turned to face a wall of immense trees, threatening and cruel. Iramov and his army waited. Again the king turned the pulsing blue stone between his fingers. The trees seemed to reach out in the dim half-light of morning. But as Codard turned to face them, they stood still as stone, sentinels against the coming invasion.

A sound stirred the king from his thoughts, and he snapped around quickly. Below, he should have seen the innumerable forms that made up Iramov's army, but he could not. Something immense—and blacker than darkest night, like the bottom of a covered well—loomed into view. It grew until the void overtook all sight, extinguishing even the sun. Drawing closer, the blackness pulsed with warning. At its center, the Death fragment glowed red.

Morrowmen shook Askon awake. "Get up," he said dryly. "Apopsé's seen something. And it doesn't bode well for your time in training."

Sun streamed through the windows. A breath of wind stirred the curtains. Askon rose, pulled on the linen shirt and trousers, crossed the room, and closed the shutters. With a start, he felt for the Time fragment. Patting his chest, he found it there, cold and sharp. "Should I wear armor for our training?" he asked, still muddled by sleep and too much wine.

"Bring your sword," said Morrowmen. "Though I don't think we'll be needing it today. At some point you'll have to respond with it under stress. For now, let's just get started with a little self-control. Your first test happens now."

Askon cinched the sword belt around his waist. It felt awkward and heavy against the feather-light linen. "Alright."

Folding his arms, Morrowmen rested on his walking stick. Under the robes, he trembled minutely. "Iramov's army—his whole army—stands at the border of Grafmark. Apopsé and I believe he intends to strike Dalstone in earnest this time."

Instantly the belt was off, and Askon was on the other side of the room, rifling through the cabinet where he had stowed his armor the night before. "We have to go. I have to go. Maybe if I use the fragment, I can get there in time." But the armor wasn't there. The cabinet had been emptied.

"No," said Morrowmen, low and raspy. His eyes followed Askon's movements closely.

Another cabinet, a set of drawers, a closet, Askon shot through them all like a whirlwind. "What do you mean *no*?" he asked. "Where are the servants? Does Apopsé trust them? They probably stole it." He could feel himself growing angrier.

"I took it," Morrowmen said.

"Why?"

"Too keep you from leaving."

Askon stomped across the room, fury rising to the surface. The old man did not move. Askon clenched his fists. "Where is it?"

"No."

"Where is it?!" Askon shouted. He thrust his hands out to grab Morrowmen's collar. But it was too late. The old man was gone, just far enough to one side that Askon wrenched two handfuls of air and then tumbled onto the floor over Morrowmen's outstretched walking stick. Faster than it should have, the floor came up to meet his face. The Time fragment pulsed rapidly.

Now Morrowmen was across the room from him. "There's nothing you can do to help John now. He will have to defend Dalstone as long as he can. Hopefully he has the sense to retreat when the time comes. They might not be able to escape."

Askon rose from the ground, a thin line of blood upon his lip. He rubbed it with a finger. "What can we do to help them?" he asked. The strange feeling of the fragment working against him began to fade.

Taking a step closer, Morrowmen pulled a small, light chair from a side table by the window. He sat heavily upon it. "Nothing. Not now. You did all you could have when you fought in the first battle. Having the Grafmark Norill as allies does more to protect Dalstone than you possibly could on your own."

"Even with the fragment?"

Morrowmen laughed. "With the level of control you have over it now? Certainly. If you listen to me, and take my lessons to heart, you may very well turn the tide of battle when it comes to us, but if Dalstone is to fall…"

"The world is how it is."

"Exactly."

Involuntarily, Askon's mind leapt back to the battle against the Lost and the reinforcements from Iramov and Codard. Just winning that victory had been hard enough. Apopsé had said things were going well in Dalstone, but how much infighting had there been since the battle? How strong was the bond between Dalstone and Brâghda's people? And would John actually be wise enough to retreat instead of fighting to his death? But none of it mattered. Emotionally, strategically, intellectually, it was all out of his control. All he could do now to help anyone was learn to control the Time fragment. Without that, Iramov would surely defeat them. Even with it, they had only the chance of winning, not the certainty.

"I'll trust what you say, Morrowmen," he said. "I need to learn how to make use of this." He held up the glowing gem. "It's time you taught me."

Like a snake through the grass, Morrowmen's crooked smile slithered over wrinkles and pockmarks, splotches, and discolorations. Finally Askon understood, and the old man knew it.

They met the others in the hallway: Thomas and Elise, Edward and Líana. Behind them came the downturned hat-brim and Apopsé's ill-fitting garments. The two couples parted as he marched through the hallway with his strange, sliding strides. As he passed Edward and Líana, the frog's-eyes studied them dubiously, lids narrowed to slits as if to say, "I hold the Sight fragment. I see everything." In the bulbous face, Askon thought he saw more pain than he did anger. Apopsé slid along the floor tiles until he reached Morrowmen. He looked up, and the wide-brimmed hat wobbled.

"I want this one," the little man demanded. His arm shot out to one side, the folds of his clothing draping down like a curtain. At the termination of the gesture, stood Thomas. He stepped forward, slowly allowing his hand to slip free of Elise's grasp. A beard had begun to darken on his boyish face. The stubble against his honest eyes of pale blue made him seem stronger, more resolute than Askon would have believed of the fresh recruit who fell from his horse between Tolarenz and Austgæta. Askon wondered how Elise felt about Thomas's growing resolve.

"My Lord Apopsé," Thomas said kneeling, his arms splayed out wide.

The walking stick came down on the outspread knuckles of Thomas's left hand. He retracted the arm, rubbing his fingers at the sting. Morrowmen hooked the end of the cane under Thomas's chin and lifted it. "Stand up. He might have chosen to throw you into the smithy fires as a sacrifice."

Elise's face grew pale with fear. She stepped forward, the fear curdling to anger, her eyes turning from merely dark to black. But the cane stopped her as well. Apopsé, who had turned to face them, stepped in front of Morrowmen.

"We do not practice sacrifice of any sort in the South Kingdom," he said.

"I was merely illustrating a valuable point for our young Thomas." Morrowmen leaned on his walking stick with the majority of his weight. "The fool boy would swear his service to the first person who gave him the opportunity, like our idiot-in-chief, Askon here." He grasped Thomas's shirt collar, hauling him up from the ground with surprising strength. "Ask what the Lord Apopsé wants you to do before you bend your knee to him."

"Uh—I..." Thomas stammered.

Whether by impatience or sympathy, Apopsé interrupted him. "I'd like to offer you a position of employment here in the palace, on a trial basis of course." With a flourish of his hand, the lord of the South Kingdom gestured for Thomas to kneel in acceptance.

Morrowmen thumped the walking stick into Apopsé's chest. "He's not going to—" But it was too late. Thomas had already lowered himself to one knee. Morrowmen shook his head. "Fine. He still hasn't said what you will be doing, Thomas. But I suppose it's your life to throw away if you wish."

Apopsé nodded, then adjusted his hat. "You may rise. I'll tell you what you'll be doing after we have had our breakfast. Thomas will breakfast with me this morning so that we may discuss the duties he will attend here in the palace. Elise, you are welcome to join us."

Elise had drawn back from Thomas and now stood next to Líana. "I've had a bit to eat already this morning, thank you," she said. "Líana and I have much to discuss and to learn from each other today. I think we will get started right away."

Askon saw a small smile creep over Líana's face. It vanished almost as quickly as it had appeared. His sister nodded. She was already dressed in the uniform of Morrowmen's agents, the light leather armor dyed mysterious purple. Her hood lay in a disheveled bundle beneath her long braid. "Yes," she said in the voice of rain upon dry grass, "but we'll be needing a uniform for Elise. We won't have the Life fragment today."

"Rickard should be around the palace somewhere this morning. Find him and he will outfit Elise so you can continue teaching her," Morrowmen said.

"My lady," said Apopsé, "I'll send a servant to retrieve Morrowmen's man. Wait with Elise in the garden until then."

"Thank you," said Líana.

"But no wine," added Elise.

Apopsé bowed graciously. "No wine, then." He turned back to Morrowmen and Askon, lifting a hand conspiratorially. "By watching your friend John, I was able to confirm that we were indeed right about what I saw in the fragment this morning. Iramov means to move against Dalstone with all his strength. Brâghda's fighters are preparing to harry Iramov's forces on the way in. It should buy Dalstone some time until the attack. I give them two days before Iramov arrives at the Dalstone gate."

Askon tried to remind himself that there was nothing he could do to help John, besides learning to control the fragment. He had to rely on his friend to do the right thing, to fight until the battle had been lost and then retreat into the relative safety of Grafmark. If John and his Darts could somehow weaken Iramov's army, it might be enough for the South Kingdom to defeat him. But that victory rested upon Askon's ability to use the Time fragment to sway the conflict in their favor.

Edward, who had stood quietly for the entirety of the interaction, stepped forward, bowed to Apopsé, then to Líana with a smile Askon found unsettling but Líana seemed to find utterly charming. "I intend to learn as much as I can about your kingdom, sir," he said to Apopsé. "From what I have seen so far, it is beautiful and strange in many ways, yet also familiar in others. If I have your leave, I'd simply like to explore the city and meet its people."

Askon found Edward's choice predictable. The prince relished the chance to understand other cultures, sometimes almost to a fault. Here though, it would do no harm. As yet they had no need for him in the palace, and his message to Codard wouldn't return—if it ever did—for several days.

"You have my leave," said Apopsé.

"Thank you," Edward replied. On his way out, Askon saw his fingertips brush lightly against Líana's hand. In response, her fingers leapt to life, reaching out to his in a ripple, the smallest finger grasping nothing but empty air. The corner of her mouth twitched into a smile.

CHAPTER TWENTY-SIX

Practice Makes Perfect

Morrowmen led Askon further down the hall to the palace's southern side. When they came back into the light, the hallway opened on Askon's left onto a series of terraced levels that fell away to a wide green sparring area and a guardhouse that seemed to have gone unused for some time.

"These are my quarters," Morrowmen said, limping along with his cane. "It's where you'll do most of your training. At one time, Apopsé's personal guards lived here. You know, the ones with the preposterous feathers. A few years ago, he commissioned a larger, more lavish place for them to live and expanded their number. The new building is on the other side of the palace grounds."

They started down the steps of the terraces, and Askon was taken by the beauty of South City. Its domed roofs of slate blue or pearl white, the many arches in buildings large and small, the white layer that made the walls shine like polished marble, all added to each other in what he thought was perhaps the most splendid cityscape in all of Vladvir.

When the terrace descended, obscuring the view, Askon surveyed the premises. The sparring ground was large, the earth beneath the sparse grass compact. The structure Morrowmen called his quarters, which appeared small from the top of the stairs, was actually quite comfortable. It had a central hall, living spaces with bunks fit for guardsmen, a simple kitchen and pantry, and one room that served as a study. Books lined the study walls on two sides with a desk in between.

After showing him the various rooms, Morrowmen led Askon back to the hall. It had no chairs or tables, just open space under the shade of a high, vaulted ceiling. "So this is where you try my patience?" Askon wondered aloud. His voice carried into the rafters and died there.

"No," said Morrowmen without emotion. "This is where you try mine."

Neither patience held. In the first few days, Askon grew more and more distracted. Using the Sight fragment, Apopsé had tracked the movements of various factions across Vladvir. John and Brâghda had fought bravely, and yet Dalstone had fallen to Iramov's forces not long after Askon and the others departed. They had been unable to see the battle as it happened on account of the Death fragment, though they knew John, his Darts, Brâghda, and her warriors had made a safe retreat into the surrounding forest.

At least the fight had delayed Iramov, extending Askon's time under Morrowmen's instruction. Then, John had done just as they all had hoped. Two days after the battle, he emerged in the wilds of

Grafmark with a strong contingent of his Darts and a great many civilians. Not far behind were Brâghda and the Norill. Between the two, they were able to attack Iramov's army when it best suited them, killing a few here and a few there before pulling back when the danger became too great. Iramov's army was vastly superior, and growing. But in the forest the Darts and Norill knew so well, his army, however large, was outmatched. John and Brâghda won small victory after small victory, while Askon grew more at ease, throwing himself into his training.

Codard and the remainders of his army had gone south but not toward Apopsé's city. They marched through the snows of the southern mountains, separating and reuniting only to divide again.

The victories in Grafmark bought weeks for Askon to prepare. Each day Apopsé would meet them in the morning, update them on the military situation and confer with Thomas or Edward—though never with Elise or Líana who almost always went first to the garden for Elise's lessons and then to one of the sparring grounds for Líana's. By noontime the women had moved on to other pursuits: helping the servants with work around the palace or spending time on the more tedious of their specialties like maintenance of gear and weaponry, sewing, or embroidery.

Sometimes, before the evening meal, the whole party would cross paths in the partitioned room full of steaming tubs. Over time, they grew more comfortable speaking across the divider about the events of the day, or speculating on the news coming from other parts of Vladvir. But these intersections were the exception rather than the rule. Most days they did not meet until they sat together at

Apopsé's table. Usually this meant the long room where the first meeting had taken place, but sometimes the lord of the South Kingdom would prepare a remote location within the palace. These dining areas almost always included a breathtaking view of South City, and with each came an opportunity to select a specific seating arrangement.

Inevitably, Líana ended up on Apopsé's right while Edward sat at the opposite corner. Each time Edward took the gesture in stride, thanking Apopsé for the meal and making conversation with those at his side of the table. But when the meal ended, it was Edward—not Apopsé—who sat under the leaves of the hanging garden with Líana.

Thomas enjoyed his newly assigned post to no end. After showing his aptitude for working with and improving Apopsé's machines, Thomas had been tasked with examining all such devices in and around the palace. If he found a flaw, Apopsé's orders were to acquire the materials to eliminate it and then do so immediately. At evening meals Thomas chattered on endlessly about the alterations he had made to this or that mechanism. To all of them accept Apopsé himself, discussion of springs and levers and wheels held little interest. Elise, of course, feigned a fascination with the topic, but it wasn't so much false attention as it was Elise being enamored by the sound of Thomas's voice.

While his young friend worked tirelessly to improve Apopsé's machines, Askon had been run ragged, beaten down, traumatized, and tormented. He and Morrowmen began each day with one of several simple forms of distraction: a device Thomas had fashioned that made a repetitive squeaking sound at uneven intervals, a feather dangling before Askon's face as he sat tied to a chair, a spout that dripped water onto his forehead, a bagful of captured flies buzzing around his head, a set of linen clothing which had been dragged through a field of thistle. There was no limit to Morrowmen's creativity. Each test required Askon to activate the fragment's power while under stress—and more importantly—to avoid becoming frustrated or angry lest the fragment pull him into its negative effect.

The distraction tests were irritating, but rarely painful. That particular stress came later in the day. Every afternoon, Askon trained in swordplay. For the first week, Morrowmen had enlisted one of Apopsé's guards to serve as a sparring opponent. It was easy. Askon defeated the guardsman with almost no effort, barely breaking a sweat, even under the South Kingdom's hot sun. Morrowmen had laughed.

Then came the real test. Morrowmen tied one hand behind Askon's back or attached heavy weights to his feet. One day, Morrowmen had somehow weakened Askon's practice sword so that it would break when the guard parried a stroke. Askon was forced to fight without armor, or by taking several direct hits before even beginning the fight. It was maddening. But the more frustrated Askon became by the unfair rules Morrowmen concocted, the more difficult the Time fragment made it for Askon to win. Slowly he came to realize that he had to stay calm, no matter how frustrating Morrowmen made the challenge. Weights on his feet became little more than an inconvenience as he leveraged the fragment's power. They were still heavy, but he had ample time to move, though at the end of the fight he was very tired. So it went with all the challenges, and just as Askon became comfortable and the fragment became useful, Morrowmen would increase the difficulty.

After the first week, Morrowmen changed tactics. He brought in Edward, forcing Askon to fight against someone he knew and someone who knew him. All of Askon's collected prowess with the fragment crumbled when Morrowmen handed him his real sword. The old man meant for Askon to fight and wound his friend intentionally. This wasn't so terrible at first, as the two had often sparred with live steel during their time in Codard's army, but when Morrowmen tied Edward's hand behind his back, Askon protested. They went on, and then Morrowmen brought the weights. When Askon refused to fight, Morrowmen whacked him with the walking stick. And when that didn't work, he went after Edward.

Every night, Morrowmen would call upon Líana, enlisting her help in healing their wounds. Her ability to use the Life fragment without aging the subject made Askon's training much more effective. Thomas had protested, citing his suggestion that the fragment might be taking years off the end of her life with each use.

"Illogical," Morrowmen had replied dismissively. "My aging can be speeded because it is an effect applied to my current state. For you to be correct, the Life fragment would somehow have to determine Líana's eventual lifespan, which is an unknowable value unless you'd like to assert that our fates are predetermined." He rolled his watery eyes. "If that's the case, then why am I wasting all this time and frustration on your half-elf friend when I could be lounging in the garden, waiting for destiny to take its all-knowing course?!"

Thomas had relented at that, though Askon maintained that the bright young man had conceded only publicly; too much worry still showed on his face.

Despite Thomas's lingering misgivings, the training went on. Líana herself reminded Thomas that she would be the one to decide whether the risk was too great, and she chose to allow Morrowmen to continue. With their permission, the old man could essentially torture any of Askon's friends right before his eyes. Then, when the day was over, he could heal them of all their wounds. The cuts were never too horrific and the pain never extreme, but even minor threats to his friends snatched the fragment's power away from Askon's grasp. Morrowmen used the technique sparingly at Líana's warning, but the mere possibility that something might happen to his friends or his sister put Askon on edge and the power out of his reach.

Some afternoons it was Edward, others Thomas. After two weeks, Askon fought Líana for the first time since the humiliating duel in the firelight of Morrowmen's camp. The result was equally embarrassing. She was faster than him, more graceful, and unburdened by the fragment's negative effects. Though not as strong as Edward, nor quite as clever as Thomas, she was by far the most difficult for Askon to fight. And when Morrowmen threatened to harm her, Askon became agonizingly useless. Just the suggestion that she would suffer any pain virtually paralyzed him, sending the world into a dizzy haze, sometimes nearly an hour passing before he regained control of himself. Morrowmen had not been pleased.

Then came Elise. With a few weeks of training behind her, she had requested a chance to work with Askon during his afternoon sparring. She could not have fought more like Líana if she tried. Though she held her sword in her right hand, all of the movements, parries, feints, and counter-attacks were pure Líana, and as such, derivative of Askon's own style. Elise captured much of the grace in his sister's sword-work, but was more than a step slower and obviously inexperienced. Despite her shortcomings, Askon had found it nearly as difficult to fight Elise as it had been to fight Líana. Not because of her skill, or even her gender, but because he wanted her to succeed and to build confidence. She needed the support in order to improve, and so, even against the least-trained member of his party, Askon continued to fail the sparring test. By the end of the month, however, he had managed to trigger the fragment's power consistently against Thomas and Edward, though not nearly often enough for Morrowmen's liking.

The final tests came when exhaustion had taken hold emotionally as well as physically. In the hours preceding the evening meal, Morrowmen led Askon into one of the sleeping rooms of the guardhouse. There he had dismantled the bunks, leaving only one for Askon and a chair for himself. The windows had been boarded over, sealed with the substance that made Apopsé's city appear white, then draped with heavy cloth that covered all four walls. Sounds inside the cramped space died instantly, and it was pitch black. Not even with his acute vision could Askon perceive anything inside the bunkhouse darkroom, not even his own hand held just inches away from his face.

In this room Morrowmen used a combination of flashing powder, loud noises, smoke, and other sensory torments to make sure that Askon did not become comfortable. Then he began the real test. He retold the worst events in the history of Askon's people in vivid detail the like of which only Morrowmen could recreate. Having seen the Scouring, the interrogations, the tortures, the killings, he was able to paint a scene in the total darkness that Askon could not avoid or ignore. Closing his eyes made no difference; sometimes he could not even tell if his eyes were open or closed.

The test was simple. When Askon lay in his bed, a lever of Apopsé's design, and Thomas's refinement, opened one of three doors on each side of the room. If Askon sat up, stood, or moved away from the bed at all, the open door slammed shut like a mousetrap. Askon could not see the doors, and Thomas's adjustments made their motion so silent that the sound of Morrowmen's voice would obfuscate the sliding mechanism. If Askon could activate the fragment—especially as he had with Brâghda and the arrow or the guards in Apopsé's palace—he would be able to search the darkened room, find the door, and exit before it closed.

It was only within the last week that Askon had been able to escape the horrific room and the ghoulish past depicted in Morrowmen's stories. His most recent attempt had been almost easy. Askon found that focusing on something important outside of the moment helped to trigger the fragment's power, as had Edward's danger from the overzealous guard or Brâghda's as the arrow flew over the field toward its target.

He was pleased with his victory, but Morrowmen had not yet finished. Outside the room, the old man produced a tray lined with sewing needles and several small bottles with the names of poisonous herbs and plants labeled in white. Askon knew immediately how these would become part of the test. In some regions, plants were ground down, squeezed, and distilled to create powerful poisons. Eating the plant might merely make a person sick, but drinking the distillation would kill even the strongest warriors. But Morrowmen's intent was not to kill Askon. Others bought or sold the distillations for use in extremely small amounts, at the end of a sewing needle, for instance. It was said that doing so would alter one's consciousness, bring about visions, and stir waking nightmares. A larger part of Askon than he would have been willing to admit wanted nothing more than for Iramov to strike before Morrowmen had a chance to use the needles on the tray.

That night, during the sixth week of his training, Askon had won a victory in all three tests: flies and dripping water in the morning, sparring with Edward in the afternoon, and escaping the dreadful guardhouse darkroom. Apopsé's servants had prepared a wonderful meal of roast chicken with a sweet starchy vegetable like a potato, fresh bread laced with sunflower seeds, and a ready supply of the honey-gold wine which they had not tasted since that first night under the cool breeze of the garden.

Naturally, Apopsé had arranged a place for himself next to Líana. Tonight, more than Askon had seen on any previous night since their arrival in South City, his sister looked sullen and even resentful at being seated next to the small man rather than Edward.

But with a quick glance from Elise, the emotion was replaced with one of polite graciousness. Edward had fully recovered from the sparring match, but his spirits were low. After weeks of waiting, it was clear that his messenger would not be coming back.

One of the great limitations to Apopsé's fragment was that he could not hear what happened at the locations he espied, only see them. So, through the deductions of Morrowmen and Thomas, they only suspected that Codard was looking for Dalkaldur. There was no other reason to go to the southern mountains, but none of them could understand what the king might expect to find there. Elise had suggested that he might also be waiting for the Lost to come down out of Ellmed, and the others agreed that likely he did, or at least that was what Iramov had commanded him to do. But the dividing and reuniting army implied that Codard was exploring the area. For what, they could not guess. Whatever it was, it had to be in Dalkaldur.

Apopsé and Thomas were in the middle of a heated argument when Askon realized his attentions had drifted elsewhere.

"What good are all of these designs if they're only for decoration?" Thomas said. His chicken was half-finished and his wine untouched.

"No," Apopsé said tipping his hat back so that it fell between his shoulder blades, hanging from the narrow string beneath his chin. "South City defends itself, it does not attack. Our walls are strong, our guardsmen well trained, and their soldiers in fit condition. I will not use my devices to kill other men. These machines benefit the people, not destroy them." His eyes bulged in the heat of his anger.

Thomas was not convinced. "You've seen what Iramov's army did to Dalstone. There's almost nothing left. You'll have no people to defend if you just allow him to march to the doorstep. Let me build something with the equipment here. We could set traps, build catapults, ballistae with mechanical loading arms, remote firing crossbows. A single man could fire five-at-a-time."

"No!" Apopsé shouted, thumping the table with his meaty little fists. "I won't have it! This discussion is over."

Thomas hesitated. "Yes, my lord," he said. His eyes pleaded with Askon and with Edward for support, but Askon's training kept him silent and Edward's politics allowed only a nod. Thomas's plans, however clever and appropriate, would have to wait.

But Morrowmen was not so reserved. "You took off that ridiculous hat, Apopsé, but haven't opened your ears," he croaked. "A city like this is well protected by its walls, but walls don't win wars. At best we'll send the guard and militia out to fight an army and lose men hand over fist. At worst, Iramov will simply annihilate your men with the Death fragment. Then how will you fight back?"

The frog's-eyes clicked, but no words came.

"That's what I thought," Morrowmen continued. "Lord Apopsé. Your machines are brilliant, even if I find them to be inscrutably superfluous. But with Thomas helping you, they've become akin to magic. Let the young man survey the city, see what he can do to improve the defenses by leveraging your best asset: these machines."

Apopsé thought for a moment. Then surprisingly, he turned to Líana. "What do you think, my lady?"

Líana bristled at the words. The way Apopsé said *my* lady made it seem as though she were more possession than person, like one of the machines they currently debated. "I—" she said, faltering. "You should listen to Morrowmen. Without him, where would any of us be?"

The blue gem pulsed on Apopsé's round forehead. He nodded slowly, almost in time with the pulse. He scratched his head, and his eyes clicked again. Along the edge of the table, his drooping sleeve hissed against the polished wood. "Very well," he said. "Tomorrow, Thomas shall survey the city in order to augment our defenses." He turned to the young man, who wore a broad smile. "You will have all the resources you require and may enlist anyone you like to help. My one condition is that your designs and plans come to me first."

Morrowmen grunted and shifted his weight under his purple robes.

"Just so that I have some say in what goes on in my own city," Apopsé said with some heat. "I won't deny him, only serve as a guide and official."

"Thank you, Lord Apopsé," Thomas said respectfully. He lifted his glass. "To a better defense!" he said.

The others echoed him, then tilted back their own glasses.

CHAPTER TWENTY-SEVEN

Sun and Sand

The next morning, Askon dressed quickly, pulling on his armor rather than the linens. A dim sun floated sleepily in the sky, its light muted behind a gray haze. No breeze stirred the curtains, and the air felt damp with humidity. Askon stretched, testing the fasteners, checking for loose straps or overlooked buckles. All was in order.

In the hallway outside his room, Edward waited patiently. Askon was under no illusion that the prince waited for *him*, however. Edward nodded a good morning to Askon, but otherwise remained still.

"Why don't you just wait for her outside her door?" Askon said, taking a place on the wall next to Edward. "Or you could knock to see when she'll be ready."

Edward shifted uncomfortably. He too wore his armor, black with the blue stag blazoned on the chest. After losing the sparring match the day before, he was determined to fight again. Askon assumed that Morrowmen would have some new trick planned to break his concentration, giving Edward an edge in the day's duel.

"That would seem much too demanding, I think, or too weak," Edward replied after a moment. "Don't you think? I wouldn't want to scare her off by always being so close. A good suitor knows when to keep his distance."

Askon let his weight fall to one hip and leaned an elbow against the wall. A hint of a smirk disturbed the corners of his mouth. "You're trying to impress her?" he said. "The prince of Vladvir, decorated war hero, accomplished politician, and would-be rescuer of his kingdom is trying to impress my sister: a half-elf from a veritable backwater who is essentially little more than a farm girl." He let the smirk reveal itself fully upon his face. "Have I got it right?"

"You do," Edward said sheepishly. His head dropped, chin nearly to chest. "But what of that?"

"Of what?"

"Líana's…situation," Edward said, his head still hanging low. "What you say is right. She is only a girl, and by rights, should still be a child. But she looks, even acts like—"

"Like a grown woman," Askon said, finishing his friend's sentence. When they had first arrived in South City, even the night he had seen them kissing under the stars, Askon had been uncomfortable with the two of them. He still was, but weeks of training with Morrowmen had strengthened his will. He knew that logically it made perfect sense, but in his mind Líana was still just a girl, in spite of her outward appearance and manner. So he said what he knew to be true beyond his personal entanglements. "The world is how it is, Edward. Much of it changed forever the day that Iramov came to Tolarenz. One of those changes is Líana. It does not matter what she was half a year ago. It matters only what she is now. I'd rather she be a grown woman and happy with you than a memory lost in a circle of white powder."

A chill drifted over Edward's face, and lifting his chin from his chest, he rose to his full height, several inches above Askon. The gray eyes of a king looked down on the green and the blue. Edward put out a hand. Askon clasped it in his own, expecting the prince to finish with the two-handed greeting he so often used. But he did not. Instead, Edward beamed broadly and wrapped Askon in a bear-hug almost as one might do to a small child, lifting him bodily off the ground. When Askon's feet came to rest again on the floor tiles, he felt three quick slaps on his back.

"Thank you," Edward said happily. "You have no idea what a relief it is to have your support!"

Askon stopped. "My support? What does that mean?"

Edward released him, still beaming. In the hand he had not offered to Askon, he held up a small shiny metal object. It took Askon a moment to process its shape. A circle. Gold. A circle within a circle. A band. A ring!

"You'll not regret it, my friend," said Edward.

Every fiber, every strand, every single particle of his being wanted to stop Edward, who had turned cheerily on one heel and marched off toward Líana's room. With an urgency he hadn't felt for many days, Askon reached out to grab his friend, to stop him from doing what he was about to do. How had he even acquired such a ring? Probably through a connection made on one of his days in town. Who would refuse to sell to Codard's son, even now?

Holding hands, fine. Secretive talks in the moonlight, harmless. Kissing beneath the stars, barely acceptable. But a ring?

Askon lunged at Edward, but the prince was not there. He was already far away, covering most of the distance to Líana's door in less than the space of a breath. Askon could not catch him, could not even speak. The Time fragment flickered hysterically on its chain, still a heartbeat, but less like a man's and more like a hummingbird's.

When Edward returned with Líana, the others joined them. Askon had managed to travel almost a full foot from where he stood when the prince walked away. When he looked up, the world settled back into its normal pace. Edward was holding a finger to his lips. He hadn't yet shown her the ring. Askon breathed deep and let all the air out of his lungs in a long sigh.

"Are you alright?" Líana asked. Over her shoulder, Edward's eyes widened.

Askon nodded with a smile. "Yes, I'm fine. Just thinking about my training today."

"Well don't," said Thomas lightly. "You've been enlisted."

Askon looked to Edward. The prince shrugged, just as clueless as Askon.

"Enlisted to work for me," Thomas continued with a smile almost as broad as Edward's had been. "I was told that I could use anyone in the castle to survey Apopsé's machines, and I mean to. You, Surveyor Askon, will be going with Surveyors Edward, Líana, and Morrowmen." At the mention of the final name, the young man's grin grew even wider. The closest to Morrowmen's intellectual equal, Thomas often arrived at a conclusion before the old man did. However, in such cases the young buck always deferred to the crow. Now Thomas would get to make the decisions, and he relished it.

"Elise will be with me."

"So, four of us and only two of you?" asked Edward.

"No, no. Elise and I will be accompanied by Morrowmen's agents Rickard and Mot. Early this morning, I sent one of Apopsé's servants out to get them. They should be back any time now."

"Why four to a group?" Askon wasn't truly concerned with the number of people as much as he was happy to have a reprieve from his training. Morrowmen showed no sign of irritation at the change of plans, and that was a very good sign. Askon thought that perhaps Morrowmen needed a break as much as he did.

Thomas was ready with an answer, almost as if he had rehearsed it. "Four group members provide maximum observational capacity with minimum distraction. Any larger and the group would draw attention to itself, further compounding the number of citizens stopping to investigate and the amount of time spent by the surveyors directing those citizens away. Not that it matters if they know we're building the defenses. It will just be more efficient to do so without interruption."

"And why compose the groups as you have?" Líana asked. She too had donned her armor, no doubt intending to work with both Elise and Askon in the sparring ring.

"Two who know the city, two who do not," Thomas replied. "You and Morrowmen both know South City well enough to get around and return to the palace at the end of your observations. Rickard and Mot will serve the same purpose for us. We go east. You go west. Start where the inner wall intersects with the outer and work your way toward the main gate. We'll meet you there."

He lifted a canvas bag from his shoulder and dropped it on the tiled floor. The heavy fabric folded over itself in lumps and creases. Reaching inside with both hands, he produced several thin volumes and handed one to each of them. With his own, he opened the cover to reveal a fluttering of blank pages.

"I might have been satisfied without these, but Apopsé requests that we document any and all locations we wish to use with descriptions as well as sketches for the desired device."

Askon's ability to draw ended at simple lines for use on military maps. He looked helplessly to Edward. "We're drawing the devices?"

"No." Thomas shook his head. "I'm drawing them. Just do your best to describe the place and its surrounding features, approximate distance from the gate and the palace and so on. If you want, you can make suggestions as to what sort of machine we might use, but I'll do another pass of the wall on my own using your notes. From there, I'll draw the final proposed additions."

He looked around. Rickard and Mot still had not yet appeared. If they had come through the mechanical palace gate, no one would have heard them. Thomas had tuned the tracks and wheels so that the gate operated in near silence. With a wave of his hand, he started for the garden. He hailed a servant, requesting food while they waited. Under the leaves and blossoms, they all ate together, eager to leave the palace grounds and explore the city.

Mot and Rickard arrived nearly an hour later, sauntering in as though time was of no consequence. Askon hadn't seen any of Morrowmen's agents in the weeks since their arrival in South City, and while he felt thin and half-starved despite Apopsé's bountiful table, these two looked as if they had done nothing but eat and drink and sleep. Mot, who had been large and thick already, had put on enough mass that Askon might have described him as soft around the edges. Rickard was thin, but not wiry and sharp as he had been when Askon first met him in Morrowmen's camp. They bowed together to Morrowmen, and Thomas directed them back the way they had come, Askon and the others following close behind.

The gate, a wonder when they first arrived, now seemed almost magical. It soundlessly slid into place along Thomas's improved track and pulley system. The lever completed the process automatically, though engaging it still required knocking to an unfortunate guard who spent his day manning the door. In Thomas's room, new experimental designs for the door lay on his desk. Not yet ready for implementation, the drawings involved a series of levers which would disengage the lock when pulled in the proper sequence. When it was complete, the guard would thank him.

On the outside, South City opened before them with its vendors hawking ornate trinkets and expensive household wares. The tiled street, already jammed with people, clacked and chattered in response to passing feet. Voices filled the air, the din of a hundred conversations happening at once. Wide, taut canvas awnings stretched over the shelves and long tables before the storefronts. Some of them had retractable sides the vendors used to shade their goods—and their customers. Later in the day, those same vendors would roll up the shade on one side of the display and extend it on another, keeping themselves cool and their patrons happy.

Above it all, the haze thickened. The sun, deadened by the bank of heavy clouds, hovered as if deciding whether it would be better to retreat again to its rest. Though Askon's cloak protected him from bitter cold or blazing sun, it did little in the muggy damp of South City's streets. It was as if the buildings themselves were sweating. He tried to ignore it and pinned his hopes on a lingering band of dark clouds in the distant haze.

After wading through the press of bodies, they came to an intersection. On either side of the beautifully paved avenue, two narrow streets snaked into the city's less-traveled regions: one going west, the other east. Thomas stopped them. A man with a wide-brimmed hat like the one Apopsé wore, bumped into him, nearly knocking him off his feet. The man turned, face scrunched with irritation, ready to scold Thomas about watching out for his elders. Seeing the well-armed party of eight standing together, he quickly scuttled away. Like a stone in a stream, the remaining passersby routed around them.

"Here's where we part ways," said Thomas. "Just follow this street until you reach the far side of the wall. If you come to a dead end—and there are one or two—just double back to your nearest left, follow the cross-street and take one more left to put you back on track." He gave them a wave and plunged into the crowd with Elise at his side. Mot and Rickard followed them. The four emerged on the other side of the human stream, then vanished into the shadows between the buildings.

Askon turned to his team of surveyors and laughed to himself at the title. They shouldered their way through the crowd and into the side street. Marten dropped lightly from an adjacent rooftop. Perched high on the leather shoulder guard, the falcon moved closer than usual to Askon's face. Marten rarely made his way onto the palace grounds, and Askon had seen him only once in the preceding two weeks. But Askon sensed that the bird watched his progress from a distance, even if he did not intervene.

The shadows deepened, and a breeze picked up through the narrow lane. Once or twice, a gust even stirred the folds of Askon's cloak. But any relief he felt at the wind, he cursed in the dust. Too much sun had made the streets of South City dry with parched grit. Now the sandy powder along the road swept into the air and into their faces, mouths, and eyes. He hoped again for rain.

Before long they came to the first of Thomas's dead ends. It was a narrow, well-lit corner where children played with sticks and a ball of some sort. They were bare-chested and shoeless, but they seemed happy in their game. From the surrounding windows, mothers watched the strangers go by, glaring with suspicion but silent with fear at the hooded faces and gleaming steel.

The eyes followed them as they reenacted Thomas's instructions. Doubling-back, the four of them found the nearest left, turned down the cross-street, waited for another left, and continued on toward the wall. Morrowmen and Líana whispered something between themselves.

In the sky, the clouds had grown so thick that it became difficult to find the position of the sun. The temperature fluctuated from stifling to bearable and back again with the shifting wind. Grit swirled into their faces once more, and Askon pulled his cloak tight around his mouth and nose to shield them from the flying sand.

"Why do you think Codard is looking for Dalkaldur?" Edward asked Morrowmen. Both men had made similar masks to Askon's, and Edward's voice came through the cloth muted and thick.

Morrowmen lowered his head as another gust swept through the street. "How should I know? There was nothing left when we deserted that place all those years ago. Why should there be anything there now?"

Askon tried to recall the story Morrowmen had told them, but the weeks had eroded many of the details. He remembered that Caled had found the Tear, that the elves had most likely been so successful because they carried some kind of disease which decimated the creatures of the darkness. He even remembered most of the verse lines on the Waterside Parchment. Then he found the detail he had been searching for.

"What if Codard could find the cellar?"

Líana, who led the group, stopped and looked back. Her purple hood had served as a mask much like Askon's cloak, but while he had a great deal of extra fabric with which he could cover his face, his sister's hood was loose enough only to protect one side. The other cheek had grown red in the spray of sand, her eyes pink around the edges. "There were shelves and shelves of books there. At least, that's what you told us, Morrowmen. Caled only took the parchment. If the king were to find that cellar again, he might find great power or knowledge in those books."

"They are the same," replied the old man. He pulled his robes tighter and limped on down the street. "Information and power, I mean. And yes, that would be a distinct possibility if Codard were to find the cellar."

Wind and dust hissed against the paneled buildings. Edward lowered his mask, his voice clear and quiet. "But, he'll never find the cellar, will he?"

"No," said Morrowmen, the word drifting away as he went on ahead of them. "We never found it again. Not with Caled's help, not with my efforts, not with an entire army's worth of elves did we ever find that place again. Your father is grasping at straws. What he really needs to do is come to us, and use his fragment to defeat Iramov, not to help him."

"He won't." Edward lifted the mask again. Líana sidled up next to him and placed an arm around his shoulders. It looked uncomfortable, she almost a full foot shorter reaching up to comfort him.

Askon fell in on the other side. "He'll want a guaranteed victory. Our side isn't that. Iramov's is the better bet. And the cellar in Dalkaldur could hold anything, even something powerful enough to defeat us all, Iramov included."

"Unlikely," croaked Morrowmen. "He won't even find Dalkaldur, let alone that cellar. And even then, the place burst into flames as Caled escaped."

"A gambler always favors the long shot," said Edward.

"So he does," Morrowmen replied. "So he does."

CHAPTER TWENTY-EIGHT

Back Alleys

The street made a sharp right turn and then a left back toward the wall. Something in the shift, moving closer to the protective ring around the city, a large building somewhere distant, or perhaps just a change in the weather, brought the wind to an abrupt halt. Relief washed over their covered faces and each lowered his or her make-shift mask.

No one else walked the narrow lane when they came to the second dead end. Askon had guessed that there would be another of the sharp right-left patterns before the street wound down into the city's lowest levels. But the way was blocked.

In front of them, a large building of three floors ended their path with finality. Thin spaces at its sides ran on into the rest of the neighborhood where shadows flicked and flitted on one of the wider paths. A rickety wooden stairway climbed the outside of the building, leading all the way to the rooftop. Askon thought he might enjoy such a view, but the entrance to the stairs was latched. He could have vaulted the handrail and slid the bolt open, allowing them access to the roof and the view, and for a moment he considered doing just that. Then he remembered their assignment and thought better of intruding on an area that someone obviously wanted to keep private.

He looked around. In the time between their last dead end and this one, Askon did not recall any place where they could have gone astray. Perhaps they had missed a turn somewhere.

Líana inspected the surrounding buildings, her purple hood casting a shadow over her eyes. "These look like the houses I saw in the half-elven quarter. Not very sturdy or well taken care of. Mostly deserted. I think I remember where this part of the city begins. If we just backtrack past the corner—"

"You'll not be backtrackin' anywhere, my dear," said a voice like a butcher's knife through a cut of meat. "Though I hear ladies as lovely as yourself do interesting things in the back rooms. That is, if you press 'em right."

The two hunched shadows had appeared behind them while Askon and the others focused on the building with the staircase. They wore black. Whatever their armor—probably layered cloth with cross-hatched stitching—it helped them to be virtually silent. Askon and Edward could move quietly in the trees, even undetectably if the conditions were right, but the creak of leather was always a risk. These men wore no leather, and they moved like it.

Líana stepped back toward Askon, Edward, and Morrowmen. The strangers kept their faces in the shadow of the overhanging buildings. Morrowmen smiled. "Get out of our way. You may pick merchants' pockets or even drive daggers into unsuspecting citizens, but we are four against your two. Live to steal another day, and stand aside."

The butcher's knife struck bone, pulled back, and sliced again into cold flesh. "See, if we was simple pickpockets, that'd be sound advice. But we ain't. And actually, pretty as your girl is there, I'm thinking a dagger in the back for you boys doesn't sound so bad. Then, when that's all done and over with," he made an obscene gesture, "we'll move on to her."

But Líana's sword already gleamed in the cloud-veiled sun. Askon and Edward followed suit.

Again the knife pulled back, this time going to the strop, the man's voice sharpening to a razor's edge. "With a sword like that at your side, you'll give the boys the wrong impression," he said to Líana, taking a step forward, out into the light. "They'll think you're a dangerous one. Tell ya the truth, it's the dangerous ones that make for the best stories the next morning."

Askon drew back, fighting against his instinct to unleash his fury upon the strangers. Morrowmen's lessons won out, and he put logic before emotion. They were still several feet away, the knife-talker and his friend. But, as the man had said, they were no simple thieves. On one shoulder, almost completely eclipsed by the fastener on the man's cowl, a thin stripe of red ran in a distinct pattern. Líana's eye might have caught the same detail, but Askon doubted it as he felt the quiet calm of the Time fragment settle over him. There on the black cloth, no more than the size of a large button, was Iramov's crimson bull.

The man in black stepped forward again, tracing every line of Líana's form with greedy eyes. He licked his lips slowly, a cruel dagger now visible in his hand. Askon watched his breath enter his chest, watched his mouth part. Whatever filth filled the man's mind would never leave his throat. The fragment's green glow stopped cold beneath cloth and leather. Askon effortlessly crossed the space between them and Iramov's assassins, then drove his blade full through the man with the butcher's knife voice. Askon ripped it free and sliced at the throat: once, twice for good measure. Then remembering the attack on Thomas's village and his overzealous use of the fragment's power, he restrained himself, letting the man fall to the ground. Soon the dust and sand mingled with blood.

They hit Edward first. He went down, stunned and limp in a heap on the ground. But Líana was there standing over him, sword to sword with another of the men in black. Horrified, Askon saw the truth. While he had been distracted by the dead man at his feet, no fewer than seven of the silent killers had descended the stairs from the rooftop, leapt the side-rail, and approached from behind.

Líana's blade arced like lightning, sending an opposing sword spinning into the street. She parried another blow, deflecting the edge so that the wielder buried it in the ground. Líana's sword slipped between his ribs and back out. She whirled around and put a foot in the first man's chest. Edward stirred below her. Askon looked back for the other man who had lingered in the shadows.

He had already gone for Morrowmen, a poor choice. With incredible speed, Morrowmen cracked his assailant with the knob-end of the walking stick before spinning it in his bony hands and driving the point straight into the man's temple. He retracted the cane and left the body lifeless in the street. Like a dark cloud, his robed form flowed over the paving stones as he ran to Edward's defense.

When Askon made his full rotation, he saw how Líana's battle had gone. The man she had kicked to the ground rose behind her. He wrapped a powerful arm about her waist and wrenched her in so that her backside pressed against him. She deflected another blow from one of the others and twisted right. The man pulled her back, lifted his knife and brought it down into the tissue around her collarbone.

"Líana!" Askon tried to shout. But it was too late. The street swirled around him, and he felt slow and dumb—an exhausted man swimming upstream just before he drowns. He fought the fragment, but the harder he struggled, the further it pulled him down.

The man wrenched the knife free and stabbed viciously into the bone. He jerked it back and forth. Líana shrieked in pain, a tortured cry of frantic terror. Time swirled by, Askon powerless to stop it, powerless to even move. She cried out again, weaker this time, and he could hear her tears. The man wrenched up on her waist with a laugh and the others stepped back. He shifted the knife again. Askon was paralyzed. Morrowmen had nearly closed the gap, but what was one old man against six armed killers? Edward writhed on the ground, his eyes opening and closing involuntarily.

The man wrenched at Líana's waist a second time, lifting her off the ground. He was enjoying himself. Then the thing was upon him, all knives and daggers, shimmering in a burst of blue and gray, screeching like a saw against steel, chill and fearsome. A howl of pain burst from the man's mouth as his face became awash with blood, and still the thing bit and tore and stabbed him. It was Marten.

With a roar, the man smashed his fists against the fluttering wings and flying talons that brutalized his face. In the brief pause, he peeled the bird off and slammed it against the ground ten feet away. Marten's wings flapped limply as he turned round and round.

The man's face was a bloody wreck: all meat and teeth and the leaking fluid of a punctured eye. He turned back to Líana who had fought against the other men as best she could. But she had not been able to stop every sword. Her armor had been slashed open along the arm. The knife still protruded from her collar, and she whimpered with each sword stroke. He stepped closer to her, reaching out with the same arm he had used to trap her before.

Her boot heel shot up hard into the place where his legs came together. He went down, hands over his groin, and died that way as Morrowmen's stick shot down into the red hole where his eye had been.

A clang echoed through the street and Morrowmen spun around. They had hit the hilt of the knife like a hammer on a nail. Líana went to her knees with a grunt and a sickly choking sound. One of the men grabbed her braid and twisted her around to face Askon. Another lay his own dagger to her exposed neck. She breathed frantically, afraid to move, her eyes wild. Morrowmen stopped.

Slowly, the dagger slid down, slicing through the leather straps that held Líana's armor in place. The chest piece fell loosely to her waist. Underneath, her thin dark shirt was soaked with sweat and dark patches of blood. The dagger hovered and the other hand came down on the opposite side. It cupped around her breast and squeezed. The man's mouth drew within a hairsbreadth of Líana's ear.

She tensed, eyes closed tight, yanked the knife free from her collarbone and shoved with all her weight up into the soft flesh beneath the man's chin, beneath the sickening sound of his breath. He twitched and wriggled convulsively, then was still. Morrowmen stepped toward Líana, but five sword points had already dotted her exposed back with red.

In a world cold and distant, Askon screamed and slashed, cursed and cried. But there was the beast, the creature with his face that hulked and snarled in the depths. It grinned at him in a terrible leer that fixed Askon on the spot. And it would not move.

Morrowmen knelt over Líana's body, crying, holding her hand. "No, no, no…" he kept saying. Out came the purple stone case, even with five swords hovering above his ancient skull of a face. He began to wave the stone over her body, but two of the men already had their hands around him, prying the old man's arms behind his back, dragging him away. He kicked and flailed violently. "No, no, no…"

A third joined them. "You're the one we're looking for, Morrowmen." He said something more, but Askon did not hear him. All he saw was the body, with its golden braid dappled in blood. And the beast with his face that would not let him go to her.

"Askon!" he heard Morrowmen call. "Do something, you fool."

Two men remained standing over Líana's body. Edward still lay beside her. "Are we taking the prince?" one of them said.

"Naw. Kill him and the other half-filth and let's go."

In his frozen torment, Askon screamed again. The beast tilted its head, pointed to Líana's limp form and the growing ring of red around it, then turned back to leer at him again. Tears streamed down Askon's face.

Beyond the beast, something sparkled. A sword. It shot up, slicing one man from navel to chin. It swirled through the air with merciless speed and power, burying itself nearly a foot into the shoulder of the second. It came free and circled around, taking off the head like a blossom dropping in a garden.

Edward looked down—all ice and stone, steel and cold fire—at Líana's body. He shuddered. Fifty feet up the street, back the way they had come, the last three of Iramov's men dragged Morrowmen kicking and twisting more weakly by the inch. One of them held the small stone case, gripping it as if it meant his life. The others pulled the old man frantically away from the risen prince.

Edward charged past Askon in a blur. The beast watched him go. The three men now carried Morrowmen over their shoulders, running flat out as he lay exhausted upon them. Edward neared. Thirty feet. Twenty. Ten. Then he stopped, stunned.

With a violent tremble, the old man's body spasmed, knocking Iramov's men into a stumble. The purple robes collapsed onto the surface of the street, limp and lifeless. The body beneath them burst into a million tiny motes of white dust.

Morrowmen, the only remaining man who could remember the coming of the elves, drifted peacefully away on the summer wind of the South Kingdom, his body and mind finally at rest.

CHAPTER TWENTY-NINE

Consequences

For a moment Edward did nothing more than stand there, mouth agape, staring at the pile of loose robes and drifting dust. Iramov's men bolted. Two steps later, Edward was in pursuit. He sprinted into the city's winding passages after them.

Meanwhile, an apathetic sun fringed the face of the beast. Askon stared back, exhausted, his shirt drenched in sweat. "Please," he begged through his agony. "Please!"

In a whirl of smoke and lingering malice, the beast was gone. Askon rushed to his sister's side. She did not move, and her skin was cold to the touch. Her face, still twisted in rage at her attacker, held its firm grip; it was the face of a fierce warrior, a dead warrior. He fell against her and the tears flowed. No beast, no fragments, no war mattered anymore. He had lost them all. Mother. Father. And now Líana too. Even Morrowmen, that vicious old crow of a man was gone.

To Askon, it seemed like hours before Edward returned. A void of velvet black drew in, blocking out hope, light, warmth. His whole world was nothing more than a broken man wailing in despair and a lifeless woman's body with a long golden braid. At first Askon listened: hoping for a heartbeat, faint and weak; hoping for the sound of breath; hoping for a pulse or color, but none came.

He shut the world out. Maybe he too could die here in the dust. If he willed it, he could end it all. Tolarenz was gone; his family was gone. For what reason should he continue?

Then the answer came, heavy and bright like a sword blade. He felt the beast in this answer; he saw its face, that vacant stare with eyes that were his own, but he didn't care. He would tear Iramov limb from mutilated limb or die in the effort. In his mind's eye, the beast grinned with insatiable hunger.

Askon reached into the neck of his shirt and pulled out the Time fragment. It pulsed its heartbeat rhythm as it had always done. Baring his teeth at its mockery, its promise of power and delivery of only sorrow, he squeezed the gem into his fist until he felt the setting pierce skin and draw blood. Then, ignoring the chiding voice of Morrowmen and the wisdom of Caled, Askon yanked hard on the silver chain.

But it did not break. The force of his effort jerked his head forward, and the chain dug into the skin on the back of his neck. Out of the corner of his eye, he saw a small lump at the side of the street. It flapped weakly, then lay quivering. Tears welled in dry sockets. He gazed down at his sister, dead. Trembling with rage and pain, he clenched his jaw, heard the teeth grate against one another, squeezed hard, and felt the gem slice farther into his palm. With everything he could muster, all the energy he had expelled against the fragment while under its power—every ounce—he flexed the muscles of his arm and neck, roaring in agony as the silver chain ripped free.

When he looked up, Edward was standing over him. He still clenched the jewel in his hand. Blood ran down the base of his palm and onto his wrist.

"She's still so beautiful," Edward said quietly. "Askon, I—"

Eyes like unnatural fire, one green and one blue, shot up to meet Edward's. "Iramov dies. Now!" He was screaming, wild, almost insane with grief. "And this?" He held up the fist with the fragment. "I'm done with it!" He let out a wail and threw the fragment as hard as he could into the building across the street. It pinged like a bell, landing next to the tremulous body of the fallen falcon.

"He may command death and darkness," Askon ranted. "But even the crimson bull must sleep. When he does, he will wake with my blade in his heart. The last face he sees will be that of a half-elf, and his screaming death will be our victory."

Edward said nothing, only stared at Líana's body. The ring of red had begun to soak into the cracks between the stones of Apopsé's street. And in places, around her lips and ears, she had grown pale with its going. Edward looked away. With a slow breath, he lifted his head, crossed the street and collected the fragment. He wobbled at its touch, nearly losing his balance, then righted himself. Marten still lay twitching in a pile of sand.

"You did well," Edward said to the bird. He opened the clasp on his cloak and cast it over Marten. Beneath the cloth there was a surge of movement, then stillness. Carefully, Edward wrapped the cloak around the falcon and lifted it like a sack over his shoulder. He turned to Askon. "I think you should carry her," he said.

With the fragment gone, there was nothing left to hold back the energy of Askon's anger. He lifted Líana's body as if she weighed no more than the bird wrapped in Edward's cloak. They left Iramov's men to the rats and the crows.

"We will not bury her," Askon said sadly as they carried their burdens back toward the palace. "I'll not have her in the ground under South Kingdom soil. A pyre, bright with heat and warmth. Then maybe her ashes might return to Tolarenz. But not until it is finished."

Again Edward said nothing, and Askon knew that his friend feared to question him. However, nothing would shift his decision. Iramov would die, and Askon would be the one to kill him. When it was over, he would return to see the pyre. Revenge would not bring Líana back, but it would bring an end to the Death fragment's destruction. And maybe then, Askon would find peace.

When they arrived at the palace, the guards quickly allowed them passage to Apopsé's main hall. Edward spoke little to them, and Askon not at all, but their faces turned white upon seeing what Askon carried. Through the silently sliding gate they went and up the several tiers of the garden. As they passed the benches on the top tier, Askon saw Edward's face shift from determination to sorrow before turning away.

They entered the main hall and found it empty. One of the doors at the far side opened, and Apopsé came sliding across the floor in his soft shoes. His hat sat askew on his head, the sky-blue Sight fragment pulsing at his brow. Tears ran down his round face.

"It's not true," he said to no one in particular. Then he saw her, lying limply over Askon's shoulder. The little man wheeled around and threw a wild punch up into Edward's face. "Prince of Vladvir!" he shouted. "What has all your military training done? Nothing."

Edward looked on, barely affected by Apopsé's outburst. To Askon it looked like he secretly hoped the little man would hit him again, as if he deserved it.

"Why didn't you protect her?" Apopsé went on, the tears breaking his speech now. "I would have given her a life of wine and sunset and ease and beauty and—"

"And she would have hated it!" Askon snapped, in no mood for Apopsé's sniveling.

"You," the little man growled. "It's probably your fault she's dead. Did you use the Time fragment? Or did you lose control of yourself once again?"

Askon wanted desperately to show Apopsé what it meant for him to lose control, but there was one thing he wanted more. He directed the anger inward, saving every bit for his grim errand.

"Where's Morrowmen?" Apopsé demanded. "We have some things to discuss. I'm not certain that the South Kingdom should be supporting either of—"

"Morrowmen is dead," Askon said flatly. "They took him. I watched it myself. They didn't kill him. He fought to get away. Then he just, died in a cloud of dust."

"I saw it as well," Edward added. "They took the Life fragment. And I wasn't able to catch up with them."

"Then what are we going to do?" Apopsé threw his hands in the air.

"First," said Askon, his voice low, "I need somewhere to lay my sister to rest. And also Marten. It is he who should be thanked most of all.

"I would see them placed on a pyre and kept until I return. I will not rest until Iramov is dead. If you should receive word that I have failed in the attempt, light the fire and wish their spirits a farewell for me."

"And how will you find Iramov?" Apopsé asked.

"You and your fragment are going to tell me."

Apopsé's eyes narrowed. "I don't know where he is. The Sight fragment conflicts with the Death fragment."

"I know," Askon rumbled. "But you can find John, and you can find Brâghda. They are hunting Iramov's men. Where they are, he will be close by."

"And if I refuse?"

"Then I kill you and pry the Sight fragment from your ruined face!"

Edward reached out with his free hand, feebly holding Askon back. Watching as the little man's face weighed his options, Askon saw the reluctant recognition settle upon it. Apopsé knew that

Askon was beyond reason, and that South City would be better off without him roaming within its walls.

Apopsé gave a curt nod. "Take Líana to your training grounds. My servants will build the pyre there. When you return, I will tell you where John and Brâghda are hiding. But they have not attacked Iramov openly before. What makes you think that they will now?"

Askon headed for the door which led to the training grounds. "Neither John nor Brâghda will know of my arrival or my plans. No one will. When Iramov is dead, and his fragment useless, the Darts of Grafmark will lay waste to his army." Askon wiped a bead of sweat from his brow, Líana's weight growing more and more apparent. "And Brâghda's fighters will kill all those who flee. They will never even cross your border, Lord Apopsé." He turned and carried Líana through the doorway. Edward followed quietly behind him.

Askon laid Líana's body on a bench outside of the guardhouse. In her left arm he placed her sword, its gentle curve arcing across her body from chest to hip. He placed her right arm in a similar position, one hand over the other. But it fell away loosely to the ground. He tried again, and it fell to the ground. After a third attempt, he put his hand to his face. He wanted it to be perfect. A proper arrangement for the gift the gods were about to receive. Did they know how precious the girl was who lay with one hand trailing in the dust? Could they see what had been lost? He leaned down, kissed her forehead, and said the word he had once forgotten.

"Goodbye."

As Askon walked slowly back to the main hall, Edward passed him with Marten still wrapped in the cloak. Unfurling the black cloth, he placed the bird just below Líana's sword-hand with wings outstretched and his body over the blade. Askon heard Edward begin to cry, heard him kiss her face hopelessly again and again. Each sound added to Askon's hatred for Iramov, strengthened his resolve to see his errand through to its end.

He did not see Edward place the ring into the palm of her right hand, did not see the prince place that hand across her chest, did not see it remain there, out of the dust and over the hand that held her sword.

"Where are they?" Askon demanded.

The little man with the frog's eyes glared at him. "If you reveal our allies' position, Iramov's army will be too large for us to defeat when he arrives here. Let John and Brâghda pick away at his numbers, and we have a much better chance of winning."

Askon wanted to reach across the table and strangle him. "I will not give away their position. And if I kill Iramov, there will be no battle at South City. Tell me where they are!"

Apopsé thumped his fingers down on a map which lay across the long table. He had led Askon through the same mechanical doors that they used on the first night in South City, now with Thomas's improvements. In the same room where Morrowmen told them of the Waterside Parchment and the battle of Dalkaldur, Apopsé would tell him how to find Iramov.

"When you took Líana to the, to—" he sighed. "When you took her away, I used the Sight fragment to find John and Brâghda. This," he indicated with his index finger, "is where Brâghda's forces are right now. And this," he lifted his middle finger and set it back down on the map, "is where the Darts of Grafmark are hiding. By tomorrow they should be," he slid his hand to the south an inch or two, "here."

"Thank you," said Askon. He reached out to shake Apopsé's hand. A scraping sound echoed in the long dining room, and the little man slid something across the table.

"Edward said you would need this."

There, its silver chain repaired and sparkling, lay the Time fragment. It pulsed green then darker green, mocking Askon, reminding him over and over of his failure.

"No." He slid it back. But in touching it, he felt the refreshing clarity he had first experienced in the hidden room of the Tolarenz town hall. His sight was sharper, his thoughts instantly more orderly. He let it go and shook his head. "No."

He took the map, folded it into a small square, and slid it into his shirt pocket. Saying goodbye to Apopsé, he headed out of the main hall and down toward his room to collect his gear. As he slipped through the door, he saw Thomas, Elise, and the others pass through the garden, obviously aware that something terrible had happened. Unable to face them, Askon stuffed his pack, grabbed the waterskins and other supplies, and silently opened one of the large windows at the far side of the room. He leapt through without a sound, the thin white curtains fluttering with his passing.

The stableboy was ready and surpassingly helpful when Askon arrived. A message from Apopsé, he assumed. A horse had been saddled and now awaited Askon's arrival with provisions for several days' worth of travel. Enough, he thought, to get there and return if his rations were spare. He threw the rest of his pack onto the horse, tightening buckles and clasps rapidly. Above all he needed to get out of the city. For the moment his anger had cooled, and he feared that any interruption might deter him from his course. So, with the saddlebags only loosely secured, he rode out from the palace grounds without looking back.

"Askon."

"Yes, Líana."

"It would be such fun to go to King's City without a hood or a cloak. Father says I should probably stay away from those places. I think I'd like to live in a city someday."

"Not everyone is as understanding as the people of Tolarenz."

"Do you think that they'll ever accept us?"

"No, Líana. They never will."

CHAPTER THIRTY

Revenge

Stone against steel. *Rasp, rasp, rasp.* Needles of green so deep they blurred to black. A wind whispering through the trunks and branches like the voices of the dead. Fluttering wings in the distance. A wolf howling far away. Crackling branches broken by creatures in passing. *Rasp, rasp, rasp.*

Alone, wrapped in the same needle-green, Askon huddled, silent but for the shearing hiss of grindstone against metal. He drew the blade to his face. Darkness was coming, and the moon glimmered on the surface of the steel. With one eye on the razor edge, he flipped the hilt, and the sword flickered out of the light. It returned, ready for the stone on the opposite side. Askon brought the two together, listening intently to the prelude to Iramov's death. *Rasp, rasp, rasp.*

"We of the elven blood believe that the sword is an extension of the self."

It was his father's voice. For days the voices had come and gone. First it was Líana: bits of advice he had given her, questions she had asked him, joys and sorrows they had shared. Then it was his mother: warm and loving, begging him to put an end to the blood and death. When, under cover of darkness, he had crossed back onto the Vladvir plain, it was Morrowmen: croaking commands, needlepoint critiques. On his first night in Grafmark, Caled's voice came and went: wise, calm, utterly controlled, all the things Askon was not. Now, on the sixth night under Grafmark's shadowed canopy, his father's voice came back. He put the stone again to the blade.

"Human instructors say this as well, I know. But the elves meant it. Not only is the sword the extension of the arm, the wrist, the hand, it is the extension of the soul, the man, the mind."

Rasp, rasp, rasp.

"You see, Askon, when you engage in battle with another warrior, the time will come when this steel must cause your opponent pain. Conflict does not always end in death, but to carry a sword and never kill is a rare thing."

Rasp, rasp, rasp.

"When this sword finally does what it was made to do, it will be only an extension of the man who wields it. Make no mistake. A sword can end the life of any man or beast you encounter, but when it is done, you will be the killer."

Rasp, rasp, rasp.

Askon eyed the blade again, the pale moon coursing up and down the metal. His face twitched in grim pleasure, not a smile, for happiness seemed farther away now than the howling wolves, more distant than the walls of South City, as far from him as the night when a single tear fell from the face of Alora, Breaker of Hearts. His face twitched again. His father was right. The sword would be an extension of the self. And though steel and leather and wire would separate them, it would be Askon who killed Iramov.

Truly, the sword was sharp before he had even begun to rake stone over steel, but in the quiet of Grafmark he had been forced to bide his time. The repetitive motion and constant reminder of purpose had become his sustenance. As much as food or water, the scraping of the grindstone nourished him in the dark. Slowly, as an artist might place the final line of paint on a finished canvas, Askon wiped the edge of the sword over his cloak and slid it into the scabbard.

Several hundred feet below, Iramov's army settled in to rest. It had been ten days since he left South City, since Iramov's assassins had cornered them in the street, since he had left Líana on the stone bench with her sword across her chest. Getting out of the South Kingdom had been easy, but finding the armies once inside Grafmark's stifling shadows was more difficult. Each of the allied groups had divided their numbers into three individual companies. They struck at intermittent times against Iramov's forces, generally by night, and never from the same place. After routing an unsuspecting pocket of soldiers, they slid back into the trees and vanished with hardly a trace.

But it had been enough for Askon. After a frustrating pair of days, he tracked a Norill raiding party as they attacked, then followed them into the depths of the forest. There, they met with a group of emissaries from the other companies who brought the news to their respective commanders. After that, locating all of the groups was only a matter of time. Askon simply waited for the current group to strike, then followed an emissary to the next, and so on.

To the best of his reckoning, they had traveled a significant distance south and almost equally east since he had demanded their locations from Apopsé. John and Brâghda were indeed slowing Iramov's progress, and his forces seemed undecided as to whether they should press on and leave the forest or remain to try and obliterate what was left of the Grafmark resistance. Askon had scouted the various locations of allies as well as enemies and scratched out a timetable based on how often the Grafmark forces attacked. Tonight would be his opening. According to his calculations, a Norill company to the northwest would strike Iramov just before nightfall the following evening. By then, Iramov would be dead, and the allies would never even know Askon had been there.

He felt confident he could return to the makeshift camp where his gear lay hidden beneath a crisscross of branches and ferns. Above him, a huge rock formation jutted from the forest canopy and into the night sky. When he had done his work, he would disappear into the forest and backtrack to the rock. He adjusted the final branch over his pack and descended the slope with footsteps quieter than the whispering trees.

Deftly he slid from shadow to moonlight and back again. The valley was a scattered collection of starved pines mixed with the towering behemoths of Grafmark's inner sanctuaries. He stalked the blackness, eyeing the flicker of torchlight where Iramov's watchmen stood guard. Stubble now grew thick on his cheeks—no razor had touched his face since the morning he set out to survey South City's walls—and he ran his fingers through the coarse hairs. He lifted the hood of his cloak and vanished, crouching further into the black. With closed eyes, he waited. And there it was. Behind the wall of his eyelids, the beast stared back at him, slavering and tremulous, snarling in the dark.

In the time he had spent surveilling Grafmark's forces he had also assessed Iramov's strategies. He knew that the central pavilion in which Lord Iramov took his counsels never changed position, whether by ignorance or arrogance. Unfortunately, it was indeed the central pavilion. Askon would have to slip past several watches before reaching the inner circle. Once there, he would have to improvise a way in.

The faraway wolf pack howled again, and Askon used the sound to creep closer to the outer watch. There were four guards at this station: two tall and slender, two hunched with knuckles near to dragging. It was said that Norill had night eyes to rival the elves, and so it seemed Iramov believed.

They stood in alternating positions: one man, one Norill, the second man, the second Norill. All of them wore armor with the crimson bull. For a moment Askon watched to see what they would do. None of them spoke. He leaned closer, angling his head for a different perspective. They were very still. Then as puppets on the string, they moved simultaneously fifteen feet to one side.

Askon pressed forward, drawing nearer than he had intended, in an attempt to see how the watchers had moved together so well without an audible command. Codard's army valued such synchronicity, but the commands to trigger position changes were always spoken aloud. These had moved without a sound.

When they came to a halt, he knew. Each of them, one after the other, fell mechanically into place like levers in one of Apopsé's doors. They stared out into the trees. Never in his life would Askon forget that stare: vacant, gaping, as though mind had been disconnected from body. It was the stare of the dead. Victor, Patrick, and Christopher had all worn the same blank, emotionless gaze when he saw them in the flash of lightning outside Dalstone. Askon had never seen the men who guarded Iramov's camp before, but the empty-eyed stare was the same.

Only this time, there was no fragment to slow him down. All his plans to slip silently into the camp without causing a disturbance burst inside him like a bubble surfacing on a still pond. The beast needed to feed; Askon would be its fangs.

Staying low, he drew his sword in one hand and the long hunting knife in the other. He would have to be quick; such abominations could not be allowed to stand. On soundless feet he floated past their vacant eyes and around behind them. Out of the darkness, he loomed up and brought both blades down into the backs of the leftmost watchers. They fell heavily, almost in relief. He kept his grip, and the blades slid out of the fallen bodies. He rounded and took the head off the Norill watcher nearest him and drove the knife into the last man's heart. Again they fell like stones.

Into the shadows he went again, all but invisible in his cloak, just beyond the torchlight's reach. He breathed deep, allowing his eyes to close as he relished the first step toward revenge. Behind his eyelids, again, was the beast, hulking and bristling, hungry for more. When he opened his eyes, he gasped. At the edge of the camp, four watchers stood as though he had never even been there: one man, one Norill, another man, and a Norill body standing headless in the moonlight.

Askon gaped and looked about frantically. No blood was on either blade. All along the perimeter of Iramov's army, watches like this one had been set. Had he been any louder in his attack, the two nearest this one would certainly have heard it. Were they all like this? Were they all the watches of the dead? He didn't have time to answer.

A cacophony arose at the watch two stations away from his. With eerie precision, the four watchers Askon had just killed turned simultaneously toward the sound. They stared their empty-eyed stare and charged off into the darkness. Other groups were rising from their rest. Whether the dead slept or not, Askon did not know. Some of those awaking had soulless eyes, while others were ordinary men responding to the sound of the alarm. Contrary to Askon's predictions, his Grafmark allies were on the attack.

The camp swirled like a disturbed beehive. Amongst dozens of enemies, Askon could not tell whether it was Brâghda's forces or John's that struck the nearby watch. Whoever it was did not do so quietly. Capitalizing on the opportunity, Askon used the commotion to cover his movements farther into the camp.

Then the second force collided with Iramov's army. Askon whirled around, almost giving up his position. A large number of

John's Darts came smashing into the camp two stations in the other direction. The tactic was new, and seemed to disorient the enemy even further. They ran this way and that, some to defend the first attack, others the second. With a strange misgiving, Askon turned back to his target. Past a row of low tents that gave way to larger and larger pavilions, he saw Iramov's quarters. Lights flickered within, and Askon thought he saw shadows moving in the glow. He crept along, moving closer, when a heavy footfall sounded behind him.

"What? Ya think yer so quiet and subtle as to prowl 'round my forest an' me not know it?" A hand yanked Askon around. "Well? Whatta ya got to say for yerself?"

"I—John?"

"Yeah, who else would it be?" John stood over him in full armor, the tree and quarrel bright on his chest. In the time since Askon had left him waving on the dock by the Grafdrek, a curling brush of black beard had sprouted from his chin. He might've been mistaken for a bear. He hunched down next to Askon.

"Alright," he said. "We've had eyes on ya since ya got here. Figured you didn't want to alert us so we didn't alert you. But now we got a hell of a mess on our hands. Yer plan better be good."

"My plan is that I sneak in and kill Iramov, then disappear without any of you ever knowing otherwise."

"Well that's a stupid plan. And it doesn't seem to have worked very well. Ya think this army's gonna stop soon as you put Iramov to the sword? Better think again. They got their orders now. There's no stoppin' 'em till they break right through Apopsé's door."

"What do you mean?"

"Simple. You saw it when ya hacked up those guards back there. They're dead as dead 'fore ya even get to 'em, and then they're live as live fast as ya can pull yer blade back out. It ain't right. But we been seein' it now for weeks. Once they get their orders, they don't flinch from 'em, not one bit. An' I'll tell ya what. If they don't keep on with it after you run a knife through Iramov's ribcage, I'm a gods damned Norill."

The battle cries rose and fell now, drawing into the distance. Askon lifted his head, turning it left and right, listening.

"They're backing away," Askon said. "I need to go now."

"Damn right ya do. Course, even though ya only gave me command when ya had nobody left that was better, I got this rabble in line. We should be able to get in there and out before Iramov's dead-faces even get back. Brâghda's got an ambush waitin' for 'em in the trees. She'll keep 'em busy."

John looked Askon up and down.

"You look a right mess. No time for it now. Where's that little trinket o' yours?"

Askon stared back, imagining that his eyes probably looked as vacant as those of the "dead-faces," as John had called them. He cast his eyes to the ground. Inside him the beast pounded against its cage, ready to capture its prey.

"It's not here," Askon said, scowling.

John was not amused. "This is no time to be jokin' around, Askon. Where's the fragment?"

"I left the cursed thing in South City. Go get it there if you want it!" he shouted.

For a moment, John looked wounded and confused. Then his face changed to hardened determination. "Right. Well, it may have saved Brâghda, but the damn thing never saved me. We can kill that bald, murderin' bastard with steel as easy as stone. Yer gonna have to tell me why ya left it when this is over, though. Hear me?"

"I hear you," Askon said gratefully. "And thanks."

"Somebody's gotta pull yer half-elf ass outta the fire."

CHAPTER THIRTY-ONE
The Beast

The sounds of battle grew distant as they followed the line of tents. They heard Brâghda spring the trap. A war cry rose and fell. The outer ring of the camp had nearly emptied when the Grafmark forces crashed in from the surrounding trees. Now the wide space felt deserted and all too quiet. Inside, patrols of guards stood ready for any threat; spears, swords, and nocked arrows glinted in the torchlight.

Askon led John around the inner circle, moving from shadow to shadow. All attention was directed toward the Darts' attacks and Brâghda's ambushes. Once inside, they made their move. The guards stationed around Iramov's pavilion were not the mindless dead; they were men, battle hardened and eager to defend their leader. But even the most grizzled veteran can be distracted, and John's plan had done just that. They watched warily the south side of the camp where the Grafmark allies had struck only a few minutes before. They saw neither the deep green hood nor the curling black beard approach from behind.

John's fist victim struggled, but he held the guard's mouth with an armored wrist. Askon's kill fell to the ground, the man's neck laid open by the long knife. In they went, drawing ever closer to the backside of the pavilion. Only two guards remained, both of them in heavy armor with shining metal plates at the shoulders and glimmering helms of polished steel. John motioned with his hands, and Askon nodded in response. With a silent count of three, Askon stepped up behind the guard and grabbed his helmet. Feeling the power of the beast within him, Askon twisted viciously, snapping the man's neck. The body fell limp as a fish into the trampled fern and brush. John's did the same, but the guard's spear stood fixedly a moment too long. Askon watched John's eyes widen as the shaft wobbled and fell onto the body of its wielder.

The head of the spear rang against the helmet. Askon flinched. John froze in place, but it was too late. The five remaining guards turned to face the sound.

And then John was out in the torchlight, openly brandishing his sword in one hand and the guard's fallen spear in the other. He sneered at them. They closed in on him. He stepped back, one step, then two. With a glance to Askon, he bared his teeth and plunged into the darkness. The guards followed, wary of an ambush.

Askon surged ahead, blocking out the thoughts that beat against his consciousness. Certainly five armed soldiers were too many for John to fight by himself. Were there more guards waiting in the darkness? But Iramov was too close. Askon tightened his grip around his sword hilt.

"The sword is an extension of the self."

The thick canvas of Iramov's tent was heavier than Askon would have imagined. A great deal of extra fabric lay piled on the ground, and Askon was forced to move through it in sections. Under the folds the world was entirely dark, and the beast loomed before his eyes, licking its lips greedily. Before he knew it, he was on the other side.

Light filled the tent. A table had been set on one side, with plates and forks and cups, as if Iramov had plans to entertain dinner guests. On the other side, a collapsible bed stood neatly made with blankets Askon recognized from the Dalstone sleeping quarters. A round glass lamp, very rare and exceedingly expensive, sat glowing on a second table. There, it seemed, Iramov tended his strategies, though it was not a cluster of papers and quills. Instead, one map of Grafmark lay perfectly flat with one quill and a small ink bottle. The map had been marked to oblivion, almost totally covered in black where Iramov had indicated locations for the Grafmark forces then scribbled them out.

The space inside the tent was large, larger in fact than the living room and kitchen of Askon's home in Tolarenz. Narrow poles dotted the interior where soldiers or captured servants had driven them into the ground to hold up the pavilion's canopy. Twenty feet from where Askon crouched near the eerily tidy dinner table, Iramov stood in the doorway. The moonlight ringed his shiny bald head and wiry body. Around his neck the blood-red sash trailed down below his belt, rippling in the shifting air. He gazed out into the night, listening to the sounds of the distant battle. In his hand the long black staff rose up from the ground. At its tip, the Death fragment pulsed red as a living heart.

Silently, Askon glared across the inside of the tent. He needed no beast now, though he felt it clinging and heaving against his shoulders, quivering with excitement at the coming kill. In his mind a series of flashes swept by: warm blue eyes that saw into one's soul, practiced hands clipping tiny trees, a grinning smile like a skin-wrapped skull, a falcon on the wing, and a long golden braid.

Chaos and rage, trembling fury, and—at the heart of it—the screaming sadness of irreparable pain exploded upon Askon's consciousness. He was flying across the empty space toward the bald head. His sword gleamed in the light of the glass lamp, and the knife angled straight for his enemy's heart. Was he shouting? Askon didn't know. Was he crying? If he was, he felt no tears. With the beast guiding his body in all its fearsome, seething power, and with all his sorrow driving the blades, Askon slashed down into Iramov's back.

"Hello Askon, whelp of Tolarenz." The voice cooed, a fringe of sneering disgust writhing beneath the surface.

Askon looked up and found his weapons driven fully into the soil at Iramov's feet, the knife all the way to the hilt and the sword halfway down the blade. The light had gone out.

"You don't even have the Time fragment do you?" Iramov crooned. "You fool."

Askon yanked on the sword with both hands, leaving the knife buried in the dirt. "I'll kill you!" he screamed, swirling the blade around his head in a wide, powerful arc. The beast roared with him.

"Hm," Iramov hummed as the blade circled around and chopped down into the earth again. "Will you?"

Askon tried to rise, but the crushing weight of the Death fragment came down upon him, forcing him to his knees.

"I think not. You seem so very angry about it all," Iramov said with a smile. "Anger is my domain, hatred my instrument. Didn't you know?" He kicked Askon hard in the face. Blood burst from Askon's nose and ran down into the trampled grass. He fell to one side.

"Oh that won't do. Get up, whelp of Tolarenz. At least your cur of a mentor stood and faced me."

As if pulled by heavy cords, Askon felt himself lifted bodily from the ground and set again on his feet. Iramov's brow had furrowed, but his mouth betrayed his enjoyment, a cat toying with a flailing mouse. Behind him in the darkness, the beast had lugged its bulk. And there, Askon realized the beast had never been his ally, could never be at all. Another series of images flashed before him: the king's throne room, the Greyarc bridge, the trees outside the Dalstone meeting hall, the fight against his sister in Morrowmen's camp, the old man's horrible attack on his shoulder, and finally the street in South City where they had killed Líana. They all had one thing in common: the beast was there. Even if he hadn't known it at the time, the beast was always there.

"Oh dear," said Iramov. "It seems he finally understands. All it took was a little push from this." He waved the pulsing red fragment, and the world swayed dizzily before Askon's eyes. The staff swung around and smashed into Askon's stomach, a blow that should have sent him sprawling. Yet he remained upright, fixed in place by the pulsing red gem wrapped in empty darkness.

"It hurts, doesn't it?" Iramov purred. "Well, I have to have a little fun with the last vermin left in all of Vladvir." He brought the staff around, slamming it into Askon's side.

"Not the last," Askon choked. "There are more."

"Ha!" Iramov cackled. "They'll be of no more resistance than the ones in your precious Tolarenz. When I have all the fragments, I will wash them away as the Scouring should have done before you were even born." The heat in his voice climbed higher.

"How stupid of you to leave the Time fragment behind. So much for the cleverness of the elves! Caled was a clever one, but he was human, only wishing he was of the filthy invaders' blood. For a while I thought that worthless scepter was the Time fragment. Even mutts show cleverness from time to time." He raised the staff, and the weight of the darkness grew, pressing Askon to the ground. Around him, moonlight, torchlight, all was blackness. It stretched out infinitely into the empty void. Before his eyes, Iramov and the beast stared down at him, their faces bathed in the Death fragment's red glow.

"The cleverness of the elves saved us all!" Iramov mocked, his tremulous voice climbing higher. "That's what Morrowmen would have told you. 'Without them, we'd all be dead.' But they didn't save us, they shackled us! It was their advice that warned not to use the fragments to our advantage. The things we could have done with such power. The things we could still do!"

With every word, the darkness grew heavier. Askon struggled to breathe. No longer did he desire to kill this man, only to run, to escape the horrible, empty, soundless darkness.

Iramov's face twisted into a grin. "When I have the five fragments, no one will stop me. We will see how clever the elves are when my army marches through into their world with limitless power at my fingertips. Alora's Tear brought them here; it can take me there. And when it does, more than just the elves of Vladvir will die." He reached down and lifted Askon's chin. "Oh, I hear that my men got to try out your little sister. The elf women always were good for at least one thing."

Powerless to move and barely able to breathe, Askon stared past Iramov into the eyes of the beast. The words should have pained him, caused him grief and rage, fed the creature that lived inside him. But they did not. Líana was gone, free from Iramov's threats, free from pain and sadness and torment. His words could harm her no more. And so Askon sucked in a shuddering breath and awaited Iramov's wrath.

"What?!" Iramov cried. "No affection for the sister you lost, whelp? Or was she just another bitch in your pack of dogs?"

The words cut deep, but he knew that for better or worse Líana was safe from Iramov's hate. He stared up into the madman's frantic eyes, the bald head beading with sweat, the fragment growing brighter in the black.

"Speak you rat, you trash, you piece of filth!" Iramov screamed, his voice climbing again, vaulting to a piercing screech.

Then he turned, and the staff shot into the air. For a moment, like a lightning flash, the darkness lifted and a sword cut down through the moonlight. It was John. His beard was matted, and blood streaked his arms, but he swung with the weight of all his strength.

The blade dug deep into the fire-hardened staff, and Askon seized the moment. He tackled Iramov, not taking the time to wrench either of his weapons free. The staff snapped as Iramov leaned against it, then clattered to the ground.

"Kill him, John!" Askon shouted, and John lifted his sword high above his head, bringing it down as a woodsman splits the block. But it never touched the insane face and bald head.

"Back down where you belong," he keened. The staff had fallen, but not all the way out of his grasp. Now the darkness swooped in like an iron carrion bird, its wicked talons crushing their faces into the earth beneath the tent. But all that was gone once again. Empty blackness reached out forever, eclipsing Grafmark, eclipsing Vladvir, Askon and John little more than tiny specks under the weight of the universe.

"No more!" shouted Iramov, his staff wobbling crazily in his hand, its foot hacked off by John's sword. "Now you die!" With a final heaving press, the darkness became complete. In the distance a wall of white rose up on the horizon. He knew that light. When it reached them, nothing would remain but a circle of white powder and a memory of who they had once been. In the flash that rolled like a tumbling wave, Askon saw Iramov, sash swirling about him, a blood soaked flag about his pale neck, his eyes wild with power and twisted delight. The light rushed toward them.

Then Iramov's form began to blur, to shiver as if through smoked glass. He looked from side to side. The light dimmed slightly. Iramov's body rippled, for a moment looking like a reflection on water. Askon met his eyes, and they narrowed to slits. Then Iramov and his swirling sash faded from view. He shouted something and raised the staff. The wave of light brightened for an instant, then went out entirely.

The pavilion was empty.

CHAPTER THIRTY-TWO
Before the Storm

Catapults lined the wall, Thomas's work. Ranks of bows that armed and rearmed themselves covered the rest of the defenses: one firing mechanism for thirty arrows. Along either side of the main gate were his crowning achievements: huge ballistae that, using the same rearming mechanic, could fire arrows as large as tree trunks within a few moments of one another. Each shaft might kill dozens of the enemy or destroy large siege engines.

Codard's men had first been spotted at the confluence of the Grafdrek and the Estelle. The guards were under strict orders to destroy the bridge before Codard's forces arrived, but they were also awaiting the Grafmark warriors, if any escaped the forest. In so doing, Codard took the bridge, appearing seemingly out of nowhere with his men, killing the guards, and crossing into the South Kingdom virtually unchecked. They settled around a grove of trees, the same grove where Morrowmen's company had camped for the night before first leading Askon and his friends into South City. If John and Brâghda were coming, the lines of communication had already been cut; they would arrive or they would not. It was that simple.

At first Edward had been reluctant to help Lord Apopsé with any preparations, military, defensive, or otherwise. The little man with the frog's eyes had berated him at every turn, blaming him for Líana's death, blaming him for Morrowmen's death, blaming him for Askon's sudden departure and likely death. But then Thomas had come along, and with his simple, unassailable logic, had convinced Edward that there was no better place for the prince of Vladvir to be than within South City's walls.

"That's where the people are," Thomas had said. "Your father calls himself the king, and Apopsé is only brave enough to take the title of lord. That means you will be king when we defeat Iramov and your father. Protect the people from a place of strength. Show them who you are."

And of course, he was right. What option did Edward have, even if he did decide to leave. Askon was long gone. By now he was probably stalking Iramov's encampment, or had already moved against him. No messages had come from the north, and they knew not whether Askon would succeed or fail. So Edward began the simple task of preparing the troops. It was what he had been trained to do. Leading soldiers had been his focus for nearly all of his adult life, and now he would use that training again. By the time Thomas had finished construction on his defensive contraptions, Edward had schooled an army in the enemy's tactics. They knew them inside and out. Unless Codard implemented new strategies, the South

Kingdom defenders could anticipate and counter every move the king's army would make against them.

On the first day, Edward had balked at Elise's involvement, but now she swung a sword as comfortably as any but the most practiced of soldiers. Her style was different, much more like Líana's and thus, more like Askon's than Edward's, yet she managed to defeat a great many of Apopsé's defenders in sparring matches. The initial victories came as the men fought reluctantly against a woman. In the end though, they held nothing back and still—on multiple accounts—found themselves defeated.

They were as ready as the South Kingdom could be, but the news continued to worsen. Edward stood on the wall looking out into the fields. Fires burned there, destroying the crops that would feed them through the winter. Stores were plentiful in South City, but farmers from all around had headed for the safety of its walls when Codard's men appeared. Now, two banners had been spotted looming on the horizon. From his vantage, Edward could not make them out, though Askon would have been able to. Sometime in the night, Iramov had joined them, and now the might of both armies stood at the ready. It would begin soon. Edward hoped the defenses would be enough.

Thomas approached with Elise in tow. He carried an armful of bread and cheese, some fruit, and a skin of wine. Looking out at the gathered host, he offered the meal to Edward.

"If battle comes today, it comes today," Thomas said.

"The world is how it is," echoed Elise. "The least we can do is enjoy one another's company. Whatever happens, Vladvir and the South Kingdom will be very different. There is no stopping it now."

Edward smashed his boot against the warm stones of the wall, his knuckles white on the rail. "We should be with Askon," he said, under his breath, "not standing here waiting for my father and Iramov to crush us. At least Askon took action. What did we do?"

Thomas motioned for him to sit. "We did everything we could to give Apopsé's forces the best chance of survival. You know, I hear that some of the refugees are actually from all the way up in the Vladvir plain. They heard that you had made your way here, and they've come to rally around you."

Edward sighed. "I'm sure they are wonderful farmers and clothiers and blacksmiths, but they aren't soldiers. If we want to win, we need more men who can fight."

Elise finished a mouthful. "Or women."

Edward turned his face downward. "Or women," he said quietly. It had been days since he had visited the training grounds; he found it too painful to bear. Initially he promised himself that nothing would keep him away, that he would visit her every day until the pyre was lit. And he did for a few. But seeing that face again and again, lifeless, was too much even for Edward's strong will. No carrion birds disturbed her—thank the gods—and no decay took away from her splendor. Even on the third day she looked exactly as she had when Askon had placed her on the stone bench.

For a while they continued, talking of the preparations and the successes that the South Kingdom forces had achieved in such a short span of time. But soon the food was gone, the wineskin empty. Thomas and Elise arose and went back down the scaffolded steps of the wall. Edward stayed at his post. They promised to come see him again that evening, but Edward knew that by then the enemy would be on the move.

They rode hard, thundering hoofbeats pounding beneath them, hour upon exhausting hour. Numbering half a hundred, the spearhead of Grafmark's forces outpaced the main column by more and more. When they had set out after their most recent hour-long rest, they judged Brâghda and the Darts, all on foot, to be a day behind. When they crossed the confluence, the evidence was clear. Codard had already been through, decimating the small contingent of retainers on the bridge. Without looking back, they rode on.

Askon found it refreshing, to ride without looking ahead or behind, to spur the animal to its limits and feel the wind on his face. Nothing held him back now. The weight of his revenge had lifted, shattered by his folly in Iramov's pavilion. The beast, he had left there to rot, whether it willed it or no. Askon would be a slave to its anger and hatred no longer. He kicked the spurs and rubbed the horse's neck, urging it forward.

Askon had never seen an army reassemble so quickly as had the Grafmark allies. The forest Askon had taken days to navigate, the Darts and Grafmark Norill slipped through like water in a channel. Within hours Brâghda had led them out. All of the horses in the

Grafmark army, save a handful, were collected and given to men handpicked by John. Those fifty would ride for South City, hoping to reach it in time with their steel as well as their message: help was on its way.

Askon's plan relied on Codard's army needing time to rest and prepare. He and John knew that Iramov's puppets needed no such luxuries. When the bald man and the Death fragment had vanished, so had nearly his entire force. The camp had become instantly empty with only a hundred or so men left behind who surrendered or fought to their deaths. From the captured soldiers Askon was able to learn that all the rest, those who had vanished with their leader, were dead-faces, as John called the warriors who had once been killed but now walked again amongst the living. Askon's best guess led him to assume Codard and the Space fragment were somehow involved in the disappearance, the shimmer and suddenness all too similar to Christopher's arrival in Shale. If they were right, Codard's timing had been exceptional whether intentional or not.

During the ride, Askon had entertained a theory about the dead men. As Iramov fought battles across Vladvir, his men took casualties, but when they fell, he turned them into the empty-eyed shell-people that now made up the entirety of his force. They went down easily enough, Askon had tested that against the watchmen. Unfortunately, they did not stay down. After they were turned, the dead men rose again and again to fight, regardless of mutilation, decapitation, whatever. Askon guessed that the dead men also made Iramov more difficult to track using the Sight fragment. At first, he had appeared as a small blackness within Apopsé's sky-blue gem, but slowly that blackness spread. Because the dead men were constructs of the Death fragment, Askon guessed, so would they expand the area which Apopsé could not see.

But none of this did them any good if they didn't arrive in time to tell Apopsé, to alert all of the South Kingdom. When the combined forces of Iramov and Codard struck the white walls, Askon's friends would be unaware of their danger. And there was something else, but Askon wanted another mind with which he could confer. He mulled the thought over, considering the possibilities, and waited for the next break. The wind lifted his hood, flapping it against his back, and the hoofbeats pounded on.

They watered the horses at a stream a few hours' ride north of the clump of trees where Codard had made his camp. They did not know it, but guessed rightly that Iramov was there too, his army of dead men ready as soon as Codard gave the word. Askon gulped at the stream, splashing his face with the cool water.

"How do ya know if there'll even be a South City left standin' when we get back?" John asked, running his fingers through his thick beard. Shining droplets dribbled out of the black coils and over his hands.

"They have a secret weapon," Askon said with a wink.

John scrubbed his face. "What. Apopsé's fragment? You said yerself it doesn't do him any good against our bald friend."

"Not the Sight fragment."

"Then what?"

Askon paused, a smile spreading over his face. His beard too had grown in, though the hairs were sparse and straight, unlike John's. Were he to survive the battle, he vowed to shave it clean. John was impatient.

"What's the secret?"

"Thomas."

Anticipating the laughter, Askon sat back as John proceeded to turn red in the face, chuckling and chortling until he gasped for air. Tears squeezed into his eyes and would have dripped down his cheeks if not for the beard. Just as Askon thought it had come to an end, the laughter overpowered his friend again, and John rolled and twisted in the high grass that lined the stream. When he finally stopped in a shuddering heap, he turned to Askon.

"You're like to kill a man with a joke like that. Our boy who spent the ride to Austgæta fallin' off his horse? The stu-stu-stutterin' stamerin' kid fresh outta training? Doesn't he have a woman to tend to these days?"

Askon grinned. "He does. And last I saw, she might even give you a second or third round in the practice ring if Líana's lessons sunk in."

John stopped cold. "Líana? You mean your sister? Askon, she's a ten-year-old girl. Even if she were alive, how could she teach anybody—"

"It's a long tale. But I'll tell you this. Líana is gone. No one can hurt her anymore. Whether or not you believe it, she taught Elise how to fight as well as anyone I've ever trained. As long as Edward hasn't taught her too much out of the king's book, Elise will be a formidable ally. And I'd hate to have her as an enemy. So, I guess that makes two secret weapons."

"I guess it does." John stood up and went back to his horse. Only one leg remained in their journey to the South City gates. How they would enter once they arrived, Askon had not yet decided. He hoped that behind the city there was a second entry of some kind. By the time they reached Apopsé, little chance remained that they would be able to enter by way of the main gate.

"John wait," Askon called. "Before we head out, there's something that's been on my mind since we left Grafmark." Askon led his own horse over to John's. The animals were exhausted, still breathing heavily even after nearly an hour's rest.

"Better get it out now. Ya might not have another chance."

"My thoughts exactly," Askon said. "Before we left, I told you about Morrowmen. I left out my sister to make it easier for you to understand."

"What, you don't trust my reasonin' skills?"

Askon smiled. John could make light of almost anything. "Morrowmen had the Life fragment, it does just what you'd expect. It heals people of any injury you can imagine. When we were attacked in the South City street, Iramov's men took Morrowmen and his fragment. They didn't know I had one. No one would have, for all the good it did us. Morrowmen died, but Edward never found Iramov's men in order to retrieve the fragment."

"Which means that now Iramov has both Life and Death." John nodded, rubbing the black scruff on his face.

"Right," Askon replied. "But he didn't mention it when he had me under the Death fragment's power. Doesn't that seem like something he would flaunt in our faces? He assumed we knew that he intends to take Codard's fragment as soon as the battle is won and that he'll take Apopsé's when he defeats him, but if he already had the Life fragment, why not say so?"

"Maybe his men never made it to him," John offered. It was a weak suggestion, but his options were limited. He tightened the straps on his saddle, checking them twice.

"That could be. But if so, the fragment is lost."

"Then where is it?"

"I don't know." Askon attended his saddle in much the same fashion as John had. He tightened the straps and patted the horse on the neck. "One of our pieces is askew on the board, and I'm fairly certain it's the Life fragment."

John laughed. "Well, game board pieces, or magical bits of lovestruck fairytale tears, makes no difference to me. If we don't get inside that wall, and get you to that jewelry of yours, we're all as good as dead. Even then, I'd call it questionable. Let's go."

Askon smiled, glad to once again have John at his side. He vaulted into the saddle and spurred the horse. Soon fifty sets of hoofbeats pounded the turf toward South City. Behind them, trudging along more than a day behind, were Brâghda and the rest of Grafmark's warriors.

Thomas and Elise never came back. Upon the distant mountains, the fringe of the world, the sun scattered the final beams of daylight. Edward's shadow sprawled before him, climbed the rail of the wall, and spilled out into nothing. Smoke churned up from the fields, here in spindly wisps, there in great roiling gouts; even with a victory, the South Kingdom would still be in danger. He paced the wall as he had done a thousand times since morning, waiting.

Across the rolling hills and burning fields, the enemy too seemed to be waiting. Edward doubted that his father had much control over Iramov at this point, but the Lord of the crimson bull would not have postponed the attack. The king however—cautious to a fault—might delay for days merely on the anxiety of coming battle. Edward was certain that it wouldn't be that long. And there was something else.

An hour earlier, one of the watchers had approached him breathlessly. "Your highness," he said. "A force has broken away from the main body of the enemy. They're moving quickly around our right flank."

"Are the defenses prepared?"

"As well as they can be, sir."

Their right flank was the southernmost part of the city. There, the wall was lower, maybe twenty feet lower, but much too high to climb. Inside, the half-elven quarter abutted the outer defenses. The shacks and run-down buildings huddled closely there, many of them actually touching one another on one or both sides. There was a small gate with a portcullis that ratcheted up to allow entry and exit from the city. Even wide open, it would be of little use to an army. So why send what looked to be a scouting party to that entry point? The left flank was always the most difficult to defend. Rarely did an army attack the right first. A feint? Exploiting the common knowledge of a left-side-first attack? Edward struggled to identify the strategy.

"Alert the half-elven quarter to either evacuate or prepare to defend their homes," he commanded.

"Couldn't someone else go talk to—to them?" the watchman said with an uncomfortable look. "A servant, or another one of their own?"

"Do it now!" Edward shouted, his gray eyes sharp as the sword on his hip. Now was not the time for petty differences. The watchman sprinted down the scaffolded stairs and into the street out of sight.

Edward swung around and strode across the wall, heading south. He passed over the giant mechanical gate and past two of the ballistae Thomas had designed. Between them a row of the automatically firing bows stood with arrows nocked to the string, a clockwork regiment. Beyond the second ballista, Edward climbed one of the forward-facing wall's three turrets. He leapt up the stairs, two at a time through the shadowy interior, and emerged atop the tower through an opening in the floor. Two watchmen waited there for the return of the third who now ran through South City's streets toward the half-elven quarter.

"Show me the splinter force," Edward said to the man nearest him. He was one of the king's personal guards, his tall white feather bronzed by the sunset.

"They're making very good time, your highness," the man said, pointing to a dark blotch moving through the city's lengthening shadow. "I'd give them little more than an hour before they reach the wall."

"Have you taken this to Apopsé?"

"Of course. What do you think they're doing?"

"I don't know," Edward said thoughtfully. "I don't know."

A quarter hour later, the soft padding of slippered feet peppered the tower stairs. Edward was still watching the black shape move across the rolling hills to the south. Unable to slide over the stones as he was accustomed in the palace, Apopsé instead stumped along awkwardly, his feet stubbing into the ground with a scrape at each step. His hat was fixed securely on his head with a sliding clasp wrought from the bone or tooth of some great beast. Under the wide brim, Edward knew that the Sight fragment glowed steadily, but its light was hidden.

"It seems all our incessant preparations did little to assuage our danger," Apopsé lisped with the same slithering sibilance he had used when they first met.

"Why is that, Lord Apopsé?"

With the tip of his soft shoe, the little man kicked a box over to the edge of the guardrail and stood atop it. The increase in height put Edward off balance, though even with the assistance Apopsé stood several inches shorter than the prince. One of the flowing sleeves shot out into the darkening air. "That. That is why."

Edward frowned. "We don't know yet what they mean to do with such a small group," he said. "Maybe they're trying to divert our attention to—"

"Or maybe you've failed again, dear prince!" Apopsé spat the final word over the barrier where the sheer stone tower dropped thirty feet to the top of the wall and down another hundred to the ground below. "Ever since you set foot in South City, we've had nothing but grief and miserable defeat at every turn."

There was no denying Apopsé's assertions, and Edward elected not to argue his own virtues. It was a discussion the lord of the South Kingdom and the prince of Vladvir had played out time and again since Líana and Morrowmen had been lost in the streets. Edward knew that if he challenged Apopsé, he would only fracture the alliance between the citizens of the South Kingdom and the refugees from Vladvir. So he held his tongue, biding his time. Perhaps when the battle was over he would press Apopsé for the respect his efforts deserved, but not now. Instead, he turned to the man standing on the box and said, "What would you have me do?"

The frog's-face curled up into a squinting smile, beads of sweat forming a slick sheen over round cheeks and wide brow. "That's just what I wanted to hear." He wagged a finger, the arm still pointing out into the southern hills. His billowing sleeve rippled in the air above the city. "Go meet them. You have some experience with the half-elves. Take any who will fight and meet this threat head-on. If we can capture them, we might question them and learn the purpose of our enemy's strategy."

"Or it could be exactly what they want. What if I'm captured? Half-elves, men, even those of pure elvish descent are little more than useless in battle with no training. We've left the half-elven quarter out of our preparations."

"You'll figure it out," Apopsé said feebly. Then, "Alright. Gared here will assemble some of my guard to fill out your numbers. But they must not be lost."

"And who will command from the wall?" Edward asked.

"I will," Apopsé replied, with a conviction Edward knew to be false. Edward doubted whether the lord of the South Kingdom had ever known anything but luxury and peace. In this battle, his military skills, if he had any at all, would prove insufficient. But again, Edward allowed the words to stand. He climbed down the stairs through the darkening tower. When he had descended all the way to the street, the city was shrouded in gray. Soon the sun would set. And after that, the siege would begin.

CHAPTER THIRTY-THREE
A Bargaining Chip

In the gathering darkness, the city loomed like faded bones. Behind it the last sliver of sun passed away; only a faint glow remained. Wind whipped through the grass in swirling gusts. Northeast of the city, the greater part of Iramov's forces had begun their march toward the main gate. The army moved like a blanket of black ants swarming over the charred stumps where they had burned the fields that had once been forest. The smoke from the fires had dissipated, filling the air with an ashy haze. Soon it would be dark.

In the south, the small company of half a hundred horsemen panted along with their mounts, watching the army crawl over the hills. The animals stamped nervously, well aware of the battle to come. Near the back of the group, several horses reared, screaming over the wind, their eyes white and darting. At the front a thick man with a loud laugh and dark beard talked with a figure hooded in green.

"How'd you know there'd be a gate over here? No, wait. It was a guess, wasn't it?"

"Always go left, John. You know that."

"And if you'da been wrong?"

The figure pointed north. "Then they would have opened the gate for us."

"So yer sayin' that if *left* wasn't *right* then we'da just been *left* outta the city until the dead-faces would'a beat Apopsé's door *right* down?"

"That's what I'm *sayin'*," Askon replied, mimicking John's manner of speech. He smiled, and the green eye glittered against the blue.

"Well we better hurry up, or all yer leftin' and rightin' won't be worth two bits. They'll have the gate down before we even reach the wall."

Askon's smile grew wider. "I doubt that. They have quite a way to go before they reach the gate. And you're forgetting our secret weapon."

John spurred his horse, snapping the reins against the tired animal's neck. His booming laugh drifted after him and away over the hill. Askon followed, digging his heels in gently and patting the beast on its neck.

"Time to go."

They reigned up just outside of bowshot from the wall. It was a long way, but John's voice was loud, even over the rushing wind.

"Oy!" he shouted, his mouth like a great bear bellowing in the deep woods. "Open the gods damn door already!"

If John's thundering shout was a bear, then the answer was a mosquito. It came from one of the watch posts along the wall. "Who's out there?" it whined. "We'll not be fooled by Iramov's tricks."

"Keep us out here and Iramov'll smash open yer front gate and put a boot in yer ass!" John shot back, the force of his words enough to blow the mosquito away.

"Prove you're not part of Iramov's army then," it squeaked.

"Oh, damn it all!" John roared. "Askon!" But Askon wasn't there. He had drawn away to the other side of the little company. "Askon?"

And then they were surrounded. With shaky hands that wielded hatchets and cooking knives, shovels and pointed rakes, dozens of shapes emerged out of the growing darkness. Though their hands were unsteady, their eyes glittered. Askon lowered his sword.

"I wish you were Iramov's emissary," said a voice on the brink of laughter. "We could have killed you where you stand with all that blustering. You'd think John would've gotten himself shot by now."

Edward emerged from the ring of terrified half-elves, a retinue of white feathered helmets backing him. Apopsé's guards stayed behind while he crossed the space, reached up, and clasped Askon's arm with both hands. "It's good to see you back," Edward said with a wide smile. It looked to Askon as though the prince hadn't smiled in years.

"I see you've recruited some new soldiers," Askon said, gesturing to the timid ring of farm hands, building maintainers, and servants.

Edward leaned closer. "Hardly," he whispered. "I may make jokes at John's expense, but if we had met a fight out here, you really would be the last half-elf in Vladvir. Well, the last man anyway. Some of the women stayed back to tend the children."

"There are children?" Askon said. "Of course there are children, what am I thinking?" He looked out into the ring of trembling half-elves and saw that indeed they had fielded almost every kind possible: old men with graying wisps of hair, boys and girls just out of childhood, women old and young. As he eyed them, they seemed to relax.

Edward turned to the trembling ring. "Thank you for your help!" he called, and each of them seemed to grow taller with pride. "Gared, lead them back to the gate. I'll stay with Askon. We need to get back inside, and quickly."

Portcullis and surrounding wall, watchers and door-guards, all were quiet when John's fifty horsemen edged closer to the gate. Edward leaned out from behind Askon's horse calling to the watchmen above.

"I have returned with good news," he said, genuine joy lacing the words. "Our friends have come to help us. Grafmark is on its way, and this is the spearpoint."

"Who returns to us?" asked the mosquito. It was louder now that they were so close but just as thin.

Edward and Askon shared a glance. "Edward, prince of Vladvir returns. Who else would it be?"

John bristled, snapping his reins in an arrhythmic pattern.

"We knew not of the prince's going, impostor. The real Edward watches from the walls."

John shifted on his horse. "He came out to find us, you stone-skulled gate-monkey. Now let us in!"

"What my friend, John of Dalstone, means to say is that I have accomplished the task given me by Lord Apopsé. And I've returned with better news than we could have hoped. Askon of Tolarenz rides with us. Tell Apopsé. He will understand."

But the watchman did not move. Instead, between the two guards standing at the top of the portcullis, a small shape bobbed above the rail and back down again. It paused momentarily, then popped up over the edge. They could not see his face, but Apopsé's hat stood before them on the wall.

"I say that prince Edward watches the enemy's movements from the main gate," he called down to them. "Who you might be, I do not know. But I can see that indeed you have brought the half-elf Askon back to South City. His eyes and cloak give that much away."

Edward tilted his head, perplexed. "Apopsé, you sent me out here to meet what we thought would be Iramov's initial strike. I've brought back reinforcements and good news. Raise the gate."

As Askon waited for the response, he sensed a difference in Apopsé since he had left to find Iramov. He looked on, hoping that the man who bore the Sight fragment could see the folly in barring their entry.

"My conscience suggests I respond in the negative, impostor. How could I give safe passage to you when the prince already stands guard upon the wall?" Once again, Apopsé's words slithered out like a serpent's tongue; however, now there was no Morrowmen to force the little man to do what was right.

"He's not going to let us in," Edward whispered.

John shrugged. "We been locked out before. What's one more time? They're all gonna die without our help anyway, 'specially without Askon."

Apopsé lifted a meaty fist over the wall. In it something sparkled. With an ungainly wobble, he lowered the hand and spoke again. "Iramov seeks two things only," he said, elongating the hiss at the end of his words, "Alora's Tear and the half-elves."

Suddenly Askon understood, and he assumed Edward would have as well. Apopsé had no intent of allowing them back into South City. He had planned to lock them out all along. Askon's luck, which had led them to the gate, had also given Apopsé the opportunity to flush out the majority of the half-elven quarter. The rest could easily be handed over. And whether it would work or not, the little Lord intended to use the skill that his country valued most—bartering—to finish the deal. He had both the Time fragment and the Sight fragment. He could give away the former and offer the services of the latter in hopes of turning Iramov's army away.

The sun's light had vanished now.

"Iramov has begun the assault. He'll weaken the wall-guards first, hoping to break them," Askon said hurriedly.

"No he won't," Apopsé said from his box. "Because we're going to offer him a bargaining chip: you."

Askon heard the snick of bowstrings though he saw no bow-men. The regiment of mechanical bows had begun to fire. Behind him, three of John's Darts went down with arrows in their chests and necks. John himself wheeled around in the saddle. "Down! Down off the horses! The bastard is shootin' at us!"

He slipped his foot loose from the stirrup, but a loop of thread caught one of the buckles. With a wrench, he tore it free and tumbled to the ground. An arrow sprouted up from his shoulder.

Askon slid off the horse, hiding behind its bulk the best he could. Edward was there on his right as another two Darts of Grafmark took arrows from the automatically firing bows. Behind them, the contingent of guards threatened the half-elves with swords and spears, indicating that the bows on the wall would find them next, were they to try to help.

Moving quickly, Askon led the horse over to John. The arrow had sunk into his left shoulder, missing the bone and pinning him to the ground. "Argh! Ya got yer wish Edward. They shot me." John grunted. "Just break it off. We'll sear it back together after I beat the stuffing outta that traitor. You think he's full o' gold coins? I bet he jingles when my fist meets his pampered little face."

Shaking his head, Askon snapped off the end of the arrow, leaving the head sticking out the back of John's arm. John grimaced and looped his belt around the useless hand, holding it in place. "Only need one arm to stab people with anyway," he said, but Askon saw the color drain from his cheeks and his jaw clench as he tried to move.

Askon looked up. The arrows had stopped. He turned to Edward. Then a wailing scream shot out from the top of the wall. Like a rag doll, one of the guards tumbled limply down, bouncing once, twice off the smooth white surface before landing in a crumpled heap. Clashing steel rattled above, followed by a thick gurgling cough. Two figures were cutting their way toward Apopsé's frantically bobbing hat.

Apopsé's hands shot up, shaking in fear. His sleeves fell as if apologizing for his mistake. The last remaining guard looked from one flashing sword to the other, trying to choose who to engage first. With a frightened stutter step from one side to the other, he rushed the smaller swordsman with a shout. Effortlessly, the rescuer spun to one side, leaving the blade behind to trip the guard. Almost as if it had been rehearsed, the blade arced wide into the torchlight on the wall and spiked into the fallen man. Askon smiled, Elise had become quite the swordswoman indeed.

She and Thomas closed in on Apopsé, wrenching one fleshy arm behind his back. Elise reached for the other, but Apopsé cocked it back into her stomach. In the ensuing struggle the sparkling silver chain whirled in his hand and slipped out into the open air. It plummeted down, the glowing green fragment trailing behind. Thomas stopped, in shock, as the jewel rocketed toward the hard sides of the gently sloping wall. Then the little man wrenched himself free. Thomas slipped, stumbling backward a step. With a sickening jolt, Apopsé shoved Elise from the wall.

Nearly a hundred feet. From the top of the guardrail to the hard-packed soil at its base, the South City wall was a marvel. The dead man's fall had been surreal, like a flopping doll, but the woman who sailed through the air now was fully alive. Below her, the fragment pinged off the hard white surface but did not break. It was close, maybe thirty feet from where Askon stood. His first instinct was to run to it, to jump up and grab it, but something held him in place. When it bounced again, it did break. The chain caught a sharp outcropping where the wall had cracked, and the gem slammed into the surface. It broke free of the setting and flew out toward the wind-whipped grass.

Askon still did not move, and Elise shrieked as she fell, arms flailing toward the white wall. She would hit it before she hit the ground. Maybe that would bring a more peaceful end. But when he looked up from where the fragment had snapped out of its setting, he saw her frozen in midair above him. He looked back down, and the fragment glowed brightly, casting green shadows up and down the wall and across the swirling grass. It too was frozen in place. Beyond it, just a shadow of Askon's memory, was Caled's open palm. *"Wait,"* it said and vanished.

The fragment still did not move. Askon watched it for a moment as it hung there, sparkling like a bright green star fallen from the heavens. Without its setting, the gem seemed naked and beautiful. It floated, unmoving against the blackening night sky and the white wall. Askon decided he had waited long enough. He sprinted toward the gate, snapping the fragment out of the air on his way by. He looked around; no way in, only up.

Wrapping his fingers around the portcullis grating, he began to climb as quickly as he could. He searched for Elise. How long would the fragment's power last? He could not say. But when his eyes found her, she had already begun to move again. Her arms rotated in slow circles, and her face grew wider and wider with fear. She was still falling.

Don't think of a salamander.

The words resounded in his consciousness, and he tore his eyes away from his falling friend. He grabbed the silver chain from where it had hooked the wall, leaned back and smashed the jewel into the setting, heedless of whether or not the stone would break. The setting was a crumpled wreck of silver leaves, barely clinging to the stone. He counted the links in the chain, and the glow of the jewel held steady. Gripping the cold metal bars, he climbed.

And then there was no portcullis left to use as a handhold. Nearly twenty feet off the ground, Askon had run out of climbing space. Elise's frozen form hung another fifty feet above him, but he dared not look.

In his mind he heard soft laughter, Líana's laughter, and recalled a warm afternoon in the Tolarenz square when she had stood clapping excitedly, no more than five or six years old, as a troop of acrobats tumbled and rolled in spectacular fashion. One had even run up the wall of Roland's house four or five steps and flipped over backward.

Askon smiled and the laughter faded. He thrust himself upward with hands and feet churning as fast as he could move them. He felt the slightly sloped surface scrape under his feet, and though he ran straight up the wall, it felt no different than crossing the clearing before the gates of Dalstone.

But halfway up, he began to tire. How long had the fragment's power been in effect? Could it even be measured? What might have looked like a split second to John or Edward was enough time for Askon to scale a hundred-foot, vertical stone slab. Suddenly he started to feel light-headed, and his footsteps came slower. Still, he stared at the fragment, counting the tiny links of chain: twenty-one, twenty-two, twenty-three.

His vision darkened, and he felt his foot slip against the wall's smooth side. Reflexively, he looked up, hoping to see the guardrail drawing nearer. It did, but to his horror, Elise was drawing closer much faster than the guardrail. When his eyes went back to the fragment, its light had begun to dim ever so slowly. Panic set in and, driving his feet hard into the smooth whiteness, he leapt for the rail.

As he passed, he reached out with his left hand and clasped Elise's wrist. Her body spun in midair as he sailed up toward the top of the wall. Askon clawed at the sharp blocks which made up the rail and hooked the lip with three of his fingers. Elise swung fluidly below him, and the fragment pulsed its heartbeat rhythm once again. He dug in, but the fingers slid against stone.

Then Thomas gripped his arm with both hands and hauled him over the rail. Askon collapsed, his head reeling. Elise fell into Thomas's arms, shivering uncontrollably. Apopsé lay where Thomas had felled him, unconscious near his box.

Rolling to one side, Askon reached out and snatched the hat off Apopsé's head. There on his sweating brow, the Sight fragment glowed blue under the flames of the nearby torches. Pitching the hat to one side, Askon ripped the crown away. It left behind pink scratches and a whitened indentation where it had sat for years on Apopsé's head.

Upon touching it, Askon felt the world shift beneath him as though the wall would come tumbling to the ground. In his ears a piercing screech swelled like metal on glass. He pitched the crown limply at Thomas. With a thud, it bounced off the young man's side and fell to the ground. Thomas knelt, and with awed reverence—Elise still enfolded in his arms—he picked it up.

"Keep that," Askon said, still unable to regain his footing. The strange feeling, brought on when he touched the crown, had faded instantly when he threw it to Thomas. But the exhaustion from his climb still held him down, and he could feel in the gathering dark of night, another force pressing down upon them. Heavier now than humidity yet somehow empty as a tomb.

Thomas looked dumbly at the crown. "Should I wear it?"

"I don't care if you eat it, just don't let him have it again."

Sky-blue light cast cool shadows over the surrounding stones. Thomas lifted the crown and placed it upon his head. Instantly, the light went out.

"It doesn't fit," he said.

"Oy!" It was John. "Are ya dead, Askon?"

"No, he's not dead," Thomas called down. Askon had been right. Thomas and Elise had indeed been the secret weapon.

"Fantastic. Now open the damned door!"

While Thomas and Elise cranked the handles to lift the gate, Askon had sidled his way over to the guardrail and propped himself against it. His strength came back as he stared down at the pulsing gem. *The world is how it is,* he thought with a sigh and looped the chain around his neck.

Over the next half hour, John's Darts and the half-elves of South City streamed back into the streets. The white plumes of Apopsé's personal guard marched along, weaponless, with swords or hatchets or knives at their backs. John's orders had been to detain them in the half-elven quarter, where without their gear, they would be less dangerous. Edward had dragged Apopsé to the top of the central tower and barred the hatch in the floor. John had demanded a chance to interrogate Apopsé, but the others feared John's definition of interrogation. Four Darts of Grafmark guarded the stairs instead.

Askon's energy had returned, but with every passing moment, he felt the power of the Death fragment growing. The torches reached only a few feet into the darkness now, and the night was far from over. He wondered if by morning even the sun could pierce Iramov's shroud.

They circled around to the front gate, still atop the wall. Askon had advised the half-elves to remain near their homes. "Iramov will come there last. He thinks that this is the only half-elven settlement left in all of Vladvir. He'll imagine it as a grand moment of death and destruction. But he'll leave the houses. Stay here and man this gate. It's the safest place in the city," he had said.

Now, standing above the heavy mechanical doors, with Thomas's ballistae flanking each side and a row of the automatic bows armed and ready, Askon turned to look upon Iramov's host.

He saw only blackness.

CHAPTER THIRTY-FOUR

Iramov

Askon's heightened vision did little to pierce the velvet shroud that encircled Apopsé's city. No stars shone above them, just the faint light of the fading moon. It hung in place above the South Kingdom's hills, growing paler and paler against the black. The extent of what he could see ended only thirty feet or so beyond the foot of the wall where puny torches guttered in the oncoming shadow. He breathed slowly, clutching the mangled setting of the Time fragment in his right hand. Iramov's forces had not yet begun their assault. But why?

It would be folly, even for an army of the dead, to stand within range of the bows and ballistae on the wall. The dead-faces would be scattered like dice on a board if one of the massive spears were to strike them directly. Whether that would stop them for good or not had yet to be proven, but it would certainly slow the attack and make breaking the massive central gate even more difficult. Wherever they were, the enemy would stay out of range until Iramov was ready to break down the door.

Thomas tinkered on one of the bow mechanisms a few feet away from Askon. His hands were black with grease and the gray dust used to make the machines operate more smoothly. He cursed, and the bow released an arrow with a *twang!* It sailed down from the wall and beyond the torchlight's reach into the field below. Thomas reloaded it by hand and continued his adjustments.

Elise stood behind him, as far from the front side of the wall as possible. Over the inner rail, a scaffold widened the space upon which defenders could stand and offered a series of steps leading down to the streets of South City. There, unaware of Apopsé's betrayal, the city guards bustled about in preparation for the attack. Here and there, white plumes bobbed as the king's commanders barked orders and directed civilians.

Next to Askon stood Edward, leaning on the rail with his face screwed up against the darkness. His long cloak hung loosely, covering his shoulders and back. He still wore the blue stag on his armor in hopes that his father's mistakes would not destroy the kingdom of Vladvir. There were still some, now commanded by Apopsé's officers, who fought with the prince, even if the king's army opposed him.

"I can't see," he said. And Askon guessed his friend meant more than just the darkness surrounding them.

Suddenly the shadow began to quiver and seethe. The dim torchlight at the foot of the wall went out, then surged back up, casting rays out into the tumbled fields only to retreat again. Askon leaned out over the rail, trying his best to see what had happened.

"Did you see that?"

Edward shook his head. "I told you, I can't see anything. It's like we've been locked in a cellar. I mean, I see you and Thomas. If I turn, I can see the streets of the city. But out there?" He pointed over the rail. "Nothing."

Askon looked again out over the South Kingdom and saw the torchlight rise and fall more violently than before. Before he could turn to Edward a second time, the cycle repeated. "Watch the torches," he said.

And so they did. Like waves upon a shore, the shadow rolled in and out, sometimes receding farther from the wall before crashing against it once more, sometimes changing only slightly. For several minutes the darkness rolled in and out. In and out.

"Thomas! Come and watch this," Edward called.

Dropping his tools and wiping the powdery grease on his trousers, Thomas trotted across the wall to Askon and Edward. He looked out into the black, then back at Askon. "I don't see anything."

"Neither did I, at first," Edward replied. "Try to just feel it. It helps to watch the torches down below us."

Thomas did as he was told. Each time the shadow rolled in again something in the blue gem on his forehead changed. It seemed to grow dull and dead in the silver crown. No light glowed there as it had when Apopsé wore it, but with the coming of the shadow, it looked more like a common river rock than a jewel.

"I see it," Thomas said. "The darkness seems to breathe. Iramov must be ready to make his move."

"That's what I thought when I noticed it," Askon said. "But it has been going on for some time now. Why hasn't the army come forward?"

Thomas rubbed his hands together; they made a swishing sound in the eerie quiet. "Maybe he's trying to intimidate us."

Far beyond the wall, in the depths of the never-ending blackness, a white orb of light burst upon the field—to Askon it could have been a thousand feet away or a thousand miles. It bathed the two armies in light for a moment, then surged over the hills and into the wall. As it approached them, Askon recognized it. "Get down!" he shouted.

They hit the stones of the wall-walk on all fours. Elise, still too nervous to approach the wall's outer edge, dropped last. Her eyes darted from side to side as if she could no longer see. She rubbed her hands across the stones, shuffling along until she found Thomas. "What was that?"

"The Death fragment," replied Askon. He lifted his head over the rail and saw only a deep nothingness. The darkness had grown and now pressed heavily against the pale white of South City's wall. "I've only seen that light twice. Once in Tolarenz, when Iramov killed Caled, and once in Grafmark where he tried to kill me and John."

Thomas looked around. "Where *is* John?"

Only a moment before the white light had flashed in the darkness, they had all been standing there together. Askon thought back. Thomas was working on the automatic bows. Elise watched him from the back of the wall. Edward had been standing next to him the whole time, and John had…Where had he gone? Askon remembered him following as they put Apopsé in the tower, remembered the orders John had given to the guards—his own men. But when they reached the main gate, where was he?

"Edward," Askon said slowly. "Did you see where John went?"

No response.

As one, the three of them looked to the prince, who knelt face down on the wall-walk.

"Edward?" Elise said in her quietest whisper. But he did not move.

Askon knelt in front of him. "What is it?" he asked, grabbing the prince's shoulder and shaking him vigorously.

Edward looked up, tears shining white against his gray eyes. In his hand was a round stone the size of a child's fist, piece for piece identical to the purple stone case of the Life fragment only deep-water blue. On one side, a small latch was fastened. Askon knew what would be inside. Edward's other hand rested nervelessly upon the paving stones. Beneath his still fingers, a small, powdery white circle had appeared.

"They're already inside," he said.

Again and again Iramov's dead-faces threw themselves at the gate. It creaked and shuddered, but did not give way. Volleys of arrows plunged down into the void. When the shafts met their marks, Askon and the others heard the *thunk* of wood and steel against armor and flesh, but there were no screams or cries of pain.

The ballistae launched their heavy arrows out into the field, one after another. Without any way to target the enemy force, Thomas directed the soldiers to rake the battlefield, hoping to crush as many of Iramov's dead puppets as possible. It seemed to be working, as the clatter of bodies and weapons peppering the wall lessened with each shot fired.

Then in the tiled square, a cry arose. Frothing Norill leapt howling onto the backs of the assembled South City guard. The creatures stabbed and sliced and hacked at the fallen bodies, sending the less experienced men of Apopsé's army back against the main gate. Then from the shifting shadows of the torchlit streets, hundreds of dead-faces emerged. They stood watching the Norill viciously rip and tear at the fallen defenders. Vacant eyes and expressionless faces gazed at the gate and cowering defenders while from without, Iramov's force clattered against the wall again and again. The dead men advanced slowly, their heads hanging awkwardly to one side, their steps even and steady.

"Edward!" Askon shouted. "We need to do something. Get up."

But the prince did not get up. He just stared at the blue stone case as vacant as one of Iramov's warriors.

Out of the shadow along the wall, John appeared, cracking his knuckles one by one.

"Where were you?" demanded Askon.

"Just checkin' on our froggy-friend in the tower," he said, flexing against his index finger. It popped quietly. "Kinda disappointing. No coins."

Edward still hadn't moved. John raised an eyebrow, looking down into the street below. "Seems we got a fight on our hands now, doesn't it? It's now or not at all, Askon."

In the square, the dead-faces marched forward, pressing the defenders farther and farther back toward the gate. The Norill fighters at their head jumped out wildly, slashing with swords and axes. Some of the blows went wide, while others killed in an instant. A few of the Norill fell as valiant spears of the South Kingdom skewered their chests. But with one sickening touch, the dead hands of Iramov's warriors would reach down and lift the fallen Norill to their feet. Each kill blunted the aggressive force of live Norill, but only added to the ominous wall of empty faces.

"Codard must have used his fragment to get them inside," said Thomas. His eyes were wide as Iramov's army drew closer to the gate. Elise drew her sword.

"We have to try to stop them," she said. "Askon, do what you can to slow them down. John, Edward, go to the right flank. Thomas and I will go to the left. How do we kill them?"

"You can't," John and Askon said in unison.

Spears and swords dropped to the ground before the gate, clanging against the carefully laid tiles. A large number of Apopsé's men had given their weapons up in favor of surrender. If the enemy on the inside allowed them to live, the rest of the army, frantically battering the main gate would not. Surrender or no surrender, Apopsé's men were as good as dead. But for now they lived. Askon watched carefully as the enemy drew within arm's length of the line.

His first instinct was to rush Iramov's men and disarm them as he had Apopsé's guards in the main hall of the palace. He recognized the strategy's weakness immediately: though the enemy would have no weapons, he would be extremely tired by the time he disarmed them all. The weapons would not come free easily, even if the fragment could give him all the time he needed. In addition to his own exhaustion, he doubted that the dead men even needed weapons in order to kill. With Apopsé's defenders already intimidated, an army that ripped limb from limb with its bare hands would be more frightening than one that used swords to the same end. As he looked the lines of his allies and enemies up and down, he felt the fragment's power begin to enfold him. The world slowed.

His second thought was to move the South City defenders to a different, less exposed position. They might again be backed against a wall, but it was unlikely for any other position to expose their backs to an army as the main gate eventually would. But if removing the enemy's weapons would be tiring, moving each defender individually would be overwhelming. So he continued to watch, and the fragment brought the world to a crawl.

Both the ballistae and the automatic bows posed too great a threat to the defenders and did too little to impede the enemy. Dead men couldn't be distracted by loud noises or fire. Then it came to him, and the world stopped.

Askon ran down the stairs, sword in hand, and crossed the square to the line of enemy soldiers. Their empty faces, like ghoulish, disinterested statues, gaped at their would-be victims. Approaching the first rank, Askon drew back his blade. He cut deep into the lower leg of the first dead man, his sword slicing clean through. He followed the momentum of the steel through the next leg, and on to the next man, and the Norill beside him, and on and on down the line. He found that one stroke could hobble several of the dead soldiers, if he timed it right. But by the end of the first rank Askon's lungs screamed in revolt, his muscles liquid and unresponsive. It would have to do. As he turned and ran, retreating to the stairway, the fragment began to pulse again.

He had climbed half the scaffolding when the others met him on their way down. John grinned through his beard while Thomas looked down on the crippled line of Iramov's men. Elise followed closely behind. The first rank lay limp, as if life had left them once again. Askon panted, leaning on wobbly legs as his consciousness threatened to surrender to his tired body. With a twitching convulsion, the legless bodies began to crawl toward the defenders, and the enemies that remained upright climbed clumsily over their injured comrades.

The defenders, surprised and confused by the toppling row of empty-faced attackers, rallied almost instantly. They roared in response and leapt out at Iramov's men, stabbing sharp spears through the struggling bodies, staking them into the polished tiles. Then the defenders advanced, seeing how quickly the opposition would fall. A group of several guards—led by a man with a plumed helmet—drove into the enemy line, attempting to break through and gain better position away from the gate. A few stayed behind and cheered at Askon, who still struggled to stay on his feet, his hands resting heavily on his knees.

"Where's Edward?" Askon gasped.

John grunted in disgust and Thomas said nothing.

"He refuses to get up," said the cold commander's voice. Elise had tied back her hair so tightly that it appeared as if it had been painted to her scalp. A thick bun stuck up from the back where she had fastened the rest, black as the shadow pressing against the outer wall. She glared at Askon. "Try if you want, but he's not coming down. Something's broken him."

Askon turned to climb the stairs. He knew what lay in Edward's hand. He knew, at least in part, what Edward would have seen in the powdered circle, but now was not the time to grieve. Somehow, they'd been given an unexpected gift, and they couldn't let it go to waste. Askon bounded up the flight of stairs that crossed and re-crossed the inside of South City's wall.

When he heard the grinding squeal of metal against metal, he stopped. Halfway up the wall on either side, great levers protruded into the night air. Guards had been placed around each, in case the central gate needed to be opened. Askon watched as the last of them fell limply to the tiled square below, fifty feet straight to the ground. The last man's armor crunched like snow under a boot. Then the second screech poured out into the night.

Somehow, while he and the others had been busy in the square, two groups of Norill had silently scaled the inner wall. They struck when the defenders had redoubled the attack. Now, with no one to stop them, they flung open the doors to South City, and the barrage of empty-faced dead poured in. Askon gaped as hundreds of them rushed over the carefully placed tiles, catching the remaining defenders by surprise, killing them where they stood. The first to die were those who had cheered Askon's assault. In seconds, nearly all of the defenders had drowned in the tide.

Then in horrified wonder, Askon watched several of the empty-faced men reach down into the trampled ranks of defenders, lifting them bonelessly to their feet. Soon, white-plumed helmets dotted the Death fragment's swarming army, and the white dove on sky-blue mixed with crimson bull and blue stag. They were headed for the palace.

Askon's heart stopped. He watched another dead hand claw its way down and lift a fallen defender into the enemy ranks. Iramov must have thought that Apopsé would hide within the palace, the safest place in South City, but the Lord of the South Kingdom was locked in the outer wall's central tower, and the Sight fragment now rested dully on Thomas's brow. The palace was empty. Then under the weight of the Death fragment's darkness, he remembered. She was in the palace. Through the garden, across the beautifully paved stones, down the tiered stairway, in the wide sparring ground, lay his sister's unburned and unburied body.

"No!" Askon screamed into the cacophony of battle below.

And there before him, once again with leering jaw and curious, cold stare was the beast. With Askon's face and its heavy bulk burdened with hatred, it planted itself before his eyes. Soon the battle and the pouring multitudes of Iramov's army faded. The darkness grew heavier, and Askon glared back at the beast.

"No," he said.

Then he was running. Up the stairs and across the wall-walk to Edward. There was no beast, only his enemy—Iramov. He hoped that his friends had followed, for they too still lived. Back in the pale moonlight of Grafmark, he had told himself that Iramov could harm Líana no more, that she was beyond the reach of the Death fragment's power. But Askon had been wrong. One way still remained.

Yet something had changed. He could stop Iramov now. Not because he hated or raged like the stupid drooling creature he had banished to the void. No. He could defeat Iramov because the screaming bald man, long ago lost to the Death fragment's insanity, and the thrashing, hulking beast were one in the same. But Caled had not been the same; Morrowmen had tried to teach Askon that. And now he understood.

Before, Askon would have charged into the swarm of dead-faces, fragment or no fragment, hoping to slash his way through as many as possible. Now, as time slowed to a crawl around him, he smiled. He would not lead his friends to their deaths. In a blink, he knelt at Edward's side and the power of the fragment fell away. Edward looked up.

"He's dead, Askon. No, he's gone. And the whole army, they've been turned into those, those things!"

"I know," Askon said. He had guessed that Iramov had made his move against Codard, but now he had proof. Whatever else Edward might have seen in the powdered circle would have to wait.

"He tried to stop him. My father meant to end Iramov's assault, but Death was too strong. He used this as he died," Edward held up the Space fragment's stone case, "trying to transport himself to me. I should never have trusted Apopsé."

Askon lifted him up from the cold stones. Edward's hand trailed behind, lingering on the powdered circle. Blackness pressed in all around them, threatening to blot out all light and all hope. Grabbing the prince's hand, Askon jerked the fragment up and held it in front of Edward's eyes.

"You know what this can do," Askon said breathlessly.

Edward nodded blankly.

"Can you use it?"

"I don't know. My father seemed to think it only works if you are truly afraid."

John thundered up the stairs. "Gods yer fast with that thing, Askon." He eyed Edward. "And you've even woken our dear prince."

"Not now, John," Askon snapped. "Go to the southern gate. Rally the half-elves there and as many of your horsemen as we can muster. Iramov will come there last.

"Why me?" John asked, as if the fighting would be better in the street leading to the palace.

"Because men follow you," Askon said. "That's why I chose you in the forest outside of Austgæta. It's why Eldred chose you to lead the Darts. It's why you were able to fire the arrow that saved Dalstone." John's face twisted at the last. Askon put his hand on his friend's shoulder. "Lead them. Away from here if you have to. They will follow you."

"And who's gonna drag your half-elf ass outta the fire if I'm gone?"

Askon smiled. "This time, I do that myself. Now go."

John gave a lazy salute and bolted down the wall toward the southern gate. Askon watched him go. Thomas and Elise came up the stairs next. Neither of them spoke, and still the dead army poured through the gates and into the streets. In the distance, through the thick blackness, Askon thought he saw them moving, nearly halfway to the palace. He turned to Edward.

"Alright. If it works based on fear, we need you to be afraid."

Edward stared out into the darkness. "There's nothing left. Líana, my kingdom, my father, even those who fled here will soon be dead. What should I fear?"

Another wave of dead men stomped over the corpses of the fallen guardsmen below. One reached down and lifted a crumpled body to its feet, adding to the ever expanding number. Askon yanked Edward to the edge of the wall.

"That!" Askon said. "You should be afraid of that."

Edward looked helpless. "What is one more enemy in so many hundreds?"

With another forceful wrench, Askon dragged Edward's head and neck around to face the palace's inner wall. He pointed, in the pulsing dark, to the sparring ground. "There. Iramov's dead army is going there!" Askon shouted. "They're after Apopsé, but they're going to find *her*."

As if a curtain had lifted before his eyes to reveal something horrible, Edward's face grew pale and sickly. Askon was certain that now the prince felt fear.

The wall and surrounding sky blurred and shifted dizzily. Beneath their feet, the ground began to sway, and it felt as though Askon stood upon a broken piece of ice amid a frigid lake. Thomas, Elise, Edward. They were all with him when the floor gave way. Then, so was Iramov, his loathsome eyes and pale bald head gleaming just inches away from Askon. He looked bewildered, but Askon could do nothing to reach him. With a sickening lurch, it stopped, and the world blurred again.

When Askon opened his eyes, terror overrode him. Edward had used the Space fragment. The fear of what the dead men would do to Líana had pushed the prince over the edge. But, just as the Time fragment had been for Askon, the Space fragment's power was unpredictable. Later Thomas guessed that it was Edward's concentration on protecting Líana that had brought them there.

Askon looked around in despair. Edward had used the fragment, but he had moved Iramov to them. And in his own worry and terror, Edward had moved them all to the sparring ground where they had laid Líana and the falcon Marten. The sound of a thousand clattering feet drew nearer and nearer. Iramov's army was inside the palace grounds.

"Oh, I couldn't have designed this better myself," said a voice of cold music. "I have the Death fragment. The cowardly father bequeaths Space to his equally craven son. The stolen Sight fragment stands atop the brow of a boy just grown into his uniform. And Time pulses at the chest of a disobedient dog, frothing for revenge. All I need is Life and Alora's Tear will be reunited once more." Through the giddy thickness of his voice, he might have laughed, but instead he only grinned, too pleased with himself to even move.

Askon wanted to kill him. Wanted to bring on the power of the Time fragment and slam his father's sword into Iramov's heart. And the steel was ready. But Iramov had given away too much. Askon had guessed it, and now he knew for certain. The lord of the crimson bull did not have Morrowmen's Life fragment. Somehow the assassins had never made it back to their leader. One piece was indeed askew on the board.

In the swirling darkness, Askon's eyes shone like flecks of green and blue starlight. A smile curled over his face. In his mind's eye, Caled stood before the sneering bald man, his palm outstretched. *Wait.*

So Askon waited, expecting the fragment to take over as it had before. The footsteps of the dead drew nearer, and the shadows drew closer. Iramov stepped softly, just ahead of the darkness and spoke again.

"It's hard to move, isn't it half-man," he spat. "Your friends are finding it difficult as well. This boy and Codard's worthless son, they won't be moving anymore. And neither will *you!*" He stepped forward, the ebony staff lancing down, and without touching Askon, drove him face first into the hard-packed sparring grounds. Blood ran from Askon's face as he lifted his head. He tightened his grip on his sword, his head swimming in the crushing darkness. Yet, Caled was still there. *Wait.*

Iramov's voice boomed now, as though Askon were an ant at the bald man's feet. *"Look at your friends!"* he cackled. *"Look what your filthy invader's blood has brought them! Death. They aren't even worthy of fighting alongside me against your precious elves. My fragment will devour them like it did your father and your cur of a leader. They and you will be dust beneath my heel."*

Iramov whirled the staff over his head, and Askon saw Edward and Thomas, their faces bloody like his in the lurid red glare. The staff made another rotation and Edward tried to rise, tried to fight. But the darkness slammed him back into the gravel and dirt. Thomas struggled, but could not lift his head. Now the army of empty faces had begun to pour into the sparring ground. Their arms and legs flapped together loosely as their puppeteer led them down the smooth stone steps. And then, the image of Caled vanished. The time for waiting was over.

Don't think of a salamander.

Askon lifted the Time fragment to his face, followed every facet with his eyes. He looked for Caled there, but saw only himself reflected in the glowing jewel. The crumpled leaves of the setting seemed tired and beaten, but the metal still shone as though no harm could come to its polished surface. He counted the links: one, two, three. And stood up.

All around him was black deeper than night, deeper than the furthest reaches of the sky, deeper than the chasm beneath Austgæta; it was the all-encompassing darkness of death. In that darkness he knew that the army of the dead waited unfeeling, unknowing, for their victory. He stepped toward Iramov, sword in hand, and examined the insanity on that pale-skinned face. He brought the blade back—one thrust would skewer the crimson bull and put an end to his hatred. In Askon's mind the grasses of Tolarenz rustled in the spring wind. The lake rippled, crystalline blue under the summer sun. He heard Roland pinging away at the forge. He smelled fresh bread in his mother's kitchen, and felt the dull ache of tired muscles when a long day's work is done.

And then the bald man's face wriggled into a tight lipped smile, the eyes growing larger, sparkling with greed. The darkness blasted Askon into the earth like a snowball against a heavy door, and he felt the clawing hands of dead men piling onto his shoulders. His sword clattered away, and he felt his arms break as his elbows drove into the dirt and grit. His breath shuddered and blood ran like rust in his mouth. He rolled onto his back. Through a net of groping fingers, he saw Iramov grinning down, and the long red scarf rippling in the dark.

"Fool. Half a man, half a waste! I do only one thing with worthless, broken animals like you. How stupid are you? Time has no power over me. Death comes for all!"

So it did. And so it does. Askon tried to move, but his arms were shattered, his face smeared in blood, the darkness so heavy that he failed even to breathe. Then instantly, it lifted, and silence engulfed him.

In the distance a rolling wave of light coursed toward him. Faster and faster it came, through the walls, through the ground, and down from the sky it rushed on. He turned to his friends, and they saw it too, racing over stairs and brightly colored flowers. It crashed upon them then, and everything was gone.

CHAPTER THIRTY-FIVE

Hands Covered in White Powder

"Askon."

"Yes, Líana."

"When we die, where do we go?"

"The gods take us and set us amongst the stars, like the Hunter, and the Cloud King, like Alora and Heraphus."

"But they're so far away. Won't it be cold up there?"

"No, it won't. The night is cold, but the stars? The stars are all of our lost friends and loved ones. They will keep us warm."

"But I don't want you to go so far away."

"Don't worry, Líana, I'm not going to die."

"No. You're not."

She stood in silhouette against the shining whiteness that engulfed the world. Her face was calm and undisturbed. For a moment, he thought that he glimpsed the same emptiness in her eyes as *they* had in theirs. But no. She just looked tired, so tired. On her shoulder, an odd shape rose up like a second, pointed head. He winced in the blinding brightness, and she put out a hand.

"It's alright," said the voice like water.

He tried to reach up, but his arms surged with pain and his head swam. He could not speak or even scream. The light was too bright. She squeezed his hand and the pain was gone.

She turned away and spoke to the blinding white light. "You will not harm him," she said, stepping in front of Askon.

For a moment there was no response, only a snuffling, chattering, choking sound. Then the second voice came. High and shrill, but still powerful.

"I'll kill you all!" Iramov snarled through clenched teeth.

"Perhaps you are the foolish one, Iramov," she said calmly. "Death has no real power over Life. Life is always reborn."

The snarling and chattering came again, louder this time, with a faint wail of fury. It was the death rattle of the beast.

"No, Iramov," she said, and the water became a downpour. "Your rage cannot help you anymore."

Iramov roared, raising the staff high above his head. The scream went on and on into the depths of Askon's mind, until he wished for nothing more than to end the sound. The whiteness swelled, making him feel lighter than the very air. And then the shape on her shoulder spread its wings and took flight, revealing not white but purple. Violet like flowers in spring, when the lilacs bloom and dangle their heavy buds for the bees of the field. Like the deepest ring of the rainbow's edge. Like the shadowy heart of a summer storm, it grew against the cold harsh light. It rose in shivering waves, pressing the white back and back and back. Somewhere in the distance, Iramov was still screaming. Then the violet ring exploded like sparks on a sword in the forge, rippling out and out forever, laying to rest the mindless throngs of the dead. When Askon looked up again, his hands were covered in white powder.

To his left lay his father's sword. It gleamed in the warm mixture of moon and star and torchlight. A few feet away was Thomas, lying face down, the Sight fragment's crown askew on his head. Edward was on the other side, his hand still clutching the blue stone case of the Space fragment. And before him knelt Líana, Marten perched on her exposed back. His talons should have cut through the skin and muscle into her very bones, but they did not. She tried to stand but couldn't. A few feet in front of her, Iramov stood dazedly, his staff fallen to the ground beside him.

The Time fragment continued its heartbeat rhythm, but the next few moments passed as though time nearly stood still. With a flash of recognition, Iramov lunged for the staff. He coiled his fingers about it, one by one. Edward and Thomas still lay unconscious— maybe dead—on either side. Iramov's lips curled into a venomous smile, and he lifted the Death fragment's staff into the air, meaning to bring it down upon Líana, to bash in her skull in her moment of weakness.

And then he looked very surprised. From his chest, a gently sloping shaft of steel sprouted, a slick film of blood covering it like wet red paint. His heart must already have been shredded, but the blade twisted, rotating almost full circle before sliding back and appearing three, four, five more times out of his chest. The arms behind the blade had tired when it finally rounded on Iramov's slumping body, burying itself the full width of the blade into his neck.

"The world is how it is," said the cold commander's voice. And Elise kicked Iramov's lifeless body to the ground.

The ebony staff, the half remaining after John's sword had split it, wobbled and fell. The Death fragment grew darker and darker until red dulled almost to black. All around the sparring area, a film of white powder coated the ground. The Death fragment's army was nowhere to be found.

Líana breathed slowly, kneeling where she had fallen after the wave of purple light. Askon rose and went to her. His arms—broken when Iramov's dead men had thrust him to the ground—were now healed. He lifted her up, hugging her tightly, kissing the top of her head where the tight braid parted the hair. She was shaking.

"Take me to him," she whispered.

Askon helped his sister over to Edward. Across from them Elise had already turned Thomas over, laying his head in her lap. Tears streamed down her face.

Edward's skin had paled, his blood gone cold. But Askon had seen this before. He would not be fooled again by a man who only appeared to be dead. He knelt beside his friend, helping Líana down with him.

"Is he?"

Líana lowered her head to his chest, listening for the heart. Then she placed a gentle finger at his neck. She let her hand rest there, opening it to cover his faded cheek. With her left hand, she wrapped her fingers in his. The ring was there, on the third finger of her hand. She bent down and kissed his forehead.

With a gasp, Edward's gray eyes snapped open. They darted back and forth, then alighted in wonder upon her face. Askon turned away then, and did not see as she lowered her head a second time, her lips meeting his, did not see them linger there till both were gasping for breath, did not see Edward grip the ring on her finger and kiss her again.

As he walked away, he did see Marten. The bird landed lightly on his shoulder, where the leather guard had sat empty since Marten had come streaking from the sky to protect his sister. But in that moment, Askon knew—in the uncanny way he always had with Marten—that he was no longer at home there. The falcon now belonged to Líana and she to him. Askon ruffled the feathers on the bird's head with a finger and smiled.

"I don't think she needs us to protect her."

Edward and Líana sat tearily holding each other on the grass while Thomas and Elise embraced with arms and legs and lips in a manner not fit for polite company. Askon climbed the smooth stone stairs. Iramov's army of the dead may have been gone, but the battle still raged in the southern corner of the city. The Lost— Iramov's Norill allies—had advanced on John's horsemen and half- elves. They were not all yet safe.

He set out alone, but when he arrived at the half-elven quarter, his friends followed closely behind. Askon had used the Time fragment to rush out of the palace grounds and through the silently sliding mechanical gate. To his surprise, the effort drained him so fully that the others had already noticed he was gone and covered half the distance before he was able to stand. When he rose, he moved slowly, his muscles dull and unresponsive. While he trudged along the winding streets, his friends drew closer and closer.

It was still dark, but in comparison to the utter blackness of the Death fragment, natural night seemed as clear as midmorning sun. All around them, ramshackle wooden buildings leaned awkwardly under the sparkling stars. Torches burned at the doors of some, but no fire had yet touched the buildings themselves. In the distance the clatter of battle echoed through the streets. They rounded a corner, Líana falling into step next to her brother, and found John's remaining forces locked in combat with a group of the Lost.

The passage was narrow, the leaning half-elven buildings on one side and the southern wall on the other; Askon assumed that John had planned it that way. John's men were few and the enemy still numbered in the many hundreds. In the close alleys of the half-elven quarter, though, the smaller force could even the odds, limiting the attackers to a front of fifteen or twenty. Slowly, John's men drew back. With each movement a few more Darts or a few more half-elves fell, and the strategy grew thinner.

On the wall above them, two guards stood waiting for the Norill to advance into range. Before them they had gathered two huge racks of the ballista arrows. Each one alone could kill a dozen Norill, and the collection would distract as well as damage the frontmost lines. Askon watched as the Norill clambered forward. John ordered his men to retreat, and as he did so, Askon saw that not only did he favor the arm which had taken the arrow outside South City's walls, but a large dark circle had spread through his armor. He looked paler than ever behind the curling beard, and he grimaced with each step.

The Norill sensed his weakness. They advanced greedily, shrieking and wailing, lashing out at those who did not retreat swiftly with the rest. John smiled as the first rank of Norill stepped into the trap. But further back, Askon saw two Norill jumping crazily, waving their long arms, shouting in their own guttural language. They pointed to the guards and piles of arrows on the wall, and the message began to travel forward through the column.

In a strange mirroring of the enemy Norill, Askon pointed to the trap. "They know what he's going to do," Askon said to the others. "We have to try to help him." Askon looked around, trying to remain calm. He could attempt to use the Time fragment again, but after its short duration and exhausting toll in crossing the palace grounds, he decided it unwise. No strategy came to him, and time rolled on.

"I have an idea," said Thomas. He, or more likely Elise, had straightened the crown to improve his comical appearance, but it tipped sideways again as he spoke. "Look at us, Askon."

And Askon did. Around his own neck, the Time fragment pulsed its green heartbeat. Edward clutched the blue stone case. Thomas wore the crown. And when his eyes alighted on Elise, she carried Iramov's ebony staff. Of course she did. The red gem at the tip of the shaft was as dead as its previous possessor, just as the Sight fragment did not glow upon Thomas's brow. Askon sighed.

The red had become almost black, just like her eyes. Then he turned to Líana.

Her armor still showed the damage from her assault in the South City street. She wore high boots of faintly purple leather that rose nearly to her knee. The same color continued to her waist, where the uniform of Morrowmen's agents ended. Her leather chest plate, they had fully removed when they laid her upon the stone bench. Instead, all she wore above the waist was a thin dark shirt. The opening at the neck had been ripped slightly wider by the knife the assassin had driven into her collarbone. There, where a deep scar should have gnarled the skin, only a round lump remained. It pulsed deep violet through the layers of skin and flesh.

Against his will, the memory flooded back. Five swords stabbed into her back as she drove the knife into her vile attacker, Morrowmen instantly at her side. The old man had touched her, waved the case over her, said something.

But no one had seen him open the case before he reached her. No one had seen the aged fingers slip down the arm to the knife-wound and bury the Life fragment in the wide gash.

"My dear, it would take a lot more than his angry little fingers to kill me. As long as I carry the fragment, I'll be just fine."

So that was the way of it. Morrowmen was gone, vanished into swirling dust as the assassins dragged him away from the fragment that had kept him alive for so many years. And they had believed him, just as Iramov had believed in Caled's scepter. Askon wondered if the two had somehow planned it all along.

"We have all five fragments," he said to Thomas finally.

"Yes, we do," Thomas replied. "These Norill worship the Tear. We can't kill them all, not even if we all had command of the power of our given pieces. But that doesn't mean we can't help John."

Finding their way through the retreating crowd was more difficult than they expected. Men, and some half-elf women, turned to face them with vicious eyes. Almost all had slowed the five of them in some way, either thinking them enemies or hardly noticing their presence, knocking Líana and Askon nearly off their feet on more than one occasion. Both found their energy flagging as they pushed to the head of the column.

Then they were out. John still limped along, wincing in pain, driving his men back. The Norill message rippled through the enemy ranks, but Askon and the others got there first. They stood before the leaders of the Lost, with all five fragments fully visible. The Norill stopped. Wonder filled their beady black eyes, and some of the snarling mouths dropped open. A few knelt instantly before the five sparkling gems, but only a few.

After the initial shock, the leaders turned to their kneeling comrades and brought their weapons down hard, stabbing, chopping, slicing, mercilessly killing any who would surrender. Askon and the others backed away, as new Norill filled the gaps.

When the ballistae arrows came tumbling down, the entirety of the Lost's command was crushed. They who had killed so easily were swatted like so many flies by the falling timbers. Askon felt the air move around his head, so close were they to the trap. Any closer and they might have been pinned beneath it as well. When the dust settled, the five still stood, though Askon and Líana only barely. Seeing the glittering gems, and the utter annihilation of their commanders, the Norill broke and fled for the main gate.

They poured out into the rolling hills of the South Kingdom by the dozens, sprinting on their squat, crooked legs. A volley of automatically fired arrows fell amongst the first swarm of escapees, but then the ammunition was spent. The rest of the Lost, still hundreds strong, ran screaming into the night along the main road to the north, desperately trying to find their way back home. South City was empty. The enemy had been defeated.

All around them, half-elves and Darts of Grafmark cheered wildly. They had climbed over the wreckage of the sprung trap, flushing the Norill out of the streets and into the surrounding hills. Askon and his friends lagged behind, either out of exhaustion, injury, or fellowship. John looked the worst. His face grew paler with each step, and a thick bead of blood ran down his chest plate from ribcage to boot laces. Finally he could go no more. He slumped against the outer wall with a grunt.

"It was my own damn fault. Should'a told those fool Darts not to bring the horses. Got backed into one and took a Norill axe to the chest." He coughed thickly, wiping his mouth with a blood-soaked wrist. "Not to mention the arrow our frog-lord stuck in my arm. Tell ya what though, you should'a seen the blood spray when I took off that Norill's head. His black-eyed friends thought twice before takin' another shot at me." He laughed weakly to himself, and the heaves descended into choking gasps.

"John, we need to do something about your wounds," Thomas said, his eyes widening in concern. "You don't have much time."

"Ah, don't bother," John choked. "I can handle a little Norill scratch." His head lolled loosely as he spoke, the eyes unfocused and bleary. Thomas reached down and cut the straps that fastened John's armor. Beneath, the damage was worse than John would ever have admitted. The axe had been of Norill make. Only their metalwork would have shredded so much skin and muscle and bone. Human and Elf weapons were sleek, meant for stabbing and slicing. Norill steel ripped and tore and crushed. They were less elegant, but repairing their damage was always more difficult. John had been the victim of many more than one Norill axe.

Blood oozed from two gashes and the combined trickle joined together to run down onto his leggings. He coughed again and the flow pulsed stronger, then weaker.

"Alright," he wheezed. "Maybe I lied. One Norill axe ain't any different than a few. They're all dead now anyway. Only took off the one head, though."

Líana knelt before John, wobbling slightly as she tried to keep her balance. She tilted her head this way then that, examining the damage. The long golden braid slipped back and forth over her back. Slowly, weakly, she reached out with her left hand, moving toward the pulsing wound.

"You're a pretty one, aren't ya?" John rasped. "What a way to go. Dead Norill all around, the leader of my own company, and a girl like that just before it all goes dark." He smiled, pawing limply toward Líana's face.

Askon only smiled. John would be John, of course. And he knew what Brâghda and Elise would say to that. Edward stood still as well, knowing what would come next, watching the ring on her hand press into the wet redness of John's wounds.

A warm violet glow rose around them, and Askon was forced to look away from the glowing fragment under his sister's skin. When the light dimmed, John's major wounds were gone, though many scars, bruises, and the arrow remained. Líana tottered in place, and Edward caught her before she fell.

CHAPTER THIRTY-SIX

The Gardens of South City

Light and warmth bathed every corner of the palace when Líana and John finally awoke. They were in the garden, the soft sound of water trickling above them. Askon and the others had removed their armor. They still wore the thin shirts and trousers from the previous night's battle, though John's were so shredded they could hardly be called such any longer.

Askon slept late, until long after the sunrise. His friend and sister slept even longer. The sun climbed steadily while Morrowmen's agents, led by Rickard and Mot, stood guard. They took their leave when Edward and Thomas woke before the others even stirred. For the last half an hour, the four of them: Askon, Edward, Thomas, and Elise had sat waiting for John and Líana to awaken. At first it seemed that they might sleep forever; their breathing and other signs of life were so faint. But as the sun climbed, so did their heartbeats and the rise and fall of their chests. John even began snoring.

Elise gathered a breakfast fit for battle-weary warriors from Apopsé's storerooms. The ever-present servants had made appearances, but showed no sign of helping Askon or his friends while their lord was still missing. Two large decanters of the honey-gold wine sat in the shade alongside an array of salted meat, fresh fruit, and day-old bread.

John awoke first. He snorted and stretched his arms, wincing at the bandaged wound where they had removed the arrow. When it healed, the puncture would scar, and John would like it. With a re-sounding *crack* he arched his shoulders, popping the joints in his back. Breathing deep through his nose, he let out a long sigh. When he opened his eyes, he saw Líana lying on the bench nearest his.

"Oh, I remember this one," he mumbled through a yawn. "Gentle touch, she's got. Tickles a little, too." He scratched his chin through the snarl of beard. "Got a ring on her finger, though. Too bad. 'Course a ring's never stopped me before."

Askon laughed as Edward approached. "That's my ring, John."

"Yeah?"

"Yes."

"Oh. Well, let me tell you, that's one fine piece o'—"

"And my sister."

John whirled, twitching again at the bandaged arm. His eyebrows lifted. "That's little Líana?" he said quietly.

"It is," Askon replied. "She saved your life. Saved all of us." He had stowed his cloak in his room along with his armor. In the white linen, he felt lighter and taller than he had in months. Tired, yet somehow stronger.

"My apologies," John said in his best approximation of graciousness. "But I'll have a hard time not recallin' the dream I had just before you lot woke me up. Vivid one, that. Gentle touch, like I said."

Edward shoved a hunk of bread into John's hand. It wrenched the bandaged arm slightly, and John sucked in a hiss. "Maybe you better eat this instead of telling that story," Edward said.

A few minutes later, Líana was awake and sitting with Edward on the bench. John had bowed low, thanking her for saving his life, and she apologized for not being able to fully restore his body. John only laughed, giving her a hard pat on the head. He said that he liked it better that way. The women he most often consorted with, it seemed, appreciated the marks of battle.

The decanters opened and the wine flowed. John seemed the least pleased with Apopsé's provisions. He called for beer and fresh meat, and when no one came to serve him, Elise directed him to the stores at the back of Apopsé's hall. John emerged, with Thomas in tow, carrying two flagons of thick dark beer suitable for a man of Dalstone. Thomas lugged what looked to be the full hindquarters of a pig and a bag filled with various herbs, salts, and spices. In the center tier of the garden, just out of reach of the blossoming flowers, John built a fire. Askon had suggested he do so in the surrounding grasses, but John took great pleasure in blackening Apopsé's perfect floor tiles. He said it would give the place character. The meat went over the fire, and all were glad for John's persistence.

Afternoon burned away, the sun hovering in the sky like a hot iron. By the time Rickard and Mot brought the first news from the rest of the city, John had already heard all there was to hear about Líana's first and second reappearances. Retelling the attack by Iramov's assassins had proved particularly uncomfortable for all and painful for most. But a solemn respect surged when Askon revealed that, to assure his sister's safety, Morrowmen had sacrificed himself.

South city was one enormous powdered circle. The power of Líana's fragment had reduced the enemy literally to dust. No memories transferred through the powder as they had in Tolarenz or when Codard sent the Space fragment to his son on the wall. The dead-faces in Iramov's army had lived their last memories long before they reached South City, and those who had been added to the swarm as they headed for the palace were only a few amongst the many. Even if someone did happen upon a freshly slain soldier's memory, it would have been filled only with an endless stream of vacant stares. The remaining soldiers and civilians had already begun washing the white powder away.

Edward kept the memories from his father's circle to himself. Askon assumed that sooner or later Líana would know exactly what the king had said to his son, and eventually Edward would share it with whomever else he chose. Likely, the words had been personal, not meant for the ears of others, so Askon let it go. What mattered was that Codard recognized his own folly before it was too late, and that Edward had been able to use the Space fragment to bring about Iramov's defeat.

Apopsé was still locked in the tower. When they tried to speak with him, he was petulant and sullen. "Give the fragment back!" he shouted, like a child robbed of a favorite toy. Of course, they wouldn't give it back. Apopsé had never been a warrior, and it seemed even less likely now than ever. But the Sight fragment would give him an advantage with which the others were no longer comfortable. Edward told him to continue in the South Kingdom as they ever had. With prosperity, the wounds would heal. Apopsé had whined at that, claiming he needed the Sight fragment in order to maximize his profits. Askon wondered if the success of the South Kingdom had always depended upon the Tear.

When evening approached, Rickard and Mot appeared again. The former took the lead, bowing before Líana then Edward. He cleared his throat. "We have two statements to make, my lady." The words sounded awkward, almost too formal in the nasally voice.

"First, on behalf of all of Morrowmen's remaining agents, I present my sword to you." He lay the gleaming short sword at her feet gingerly. "We followed Morrowmen to protect the Life fragment and its bearer. Now we would do the same for you." He bowed again slowly, and Mot followed with a jerk, as though he had made the same mistake in a prior rehearsal.

"I would be honored," she said. "Though it is strange that your new leader was only recently your youngest member."

Mot laughed stupidly. Rickard gave him a slap. Then they both stood up.

Edward eyed them suspiciously. "You said there was something else?"

Rickard nodded. "There is. And this would be best handled by Askon or John—meaning no offense to yourself of course."

From one of the stone benches, where he had reclined for the last hour, his eyes lazily floating between open and closed, John hollered back at Rickard. "Eh? Wha'dya want! Can't ya see I'm asleep? It's not like I didn't spend last night tryin' to get myself killed."

Askon, who had been standing with Edward and Líana all along, shrugged off John's comment. "I think he means you should just tell us and get it over with. What is it?"

Rickard leaned forward, glancing about as if someone might hear him. "There are Norill at the gates."

John perked up. "Are they wearin' the Tree and Quarrel?"

"They are," said Rickard.

"Ha! That'll be Brâghda then. Well, let 'em in already." John scrambled to his feet. "Can't let her see me sweat. I need a new bandage for this gods damned arm. C'mon Askon, she might have news for us. Not to mention the rest o' my boys!" He pulled a fresh bandage from a collection near one of the benches, sliced into the old, and tossed it out onto the grass. "Let Apopsé deal with that when we let him out," he laughed. Then, he looped the clean linen strip around the puncture in his arm and headed down toward the palace's mechanical gate. Askon followed him.

When they reached the city's main gate, Brâghda waited impatiently outside, as Askon knew she would. The guards seemed irritated at her presence, but John cured them of that quickly enough. He shouted orders and flailed his good arm, cursing them for not knowing an ally when they saw one. Luckily no one had been foolish enough to fire upon them.

The huge mechanism rumbled to life, and the doors swung open. Norill streamed in, just as they had on the previous night, but these looked wary and awestruck rather than ferocious or expressionless. Behind the Norill came the rest of the Darts of Grafmark. They looked exhausted. Askon wondered if any of them felt it unnecessary that they had marched all the way to South City only to find the battle already won.

John sauntered up to Brâghda with his thumbs hooked in his belt. "Seems ya took yer time gettin' here. Fancy that. We get all the fightin' done, even get the cleanup started, and then you bring in the reinforcements. Aren't ya a little late?"

Brâghda's deep dark eyes rolled back into her head. She breathed slowly in and out, and walked past John without a word, the little bones in her jewelry clattering as she went.

"Elf-kind," she said, bowing to Askon. "I bring news to the city with the white wall."

Askon bowed in return. "And what news does Brâghda, daughter of Bur-ghân bring?"

The Norill leader's face curled into a smile at this. She tilted her head, and the little bones rattled again. "The Lost are destroyed," she began. "We marched hard to reach the city with the white wall, but could not reach it in time. Still many hours away, we rested for a final march. Our watchers sounded the alarm in the night, bands of the Lost were fleeing to the north.

"The Lost did not stand long against us. We killed many and more. They gave battle and did not surrender, but never did they rally under one command. Before long, nearly all were dead. The others fled north, but they were too few to harm any war bands left in Vladvir. Too few."

"That is welcome news indeed," Askon said. "Thank you, Brâghda. Without your help, Iramov would not have been defeated." Askon put out a hand, and she clasped it with hers.

"At least Eldred won't have anything to worry about," said John. He turned to Askon. "We left him with the rest o' Dalstone's people near Vitæsta. By the time we get back, he'll have the place set to rights. It'll be like we never left."

Askon nodded. "I'm glad to hear he survived the battle, and that you'll have a people to come home to, John. But I need to ask a favor."

"Yeah?"

"Will you take Brâghda's fighters to the half-elven quarter? I think that the two groups might get along surpassingly well, given the right introduction."

Brâghda led John to one of her commanders, whom John already seemed to have been acquainted with. He enfolded the wiry Norill captain in a bear hug, and Askon remembered the man who practically spat upon the prisoners at Austgæta. How could he have changed so much? Under the proper circumstances, it seemed, anything might be possible. Askon watched as John led the Grafmark Norill down toward the half-elven quarter.

Brâghda ambled up the street to Askon again, her bone jewelry clicking and chattering. At first, she didn't say anything, only watched with him as her people disappeared into the alleys.

"Is there something else?" Askon said after a moment.

"Yes."

He waited for a response. For a while, none came. Then, as if it somehow embarrassed her to ask, she grabbed his shoulder.

"Is Elise well?" she said timidly. It was a new experience. Askon could not remember Brâghda ever sounding anything but supremely confident.

"She is. Would you like to see her?"

"I would. Thank you, elf-kind."

They walked slowly back up toward the palace, she detailing the full span of the battle against the Lost and he explaining the events that had driven the creatures screaming from Apopsé's city.

Elise nearly tackled Brâghda when she appeared at the foot of the hanging gardens. Askon had not known how close the two had been. It was almost like the meeting of parent and child. No more than a moment had passed and Elise was dragging the gangly Norill leader up the tiered stairs to their collection of food and drink. Elise's dark hair, now hanging loose around her face and shoulders, spun and floated as she excitedly described her victories. And then Askon understood. Brâghda was the only other female warrior that Elise had ever known, save for Líana, and the latter had been quiet and distant since she ended the Death fragment's assault. In Brâghda, Elise had not only a rescuer from her old life, but a kindred spirit.

After the sun set behind the faraway mountains, Brâghda said her farewells and followed Mot down to the half-elven quarter with the rest of her people. The Darts had taken up residence around a tavern John decreed to be in the best post-battle condition. He was unlikely to return until morning.

Stars blanketed the sky, the pale moon clear and white amongst the glittering black. Five forms lingered in the gardens after all the palace had given itself up to sleep. Sounds of celebration jangled through South City: high musical wails, raucous laughter, rhythmic applause. They could hear it, however faint, but they did not heed it. For them, wine and friends and laughter had their limits; Alora's Tear was now their burden to bear. One by one, they removed the five fragments.

Edward lay his down first, the stone case with its clasp popped open, the deep blue gem glowing faintly in the black velvet interior. On the other side of the small, three-legged table, Askon placed the silver chain and the pulsing green Time fragment. Time and Space, alike, but ever in opposition to one another. Elise came next, leaning the broken ebony staff against the table's rounded side. The Death fragment seemed to come to life as it drew closer to its siblings. It did not glow as the other two did, but a faint inner light smoldered there quietly. Then the crown came off Thomas's head and went to the center of the table, the sky-blue Sight fragment also kindling alongside the others.

Finally they all looked to Líana. She had been waiting for the moment with some anticipation. Askon had seen it on her face, seen it in her fidgeting hands. She had slid Edward's ring on and off her finger a dozen times since the solemn proceedings had begun. Now her eyes, one blue and one green, darted around the circle. They fell upon Edward last.

She lifted a hand, placing it lightly over his eyes. With the other, like a striking snake, she produced a knife from beneath her side of the bench. Not even Askon had noticed it in all the time they had sat together that evening. Unflinchingly she buried the blade in her collarbone. A muted whimper of pain escaped her lips, and Edward tried to pull her hand away. With a squelch she pried the stone out of skin and flesh, tears forming in her bright eyes. Askon turned away.

Their shadows grew longer as the purple light rose behind them. When Askon turned back, the Life fragment lay glowing on the table opposite the faintly red gem at the end of the ebony staff. Life and Death. Líana lay with her face buried against Edward's chest, her arms laced around him. The knife wound was gone. Her braid fell over her shoulder and tumbled down onto his linen leggings. She was smiling.

"So there they are," Askon said emptily.

"You mean, there *it* is," Thomas corrected.

"I suppose so. Only a few months ago I didn't believe Caled when he told me that the Tear was real. Now, with so many gone, I can hardly remember a time when it wasn't."

"What do we do?" Elise asked. It was the question that none of them wanted to pose, but that all of them knew had to be answered.

Edward sat up, adjusting Líana's position on his shoulder. He sighed. "My father meant for me to have his piece of the Tear. His memories told me as much when the fragment came to me on the wall. And I know that Caled meant for Askon to have the Time fragment. Morrowmen felt the same about Líana. I think her abilities bear out his decision."

"And what about us?" Elise seemed unsteady, as if she thought he might take the staff away.

"You were certainly meant to have the Death fragment, Elise," Edward continued. "And you earned that right. Líana would be dead if not for you. But—"

"But what?"

"The Death fragment does not come alive for you as the others do for Líana, Askon, and myself. The same can be said for Thomas and the Sight fragment."

Askon pressed his fingers together in front of his face. He tapped them against his lips slowly. "The Greats," he said.

And now Thomas was out of his seat, telling it all as if he had been there himself. "It's like Morrowmen told you, Askon. The Greats decided what ought to be done with the fragments. The Tear was only ever separated because the lords of Vladvir feared anyone having so much power to himself. I say we continue their tradition, as it appears Morrowmen wanted us to. We'll be spread across the map. Elise and I will return to Dalstone with John and Brâghda. Edward will make for King's City, where I'm sure his bride and his people will follow him. And you—"

"And me?" Askon asked wearily. Where would he go? What was left for him to do? Iramov was dead, the Tear fragments in the hands of people he trusted with his very life. Apopsé's military strength—whatever there had been of it—was gone.

He gazed up into the glittering light of a million stars. He saw there the Breaker and the Mender, their fingertips touching. All around them tiny specks shone steadily in a veil of black. And he knew where he would go. But she knew it first.

"You'll go home," said Líana.

Epilogue

Autumn in the valley brought with it a rush of color. Reds and yellows dotted the summer's fading green. Cool fog drifted in banks that curled about the lake like a blanket against the oncoming winter's chill. Geese chorused above the water, speeding away to their nests in the south over the Greyarc, over the confluence of the Estelle and the Grafdrek, over South City and beyond, all the way to the sea.

Leaves rustled under the garden oaks. So quiet were the onlookers that even the gentle *snap* of a leaf releasing its grip on the branches of summer resounded. A low hedge surrounded the guests of honor, while the farmers and smiths and weavers watched from beyond the bristling ring of green. Behind them, the garden wove a labyrinth's way, a series of living arches. In the center of the hedge, two figures stood on a dais.

On the right, was a man tall and stern of face, gray of eye. From within he radiated a warmth and power beyond any other in attendance. He wore a tunic dyed black and leggings of the same. A short cape draped his shoulders, falling to one side in a ripple of deep blue, upon it a silver stag was embroidered in the finest craftsman-ship. Edward was Codard's son, but not Codard himself. No longer, he had decreed, would the king's emblem be black.

Opposite him, shining to dim the sun, was a woman lean of features, her smile cool as an autumn stream. Here, in this very val-ley, she had been born. Not more than a few hundred feet away, she had cast herself into the inferno of her childhood, and there nearly perished. Now, what seemed ages later, she stood on the dais, a ring of white flowers encircling her head, trailing down through her golden curls. She wore no braid today. Only white.

They wore rings, the two on the dais. Both were of elaborate silver, with snaking vines and tiny leaves etched in the bands. The gemstones were glorious, one deep-ocean blue and the other purple as camas buds in spring. In unison, the stones grew brighter and darker, breathing together as their wearers breathed together.

Before them, in the failing rays of sunlight, three men stood sol-emnly. Those on either side were old, their hair shining silver-gray, their beards thick and neatly groomed. They had come from far away to witness the day's proceedings. The leftmost, and oldest, was Eldred of Dalstone. He had left his city in the hands of the Darts of Grafmark, though no enemies had yet challenged the Tree and Quarrel since the defeat of the Lost. On the right was Havard, the Grandfather of Shale, in his rough brown robes, a thick rope tied about his waist. He represented the people of the Vladvir plain, the king's subjects, from the city walls to the fields to the northern watches where Austgæta and Norogæta had fallen.

In the center was a figure cloaked in green, but no hood shadowed his face. Upon his chest, for all to see, hung a glowing green jewel wrapped in a silver setting not unlike the bands of the couple on the dais. His eyes sparkled, one green and one blue, the representative of the remaining half-elves of Vladvir who had come to this place in hopes of beginning anew. Today they would give one of their own into the hands of Vladvir's king, a king who recognized their sacrifice, their value, a king who honored their friendship.

"I come before all of you on this day to ask a favor," said Edward, his voice loud and strong, thick with pride and awe. "Your people have given Vladvir a great gift, one that I treasure above all, one for whom I would give away kingdom and crown, wealth and comfort, even health or life."

Across from him, color bloomed on Líana's cheeks.

"But those who gave her to us are gone," continued Edward, his voice softening. "Líana, daughter of Teral, has agreed to marry me."

Applause.

"Who speaks for her father today?" Edward asked.

"I speak for Teral." Askon stepped forward. "As do the people of Tolarenz."

The surrounding crowd roared to life. Cheers and whistles echoed through the rustling leaves of the garden. The applause rolled on for nearly a minute before Askon was able to quiet them again.

And so it began. The marriage of Edward and Líana. Never before had one of the Greats been wed to one of the elven blood, never before had two of the Greats married one another. Such elven and human pairings were less rare at times throughout Vladvir's history, though only with the common people who worked fields and orchards, forges and mill wheels. Now from the throne to the very earth, Vladvir would accept all of its people. Even the Norill could now walk freely from Vitæsta to King's City to Tolarenz, though they seemed to prefer the shadows of Grafmark's towering trees.

When the ceremony had finished, and the witnesses of Dalstone, Tolarenz, and Vladvir's many villages had given their approval, Edward kissed Líana under the tall oaks of the town hall garden, much the same as he had done under the South Kingdom's stars. Much as he would for a very long count of years.

No expense had been spared. Edward made certain that Askon had everything he needed to give Vladvir's most heavily burdened people a night they could remember. In truth it was a series of nights, but this, this would be the centerpiece. Of course, in King's City, another celebration would be held in honor of the arrival of the new king and his queen. But for now, all joy and mirth radiated from the ring of little mountains.

Long vines of white flowers draped the cavernous main hall. They dangled between rafters and twined around support-columns. Along the intricate carvings, the vines looped and curled, accentuating the depictions of the city's founding and the various employments of its people.

On one side the hearth roared red-orange, and sparks popped and hissed within its blackened stones. Not so long ago, Askon had been surprised in the night at that very hearth. He hoped that somewhere in the stars Morrowmen could see the happiness he and Caled had wrought.

Over Caled's powdered circle, they had sewn his light-blue cape. It looked like a pool of sky fallen to the floor. On it they had embroidered, "Caled, Knight of Vladvir, Builder of Tolarenz." No one stepped nearer than arm's length.

Tables stretched to the innermost side of the hall where Edward and Líana sat with Askon, Thomas, Elise, and John. The other guests filled the tables and clattered across the floor near the entryway where music rang from strings and pipes as fine as Tolarenz could provide. John, bold as ever and already mildly drunk, had risen from his seat to approach Líana.

"My queen," he said in his best courtly fashion, "I'd like ta' give ya this one last chance to see how a real man shows a lady the art o' the dance, before ya go riding off to yer silver spoons an' silk cushions."

Líana reached up and tugged on the snarl of black beard. "We'll see how that turns out if you manage to stay on your feet."

She slid out from the table, her hand trailing lightly against Edward's arm, and skipped down the rows of tables toward the music. John followed with his arm outstretched, tripping clumsily over one of the benches. He would have fallen, but she caught him as if he were a stumbling toddler and set him right again. With a smirk, she twirled away into the crowd, and John waded through behind her.

While they watched, another man had appeared. He was less drunk, but equally bold. It was Eldred. For a moment he stood quietly before clearing his throat. They looked up. He ran a hand through his silver hair. "I never got the chance to thank you for what you did against Iramov," he said to Elise. "And after talking with Brâghda, I think an apology might be in order as well. I'd like to do so. May I have a dance so as to offer my humblest apologies? Dalstone should never feel unwelcome to its own people."

Elise nodded and went away with Eldred.

Thomas let out a sigh. "I'm glad he finally did that."

"What do you mean?" Edward asked, his eyes on Líana and John. He smiled. She spun in and out of the swirling crowd while John thumped along, two steps behind.

"Since we arrived in Dalstone, after the battle, Eldred has said almost nothing to her. Without her, we'd all be dead. Who knows how her life would have gone if Brâghda hadn't brought her to Vitæsta. At least now, she can feel some sense of gratitude."

"Indeed," Askon agreed. Across from them, Líana and John continued their amusing game of cat and mouse in which the mouse thought he was the cat. Eldred and Elise danced more formally, each pausing to speak to the other in turns. Askon turned back to his friends. Edward was rubbing his hands together, looking pale when he ought only to have looked proud.

"What's the matter?" Askon asked.

The prince waited a moment, his eyes still following Líana. His brows pinched together then relaxed, and he opened his mouth to speak. Nothing came out. Behind them dishes clattered and laughter boomed two tables away. Edward closed his eyes. "I need to speak with the two of you," he said, as if revealing a long-guarded secret.

Askon looked over at Thomas. "So speak to us," he said.

Edward looked around, across the hall to Elise, and finally back to Líana. "Not here." His voice had fallen to a whisper. Askon barely heard the words over the din. Edward rose from the table as Líana passed once again into the crowd and as Elise was eclipsed by Eldred's wide shoulders. Askon and Thomas followed him to the back of the hall.

In contrast to the light from the fire and the noise of the revelry, the narrow hall at the back of the building seemed eerily quiet. Along the far side, Edward felt up and down the wall panels, searching for something. Askon drew closer with Thomas trailing closely behind.

"Where is it?" Edward asked the wall. Then his fingers found the latch. He pulled and the hidden door to Caled's study—now Askon's—slid open. They slipped inside.

Fading sunlight filtered down through the elaborate crossbars of the skylight into the small room. Since his return to Tolarenz, Askon had removed some of the furniture and items from the study in an attempt to make it feel like his own, but Caled's memory still remained. Edward felt along through the dim light, again searching. He found an oil lamp and handed it to Askon.

"Light it," he said.

Askon drew back. The words were a command, not a request. It was unlike Edward to speak to him in such a way. With a suspicious look, Askon retrieved the tinderbox and lit the lamp. He handed it back to Edward.

The light pulled away from Askon and came to rest upon the low table at which he and Morrowmen had sat with his sister under a thin white sheet. Askon still kept the finely upholstered chairs as well as an additional pair on the opposite side of the room. Edward motioned for them to sit. They did.

He crossed the small space and retrieved one of Askon's new additions. It was full and soft, as were the others, but it lacked a certain skill in its carvings and quality of fabric. The half-elves of the South Kingdom had spent most of their lives as servants to Apopsé or other wealthy people of South City. Many of them had no other trade. One day they would weave cloth as fine as that which wrapped the older chairs, but for now only the first buds of that flower had formed.

He sat heavily, the chair creaking beneath him. With a frown, he balled his hand into a fist, staring at the pulsing blue Space fragment. The hand opened and he twisted the ring from his finger, setting it against the table with a *clack*. Gesturing to Askon and Thomas, he waited for their fragments to appear.

Thomas dutifully produced his own. Even before they had left South City, Thomas had decided against the crown. He left it for Apopsé and carried the Sight fragment in a leather pouch back to Dalstone. When they arrived, he set to work designing his own vessel for the precious gem.

He wore it today. On his wrist was a thick band, wrought in the same silver as the rings and Askon's chain. The clasp was an intricate series of loops and hooks driven by springs and clicking sprockets. How Thomas had been able to fashion metal pieces so small was a wonder to Askon, but the bracelet clattered together automatically, and spring-loaded catches along its width housed equally small tools and knives Thomas used in his mechanical constructions. Dalstone, it appeared, would soon be just as mechanized as South City.

When the chittering clicks of his bracelet came to a stop, Thomas thumped it too upon the table. He smiled.

"I need to see the stone," Edward said, his face still dark.

Thomas reached down and pressed another catch. The bracelet clattered and clicked, then sprang open like a clamshell, a miniature version of the old stone cases Morrowmen and Codard had used. Thomas twisted the open clamshell and the Sight fragment fell onto the table with barely a sound.

While Thomas had gone through the complicated process of removing his fragment, Askon had put his own to use. In the lengthened moment, Askon read Edward's face, the subtle movements there, his eyes as he watched the Sight fragment tumble out onto the table, his fingers and arms as he waited for Askon to act. In that face Askon saw he hadn't been far from the truth when Edward had asked them to come away from the table. His friend did indeed have a secret to tell. And there would be consequences for doing so. It seemed his concern was mostly for Líana and Elise, as his eyes returned to the wall again and again. Through that wall, the dance would soon be over, the women wondering what had happened to the men. Askon let go of the Time fragment's power, then lifted the chain over his head.

"Alright," he said, setting the stone onto the table. "Out with it."

Edward laced his fingers together. He looked haggard, hardly the happy groom he ought to have been. "I have to tell you this before Líana and I go back to my father's city."

"Your city, you mean," Thomas corrected.

"I suppose, yes, my city—our city…It doesn't matter."

"Of course it matters," Thomas continued. "You're the king now, and since you're the—"

"Enough!" Edward shouted. He brought his hand down against the table, and the fragments rattled against the surface. Askon leaned back, wary of his friend's unusual temper.

"I have to tell you," Edward went on, "about what I saw when my father sent me the Space fragment." He scooted his chair forward. "I saw what I told you I saw, Askon. But there was more. I hadn't had time to consider what I would tell you. Now I have decided."

Askon smiled. Edward had many qualities, but one seemed to win out over the others time and again. When confronted with a difficult problem, he always did the right thing, regardless of the cost to himself. The fact that it had taken him nearly two months since the battle to tell them, meant it must have been a particularly costly decision.

"My family," Edward began, "has cared for the Space fragment since the breaking of the Tear. Caled and Morrowmen may have been alive all of those years, but even they did not know all the powers of all the fragments. They were limited, by their personalities as well as by the pieces they carried. Both were surprised, even after all that time, to see what Iramov was capable of with the Death fragment. And both would be surprised to discover what my family has known for several generations."

Askon shifted in his seat, carefully studying Edward's face. The Time fragment glowed brilliant green on the table.

Edward continued. "As we know, the fragments conflict with one another in various ways. Life will not heal in the presence of Time. Sight cannot observe the movements of Death. Death heeds not the powers of Time and so on. My father made clear to me through his message that in addition to these, Space cannot move the bearer of Time from place to place."

Thomas frowned. "But that's not true. You moved Askon during the battle with Iramov's army."

Askon had already answered the riddle, but he chose not to speak. He imagined Caled's figure as it had appeared to him during the fight with Iramov. *Wait.*

"I did," said Edward. "But we also know the abilities of the fragments change with their bearers. My father was in opposition to Askon, perhaps he could not move him as a result. There is more, however, as Morrowmen and Caled already knew these truths.

"At the breaking of the Tear, my ancestor possessed the greatest share of lands in Vladvir, as does my family to this day. As such, he was given the task to set each of the gems into their respective cases: Time in the silver chain, the stone clamshells for Life and Space, the crown for Sight, and the staff for Death. When he did this, he had the unprecedented benefit of holding all of the gems at once and in several combinations as he set each one into its vessel."

Thomas stared at the three fragments glowing on the table, dark blue, green, and a tiny flicker of pale blue between them. "One of the combinations was this one, wasn't it?"

Edward nodded. "It was. Just as the fragments can negate one another, certain combinations can augment the powers of each on its own. That is the secret my family has kept for all the many generations. My father kept it from me till the very end. What's more—and this is the last memory my father gave to me—my family knows what we will see with this combination." He pointed to the three gems on the table.

With a huff, Thomas folded his arms. "We won't *see* anything," he said. "I haven't been able to make that stone do anything other than look pretty in its bracelet."

Askon leaned forward. "Maybe here, with us, you'll be able to make it work."

"If it shows what my father said it shows, then we have to make it work."

One by one they put their hands on the table, each man clasping his fragment in a closed fist. They drew them back to the edge and light began to pour through their fingers. Askon kept calm; he had no reason to be afraid or even nervous, regardless of Edward's concerns. He and his friends controlled all the pieces of the Tear.

All around them, the world came to a halt. Nothing moved, not even the dust in the air. Suddenly the ground ripped away, and they stood over a vast empty whiteness. For a moment, Askon recalled the wave of white light Iramov had summoned with the Death fragment. But when he looked up, he saw an endless blue sky and gleaming yellow sun. Still, nothing moved.

Across from him, the others sat in the same configuration as they had in the hidden room behind the main hall, but the chairs had vanished. He stood up, and seeing him do so, Thomas and Edward rose as well. They looked around at their frozen surroundings. Wherever they were, it was difficult to see. Askon put a hand on Thomas's shoulder and, like blinking eyes blurred by fog, the image became clear.

It was not a pure whiteness over which they stood, but an immense blanket of cloud. Here and there, mountaintops poked up like the tips of gray nails in a poorly built floor. Thomas opened his eyes, gasping in terror. He flailed his arms and clung tightly to Askon. The clouds and mountains again became a blur.

"Close your eyes, Thomas," Edward said. "We need to see this, and your concentration controls the power of Sight."

Thomas did as he was told and the cloudscape came again into focus. It spread out for miles upon countless miles. At the farthest reaches of the clouds, Askon thought he could see a thin ribbon of river slicing through wide golden fields. They were standing over the southern mountains. He looked down.

Directly beneath their feet, a huge circular bowl lay open to the sky. Over it, no clouds came. In its center, like a giant flashing mirror was a wide lake. Askon could not tell how high they were, but judging by the thin streams leading into it and the building that stood on one side, the bowl had to be nearly three times the width of the Tolarenz valley. He tried to grasp its vastness.

And then they were falling.

So quickly that Askon could only remember his speed in vaulting the South City wall and his crossing of the Dalstone battlefield, the floor of the bowl rushed up to meet them. Down, down, down they went, the jagged rocks and motionless lake rising faster and faster. Askon tried to keep calm.

As he struggled against his fear, he felt no wind against his skin, no cold above the snowy mountains. It was as warm as it had been in the Tolarenz hall. They stopped abruptly, only inches from the water.

The lake lay motionless, almost as if it were frozen. Then they saw something move. Out of a small clump of trees and brush, a frightened form stumbled and fell into the short tangle of grass. It lifted its head, breathing rapidly, looking from right to left. Askon wondered if he had lost control of his fragment, but the figure's movement held his attention.

She rose. Yes, Askon thought to himself, she. But her rise was only to her knees. She scrabbled through the grass, one arm looped around something thick and brown. She came closer. Askon reached out to stop her, but Edward stayed his hand. She crawled by as though they were not even there.

A few feet away, still a good distance from the water's edge, she stopped. Askon walked slowly up behind her. She was digging frantically, shreds of grass and dirt flying into the air. Then she found what she had been looking for. Her hands stopped and she lifted the lid of a chest or trunk that had been skillfully covered with sod. It blended perfectly with its surroundings. She peered inside.

Warm light spilled out of the chest. It bathed her face, and Askon struggled to see her clearly. In the light her skin seemed red at first, but warmed to a subtle brown slightly darker than Askon's own. Her eyes, dark and warm, so unlike Elise's which were cold and nearly black. A dainty nose stood like a little bulb upon her face, and her lips were soft pink. And yet all of these were little more than smudges in the vague image. Then for a moment, as all three focused their eyes and wills, came clarity. Around her forehead she wore a circlet of copper-red metal that folded into her chestnut hair. With one hand, she slipped the loose straight hair around a pointed ear and stared into the light of the partially open chest.

"She's a half-elf." Askon's voice died inches before his face. The girl did not seem to hear him.

He leaned over her shoulder as she unwrapped the brown bundle and placed it on the grass near the chest. It was a book.

The Book of the Tear was printed on the cover in fine golden letters. But much more interesting than the title, was the second line: *A History, by Thomas of Dalstone.*

Thomas and Edward had gathered around the frantic woman now. Eyes wide, Thomas had seen the name. He shook his head vigorously. He might have said something, but Askon could not hear or understand it. Edward pointed back to the open chest.

The light dimmed and the girl opened the book to a page halfway from the end. On it were several rough sketches, blurry and difficult to see. Thomas had lost his concentration after seeing his own name printed on the book.

Askon looked back into the chest, where he could see more clearly. Instantly, the image shattered like a reflection on water after a heavy stone breaks the surface.

They were back in the hidden room once again, but Askon had seen what the girl had placed inside the chest. Three of them were already there when she arrived. The first, a thick bracelet of silver with a blood red gem glowing in its center, and beside it a nearly identical bracelet with mechanical clasp. The third was a ring engraved with vines and leaves, a dark blue jewel pulsing in the setting. The last, the one she had placed while Askon and his friends watched, was a finely wrought silver chain with a pendant of vines similar to the ring. A deep green glow filled the dark interior.

Askon had seen one final thing in the shattered reflection, in the valley he was certain must be Dalkaldur. The copper band on the woman's forehead was inscribed with a single word: Alora.

Acknowledgements

Sharing *Fragments* and *The Elf and the Arrow* with the world has been a wonderful, surprising experience that continues to bring me joy each time a reader tells me about having read either book or each time a review appears on Amazon, iBooks, or elsewhere. For so long, I never thought that anyone besides my closest friends and family members would ever read the story of Askon, Líana, Morrowmen, and the others. Hearing someone speak of Austgæta or the Norill is still surreal, unexpected. I think (if only for a split second) to myself, *How do you even know about such things? They're figments of my imagination!* And so they are, and so they aren't, not anymore.

Now, with *The Voice like Water*, Tolarenz, Vladvir, South City, and the rest are places that my readers have gone, the people who live there are people my readers have met and cared for, even cried for. So my first thanks go to the readers, who made the characters and places in my mind real and who now do so frequently, whether I meet you online, at a craft fair, at a book signing, or every day in my classroom.

Also to Liz Wilmerding at Palouse Digital Press and all the other authors there who have been supportive of my work, who have graciously invited me along to panels and readings. I might not have ever done those things without you.

Thanks to my family, who have not only read the books again and again, but who have tirelessly advertised, sold, and given copies to every person who will listen. Sometimes more than once. And as this is the end of the first trilogy, thanks to Pops for reading the earliest (and somewhat unrecognizable) drafts, and to Grandma Jeanie for reading the later ones that still needed a great deal of work, and to my friend Scott Boren, for being the first beta reader, and who has been patiently waiting to see what happens with the chest and the girl in the copper circlet.

And last, again, more times than I can say or anyone would ever be willing to hear, to my wife: Kel, without you, in *so* many ways, there simply is no book, no second draft, no first draft, no Tear, no story at all.

Thank you.

About the Author

Nathan spends most of his working days with the students of Genesee Junior-Senior High School in Genesee, Idaho. Whether it's essay structure, a classic literary work, or the occasional impromptu dance routine, he strives to keep students interested in the fun and the fundamentals of the English language.

When he's not teaching, he wears a number of hats, though the one that says "Dad" is the most careworn and cherished (it says "Husband" on the back). It hangs on a hook in a house where music is a constant and all the computers say "Apple" somewhere on their *aluminium* facades. From time to time it is said that he ventures into the mysterious realm called *outside*, though the occasion is rare and almost exclusively upon request by son or daughter.

Sign up for Nathan's newsletter:
www.BarhamInk.com/subscribe

Connect with Nathan:
Twitter: twitter.com/natebarham
Blog: natebarham.com
Facebook: facebook.com/BarhamInk